Beyond

the

Beaded Curtain:

A Gay Male Anthology of Firsts

BarbarianSpy

FOR LITERARY HEAT

This book is copyright © habu 2012
Published by BarbarianSpy in 2012
Cover design © S Bush 2012
Cover images: Young Man © Kirill Zdorov | Dreamstime.com,
Beaded Curtain © Photochris | Dreamstime.com
ISBN: 978-1-922187-20-8
All rights reserved

BarbarianSpy
Jindalee St
Toronto, NSW
Australia

Beyond

the

Beaded Curtain:

A Gay Male Anthology of Firsts

by

habu

Contents

Introduction

What gay male can ever forget his first full-blown sexual experience, which can be a particularly memorable first time given the conventions of society? It can be the culmination of long-held frustration, or it can be casual and come as a complete surprise. It can be traumatic, or it can have been sought. It can be imprisoning or releasing, disappointing or far beyond the wildest dream. It can be prearranged or ritualistic, or it can be spontaneous and unexpected by both parties. The experience can be instigated by a predator, a new lover, or a savior, or it can have been initiated by the first timer himself. The situation and venue can be sordid; or off-the-cuff convenient; or involve silken sheets, candles, champagne, and prolonged seduction and foreplay. But for most men, the one thing it cannot be is forgotten.

This anthology provides a treasure trove of thirty-six short stories of separate, varied "first time" gay male experiences, from the stalked to the long anticipated, from the romantic to the brutal, for the young or not so young. The one central theme of all of these stories, however, is that the experiences depicted all result in the beginning of a new lifestyle, not the ending of a world.

The title for this anthology is taken from a motif habu often uses in his "first time" stories, likening the irrevocable first step into the world of gay male encounter in its fullness to a step beyond the beaded curtain, sometimes with an actual beaded-curtain doorway that the protagonist steps beyond to his initiation appearing in the story itself.

This is an expanded relaunch of the eXcessica anthology, *Across the Threshold.*

Beyond the Beaded

Curtain

Fuck Julia, I was screaming in my head, as I pulled on my jeans and a dress shirt and my leather vest, slammed through the apartment door, and stabbed at the buttons on the elevator door.

She didn't feel satisfied. *she* didn't feel satisfied. Well, what about me? She didn't satisfy me either. Maybe I could satisfy her better if I ever was made to feel satisfied.

Well, fuck Julia, I muttered as I slammed my fists against the metal elevator walls while it descended twenty stories to the street level below. I'd told her I needed smokes and dressed and headed for the door before she could go into that litany of how Jim had fucked her so much better than I did. Well, fuck Jim too for that matter.

I hit the streets. It was drizzling rain, and I knew I couldn't just walk it off. I didn't really need smokes, but I sure could use a drink. There was a bar up ahead, Big John's. I'd never been in there, but it was beginning to rain harder now, and

I couldn't go back to the apartment—not just yet. Anything but facing Julie's mocking eyes right now.

I pushed the door open and entered the smoke-filled room. A rock band with a sound much too big for the size of the room was doing its thing over in the corner. The first thing I realized, though, was that there were nothing but men in the room. Not a woman in sight. Well, that wasn't all that bad. If I looked into the eyes of any woman just now, I'd probably only see Julia's mocking eyes staring back at me.

A skinheaded guy who appeared to have far more muscles than brains motioned me with a big smile to a seat next to him at a table, but I just smiled weakly back at him and moved slowly toward the bar at the far side of the room. I passed men dancing with men. I surprised myself by not being the least bit turned off by this; in fact, I felt a little thrill, like I was going on an adventure—like I was detached from my body and somehow sparring with Julia across the divide between this danger-filled smoky room and the sterile environment of Julia's and my apartment up in the clouds not more than two blocks away. This was a whole new world to me. Maybe I'd check out this world a little more closely.

I leaned up against the bar and ordered a beer and then turned and watched the rock band and what was going on around me for a while. This was obviously a pickup joint at the height of its evening activity. Connections, some of a blatantly intimate sort, were taking place all over the room. For some reason I found this exciting, even sexually arousing, in a way that I didn't find Julia arousing. It didn't take long for me to realize that some of the men were starting to buzz around me as well, sensing a new player in the room. I became a little embarrassed. I wasn't really planning on being a player; I was just playing on the edge of this world, observing it, considering the "what ifs." And I hadn't the foggiest notion of how to play here even if I had intended to do that.

I ordered another beer. I momentarily wondered how long I could stay away from our apartment on the pretense of buying a pack of cigarettes, when it hit me that I didn't really care. Fuck Julia. I downed my beer and ordered another.

I had waved off several guys in obvious search of a pickup when the mystery man appeared at my elbow. As time went on, the Rock band was getting louder, the beat getting heavier. I knew I was drinking too much; the beat of the music was beginning to transfer into my head as a headache.

Tall and dark, with curly hair cascading around his head, he moved into the empty stool beside me I had been protecting to keep some distance between me and the circling crowd. His eyes seemed to be violet. He had a mustache that met his sideburns and a sensuous mouth with an engaging, ready smile. There was a small scar running down his chin that made him seem a little dangerous and kept that question in my mind of what the story was there.

He trapped me with his eyes, and I couldn't lie when he asked if I was alone and if I'd let him buy me a drink. We didn't really say anything to each other, but, although there were loud conversations and music and the smoke of cigarettes all around us, I felt that we were the only ones there. I could hear my heart beating, and I thought I could hear his as well, moving to match the rhythm of mine, matching the rhythm of the band music. It wasn't long before he had his arm around my shoulders in a possessive manner, and on my fourth drink and his second, his arm had drifted down and he was cupping my buttocks with his broad hand. I let it stay there. I was feeling dangerous and exhilarated and aroused all at once, something I hadn't felt with Julia an hour earlier. Above all, I was feeling wanted and desired. I'd play the game for a while longer and then leave and get those smokes and see if I could transfer these feelings into another go at Julia, this time feeling a little more aroused because of my visit to this bar.

All the time he was holding my eyes with his. He set his drink down, fished the cherry out and put it up to his lips. I watched him slowly draw the cherry in, move it around his mouth, and produce the pit in between his lips with that smile of his. He obviously wanted me to do something, so I reached over and went to take the pit out of his mouth with my fingers, whereupon he captured my thumb with his lips and drew it into his warm, moist mouth cavity.

At the same time, I felt his hand on my thigh. He held my thumb inside him while his hand moved to my crotch, and he felt the full engorging length of me with his hand. I could feel his intake of breath, clearly pleased at what he had discovered. I was pleased that he was pleased. I sensed the growing danger here, though. Just how close to the edge was I here? And on which side of the edge? It was about time to put an end to this pleasant little fantasy I'd entered and return to my world.

He released my thumb and gave me a broad smile. I rotated my hips, in a half-hearted attempt to get free of his grasp. He was moving too fast, but I wasn't sure I minded. All I could think of was punishing Julia for those mocking eyes of hers. She didn't want me? Well, here was someone who was showing he wanted me—even if he was from another world altogether.

His hand traveled with me as I rotated my hips, intending to shake his grip off. Misjudging my intentions, he grasped my cock through the fabric of my pants, and his other hand squeezed my butt cheek, holding my hips in place. It was obvious where he was going with this. I relaxed, giving up, bordering on the intoxicated, whether by the drink or the promise of some form of satisfactory sex as a punishment for Julia's mocking eyes.

He pulled away from the bar and led me around the bar by an elbow. I was drawn through a doorway covered by a beaded curtain into a alcove with dark velvet walls. We were just a beaded curtain away from the raucous, revolving crowd and the steady beat of the music but were fully private in our own world in that dark alcove.

He pushed my back to the wall just beyond the beaded curtain and leaned his hips into mine. I could feel the strength and urgency of him as our crotches crushed against each other's. He held me with his eyes again, as his face came to mine. He pressed his lips onto mine, opening me to his urgency and his surprisingly sweet kiss. His mustache tickled my nose. It was time for me to put a stop to this brief fantasy—to stay on my side of this divide. But, although my mind was screaming "break and escape," my legs felt like lead, glued to the spot.

I sensed that it was too late, that I no longer could pull back, and decided to go with the flow, to see and sense what this world looked like, if only for a brief time. I could always go back to my world. I'd probably be better with Julia when I'd seen and been able to reject this world.

His hands were working on the buttons of my vest and shirt, which he pulled off my body and dropped beside us. He quickly pulled off his T-shirt, and we were bare chest to bare chest. I ran my hands up his sides and onto his pecs. He was in magnificent shape, obviously a bodybuilder, and was covered with dark curly hair. I pushed my fingers through his curly chest hair and found his nipples, both pierced with rings. I let a hand follow a trail of hair down his washboard abs, finding another ring in his navel--curly hair everywhere. I wondered if it continued on down. But I wasn't in a hurry. This would be my one fantasy encounter. I might as well make the most of it.

He was in a hurry, however. This was all moving just too fast for me, but I couldn't have stopped it now if I'd tried. He had me trapped with those violet eyes. He had one hand on my crotch again, and with the other one, he was unbuckling my belt, pulling down my zipper, pushing my pants and briefs off my hips and encasing my stiffening cock in his fist, skin on skin. He quickly had his own cock out, and he held them against each other; mine was being measured with his. Mine was a good size, but neither as long nor as thick as his was. He encased both of our cocks in his hand, mine lying atop his. I sighed, letting my hand travel on down below his navel, through curly hair and sliding across the underside of his cock and finding his heavy, hairy balls. He reacted with pleasure, intensifying the sucking motion of his kiss, his exploration of my mouth with his searching tongue. I could have continued at this stage for some minutes, maybe even have left the whole encounter here, but he obviously couldn't.

I gasped as he disengaged from our kiss and quickly worked his lips and his tickling mustache down my neck, over my pecs, down my sternum and abs and belly, through my pubic hair, and to my cock, which he took into his mouth and started to work back and forth in a frenzied manner.

I grabbed his head, burying my fingers in his hair, in an involuntary maneuver to stem this full assault on my body. He roughly grabbed my hips with his hands to hold me steady, and when I relaxed and gave into his victorious breach of my crotch, he moved his hands around to cup and dig into my buttocks, still holding me firmly in place while he pumped my rod with his mouth. He pulled his mouth up to where he just held my glans in his mouth, sucking hard, flicking his tongue around my piss slit and then forcing the tip of his tongue into my slit, tongue fucking me there, in that smallest of all entrances to the body.

I groaned and tried to escape, but his hands, digging into my buttocks, held me in place. His strength was incredible, and I was weak from the buzz of the drinks. He slowly swallowed me whole again, his teeth scraping down the sides of my penis as he drew me in, applying pressure all the way in. I couldn't help letting loose soft moans and writhing under his attack. It all was surreal, a party blithely going on in the bar, and a mad man beating down my defenses and eating me alive just beyond the beaded curtain. I grabbed his massive shoulders, beating on them, scratching at them, trying to push him away from me. But all of my efforts were fruitless. His brutal mouth began his pumping of my cock again. The beat of the band beyond the beaded curtain was steadily increasing, and his pumping of my cock matched the rhythm of the band.

Without lessening his pumping of my cock with his mouth and tongue, he took my balls in the fingers of one of his hands and rolled and pulled on them, causing me to give out little yip, yip sounds and to moan more deeply. The fingers of his other hand had found my asshole, and I lurched and writhed and increased my moaning as they worked their way into my ass, not giving me time to adjust, plunging past my sphincter muscle and finding, and roughly rubbing my prostate. Not long after this, I came under his unrelenting onslaught. He just took my cum at the back of his throat as I spasmed three times and went limp against the wall. His hands went to my hips and worked their way up my sides and onto my pecs, He was digging into my chest, nipping and kneading my nipples. I begged him to stop, to let me rest.

He just laughed and told me to turn around and to spread my legs, which I did, meekly, at his sharp command. I felt his hands roughly spread my butt cheeks, and he had his mouth and tongue at my asshole, licking, rimming me, and pushing in. One hand went back to kneading the muscles in my belly, the other one was working my cock and balls.

He had me all wet and moaning again in a short time, when, without ceremony, he spun me around, lifting me up the wall with his strong hands, got his arms under my legs, and folded my knees up so my feet were completely off the floor. I was crying out for him to stop or at least slow down, but the noise in the bar was so overwhelming that there was no one to hear me or to come to my rescue.

I felt the knob of his huge, erect cock at my asshole, and I tried to lurch and escape him, without success, as the head entered me up to the rim of the glans. He stopped then, but only briefly, as we gasped and panted in unison. He captured me with those violet eyes again and commanded me in a hoarse whisper to kiss him again. As our lips met, he brutally pushed mine open with his and buried his tongue down my throat, stifling any screams of pain and pleasure I might have given, as his long, thick cock slowly but steadily pushed its way up my ass canal, keeping just ahead of my ability to stretch to accommodate him. When he was in up to the hilt, he started to pump me, keeping time with the beat of the band beyond the beaded curtain, slapping and ramming my back against the velvet wall with his thrusts, and didn't stop until he had cum.

When he was finished, he let me slide to the floor and then stood over me, smiling that smile of the conqueror and holding me with his violet eyes, while he adjusted his clothes. He told me that he'd enjoyed me immensely and would like to see me again. He flipped a business card down into my lap, and then he was gone. And I was again alone in the alcove, with the sounds of a raucous party drifting through the beaded curtains. The band had stopped; was probably on break. My whole world had also stopped.

As I lay there on a heap of sore but strangely satiated flesh on the floor, trying to come to grips with the brutal but glorious sexual encounter I'd just had, I also was coming to a realization that maybe the problem with Julia and me wasn't Julia and her mocking eyes at all. Maybe I was meant for something different than Julia. But did it always have to be this brutal, and, what concept was I striving for, both intimately personal but also impersonal at the same time? I had no idea where I fit now, but after what I'd just experienced, I couldn't honestly tell myself that I could go back to the other side of that beaded curtain, to Julia, ever again now.

Honey Hollow Swimming Hole

I'd read about the Honey Hollow swimming hole on a naturally dammed section of Cunningham Creek in the *Baltimore Sun's* travel section, and I'd never heard of it before, even though it was just up the road from Thurmont, where I lived. I'd heard of the Honey Hollow Reservoir, of course, because it provided water to Thurmont. It was up in a fold of the Catoctin Mountains, and the paper said it was a beautiful mile-and-a-half hike up beyond the reservoir to a naturally fed, rock-bottom swimming hole that harkened back to our grandfather's era.

I decided right there and then I'd check that swimming hole out. I did so first in July, and although the hike lived up to its hype, the swimming hole was crowded with families with young children and a group of smart-alecky high schoolers, and so I put swimming there on a backburner.

Today I'd gotten my chance, though. After a mid-September cold snap the previous week warning us of the approach of autumn, this week was in the 80s. The apple picking had been wrapped up at Collins's farm, so I'd settled on today to make another go at the swimming hole. It was midweek and the families would be busy doing something else, and all of the kids would be back in school anyway, so I had reason to hope I'd have the swimming hole to myself.

As I pulled up to the parking area above the reservoir dam and at the foot of the fire trail leading up into the fold in the mountains, I had to pull in close to a humongous black Dodge Ram, because a large tree had fallen into the parking area and had left little room for parking. Still, there was only one vehicle here, so chances were good that I'd be able to get in a swim without fighting a crowd. My Toyota pickup looked tiny and vulnerable beside that big old Dodge Ram, and I couldn't help but think of Sydney Collins, the farmer who had hired me since spring to work in his orchard. He had a Dodge Ram too. It wasn't black, though; it was red. It had a logo on the side like this one. I looked at the logo of this truck as I wedged myself out of the driver's door of my pickup, but I was too close in the scant space between the two vehicles to make it out.

Anyway, seeing that truck, especially there nudged up to my small pickup, reminded me that I was going to have to do something about Sydney Collins pretty soon. He was beginning to crowd me in; I'd have to decide.

I crossed the boulder-strewn creek bed that would be under an impassable torrent down to the reservoir on rainy days. And as I started the ascent up the rock-bedded fire trail running through a forest of lush oaks, hickories, and tulip poplar trees, already starting to change color, I thought about where I was— and how I'd gotten here.

I'd graduated from high school in June and was all ready to enter Mount St. Mary's this fall, when the roof caved in on my family. My dad's military police unit, the 115th, that had been on security duty up at the president's Camp David retreat, had been called to Afghanistan. My mother had taken his absence and the danger he was in so badly that her nerves had forced her to cut back her hours at the supermarket. So, I'd done what I had to do. I'd put off going to college to stick with the family until Dad could get home, and I had gotten a job as quickly as I could.

Mr. Collins had been a godsend—well, in that respect, at least. He'd taken me on immediately to work in the orchard and said he'd find something for me to do even after the harvest was in. He said it was the least he could do to support my dad and the rest of the troops that were over there in Afghanistan. The pay was all right, and the work helped me to trim down and muscle up better than spending money at a gym would do.

I'd caught on real fast, though, what Mr. Collins's real interest in me was. He wasn't married and had some of the other guys working for him living up at the house. I overheard them talking, and I paid some close attention to how they related to each other, and so I knew pretty quickly what Mr. Collins was like and what he expected of his hired hands. I wasn't shocked or put off, really. Just conflicted. I'd had some confusion about what I wanted and was like myself in high school, but I'd never been brave enough—or fool enough—to go anywhere with some of my thoughts.

Sydney Collins brought those thoughts back, though. He was old from my perspective, but he probably wasn't all that old. And he was a rangy, solid guy. Not handsome by any means, but not ugly, either. I guess a woman would have called him sexy enough. I just didn't know.

What I did know that Sydney Collins was, though, was a touchy-feely sort of guy and one with something on his mind that included me in his plans.

The day before I'd come up here to check out the swimming hole again, he'd more or less trapped me at the fence while I was watching the new, sleek black mare he'd bought trotting around at pasture. He'd come up close beside me and put his arm around me in that real friendly manner he had.

"You like her, Jake?" he asked. "I hope so. She cost me a good penny."

"Yep," I answered. "She looks mighty fine. Ridden her yet?"

"No," he responded. "She's still mighty skittish about that. She's fine quality and needs to be brought along proper. I'm bringing in a horse handler to break her in for me. I want her to want to be ridden by me when I first mount her. Everything worth riding is worth breaking in just right."

We paused, admiring the mare—in fact, admiring the whole beauty of the green pasture land on the gentle slope

21

between valley and mountain, with its white fences and azure-blue sky. Everything would have been perfect if I wasn't so aware of that arm Collins had draped around my shoulder.

"Why don't you come on up to the house with me, Jake?" Collins suddenly said in a low, husky voice. "There's something I'd like to show you."

"Sorry, I can't today, Mr. Collins," I answered. My mind raced for a reason. "My mom needs me to pick up the girls at school this afternoon. She can't do it today. Maybe another day—"

"Fine," Collins said a bit stiffly and removed his arm from around my shoulder. "Maybe another day. It can wait. But not tomorrow. I understand you aren't coming in to work tomorrow."

"That's right," I said. "I need to do some thinking, and I've heard there's an old-fashioned swimming hole up above Honey Hollow Reservoir. I'm thinking of hiking up there tomorrow afternoon."

"That sounds like fun," Collins said as he turned to walk on up to his house. "It's supposed to be a hot day; do some skinny dipping up there for me, you hear?"

Skinny dipping at the watering hole. That reminded me as I picked my way over the rocks of a stream bed intersecting that fire trail that I hadn't thought about bringing a swim suit. Well, we'd just have to see what was what, I thought, as I passed the half-way point between the parking area and the swimming hole. A brush-choked clearing was off to my left by the fire trail. The remnants of a stone fireplace told me that someone had once lived up here—maybe had been born in a cabin here and lived their whole life here and died here, leading a normal, dull life. I wasn't sure I wanted to do that. I wanted some risk and danger in my life. I wanted to know that I had lived life to the hilt. That was kind of hard to do in Thurmont, Maryland, though.

And speaking of that, as soon as I came up onto the swimming hole, I knew I wanted to swim in it. It was deserted today. The creek bed was a good bit down from the fire trail, and it would take some risk and effort just to get down to it. The swimming hole was in a gorge of sorts lined with great slabs of gray rock that jutted out here and there at square angles, like it had been quarried. But it had been nature, not man that had quarried it. The swimming hole itself was just a slightly wider section of the creek bed and had three chambers that I could see from the trail far above it. Three different rock-walled "rooms," the first one down more private than the lower two. I couldn't see what was farther up the creek from this cascade of rocks, because what would be the wall on that side of the upper chamber was maybe a twenty-five-feet high rock cliff with a waterfall noisily feeding the upper swimming hole. At the same level, naturally arranged piles of large, square-sided slabs of rock separated that chamber from the next. And then there was another drop of about fifteen feet, with a waterfall down to the lowest swimming hole. The middle chamber was the largest and looked like the cleanest and the most easily accessible one from here, so I picked my way down the side of the ravine to the terracing of solid rock surrounding that area and stripped off my shorts, T-shirt, and briefs and eased myself into the water.

It was like heaven in the water, and I just laid back and floated and luxuriated in the solitude.

It was a false solitude, though. I heard, or rather sensed, a shifting of pebbles on rock and looked over to the side of the swimming hole. I wasn't alone. A man—not old, but not young, probably ten or eleven years older than I was—was crouched down on his haunches and staring at me. He wasn't looking menacingly and he didn't scare me, but he was looking pretty hard at me. And there I was, naked, in a clear-water swimming hole.

"How's the water?" he asked in a low, melodious voice. Not threatening at all. His was a warm and interesting voice.

"Ummm. It's pretty cold," I said. And then I nonsensically went on. "I . . . I thought I was the only one here."

"Otherwise you wouldn't be skinny dipping, I guess," he said. He followed this with a friendly smile. He was a handsome man. Well-built from what I could see—at least his chest and arm muscles were bulgy against the fabric of his T-shirt and showed that he wasn't afraid of manual work. Dark complexioned and with dark hair and hazel eyes that contrasted with his skin tone and that danced when he spoke. He had a slow-starting smile that exuded confidence and good will.

I strangely felt calm in his presence even though the mere thought that I was naked in the water before him made me twitch nervously every couple of minutes. I was lost between wanting to talk with him, to hear the cool, calming tone of his voice again, and wanting him to go away so that I could dress and escape from here.

"No, no," I answered. "I don't usually do this sort of thing."

"No, I didn't think so. But there's no harm, is there? We're all alone up here in this beautiful setting, and it's a sweaty walk up that trail, despite the tree overhang. And it's a hot day. This swimming hole is made for skinny dipping, don't you think?"

"Yes, yes, I guess it is," I responded.

"In fact, I'm hot from the hike, too. Just seeing you in that cool water makes me feel hot out here on this stone ledge. I think I'll join you, if you don't mind."

I did mind. I very much minded. But I was tongue tied. He had as much right to be here and to swim in the hole as I did. I tried not to watch as he stripped off his jeans, T-shirt, and boots—he hadn't been wearing any briefs—and rose to his full height before jumping into the water. But of course I looked. He was very well put together indeed. Darkly tanned skin everywhere but where low-riding jeans shorts would hit. He obviously worked out of doors. And the paleness of his pelvis area highlighted a low-hanging dick and heavy balls that were covered in curly black hair that trailed all the way up his groin, belly, and sternum and parted and flared out across his well-muscled chest. His forearms and legs were well covered with curly black hair as well. Altogether a well-constructed, graceful package.

A splash of water and he was in the pool as well.

"Oh, you're right," he said with a sputter. "It's cold in here all right. We probably should huddle to keep from freezing."

Just the image of that set my teeth to chattering—and it wasn't from the cold. I clumsily moved through the resisting water to the other side of the pool from him. There was nowhere in this pool that was far from anywhere else in this pool, however.

"Ah, come on, I was just joking," he said. "Besides, I can tell you liked what you saw. The coldness of the water should be having the opposite effect on you than what I can see."

His voice was still calm and soothing. Incongruously, It was full of innocent playfulness too. I felt embarrassed and on the defensive that I was upset by what he said. And, damn, it was true. I was getting hard. And I couldn't hide it very well. The water this high up on the mountainside was pristine clear.

"So, I'll bet you've never swum in the nude with another man, have you?" the stranger asked, as he turned on his back and floated. I could clearly see his well-toned body and big, flopping penis right at the surface of the water. "I'm Lance, by the way. Lance Stevens. And you're . . .?"

"Umm, Jake, Jake Henderson," I said. It was like he was playing me. Sticking in something provocative and immediately taking the edge off it with something friendly and nonthreatening. All the time getting to know me better, though, getting more intimate.

"Jake. That's a good name. Live around here, Jake?"

"Umm, yes, just down the mountain, in Thurmont."

"In high school, Jake? Cutting classes are you?"

"Uh, no, I graduated last year. I should be starting college now, but my dad's in Afghanistan, and I have to work until he gets home." I had no idea what I was telling him all this. He was just so easy to talk to, despite the awkwardness of this situation.

"Ah, already through high school. Old enough then."

Old enough? Old enough for what? I asked myself. But I knew why he asked; I just didn't want to admit I knew. I was beginning to feel all tingly inside, and my cock hardened further and started to twitch.

"Lots of girlfriends, I'll bet. A good looking, strapping lad like you must get prime pussy every Saturday night."

"Ummm. No, nothing like that," I said. I was backing away without really realizing it, but I had come up close to the rocky edge of the pool. I was backing up because Lance had righted himself from his float and was drifting closer to me.

"So, ever done it with a man, Jake?" Still that "I couldn't possibly be saying anything improper" tone of voice he had established.

"No, no, of course not," I croaked. I meant to yell it out, but all I could manage was a croak.

Lance waved his hands in the water, moving a bit away from me, giving me more room. As it was, I was having trouble breathing—and that had nothing to do with the cold water or the thinness of the air at this altitude.

"But you've thought of it, of course," Lance said in a frank tone as if there was no more reasonable thought for a young man to have. "I mean we all have, haven't we, if we're honest with ourselves? And it's just the two of us up here in this remote spot. We can certainly be honest with each other. I mean I fuck women a lot, a couple a week easily. But sex is sex is sex, and a man has got to have his sex, right? When there's no woman available and I need to get it off, any sex is good sex. Haven't you found that too?"

Still that calming, ultrareasonable, honey-toned voice. Openly talking of things I'd barely allowed myself to even think about. And doing it so well that I didn't even really notice that he had drifted back to where he was very close to me and had the fingers of one of his hands brushing my upper arm just below the surface of the water.

"Ummm, ummm," I answered. I fully realized I wasn't being coherent at all. This was all just so overwhelming. He had that lulling voice of his. And the image of him standing there, on the rock, nude, achingly beautiful of body, stretched out and ready to jump in the pool was emblazoned on the back of my brain.

"So, don't tell me you haven't thought about it, Jake. We all do, of course. Don't you?"

"No . . . Ummm, yes, I guess so now and then."

Wrong answer. The hand that wasn't using its fingers to brush my arm was now tentatively fondling my cock. And my cock was responding, not paying a bit of attention to the signals of confusion and muddleheadedness and panic that were racing around my body.

Lance was still lulling me with a nonstop soothing chant in the sing song voice of his. He was pulling me with him through the opening in the rock into the first, higher, more confining, more private pool—the pool with the cascading waterfall that filled my ears with the sound of rushing water. I was crying out as Lance's hands raced across my body, finding curves and crevices and making me tremble and twitch and feel oh so aroused and concerned and needy and reluctant and violated all at once. The splashing of the waterfall dulled even to my own ears my cries and moans of receding protests as Lance turned me and hunched down and made a lap to accommodate the mounds of my buttocks. My own cries should have steeled my defenses against the feel of his strong, throbbing cock running under mine and his fingers pinching at my nipples and his teeth nipping at the hollow of my neck as he pulled me closer into him and let me feel the heat and inviting hardness of him. But the noisy splashing of the waterfall covered all of that, dulled my senses of what the cries should have alerted me to.

I did clearly hear the cry of pain and invasion when Lance lifted me and settled me down on his cock head and forced his way past my virgin ring and ever so slowly and relentlessly filled me to capacity to the bottoming depth deep inside me. But it was too late then for cries. And there was no one else in this forested fastness to hear me or to come to my rescue or to witness this passing beyond a threshold that I never again could regain.

My whimpers of pain and violation slowly receded into cries of passion and urgings of filling and satisfying as Lance lifted and lowered me in that watery swirl on his powerful tool. He nuzzled my cheek with his lips and continued to whisper calming words of endearment and encouragement to me, as he lifted me up and down on his manhood with strong hands on my hips. I arched my back in the taking, first, stiff as a board, but as I realized both that I had now given up all there was to surrender and that I not only could now accommodate it but also was enjoying it, the tension flowed out of my body and I began to match the rhythm of the fuck. Sensing I had melted to

27

him, Lance nibbled at my cheek and I turned my head to him and let him possess my mouth, making my surrender, my acquiescence, my complicity complete.

He settled me down into his lap, his dick far up into me, just holding now, as he moved a hand around to my cock and stroked me off until the water around us was cloudy with my cream.

Then he raised out of his crouch and moved through the water, still buried deep inside me, back to the middle pool. He moved over to the side of the pool, near where our clothes lay. He made a cushion of sorts with my clothes on the rocky ledge dropping right at the side of the pool and, pulling me off his tool, turned me and laid me gently down on my cushioning clothes on my back. He was standing in the water between my legs then. He lifted and spread my thighs, pushing my knees up into my torso, with his strong hands, and slowly slid his cock back inside me and fucked me, fucking and fucking and fucking until I felt him give a little lurch and then pull his cock out and shoot his warm cum on my belly.

He came up on the rock and lay stretched out beside me then and cradled me in his arms and rocked me back and forth gently while soothing my soul with his thanks for giving my virginity to him.

"Do you come here often?" Lance asked in a low voice. "This is my first time here, but if you—" He was fingering my hole with a tantalizing finger and I had every reason to believe that he would have taken me again right there if I'd asked him to.

"Maybe," I said. "I'll have to think about it. This is just all happening too fast, though."

Lulled by that rich, calming voice of his, I slept then, luxuriating in the feel of his strong, callused hands gliding across my young, heretofore innocent body. When I awoke, he was gone from the pool. And when I had dressed and slowly worked my painful way back down to the trailhead parking area, the big black Dodge Ram was gone as well.

Within a half hour, though, I saw it again. I decided to stop by Collins's orchard to check my work schedule before going home, and I was about to pull into the farm road when I saw that truck again in the farm yard. I could make out Lance sitting in the driver's seat and there was Sydney Collins leaning up against the window, looking up into the cab and smiling and laughing at something he was discussing with Lance. I pulled my truck up to the side of the road, where the branches of the trees blocked me from the view of the farm yard but where I could get a good look at what was going on there.

I saw Collins transfer a thick envelope to Lance's hands, those hands that only recently were unlocking my virginity and touching me in my most intimate recesses. Collins stood back, and Lance got out of the cab of his truck and the two slowly walked toward the pasture, toward where the new, black mare twitched and skittered about, waiting for someone to break her in to be ridden by Sydney Collins.

I could clearly read the logo on Lance's truck now. It said "Lance Stevens, Horse Handler."

I got back into my Toyota pickup and started toward home. No use crying over what was lost. I somehow knew I was moving in this direction anyway. I just needed someone to break me in right, to get me past the skittish phase. I knew now that the next time Collins asked me up to his house, I would go with him. And that this wasn't my last visit to the Honey Hollow swimming hole, either.

30

Big Birthday Wish

I was an impressionable teenager and prone to fantasies I couldn't shake. And, like any teenager, I was raging with hormones. One such fantasy was Mr. Walker, who lived down the block from us. He was a former Marine in his thirties, who worked hard to keep himself in tip-top shape. He was a runner, and I'd frequently see him running around our neighborhood, wearing no more than skimpy shorts and running shoes without socks. He wasn't muscle bound by any stretch of the imagination, but he was finely built, and there wasn't an ounce of fat on him anywhere. His buzz cut and exercise regime screamed that once a Marine, always a Marine.

The first thing that started me to fantasizing about Mr. Walker was his wife. She was a cute little blonde thing who always looked so satisfied with herself and who popped out a baby every twelve or thirteen months or so. In my adolescent mind, this suggested to me that every minute Mr. Walker wasn't out running, he and Mrs. Walker were in their bed "doing it"— and that whatever he was doing in bed satisfied Mrs. Walker a lot. The mere image of that turned me on. As I said, I was suffering from raging hormones then, and I found myself fantasizing about being in bed with the Walkers—for several weeks about being in bed with Mrs. Walker, and then for a while with both of them, and finally, distressingly, I fixated on being in bed with just Mr. Walker.

The Walkers belonged to the same community club my family did, and in the summer of my sixteenth year, I found myself at the pool the same afternoon the Walker clan was there. Mr. Walker looked mighty fine poolside in that Speedo of his. He was in the shower of the men's locker room soaping himself up when I entered the shower after my swim. A lump went to my throat. His body was magnificent—all sinew and muscle in motion and rolling veins lacing his body, having been pushed to the surface by his muscle and lack of any fat in which to hide. My eyes went directly to his dick, which was the biggest and thickest I'd ever seen as it plunged out of a clump of red hair at his groin. I hadn't thought of Mr. Walker as a red head; his buzz cut was just too short to tell from that, and the rest of his body appeared smooth and hairless from a distance. I could see now, when he was soaping himself all over, that he had tufts of red hair at his pits as well. My own cock came to quick attention at what I was seeing.

Mr. Walker obviously saw me staring at his package as well as what my own dong was doing in response.

"Hey, you're the kid living up the block from us, aren't you?" he asked in a pleasant tone, not bothering to stop soaping around his dangling dick.

"Yeah," I managed to burble out. "I see you running in the neighborhood sometimes."

"Well, how old are you, kid?" he asked straight out.

I told him.

"When's your birthday?" he then asked, which seemed a strange question at the time.

I told him that too.

"Well, on your eighteenth birthday, we'll meet again," he said. "Until then, keep yourself clean, ya hear? And you could stand to do some running of your own." With that, he rinsed off and left me and my boner alone in the locker room shower.

I started running after that, but I never stopped fantasizing about Mr. Walker.

On my seventeenth birthday, I was out running a woodland trail. I'd gotten myself in great shape with my running, and I was grateful for that little nudge Mr. Walker had given me a year earlier. I was doing real well on the cross-country team now.

As I was steaming down the trail, I heard another runner coming up behind, someone, incredibly, who was opening it up a lot faster than I was. When he came up level to me, I saw that it was Mr. Walker in his skimpy shorts and sockless running shoes.

"How's it going, Sport?" he called out to me in a voice that showed no signs of breathlessness. "Happy birthday. Today is your birthday, isn't it? I remembered right, didn't I?"

Besides being breathless from the exertion of running myself, what he was saying—having kept track of my birthday like this just from a chance encounter at the swimming pool—bowled me over so that the most I could do was mumble an affirmation that today, indeed, was my seventeenth birthday.

"I see you took my advice on running," he said with a grin. "Lookin' good, Sport. As I remember it, it's just your seventeenth, right?"

I took a little umbrage at the "just seventeenth," but I responded with a "yup."

"See you on your eighteenth," he responded with a little laugh. "Keep clean." And then he was off in front of me, leaving me in his dust as if I weren't even flat out running myself.

This encounter didn't cut down on my fantasy time about Mr. Walker for the next year.

It was my eighteenth birthday, and I was moving up the walk to my house after school, when a big SUV with smoked windows stopped beside me, and the passenger window rolled down. I came over and looked inside. It was Mr. Walker. He was wearing a loose, long-sleeved shirt, worn blue jeans, and shiny black boots.

"Happy birthday, Sport," he said with a big grin. "Climb in."

I opened the door and climbed in. As the door shut, he rolled up my window. We were alone now, in his big SUV with the smoked window. Although I don't remember ever seeing this van in his driveway. I wondered if it was his or if he'd borrowed or rented it. And then I wondered why he'd do that.

Without fanfare, he took my right hand by the wrist and brought it around and laid it on his basket. I could feel him hard and massive through the worn material of the blue jeans.

"This can be your eighteenth birthday present, Sport, if you still want it," he said in a husky voice. "You wanted it two years ago. Do you still want it, Sport? I won't go any further unless you want it. You don't want it, you can get out of the van right now."

"Yes, oh yes," I managed once the frog had been cleared from my throat. He'd remembered. I knew I should say no and just get out of the car and bury myself in a safe, normal life. But this had been my fantasy for years.

"Well, then, let's take a little ride. Buckle yourself up, but you don't have to take your hand back, if you don't want to. Here, let's give it some air." He pushed my hand to the top of his thigh and worked his zipper down. Then he went back to putting the SUV into gear and driving away from the curb. I worked my hand into the gap in his pants, not believing I was even doing this, imaging it was happening to someone I was watching from across the room, and his big plump dick just popped out of his pants. I gently ran my hand up and down and around it as we drop into the countryside. It had this large, popping vein running up the underside. His dick got impossibly large and hard as we drove along, and I was smearing some precum around the knob of the head when we pulled up to a small cabin in the woods, well off the main road.

"Gee, is this cabin yours?" I asked. It was really small and really isolated. The trees came almost right up to the side of it at one side and in the back, so that it seemed to be tucked under the overhanging tree limbs. I bet it would be impossible to see from the air. At the side of it, almost at the back of the house, I spied the tail end of the sports car I usually saw him driving peeking out of a lean-to shed.

"Yes. This is my special place. I keep it and my van here for special occasions."

Mr. Walker was actually breathing pretty hard when he came around to my side of the SUV, pulled me out with a strong hand on my wrist, and guided me to the door of the cabin. I was wondering if he had been fantasizing about me that past two years as much as I had been fantasizing about him. He certainly had made a point of knowing exactly when we could do anything about it.

He unlocked and pushed open the door to the cabin, but then he turned and looked hard into my eyes.

"Last chance, son. We can go back now if you're scared. I like to do this kind of special like. This probably won't be like anything you'd imagined it to be. Birthdays should be memorable, I think."

I just set my jaw and moved closer to the door. He got the message, and spoke again, in a softer voice.

"I can see you've kept up with the running as I suggested, Sport. But did you keep clean too? You do understand what I mean by that, don't you?"

"Yes," I answered faltingly, trying to keep my eyes connected with his. "I mean yes to both. I understand, and I've kept clean."

"Good," he said with a satisfied tone. "It's better, it feels better, if cleanliness can be assumed—if nothing has to get between skin and skin. If I had too, I could use protection, but it just isn't the same. Especially not for the first time for the other guy." While I contemplated if I'd really understood what he meant, he put the palm of a hand in the small of my back and guided me to a door. He opened this, and we were descending stairs to a basement. The door at the bottom of the stairs was locked, but he unlocked this and pushed me into a small, square room. The walls, floor, and ceiling were a stark white, and in the very center of the room, prominently located, was a black leather sling suspended from overhead beams by strong chains. Half way up each chain was a black leather cuff, now open, padded on the inside.

I just stood and stared at this. Something inside me was stirring. This was beyond my fantasy, but I found that it was turning me on. I heard the door close behind me and the key turn in the lock, but I just couldn't take my eyes off that black leather sling. When, at last, I was able to do so, I turned and my eyes popped open.

Mr. Walker had taken off his shirt and jeans and stood before me, nearly naked. He was still wearing the black boots that came up above his bulging calf muscles, but, beyond that, all he was wearing was a black leather harness criss-crossing his chest, studded with silver studs, and studded black leather wrist bands and bands around his biceps. His horse-hung cock was at full staff, and he was wrapping a black leather, studded cock ring tightly around its base as I watched.

"Strip, Sport," he said in a throaty voice. I just stood there, mesmerized by the sight of him.

"I said strip, Sport," he said more insistently. His voice had a hard edge to it I'd never heard from him before. "And climb into that sling. I told you this would be special. But it won't be any more dangerous than any other way you might have done it. You're lucky it's me as eager as you are for it."

I then did as he directed, somewhat self-consciously pulling off my clothes and hunching over before him, trying to cover my manhood without any real means to do so.

"Stand up straight, Sport. Push it out. Ah, very nice. Very nice, indeed. It was well worth the wait. Now, into the sling."

Not knowing quite how to get into the sling, I walked over to it and turned around, and tried ineffectually to hoist my butt up into the contraption. Mr. Walker walked over and lifted me with strong hands at my waist, as if I were a rag doll, and plopped my ass into the sling. He then walked around to above me, and took, first one wrist, and then the other, and locked them in the black leather cuffs up the chain. He repeated this below, with my ankles, and there I was, spread-eagled helplessly in the sling. The bottom edge of the sling cut into my buttocks just where the small of my back flared out to my butt cheeks, and the upper edge hit between my shoulder blades.

Mr. Walker walked away from me and the lights went out in the room, to be replaced by colored lights, beamed from several positions, swirling about the walls, ceiling, and floor, in undulating waves of blue, green, red, and purple.

Mr. Walker was above me now, pushing my shoulders down and then taking my head in his hands and pushing that down as well. He had his enormous cock at my mouth, pushing at my lips from above, and then he was inside my mouth, and fucking my mouth in ever more insistent thrusts. I didn't have to do more than gag for him; I *couldn't* do more than gag for him, either, because I was completely trussed up and at his mercy. Left to my own, I wouldn't have known what to do anyway. But he told me what to do.

"Just relax, Sport," he said. "Open wide, unlock your jaw, and get your tongue below it and let it slide in easy. Ahh, yes, like that. Ahh, yes, a sweet mouth. Teeth out of the way, lips closed tight on it. Yes, that's better. Take it all, now. You can do it. Just loosen up and relax. There, just a bit more. Ahhhh, yesss. Feel the studs of the cock ring at your lips? That means you've taken it all. Now, letting it slide in and out. Yes, like that, in and out. Ahhhhh. Ah, AH, AHHH! Hot Damn!"

I and started gagging again, as his cum burbled up in my mouth and overflowed on my chin. He pulled right out of me than, and his lips and tongue were at mine, cleaning me of his jism, and kissing me now.

He leaned his face into my ear and whispered to me. "That was nice, Sport. I think you're going to learn to give head real good. But I bet what you really want is your birthday present. I'm going to give that to you in about fifteen or twenty minutes. Gotta reload from that nice blow job. Won't take long to reload. Got some good advice for you on that. Eat healthy, live clean, stay fit, get plenty of sleep, and fuck often with a lot of variety, and you can keep your reload time down. Now, I'm gonna do you. It'll hurt at first, but I'll take you to heaven. You're lucky it's me the first time. I'll treat you right."

He walked away from me, and the next I saw he was below me between my spread-eagled legs. He held my balls in the palm of one hand like they were eggs he was about to crack, and he lowered his lips to my throbbing cock, licking it all over and then going down on it with his mouth. I almost lifted out of the sling in response to teething and sucking he was doing on my cock. The meeting of fantasy and reality were just too much for me, and I shot my load down his throat in short order. I was embarrassed that I'd cum this quickly, but Mr. Walker seemed to be pleased. At least he gave me a big grin.

"Nothing like the wad of a young stud," he whispered. Then he moved his lips and tongue to my asshole and wetted me up real well there. All the time he was sucking and rimming me, he was encouraging me to tell him what I liked and what I liked better, and, although words pretty much failed me, I think he got the answers he needed from the differing timbres of my moaning and groaning.

After a short while, he seemed ready to go again, because I saw him rise up below me and I felt the head of his cock at my asshole. It was just pressing at my asshole, with its head rocking back and forth, straining the rim, and I already felt I wouldn't be able to take him. My torso and limbs went rigid, and I arched my back against the sling.

"Relax there, Sport," he was saying. And then he left me for a minute, and when he came back, he had a black rubber plug with straps attached to it, which he plopped into my mouth, pushing my tongue down and filling my mouth, and he then pulled the straps around my head and tied them at the back.

"That isn't to keep you from screaming, Sport. You're going to want to do a lot of screaming, especially at the beginning. But we're way out here in the woods. There's nobody to hear your screaming. This is to keep you from biting your tongue off."

He went around to below me again, and with a sudden thrust of his hips, the head of his cock was inside my ass. I screamed in pain and went all rigid again. There was no sound, however, beyond a muffled grunt of pain, and I was biting down so hard on the rubber plug that I thought my teeth surely would bite through and meet.

"Not much else to do at the start, Sport," Mr. Walker was saying. "Your ass is new to this, and my cock is extra big. Trust me, it's going to be bad for a few minutes, but then it's going to get very, very good. And keep remembering that you wanted this. Ugh!" And with that his cock head and breached my virginal ring, and he held there.

"The worst is passed, now," he was saying. "The rest will be easier, especially if you'll relax and let all of the tension flow out of your body."

He placed his hands on my belly and worked them up to my pecs, massaging me, helping me to relax. They came back down and then glided up my outstretched legs.

"Breathe deeply and regularly," he was saying. "And as I snake up you, take short, panting breaths. It will help. But however you breathe, remember to continue to do it. Don't hold your breath. This is your eighteenth birthday. I want to give you the fuck of your life."

I watched his strong, thickly veined hands, with those sensuous fingers, gliding across my body. One came back to my belly, palm down, and his finger spread out on my abs. I watched that hand, rising and falling as I breathed, and I relaxed as I could see my breath becoming more regular. And as I relaxed, his cock started its long, slow journey up my ass canal. My ass walls were welcoming it, the muscles moving in waves and closely caressing his pulsating rod.

"Nice, very nice," he was murmuring. "Your ass wants me, I can tell. It's making love to my cock. You're tight and sweet. Everything I'd imagined. There, can you feel them? The studs of my cock ring are at your asshole now. You've managed me; I'm all in."

And I could feel those studs, and it didn't hurt so much anymore. And I was exhilarated that he was all in me, fulfilling my fantasies. He'd told me it would be a lot easier and less painful the next time, and I believed him.

He lifted his hands and wrapped them around the chain and my bound ankles now and started the sling in motion. My ass was being stroked, but it was happening by the motion of the sling Mr. Walker was setting with his hands. The swinging of the sling increased, both in arc and in speed, and soon Mr. Walker's pelvis also was in motion, and he was fucking me in deep and long strokes. He was losing control of himself and giving me a wild ride, as I watched the motion of the studded leather harness across his chest. At length, he gave out a primeval scream, and I felt his cum jetting off deep inside me, and backing up along his buried cock and dribbling out of my asshole.

"Happy birthday, Sport," he exclaimed to me with a big grin, and then he helped me out of my bonds and the sling and supported me in his strong arms as we went back up the basement stairs to a small table in the kitchen. There he pulled food out of the refrigerator, and we both sat there, naked, at the kitchen table and ate like we hadn't seen food for a week.

After he'd had his fill, Mr. Walker winked at me, and said. "Think it's been twenty minutes again, Sport. I can feel the power coming back. And my birthday is coming up soon. Let's see if I can find a present too."

He pulled me up from the table by the wrists and marched me into a small bedroom that took up the other back corner of the house from the kitchen. He had leather thongs out and, after pushing me down on the bed on my belly, he tied my wrists together and strapped my arms to the rods at the center of the brass headboard and then tied my legs, from the ankles, to the opposite bed posts at the bottom of the bed. He then came up behind me and between my legs on his knees, and a felt that big, hard cock at my backdoor again. He lifted my pelvis with his hands on my hips and skewered me with his cock in one long gliding motion, having already stretched my ass to his specifications not more than an hour earlier. I gave him plenty of noise, while he rode me like a show bull. And rode me and rode me and rode me.

When he'd shot his load, he reached around and released my arms and legs and then went over on his side, pulling my butt into his pelvis. We cuddled and kissed and joyfully explored each other with our hands until he'd reloaded again and then he lifted my leg, nuzzled his pelvis under my butt, and took me in a side split one more time, this time more gently and languidly, as if we had all of the time in the world to meld to each other.

It was near dusk before we had finished fucking and had gotten cleaned up. Mr. Walker drove me back into town in his sports car, exchanging that in the shed for the SUV we'd driven there in. He left me off a couple of blocks up the street from my house and then just drove on by my house and into his driveway before I reached our section of the sidewalk. He was greeted at the door by his pert little wife, who kissed him, and I saw him give her a little pat on the butt as they turned and went into the house. I wondered if he would take her straight to their bedroom and feed that enormous cock into her just like he'd done with me, and a little jolt of jealously shot through me. I knew then that Mr. Walker wasn't a habit I'd be giving up anytime soon.

My family held a grand eighteenth-birthday party for me that evening, oblivious to the fact that I couldn't bear to sit on the hard dining room chairs for any length of time. My gifts from that significant birthday were memorable—my parents gave me the keys to a red Mustang convertible—but none was as memorable as the gift Mr. Walker had given me in that cabin in the woods.

I followed him around like a puppy dog for a couple of weeks, begging for him to take me to the woods again, but he just smiled and told me that I needed to move on—that it wasn't my eighteenth birthday or my first time anymore so he wasn't all that much interested. I kept taking drives around the countryside, trying to find that cabin again. But I never did. I even followed him in his sports car a couple of times, but he was always just going shopping or to the gym. I did, the next summer see the SUV—or what I thought was Mr. Walker's SUV—over on East Main Street, and a young guy getting in the passenger door, but that was pretty much it for Mr. Walker.

Across the Threshold

I wanted it. I knew I wanted it, and he knew I wanted it. I just couldn't take that step over that threshold—and I kept fooling myself about wanting it.

He owned the exercise facility with another guy. Jake and Ted. I knew they were a couple. I knew that before I signed up for a membership. Jake was the muscle part, the trainer; Ted, a good ten years younger than Jake and maybe three or four years older than I am, was the bookkeeper and the one who saw to it that the gym was kept clean.

Gay guys went to that gym. I knew that before I signed up for a membership. Still, I went there with a little sense of a thrill. I was too frightened to go over that threshold myself, but, still, I could have my thoughts and my fantasies. They didn't hurt anything. I didn't really want to even see them "doing it," I told myself. I just got a little arousal off of watching the guys work out in the gym and knowing that they probably then went off and did it. I could take care of myself, at home, after that little arousal at the gym, on my own bed. No strings, no risks, no decisive changes in life.

There were two types of guys going to Jake and Ted's gym. Young guys, like me, going there to get cut and keep themselves cut and maybe cruising each other a bit—and/or, also like me, fantasizing about what could be if we'd take the chance. These guys worked out hard. And then there was a group of older guys who sort of worked at working out but hovered around the periphery of the hardcore training, sniffing around the younger guys, looking for a hookup. All of these guys were in pretty good shape too. Jake didn't allow any slouches in his place.

I thought the older guys standing around and ogling would be too much for me, would prompt me to stop playing this little game I was into of running up to the edge of the unspeakable and then running back to safety. But after the first night, I found that a little arousing too. I found I liked to be watched and assessed while I was working out.

As I got more comfortable with the scene at Jake and Ted's, the older guys got more comfortable—and forward—with me too. It wasn't more than three weeks before one or two of them started asking me if I'd like to come over to their place sometime and watch a game on the television. They asked this after a conversation where they sniffed out what sports and teams I was into, which, amazingly enough, were always the sports and teams they liked as well.

As I got in better and better shape over the weeks, Jake started showing more interest in me to. He started giving me pointers on getting the most, the best definition, out of the equipment. And he increasingly was hands on, keeping in touch with me as he spotted me in an exercise or showed me the proper way to use the equipment.

Jake had to be pushing forty, but it didn't seem to be pushing back too hard. He'd been an actor in a daytime television soap and then had done commercials for a national brand of exercise equipment. The strength of his business was tied up in how well known he was as a exercise guru and how good his body looked—that and, with most of his current clientele, because he was openly gay.

I don't think I ever admitted to myself that this was why I picked out his gym from all the others in town. I didn't even admit to myself that I liked my body the way it was now than before I started the gym classes; I hadn't really felt the need for better definition, tighter abs, and bulging chest muscles and biceps. That's pretty much what I was getting, though. That and the little thrill of standing on the threshold of something and not letting myself topple over.

The not toppling over part got harder, though. The older guys sniffing around the edges of the younger guys didn't stop trying to relate to me, and then Jake was showing direct interest too.

It started with him suggesting that he could give me extra help on the machines in greater demand after hours if I wanted to stay over—which I said I couldn't. Then he tried the "come over sometime and watch the game on television" routine, which I politely turned away as well.

He moved on to getting more direct than that. A night when the crowd was sparse and I was working over in the corner, bench-pressing weights, he came over to spot me. While I had pretty much my limit of weights over my head with one of his hand hovered under the bar in case I faltered, he put the other hand on my basket and copped a good feel.

"Jake! Whatcha doin? Stop that." I was in shock even though I'd thought about this very action for weeks.

"Relax, Stud. I know you want this."

"Shit no, Jake. What makes you think that? Stoppit." He hadn't stopped it; his hand was still on my basket. And I was still on my back on the bench. I did set the barbell down into the stand, but I just kept my hands wrapped around it. Jake lowered his spotting hand to palm my belly and his other hand went down to the hem of my shorts and was dipping under that and starting to work up my thigh.

"I know what you come in here for. I see you watchin'. I see the effect it has on you when others are watchin' you. Stop playing your game. You want it."

"Noooo," I said. it was almost a whimper. "I come here to work out. Stop that." The fingers of his hand had reached the edge of my jock cup under my shorts.

I gathered my strength and pulled out from underneath the barbell frame and bounced off the bench and away from temptation.

"Gotta go. Late for somethin'," I mumbled and fled the floor, leaving the gym without even going to the showers.

I was back the next night, though. Jake knew I would be. He gave me those looks that told me he knew I would be back, that I'd come back to him, all the time I was exercising on the floor. He didn't come over to me, though. He stood his distance away from me and just gave me those "I've gotcha" looks. I told myself he certainly didn't have me. That I'd paid for my membership here and wouldn't stop coming just because I got propositioned. I told myself I came here for the exercise, not to teeter along the edge of temptation, afraid of crossing the threshold.

After exercising, I took a cold shower and then went straight into the sauna. Just me and one of the younger guys. He was stretched out on one of the top shelves, on his back, a towel loosely wrapped around his hips. His arm was thrown over his eyes as if he was planning to take a nap there. The sauna at Jake and Ted's wasn't like most saunas in gym facilities. It was warm but not so hot that you couldn't stay in there for long periods of time. This, of course, defeated the purpose of a sauna, but the sauna at Jake and Ted's wasn't meant to be used like the normal sauna. I knew it was a sex room. I'd pretty much avoided it up until then and hadn't really seen any sex going on in there, but I'd had the older guys ask if they'd see me in the sauna later and seen the expression on their faces, and I knew.

I told myself when I went into the sauna that I just wanted to try it out that evening. I also told myself that just because I'd caught Jake watching me when I came out of the shower and then turned toward the sauna door rather than to the door to the locker room as I usually did that the look and my action didn't mean anything. I told myself that.

When I entered the sauna and saw the other guy in there, I went up on the second of three shelves directly opposite him. I leaned back in the cedar paneling and closed my eyes.

When I opened my eyes, I saw that one of the older men had entered the sauna and was sitting on the second shelf across me at the foot of the younger guy reclining on the third shelf.

After I few minutes, I noticed, with fascination, that the older guy had a hand on one of the younger guy's feet. The younger guy didn't even flinch. But then I saw the younger guy, his arm still flung across his eyes in apparent sleep, widen the

46

stance of his legs and raise his knees a bit. The older guy, who was still holding onto the younger guy's foot had a clear shot from where he was sitting of the younger guy's crotch under the spread towel, and the older guy was closely taking in the view. He obviously liked what he saw, because he let his own towel slip open and he was fisting his cock with his free hand.

I decided I'd better clear out at this point. This was more reality than I'd ever seen before.

I turned to climb down off the shelf to leave, but there was another figure in the sauna now. Jake had come in, completely stripped and sat down right next to the door. His body was still something to take notice of, even as old as he was. And his balls hung heavy and his cock swung low as I saw him stand after I had sat back down on the bench, not wanting to pass him. When I was back in place, he took two steps over to the other older guy and handed him a small square foil packet.

Jake then backed himself to the shelf by the door, gave me a wide smile, and held up another condom packet. The unspoken "this is for you" was unmistakable in his look. I shriveled back in the shelf, my butt twitching. Trapped. Confused. Trying to decide what to do next. Knowing that all of that didn't matter. Knowing where this was going.

What I did next, struggling for time to make a decision and take an action, was to look back at the couple across from me. The older guy had slid along the bench closer in to the younger guy, on the shelf below him. The hand that had been on his foot now was all the way up onto the younger guy's thigh and was still traveling. The younger guy maintained his "I'm not even here" arm-across-eyes pose.

Even while it was happening, the younger guy was maintaining a "nothing was happening" pose. Somehow I had to laugh at this, if only nervously and deep inside me. Wasn't I on that same path? Didn't I know that I had been on that path for weeks? Where was this threshold I was afraid of crossing? Still ahead of me? Or was it weeks behind me already? Had I made the decisive choice weeks ago and was just wasting time now? For some reason, those thoughts made me feel calmer. I just let the tension drain out of me, and I turned my eyes back to the couple. The older guy had a cock in either hand now, and he was gently stroking both. The only change of pose of the younger guy was that he had lowered his outer leg to the second shelf, beside the torso of the older man and his towel had slipped away so the stroking of his cock was in full evidence.

Jake had seen the tension drain out of me and had guessed correctly what that meant. he moved to the shelf below me, pushed my towel off my thighs, and took the tip of my cock between his lips.

I had no more fight in me—either with myself or with whatever Jake wanted to do with me. I knew now I was going to be fucked before I left this sauna. And, if so, I might as well enjoy the experience. And what he was doing to my cock with his mouth was taking me into a world of pleasure that was beyond anything I had fantasized. I put my hand on his head, running my fingers into his hair, massaging his scalp as he massaged my cock with his soft mouth.

The older guy was up on his knees hunched over the younger guy's pelvis and sucking his cock now too. He had fingers buried in the young guy's ass, which was moving up and down in a rolling motion. I wasn't the only one in the sauna who was going to get fucked.

Jake was lifting me with strong hands around my waist up to the third shelf and pushing my thighs up into my chest, rolling my hips up. His lips were working more than my cock now. He was teething and sucking on my ball sacs and letting his tongue run down my perineum to my rim.

Oh, gawd that felt great. I was whimpering and sighing now. I felt my body go to jelly; I was trembling all over. He was tonguing inside my ass. Oh, gawd. Why had I taken so long to get here? This was paradise. I felt the juices rising inside me. I couldn't embarrass myself and shoot off this fast. But then I did.

I looked over at the couple across from us. They were both on the third shelf now. The young guy was on his knees, on a folded towel, his right side facing me. His chest and cheek were plastered to the cedar shelf, and his raised butt was being split by the covered cock of the older guy, whose haunches encased the younger guy's hips and whose shoulder blades were using the ceiling above him to leverage the rhythm of his fuck. A doggie fuck.

I watched in fascination as the whitish rim of the condom appeared and disappeared in the young guy's ass. The younger guy no longer was feigning sleep. he was gripping the rim of the shelf with his outward hand to maintain stability and stroking his cock with his other hand. The white rim of the condom appearing and disappearing, appearing and disappearing. And his mouth was slack and emitting groans and grunts. His eyes were wide open, watching me.

Watching me get fucked now. I barely had time to ache for the appearing and disappearing of the rim of that whitish condom inside me as well when Jake had pulled me from the third shelf to the second and scooted in under me and was bringing me down, facing the other fucking couple, into his lap—slowly onto his hard, possessing cock.

This first possession was painful, and I felt stuffed and stretched and trapped all at once. But it was also exhilarating. The threshold broached, the final threshold evaporating. No more wonder, no more wanting it and running from it. No more pretending. The deeper Jake plowed, the more I wanted it, the higher the arousal, the deeper the feeling of release—free after all this time from the lying to myself and toying on the edge. And enjoying the feeling that Jake wanted me and was enjoying me—all those young studs on the gym floor, and Jake was here wanting me. Jake pitched me a bit forward, pressing his throbbing dick hard against another wall of my channel, causing my channel to ripple in the new, intoxicating sensation. He was covering my pecs with his hands, using his fingers to pinch and roll my nipples, sending electric shocks straight from my chest to my reawakening cock. I flung my arms back and laced my fingers in the hair at the back of his head, bringing his lips and teeth to between my shoulder blades. He was rocking me back and forth on his pelvis. Sending me . . . over . . . the . . . moon.

I looked wildly over to the other couple as I was being moved up and down in Jake's lap. A harmony of sounds bouncing off the sauna walls from the moanings and groanings and murmurings of four male voices. The lust of taking and being taken—fully and joyously. The younger man's gaze was plastered to mine, his eyes swimming in sex, sharing in the incredible experience, as if he was having sex with me as well.

We were being FUCKED—together; we were sharing the most intimate of experiences.

Jake was gathering me back into his chest. One palm remained on my chest; the other glided down my torso, across my belly, and my cock was being fisted and stroked hard. I was hard again. The feeling was beyond description. Jake's lips were in the hollow of my neck and he was sucking hard. I writhed in his grip, moving my hips, feeling him sink deeper and deeper.

I looked over and all I saw now was the trim back of the older man, with the tanned legs of the younger man extending out from his sides, the older man holding the ankles of the younger in his fists. The younger man wedged into the second shelf, facing me, and the older man standing on the floor, between his prey's spread legs. His butt cheeks contracting and puffing out as he used them to regulate the fuck. The sounds of the young man being taken deeply, no longer nonchalant, crying out for the full fury of his master.

I gasped in a big intake of breath, thrusting forth my pelvis, Jake riding the wave with me, me shooting ejaculate off across the sauna chamber toward the pulsing dimpled butt centered between the moaning young man's thighs. The bulb of Jake's condom bubbling up, Jake's cry of release very soon after my own. The collapsing against each other.

I looked up from my semen-drowned stupor, and the older man was gone. The younger man was collapsed on the second shelf, drawn into himself like a rag doll. He looked up when he sensed me looking at him. A sloppy grin.

When I had showered and dressed, the younger guy was waiting for me outside the gym door.

"Wanna have a beer over across the street?"

"Sure, why not."

Later, in his apartment, I fucked my first man, him patiently guiding me in what to do, until I reached the throes of frenzied passion and let nature take its course.

I stayed away from Jake and Ted's gym for two days, but then I was drawn back. Jake seemed pleased to see me, and I knew he'd meet me in the sauna if I sent the signal. But before I got any closer to that, I was engaged in conversation with one of the older men who was always floating around the edge of the circle of serious body builders. He was good looking in a clean-cut, office manager sort of way. Just the sort of guy I'd like for a supervisor.

We started talking about sports. We both liked football. We both were fans of the Redskins. The Redskins were playing in the Monday night televised game that evening. Would I like to come over and watch the game with him?

"Sure, why not."

The game was running on the television, but I could only hear it, because my belly was folded over the top of the sofa in front of the television, my knees were wedged in the back of the seat cushion, my legs were spread, and my clean-cut guy host was covering me closely from behind and fucking hard down into me from the rear.

Crossing thresholds left and right now.

The Other Side of the Island

"There, is that better?" Peitr whispered into my ear.

"Uhh. Yes, yes. That feels great," I answered, and my words turned into a soft moan.

"Yes, I can feel it in your body. You are a lot looser now. You are moving with me more smoothly. Is it because of the release of guilt?"

"Yes," I whispered. "This helps erase the guilt. It's as if none of this is something I could do anything about now."

"I thought so," Peitr whispered, and he began to move his cock inside me, dragging the head of his crocked dick along my ass canal at seven inches of depth, making my hips join in his motion. My eyes went to the ceiling paddle fan above us, gauging the thrusts of Peitr's hips against the flap, flap sound and movement of the paddles. I tugged a bit on the two silk scarves lightly tying my wrists to the headboard above me, seeking assurance that I was at least symbolically imprisoned and psychologically couldn't do anything to defend myself.

Peitr's strong, solid Dutchman's body was closely covering mine on the bed, nipples to nipples and belly to belly. His legs covered mine, and I had my heels wrapped around his ankles. His arms covered mine, and he held his hands around the silk knots at my wrists, giving yet more of a comforting feel that I had no control over this. Only his hips and my pelvis were in motion, as the flap, flap of the ceiling fan above the brass bed moved what air there was in this dim-lit cabana across our naked, sweating bodies. Beyond the closed louvered doors, the heat and the jungle of the Caribbean island assaulted the small hotel cabana, trying to invade our sanctuary. Strange bird calls screamed their annoyance that they couldn't get at us in our secret hiding place.

What a difference two days had made. A long weekend, but Cindy had to go north, into snow country, on business, and the winter had gone on just too long in the mid-Atlantic states. I'd had enough of the snow for the year, so I headed for the Dutch Antilles, and more precisely for the remote resort island of Cayo Grande, in search of sun, sand, and adventure. I had found all three in abundance, and the latter beyond my wildest notions.

Peitr had been the local Dutch guide I'd hired for a day of deep-sea fishing. We drank all day and cavorted around in our skimpy Speedos on his boat. We downed beer by sunlight, shared a couple of bottles of wine over our shell fish during the sunset, polished off a bottle of scotch under the moonlight, and I had awakened this morning with my back cuddled into his chest, his arms wrapped around me, and his dick seven inches up my ass.

I hadn't wasted my anger. I hadn't been sober to have made such a decision; if it had hurt too much, I hadn't noticed; and I'd always wondered what being with another male would be like. Unfortunately, at this point, I still didn't know what it was like even though I'd done the deed, so I was quite willing to find out when both Peitr and his peter had awakened and he'd started pumping me again.

Peitr, who obviously had not been nearly as drunk the night before as I had, remarked on how tense I was this morning in contrast to the wild fucking we'd engaged in the night before.

I had to take his word for the wild fucking part; I hadn't remembered a thing about that. It had been his suggestion then that I be put under a mild restraint, and I agreed, and it had worked a charm. I was enjoying this fuck, and I wasn't feeling guilty about it.

After we both shot our loads, Peitr untied my hands, and we glided our hands around on each other's bodies, trying to cool down under the flapping ceiling fan. Peitr lifted his lips from one of my nipples, crooked his chin on my shoulder near an ear, and asked me, "Have you ever done it with a black man?"

"No," I responded. "I've never done it before with any man before you."

"We have some magnificent native black men on this island. Have you ever thought of doing it with a black man?"

"No. . . . Well, yes, actually, I thought about that in college a couple of times. But I grew out of that."

"And now? The thought of a huge black cock churning around inside you? Does that sound pleasant, like a Caribbean adventure you might like?"

"Yes." Well, I had to be honest.

"I have business at the resort all day tomorrow. Why don't you take my boat out? Did you see that big rock formation coming down to the sea when we were about half way around the island yesterday?"

"Y-e-s-s," I answered.

"Pull into the beach just beyond that rock formation from here. You will see such a big, magnificent black man there. You will recognize him when you see him. Tell him you are interested in a waiheilah. Give him a fifty-dollar bill and ask for a waiheilah. Can you repeat that? A waiheilah."

"A waiheilah," I repeated. "OK, yes, I'll give that a try. Now, let's shower and eat and hit the beach. If I don't come home with a tan, Cindy will be suspicious."

The next day, I packed a small gym bag with shorts and a T for when the sun got too hot, struggled into my Speedo, and went out in Peitr's boat as he suggested to motor to the other side of the island. I found the little cove on the other side of the rock formation that came down to the water and pulled Peitr's boat up to just beyond the tide line. I looked around and saw nothing. But then, when my eyes adjusted in the sunlight, I saw that there was a grass hut of a pretty good size beyond the fringe of palm trees, and on the sand side of those trees, but in their shadows, was a long dugout canoe. And in the canoe, his massive back and shoulders turned to me, crouched a black giant of a man.

I knew instantly that this was the man Peitr had told me to seek out. I walked up the sand toward him. Something told me that he knew I was there and was approaching him. As I got closer, I noticed something very strange. The black giant wasn't alone in the boat. I realized that someone must be laying on his belly in the boat under the black man, because I saw two forearms dangling over the sides of the boat in the bow on either side. And they were of a very fair-skinned man. As I got closer, I saw a mop of bright-red hair on a head that rested on one seat slat near the bow of the boat. Following on behind this were the freckled shoulders of a lithe, sinewy man, whose hips rested on another seat slat toward the stern of the boat. The black man was crouched behind and above this seat slat, and, as I drew neigh, I could see that the black man, who had one beefy fist planted in the small of the redheaded man's back, was pumping the most huge, blackest cock I'd ever seen in and out of the redhead's ass.

I stood there and watched in shock and awe for the longest minute, feeling my own cock coming to life at what I was watching. The redhead turned his face to me, and I recognized the Scandinavian tourist who had returned from the sea on Peitr's fishing boat the day I engaged Peitr's services.

"Yes, may I help you?" the black man asked me, without interrupting his rhythm, in a polite voice with a Dutch accent that resonated across the cove even though he had spoken in a soft tone.

"Peitr sent me," I stuttered out. "He told me to give you this money and to ask for a waiheilah."

"OK," the black man grunted and gave me a broad smile with flashing white teeth. "Excuse me," he said to the redhead and pulled out of him and rose and stepped out of the dugout.

I drew in my breath. He was completely naked, except for a thin leather belt around his waist attached to a knife sheath that ran down his thigh and held close to his leg with another thin leather strap around his thigh at the bottom of the sheath. He was magnificent, just as Peitr had said he'd be. He was nearly seven feet tall and had European features but was black as ebony. This happy combination no doubt resulted from many generations of mixed breeding on this small island. And everything on him was big and round and curvy and rock solid, something that a bodybuilder would have paid big bucks and invested most of his youth in at a serious stateside gym to obtain. The biggest part of all on him was his dong, which jutted straight and long and thick and dripping with precum out from his body in honor of what he had been engaging in when I had arrived. His big heavy balls were swinging freely between heavily muscled thighs.

"Come over here with me, please," he told me. And he led me to the edge of the sand beyond the bow of the boat and took, first one of my wrists, and then the other, and tied them to cuffs that were chained to two palm trees. My arms were now chained out and above my head between the trees, and I was turned, helpless now, facing the boat.

"I'll be back shortly," he said, "This gentleman has a bit more time left on his hour." Then the black giant returned to the dugout, crouched behind the Scandinavian, and thrust his blunderbuster back into the redhead's ass. The redhead screamed out in ecstasy and set his hips churning as the black giant plowed him with deep strokes that brought his cock all the way out to the surface only to be quickly buried to the hilt. The black man only stopped long enough to slowly revolve the redhead on his cock and onto his back and then to start pumping again. The redhead yelled in delight in whatever language he preferred and brutally stroked his own cock until he'd shot his load all over the black man's belly. Then he just laid back and enjoyed the rest of the long ride and threw his head back and yelled in sheer delight as the black man no doubt came inside him.

Leaving the redhead lolling there in the dugout, the black man rose out of the boat and walked over to me in fluid, catlike motions. He stood in front of me and drew a thick-bladed knife out of the sheath on his thigh. Adrenaline pumped through my veins. Was he going to cut me? Here, in front of the Scandinavian, who now was avidly watching us. The redhead was now slouched, facing us, on the seat slat at the stern of the boat, with his back resting on the stern and one hand firmly wrapped around his dick.

But the black man wasn't cutting me. With two swift slashes, he cut the fabric of my Speedo at the hips, and the bathing suit dropped to the ground. The Scandinavian smiled broadly and licked his lips. The black giant sheathed his knife, knelt in front of me, and began tonguing and kissing my cock, which had been fully engorged from the entertainment he had been putting on with the Scandinavian fellow. I writhed in front of him, my wrists pulling at my bonds, and the redhead pulling vigorously at his prick, while the black man deep throated my cock and rolled and pulled on my balls. His hand continued on past the root of my cock, under my balls, and a long, plump finger found my asshole. I gasped in surprise and pain as he entered me there. The pad of his finger found my prostate, and, in quick order, I shot off down his throat in a lurch and a spasm. The redhead was thoroughly enjoying the show.

The black man rose and moved around behind me. He noticed the redhead lounging in the dugout and spoke to him sharply in some language I didn't understand. The redhead spoke back to him in a wheedling voice. He fished around in a pile of clothes at the bottom of the boat and came out with a wad of money that he waved in the air. Another verbal exchange between the two, and the redhead threw the wad of money out on the sand between the bow of the boat and where I was hanging. He then settled back in the dugout and resumed slowly beating himself off and watching the show.

The black man was behind me now, his hands on my hips, his thumbs pulling my butt cheeks apart, and his tongue searching in my asshole. We were both grunting as he slobbered into my hole and got his fingers in there. He was pretty brutal about this at first, but he seemed to come to realize that I hadn't had much attention in that department and became more gentle and caressing in his touch. His tongue was driving me crazy, and I was softly moaning for him and swaying my hips. I slitted my eyes and watched the hazy horizon where the azure sky met the cobalt sea. I was being mesmerized by the shimmering sea, nearly drifting off into a pleasurable sleep.

But I was awakened out my reverie by the sense that the black man was trying to get me to lift my legs. But I didn't know where I was supposed to be lifting them to. I felt the heel of one foot slip into a close hold on the side of one of the palm trees I was lashed between, at just above the level of my waist. I looked down and saw that there was a wooden foot holder nailed into the tree at that point. I understood now, and raised my other leg up to the foot holder on the other palm tree. The black man, who was much taller than I was, now had his strong thighs below me, and I felt the head of his cock at my asshole.

I gulped and let out a hiss of pain as he entered me with the head of his cock. He was so much thicker than Peitr was. I felt that this bulbous head was going to split me apart. But Peitr had been right. Once I'd seen this big, black tool, I'd known I wanted it inside me. The black giant rotated the head around just inside my hole as I accommodated to it. I huffed and puffed until the head got beyond my sphincter muscle, and then I felt like it would be OK, that I could manage him. He wrapped a strong arm around my belly, and the hand of his other arm went to my nipples, which he squeezed and rolled. I laid my head back into the hollow of his chest at the shoulder and moaned.

"Is it going to be all right with you?" he asked in a polite tone, his rich baritone voice echoing around the cove. "The thickest is in now. I sense you are new at this. I can manage without taking the big part of me through there, if you like."

"Yes, yes, I'm all right now, I think." I whispered to him. "I don't want you to stop. I want this. That big, black dick. All of it. In me."

And then I felt his thigh muscles tense and he was sliding that big, black, glorious cock up into me to the hilt, my ass walls undulating in appreciation as he glided in. His arm tensed around my belly and his fingers dug into my nipples. I arched my neck back and screamed to the swaying tops of the palms. The redhead applauded, as the black giant skewered me to the end and then began pumping me, shallowly at first at the deepest level, and then with longer strokes that brought the rim of his cock head to my prostate before he dove again.

After a good fifteen minutes of this stroking, the black giant pulled out of me and came around to where he was facing me. He was grinning, obviously very pleased with me. He gathered up my legs, pulling my heels out of the holds on the sides of the palm tree, had me wrap my legs around the small of his back, and then got his hips under me and entered me again from below and pumped his cock up into me like a piston. I arched my back, forced my hips up, close, into his pelvis, and threw my head back and watched the palm branches swaying against the azure sky again. The black giant palmed my butt cheeks. His lips came down to my nipples, and he sucked and rolled and nipped those with his tongue and teeth.

I heard a little cry and looked to the dugout, where the redhead was spouting foamy white cum into the air. Nearly simultaneously, I shot off another load of my own up the black giant's abs, and he flooded my insides with a very frothy Caribbean welcome.

While I was motoring Peitr's boat back to the other side of the island, I was grinning at the thought that if Peitr was fishing for a good fat tip for the weekend, he had not been fishing in vain.

Tea of the Full Moon

"My, look how big and strong you've grown, my son," Arata's mamasan said with pride as she folded his kimono just so over his powerful, straight body. "The time is near for you to enter Lord Oraruto's service."

Both mother and son turned at the sound of the wheezing and hacking cough of the old one. Something they were saying had awakened her and set her off.

"Beware," she cackled, shuffling up to mother and son. "Don't listen to this woman, my grandson. And beware of the tea of the full moon."

"This 'woman' is your daughter, old one," Papasan exploded in anger from across the tatami mat. "You will speak of her with respect. She has the family interests ever before her."

"Family interests?" the old one spat out in derision. "What are Yamashita interests to me and my blood? You were ever the climbers. You would do anything to be in Lord Oraruto's good graces."

"And perhaps the disgrace of your family has its origins in not pleasing our daimyo," Papasan spat back. "Now be gone, you old crone. Your advice is not needed here."

The old woman shuffled across the mat and disappeared behind a bamboo screen, but not before turning and pointing to her grandson and declaring once again, "Remember what I said of the tea of the full moon. Beware."

When she was gone, Papasan looked over his handsome, strapping son. "Yes, I think your mother is quite right, Arata. I think it is time. Go to the family chest, Susumu, and help Arata pick out the finest of the family kimonos. And thank your mother, Arata, for thinking of and planning for your future and ours. I will climb the mountain to the castle and offer your services to our lord."

"Arigato, Mamasan," Arata murmured, not fully understanding why, only knowing that the Yamashitas had always served the daimyo of the Tokushima on the island of Shikoku—and always would.

A few short weeks later, Arata was called for. He went around to his family members, saying his good-byes and gathering their best wishes. His mamasan's eyes were watery with the momentousness of the occasion, and his papasan's demeanor showed him that this was a time for steely resolve.

There was no old woman to see him off, though.

"Where is she?" Arata asked with concern. "Is she not well? I cannot believe she would not be here to wish me good journey."

"She has gone to visit her family," Papasan said with a set mouth. "There was no need for her to be here."

The fine silks of Arata's many-layered kimono rustled in harmony with the sighing of the swaying pines as he mounted the stone steps to the castle. He was a fine, well-muscled young man, and he moved quickly and with grace. He required no light, as the moon was full, beckoning him to the top of the mountain, to the daimyo's castle in the rustling pine forest.

Soon he was standing at the lowered drawbridge over a dry moat surrounding a high stone wall. The large wooden gates closed with a sense of finality after he had passed through them and was searched for weapons in a small courtyard just beyond. The grinding of the gates shut seemed to mark the separation of early life working in the fields, teasing the difficult land to yield succulent rice, and a life of privilege and opulence inside these walls. The plans and maneuverings of his clan, the Yamashitas, to have him accepted into the service of the daimyo had been intricate and delicate. Only the best-formed sons of the most worthy families were accorded this honor.

Arata was brimming with pride and curiosity and anticipation as he was led down the courtyard and entered yet another heavily gated entrance set at a right angle to the first at the outer end of the courtyard and entered into a wondrous world of delicate wooden pavilions interlocked and rambling across and melding with a fairytale landscape of gardens and groves of trees and rippling brooks and moonlit ponds.

He was guided through a progression of pavilions along a wooden walkway and into the center of a small grove in which old-growth bamboo shoots grew close together around a wooden platform jutting over a small, exquisitely designed pond. This obviously was a very private place. A tiered roof on slim wooden posts provided a covering for the platform, although there was an opening in the middle of the roof through which moonlight streamed down and concentrated on a single squat table between two billowy silken pillows. The hint of another pavilion nearby was the source of quiet, lilting music from a lute, which harmonized well with the sound of water passing into and out of the pond at some unseen source.

Seated on one of the cushions in a billowing pile if rich silk was the daimyo himself, Lord Oraruto. Arata recognized him from seeing the lord's lavish parades up and down the mountain road whenever he traveled to the faraway court in Kyoto.

Lord Oraruto was a magnificent sight. Towering head and shoulders over anyone else in his retinue, he had a strong, stern face and was reputed to be perfectly formed. He certainly was battle tested; a warrior among warriors.

Now, however, he was alone on the tatami mat laid over the richly polished wood of the platform and seemed to be lost in deep contemplation. No one else was there, and when the escort had motioned Arata to the other cushion at the table, the two seemly were entirely alone, although Arata could sense lurking eyes of those ready to respond to the daimyo's every wish.

Arata had just arrived to take up service with his lord and he already was alone with the great daimyo. He was almost overcome with the honor of the occasion and the privilege that was being bestowed on him by a private audience.

The table was bare except for an exquisite tea set. Two squat tea pots and two cups, matched and intricately carved.

The daimyo said nothing. He just poured tea from one pot in a cup for himself and tea from the other pot into a cup set in front of his young visitor. A beam from the strong full moon poured through the opening in the pavilion roof and spotlighted the tea set.

Arata felt overwhelmed. His lord was offering him tea by his own hand. There was little in life more significant than this. This was nothing less than a marriage contract. Through this ceremony, Lord Oraruto was accepting the Yamashita clan's offering of their fairest son to the service of their lord.

Lord Oraruto motioned for Arata to take up the tea cup and to drink, and Arata did so with trembling hands. In turn, Lord Oraruto took up his own cup and drank deeply from it. He was watching Arata carefully, though, as he drank his tea. And when the young man had finished, Lord Oraruto immediately poured him another cup and bade, with hand signals, for the young man to drink up, which he did.

The tea was sweet and intoxicating on Arata's tongue. He wondered where such a wonderful drink came from. It was putting him into a dreamy state, and he felt his senses sharpening. He felt almost as if he could rise and float over the fairyland set inside the daimyo's far-flung castle.

Lord Oraruto was smiling at him now, and Arata began to hear a slow, dull drum beat mixed in with the lute music from across the pond—or was that just the pounding in his ears or of his heart?

The tea in the pot set aside for Arata was drained into the cup, and Arata drank the last of it, hungrily. Servants rushed in and swept away the table and tea set, but Arata hardly noticed their coming and going. His mind was dissembling, and his thoughts were fleeting. He was floating above all this and briefly hoped that his altered state of mind wasn't being noticed by his lord. He was slightly embarrassed, not being able to hold his tea. He had grown up on much stronger drink than this. He had no idea that tea could be so intoxicating.

Lord Oraruto had moved his cushion quite closely in front of Arata now, so that it was positioned where the tea table had been.

From the folds in his heavily layered kimono, the daimyo produced brush paintings on rice paper and turned them for Arata to examine. Arata blushed at what was being depicted in these paintings, but he was involuntarily aroused as well. That tea and its effect on his senses had dulled his natural aversion to what he had seen. He had seen such drawings before, but they had been very crude, not beautifully brushed as these were.

His eyes drank in the exotic couplings being presented on the rice paper, and he felt his body stirring as it did when he watched the young women of his village bathe themselves from the secret observation posts that he and the other young men had developed over generations of village life.

He heard more than felt at first the rustling of the silks. Those of the daimyo as his hands drew out of the folds of his kimono and then of the silk of his own kimono, as the daimyo pulled away the folds—just enough for his hands to slip in.

More rustling and Arata felt strong hands on his body inside the billowing layers of silk. He felt he should be doing something in response, in defense, but the drugged tea possessed his mind and opened his sensitivity to the pleasure of touch, and his eyes could not tear themselves from the erotic paintings that had been placed before him. And arching over all of that was his sense of history, of the many generations of Yamashitas, whose fortunes now rested on him. The Yamashitas were being honored and given good fortune. He was being honored and given good fortune.

He felt the silks being pulled gently apart across his chest, and a single puckered nipple was exposed to the evening breezes and then, just as quickly as it appeared, it was covered with the daimyo's lips.

At the same time, the daimyo's strong hands had parted Arata's inner thighs and were taking possession of the young man's hardening cock.

Arata let the erotic paintings slowly slide out of his hands and he began to struggle mentally over what was happening, loving the touch on his cock and the sucking at his nipple, but knowing that this somehow shouldn't be happening. He was murmuring, thinking he was asking for this to stop, if only for the moment until he could adjust to what was to happen. But it came out more as sighs and moans. His mind was not yet fully lost, but his body was. He was responding to the daimyo's touch on his cock, rising to his touch and beginning to undulate at the hips. The beat of the drum seemed to meld with his responses to the touching. It increased the beat in both rhythm and intensity.

Lord Oraruto moved one of his hands away from Arata's member long enough to take his young "offering's" hands and guide them into the folds of his own kimono, placing them on his own strong, erect phallus, giving his young recruit a good notion of the power and strength and determination—and intention—of him.

More rustling of silk and the kimonos became one pile of rich fabric now, patterns and colors melding together, still covering the two men fully except for that one nipple being brushed and suckled by searching lips.

But underneath, inside that merged collection of layers of silk, two bodies had come together. Arata was sitting in and straddling the daimyo's lap now and the daimyo was holding their erect cocks together and stroking them in unison. The beat of the drum increased, overpowering the strains of the lute, becoming louder and more insistent in its beat.

From somewhere in the folds of his kimono, the daimyo produced a magic lotion, a lotion he was now rubbing into Arata's virgin, puckered hole, making it loosen and widen and become a bit more numb. He was biting Arata's nipple now and fingering the young man's hole, taking slow but steady and relentless possession of his new offering with searching fingers.

Arata gave a muted scream of pain and filling as the daimyo lifted his hips with both of his hands, skewered him firmly on his powerful cock, and pulled the young man deeply into his lap.

The young offering arched his back, and his face turned skyward and was bathed in the beam of the full moon streaming through the opening in the pavilion ceiling as he began to move his hips, meeting the natural rhythm of his lord with that of his own, his fears and concerns melting away in a natural, primeval motion tracing its way up through the ages.

Rustling silk. Thrust. Moan. Drum beat. "Beware the tea of the full moon." Thrust. Groan. Drum beat. "Beware the tea of the full moon." Thrust. M-o-a-n. Drum beat. "Beware . . . ." Aiyeeeeee.

Clouds and Rain

I didn't believe the Chujen, and I was confused. I was being trained for clouds and rain at the spring festival, as was Bao. My training and preparation had been exacting, and I had already pleasured with the kiss of the yangchu act most of the important and famous men who would be bidding at the seed sowing ceremony to take me into my first clouds and rain. But all contact with these jen had been under the watchful eyes of the master of the House of the Green Dragon, the Chujen, to ensure that I remained pure of the clouds and rain and did not lose my chenchieh, my chastity, until the ceremony. The Chujen had said I had done admirably well with the wiles and enticements that had been taught me and that the bidding and the bidders themselves were in a frenzy of anticipation.

But one night, weeks before the spring festival, the Chujen said my time had come early—and that of Bao as well—and I had been roused before dawn the next day and bathed and shaved clean of everything but a silken skein of pigtailed hair at the back of my head. I had also been perfumed, powdered with the enticement powder, and—when what I thought was just one of Chujen's cruel training exercises and teases turned to the horror of possibility—shown that I would be clothed in the shimmering red brocaded robes of my clouds and rains ceremony.

Chujen had told me of the Kueilo, the foreign ghosts, who had appeared off Haikou inside a monstrous chu'an, floating beneath a billowing cloud. But I didn't believe him or understand what this had to do with me and Bao.

"This is far greater than the spring festival, Gaopu," he had said. "This spreads the renown of the House of the Green Dragon all the way to the feet of the Shengchang of Hainan."

I knew nothing of the governor of our island province and cared even less, but the Chujen slapped me for my pouting insolence and continued.

"The Shengchang has been put into a quandary, and he has come to me for a solution. This is an opportunity of generations. And you could not be more honored if your chenchieh could be renewed every spring for the highest bidder. In fact, with the favoring of the Shengchang, the bidding on you should go up now, although I will have to do some fast training and preparation of another for the spring festival."

I opened my newly rouged lips to speak, but, seeing the expression on my face, the Chujen slapped me again, sending clouds of white powder into the air and a flurry of house servants scurrying about to repair the damage to their hours of work on my face. As luck had it, I still was naked in the wake of the powdering. I would have had better luck if I already had been wound into my red robes. Chujen wouldn't have dared ruin those with the spray of white powder. As it was, he was wasting a fortune. The intoxicating, yangchu-hardening powder was a dear commodity.

"If you are successful, I may send you to Haikou, to the Shengchang, who has made certain requests. He is the one who selected you for this assignation. If not, I will turn you out into the streets of Xinzhou, where the fishermen of the town will know what to do with you."

I remained unimpressed. He often threatened me with the randy fisherman of the town below our cliff. He had invested too much time, effort, and treasure in me for that to be a real threat. At the worst he would sell me to some dried-up ancient with no seed, flatulence, fish breath, and a limp yangchu.

"We are to provide delay," Chujen informed me. "You are to make the Kueilo—the foreign devil—who appears for you to dally as long as possible. The Shengchang does not know if the vessel is a shangchu'an or a chunch'an, a merchant ship or a war ship. There have been rumors of these Kueilo appearing at the fringes of the Central Kingdom, but never here. In either case, they must be made to turn away or go down to the depths of the sea. The Shengchang has sent queries to the emperor, but the situation is momentous; he must know if he can simply kill them or not."

I adopted my humblest look and kowtowed at the Chujen's feet. "But I don't understand, Chujen. Why are they coming here to Xinzhou? We are simply the pleasure resort for Haikou. What do we have to do with such momentous affairs?"

The Chujen patiently tried to explain, which in itself made me worry. Such reasonableness was not in keeping with the Chujen's nature. "Panicked for delaying tactics, the Shengchang saw the eyes of the Kueilo's Ch'uanchu, ship's captain, light up at the offer of a respite of clouds and rain—with a courtesan such as you. And he chose the House of the Green Dragon over other pleasure houses. And the Shengchang insisted on purity—in short, our spring offerings for the seed sowing ceremony—you and Bao."

Still I did not believe the Chujen. Still I thought this was some sort of conditioning joke he was having. That it was all part of the ritual. What did the outer world have to do with our small pleasure house high on the cliffs over the Xinzhou lagoon?

But later that afternoon, as I reclined on pillows on the veranda of the Vermilion Pavilion overlooking the sea, trying my best not to transfer any of the enticement powder to the red brocade of my ceremonial robes, I began to believe. I could not believe what I was seeing at first. A giant sea bird slowly appeared from around the eastern point of rocks and glided toward the lagoon, guided in by a red barge of the Shengchang that I recognized from his earlier visits to the House of the Green Dragon. A towering, black-wood vessel driven by billowing clouds of white gossamer.

Bao was by my side, in robes of darkest emerald blue. He shrank from the sight of the giant, floating bird and began to

71

breathe heavily. But I was mesmerized by the sight. And aroused. I had always been scolded for my fantasies and attraction to danger, but these were the same traits that had me here, at the pinnacle of empowerment. There was no more luxurious life or power over powerful men than the life of a clouds and rain master.

As Bao's nervousness grew with the far-off vision of figures in strange, black, close-fitting clothing roping down into the House of the Green Dragon launch that had been sent out to their vessel to fetch them, my interest and curiosity grew.

For what seemed to be hours but was only a short time, we could hear the Kueilo being ceremoniously welcomed in the reception rooms below us. We heard the wheedling, smooth tones of the Chujen, covered by a raucous cacophony of hard, guttural sounds from the Kueilo. It was obvious that neither understood the other, but as the voices of the foreign ghosts grew louder and their speech slurred, we understood that the Chujen had managed to place them under the spell of our special wine, spiced to loosen nerves and cares and enervate the yangchu.

And then two of them were there in the entrance to the Vermilion Pavilion, one on each side of the Chujen, and with a semicircle of slack-jawed and murmuring tunic-clad house servants behind them.

They were both monstrous. The taller of the two, quite evidently the Chu'anchu, was a Hungmao, a red-haired devil. I had read of such in the classics, but they were monsters from beyond the pale. He stood there, a full head taller than the Chujen. And such a head it was. Fully encircled with bright red, curly hair—on top and down the sides and under his chin and his nose. Broad shouldered and thin waisted, he was swathed in clinging sweat-soaked, rough black coat, under coat, and leggings and heavy black, shiny boots, which were not just exotic, but they also must be stifling in the heat of our subtropical island province. I could smell him from here. A meat eater. Underneath the hair and clothing, I could see that the man was of palest hue, the source of the name that had been given to these recent interlopers on our world—THE world: ghost.

The other man, not much taller than the Chujen, but much thicker, all hard muscle, in the body and similarly clothed to the other Kueilo, stood beside and slightly back from the Hungmao, another signal of who was the most important. This second foreign ghost had hair of the tawniest gold, not an auspicious color. We had legends of other such golden-haired men visiting from the outside side, across the deserts to the west, in times past. But they had been famous for their cruelty, and we had absorbed and destroyed them as they deserved. This Kueilo standing before us, one step back from his Chu'anchu, exuded this sense of cruelty. He had a gold ring in one ear and a black patch over one eye, and a leering stare that bore right through Bao and me.

Bao shrank against me, but I looked out at the Kueilo with disdain and with a haughtiness that I had been taught drove some men wild with wanting. I felt all tingly, ready for the challenge of my Shengchang. But the men smelled to high heaven. Before I could stomach even pleasuring either one of them in a kiss of the yangchu act, they would have to be cleaned. And I told the Chujen so in no uncertain terms. His eyes flashed, but he realized, I am sure, that there were limits to what I could do with an unwashed meat eater. Besides, as I was soon to find out, he had already anticipated that need.

As soon as I had spoken, the eyes of both Kueilo focused on me and both smiled that smile I had already seen a hundred times at the House of the Green Dragon. They both wanted me. But it was the pale blue eyes of the Hungmao Ch'uanchu that I met with mine, and I knew in an instant the pairings were settled.

If I had known beforehand what happened then, I would have acted differently. But the future, even the immediate future, is not for solitary Chungkuojen—Chinese man—like me to know—this is knowledge reserved to the emperor or at least one of no lower in the order than the Shengchang.

The Chujen motioned for Bao and me to rise and part. I was waved toward the eastern chamber off the Vermilion Pavilion and Bao toward the western chamber. The Chujen nudged the Hungmao toward the east and the golden Kueilo toward the west, which they both immediately acknowledged and acceded to. The house servants split behind the Chujen, one half gliding toward the eastern chamber and the other half toward the western chamber.

I heard Bao mutter a cut-off exclamation as he and the golden Kueilo both reached the entrance to the western chamber. This was unheard of—for a clouds and rain master to say anything at this stage of the act—and my head snapped around at the sound. The golden Kueilo had already laid hands on Bao. When Bao involuntarily shrank away from him, the golden Kueilo backhanded him across the cheek with such a mighty blow that Bao was propelled through the entrance of the eastern chamber. The golden Kueilo turned and gave the house servants moving in his direction a menacing look that stopped them dead in their tracks, and they retreated, backing away from him and bowing low at the waist.

My eyes went to the Chujen for reaction. Under normal circumstances, he would have used his martial arts skills to neutralize such a crass and out-of-control patron. But, though I could see that Chujen's jaw was set and his body tensed on the edge, he did nothing. That's when I knew this was a reality. That all he had said about the directive from the Shengchang and the importance of delaying the Kueilo's return to Haikou was true. True and necessary. Important. Perhaps vital to maintaining civilization as we knew it.

The sounds from the western chamber were rending. The tearing of cloth—which I could see was tearing equally at the Chujen, something I could well understand, knowing the price of a spring ceremonial robe—the crude gruntings of the Kueilo in immediate and full rut, and the cries of Bao, cries that were unthinkable in the House of the Green Dragon, told me in no uncertain terms that the clouds and rain had already started in the western chamber and that Bao' chenchieh—his chastity— was as good as undone already. I knew that any delay was now entirely mine to provide.

At the doorway to the eastern chamber, I turned and looked up into the pale blue eyes of the Hungmao and tried to convey with every fiber of my being that he would have me but not in the way and at the pace that the golden Kueilo was having Bao. He seemed to understand, and I was heartened to get the

74

impression that he took his pleasures at a much more easy pace than his compatriot did.

At the interior end of the eastern chamber was a bathing tub with steaming water in it. At the open end overlooking the Xinzhou lagoon was a pallet of red silk with mountains of red silk pillow cushions, the home of the clouds and rain, where I would lose my chenchieh.

The Hungmao stood in the center of the room, an amused look on his face, and his arms outstretched and legs in a wide stance, as the house servants slowly but methodically figured out how to unclothe him. The Chujen stood in the doorway from the Vermilion Pavilion, watching the Hungmao being disrobed. He would stand there and observe until the completion of the first clouds and rain. It was his duty to do so—to observe and record the time and place of my loss of chenchieh. It would be marked in vermilion ink, the highest honor—at the pleasure of the Shengchang. Even higher than a link to the spring festival seed sowing ceremony would have been. It added stacks of hsienchien, cash, to my worth for each subsequent clouds and rain assignation.

The Chujen obviously could not observe the moment for Bao, which, from the sounds from the other chamber had already taken place and was moving into a second taking, but the Chujen was a modern jen of practicality. He would simply record what he hadn't actually seen, and he knew that I would not naysay him, even though it was my duty to do so. He knew that I would not subject Bao to that dishonor and loss of future status.

My eyes were also on those of the Hungmao. His eyes were focused on me. He wanted to see my reaction to his nakedness. And, trained as I was, I was already prepared to respond with embarrassment and awe. I was trained to do this for a eunuch or castrati, if faced with that in this situation and they had been given access to me by the Chujen. I needed no training to fall back on, though. The Hungmao was huge in ways I had never seen before. His body was well formed and hard and bulging in muscles, obviously from hard, honest work. He was covered in red, curly hair everywhere. And his yangchu was the heaviest and longest I'd ever seen.

I gulped and my eyes went wide open and my jaw slack—all movements I'd been trained in to please the jen I'd been given to, but movements that came naturally under these circumstances. And my reaction pleased the Hungmao, which I could readily see as his yangchu rose parallel with the matting under us and filled out impossibly larger.

He went into the bath with the help of the house servants. A couple of these carried off his clothing, undoubtedly to be double boiled, and the other house servants began scrubbing him in earnest. The past year's spring festival master, Wangan, glided into the room with willowy stride and knelt beside the tub. His hands went into the soapy water, and I watched the Hungmao's eyes slit and the pleasure fan out across his face as Wangan enclosed his hands around the Hungmao's yangchu and began to stroke.

It was my time then. I stood there, between the tub and the sea, between the Hungmao and the pallet of my chenchieh farewell and untied my obi and began to slowly unwind my red ceremonial robe and the deep purple under robe. I took a long time doing this, and the Hungmao's eyes were glued to my form the entire time. I could hear him sighing from where I stood from the ministrations of Wangan's delicate, expert hands and fingers on the Kueilo's yangchu. Almost as if not realizing what he was doing, the Hungmao had one hand searching inside the folds of Wangan's robes, where he obviously found what he was looking for and was stroking it. His other hand was lifted above his head and had snaked into the tunic of one of the house servants scrubbing at him and had exposed and was tweaking a nipple.

After a slow, orchestrated, long-practiced performance of revealing myself, I stood there before him, the folds of the red and purple robes swirling around my feet, my hands on my hips and swaying ever so imperceptibly from side to side. I was perhaps half his size. Lithe and willowy, but muscle hard from years of ever-higher-level tai chi practice. Naked and completely shaved, and I possessed the pert little yangchu and ball sac that Chungkuojen so highly prized in their clouds and rain masters. I worried briefly if this would please a Kueilo as well, but the look he cast on my revealed body left no doubt that he did. As was

76

wanted in a spring festival master, I had the years of an adult but the body of a youth.

The Kueilo lost all interest in Wangan and the house servant and, indeed, in his bath, although, happily he had been scrubbed sufficiently already. He rose up and stepped out of the tub. Wangan had done well. That and the effect of my own disrobing had caused the Hungmao's yangchu to rise and fill out to rival the most virile of the stud horses in the House of the Green Dragon's stables.

I moved breathlessly to him, kneeling before him and gently enclosing the base of his yangchu in my small fists, one above the other, and still leaving more than I thought my mouth could accommodate. In a rustle of naked feet and soft silk, I sensed more than heard Wangan and the house servants evaporate beyond the bamboo screens.

For the next several minutes, as the Hungmao sighed and growled and rocked back and forth on the pads of his gigantic feet and breathed heavily and noisily, he moved my head between his enormous paws while I entertained him with everything I had learned in the art of the kiss of the yangchu.

He was getting bigger and bigger and was pumping ever more rapidly with his yangchu inside my mouth. My hands went to his heavy orbs. I could hardly enclose them in my hands, they were so large and tightly balled. None that I had handled before now were anything like this size. The Kueilo was a monster of a man, and I was wondering if he was typical of his people or a monster among them as well as I felt his bulbous knob pressing against the back of my throat.

I lightly squeezed on the orbs, wanting him to drain himself now, before the clouds and rain, to delay that by the time he needed to recover for another seeding. Every moment of delay was precious time. I understood that now.

But, with a roar, the Hungmao, pulled me up and off his throbbing yangchu. He turned me and pushed me down on all fours, and I understood that he was going to invade me right there and then.

That could not be, though. Our customs and rules were quite explicit. I must lose my chenchieh on the red pallet across the chamber. I heard Chujen quietly exclaim, obviously making

77

the same point. But I didn't need him to remind me of the ceremony requirements. I had been studying these for four season cycles.

I broke free somehow and half crawled and half scuttled toward the red pallet. The Hungmao misinterpreted, assuming, I'm sure, that he had frightened me too much and that I was trying to escape. The renewed cries from the other chamber across the Vermilion Pavilion only added credence to this thought. Bao was being plowed hard and roughly now, as he was loudly and plaintively complaining of—just like a stable boy, completely wiping away his dignity and social status. I could only hope that only the Chujen and I remained to hear of his dishonoring—that the house servants were well beyond hearing. But I knew that was hopeless thought. All that comforted me was knowing that any house servant heard gossiping about this night would lose his tongue—and maybe his yangchu as well.

The Hungmao reached me and toppled me down on my belly in a cloud of white powder as I reached the red silk pallet. I did manage, however, to pull up onto the pallet on my hands and knees as the Hungmao encased my hips between his strong knees.

I heard the rustle of the Chujen's robes as he decorously approached with a pot of scented clouds and rain ointment and calmed the Hungmao long enough to convey that he was trying to aid the inevitable act. The Hungmao held me down on all fours with one arm wrapped around my chest as he crouched over me and invaded my tight and virginal anus with lubricated fingers while the Chujen worked ointment on the Hungmao's prodigious, throbbing yangchu.

I had the sense then of being in the embrace of a silken-pelted bear as the Chujen faded back to the entrance of the chamber and the Hungmao held the bulbous head of his yangchu to my back entrance in an encasing, directing fist.

The Hungmao panted hard as he worked himself inside me, and I panted even harder and suppressed my groans and moans as best I could as he did so. The groaning and moaning was meant to be saved for later, when the patron was fully saddled and was stroking and needed to hear that he was the master of the Central Kingdom.

But I could not help it. I cried out in pain and invasion, nothing like this having been part of what I had learned over the last four season cycles. Although, to rights, no one involved in my training could have been known that I was destined to lose my chenchieh to a monster horse foreign ghost yangchu.

"I must not faint," I kept repeating to myself. "I must pleasure him with my body for as long as possible." I gritted my teeth and took him inside me and clenched my entrance muscles as I had been taught and listened in triumph to him gasp in pleasure at that. And then, as he sank in and in and in, I tried, through the wall of pain, to conjure up all of the exercises I had learned to control the muscles inside me. To make them ripple around and across his yangchu, to make internal love to his manhood as I had been taught to do. The clouds, the important clouds before the rain—the beating of one cloud against the other, the friction that brought on the rain, with the greater the cloud beating, the greater the rain.

He groaned and gasped in pleasure and his lips went to the hollow of my neck, where they ingested the enticement powder. He murmured and sighed and moaned and I felt the powder working in the impossible reality that he grew even larger inside me.

His horse yangchu slid back and forth, shallow and then deep, to the surface and then diving down, down, down and holding as my muscles contracted around him and worked on his yangchu.

I could hear Bao screaming out that he was being split asunder and that his insides were being flooded—again—from the other chamber, and I began to wiggle my hips, no longer in as much pain as at the beginning. Something else was moving inside me now. Wanting. Actually wanting this clouds and rain. I was working the clouds—the touching and the sighing and the moaning and the movement under him and back against him as he thrust, meeting him thrust for thrust now. Listening to his ragged breathing. Giving him the best clouds he had ever received. Living up to the reputation of the House of the Green Dragon.

Then the rains came. The Hungmao cried out in ecstasy and the rains came. Deep inside me. He collapsed on top of me,

79

pushing me down on my belly on the red silk pallet, and I heard the rustling of the Chujen's robes as he left us, his official duties finished—back to his dark room and is vermilion ink and his triumphant collection of a favor from the Shengchang, a favor that could sustain the House of the Green Dragon for generations to come.

I heard Bao sputtering and crying out from the other chamber. That his wrists had been tied and he was doubled over the rim of the unused tub and was being roughly entered again and again and again with his head forced under the water and only lifted again by the fist of the monster in his hair when he no longer could breathe—again and again. That the golden Kueilo smelled vile and cruelly bit and had a yangchu thicker than the pillars in the Vermilion Pavilion. That his rains were a flood. But there was nothing I could do for Bao now. I had to delay the departure of the vessel. And I knew it would not leave without its captain. Perhaps if I could detain him even for a night.

The Hungmao rolled off me and he lay on his back, still panting. Gathering all of the resolve and resources I could, I sat up and moved my head over his heaving chest and started to lick his nipples and set his red chest hair aswirl. My hands danced over his torso and down to his yangchu, still huge but now in repose. I needed to coax him into clouds and rain again. I needed him to believe that only with me could he accomplish rapid recovery and multiple clouds and rain. Wanting to stay with me as long as possible. I knew this was vital to the pride of any man, Chungkuojen or Kueilo. All the same in the vanity realm. Entice three clouds and rain in an assignation, and the man is yours forever.

I put an arm around his neck and lifted his mouth to my nipple. He sucked and licked while I worked my other hand across his cheek. I moved his mouth around the nipple, coaxing him to ingest more of the enticement powder, which he did. This had the desired effect, in consort with my stroking, on his yangchu. He was regaining virility. I stroked the slit in the head of his yangchu with the tip of my finger, and he gasped and began to writhe in pleasure, his life's fluid beginning to bubble up onto my finger. I would feel him trembling at the knowledge that there would be a second clouds and rain so soon after the first. He already was nearly mine.

After I'd heard the last gurgling cry from Bao from across the Vermilion Pavilion, followed by an ominous silence, I felt more than saw the presence of the golden Kueilo at the entrance to the eastern chamber. I could hear his ragged breathing. I knew he was watching the Hungmao and me deeply entering our second clouds and rain.

The Hungmao was kneeling, sitting back on his calves and facing out toward the sunset over the Xinzhou lagoon. He was holding me, like a small doll, in front of him, me facing the lagoon as well, my knees leveraging off the surface of the red-silk pallet, body arched out, and my anus sliding up and down on the Hungmao's rejuvenated yangchu. Up and down, endlessly. I no longer was in pain. I was enjoying the taking. I wondered if I would ever be swallowing a member this large ever again. Stretching for him. Perfecting the skills of internal muscle massage of a throbbing horse yangchu of impossible size and strength.

The Hungmao was sighing and groaning contentedly.

A shadow fell on me and I no longer could see the lagoon. What I saw now was a short, thick yangchu jutting out of a thick thatch of golden hair. I almost gagged at the thickness and smelliness of the second Kueilo's yangchu as he pushed it between my lips. But this was no time for niceties. I gave him quite satisfactory kiss of the yangchu attention too. I was determined to keep them here as long as possible. If Bao had failed, I could only try to succeed.

The golden Kueilo grabbed my pigtail and forced my head back and he pushed hard down inside my mouth with his yangchu. The Hungmao, between pants of his own spoke sharply at the golden one in that ugly guttural language of theirs, though, and the golden Kueilo released my pigtail.

The virile Hungmao was still sliding me up and down on his yangchu when the golden one released his seed inside my mouth. He brought his mouth down to mine and sucked his fluid from inside my mouth in a lips-on-lips invasion that we almost never performed between men at the House of the Green Dragon. But if it delayed their parting for even a moment,

81

I would do it. I returned his kiss and stifled my surprise and pain when he bit me on the lip.

The golden one knelt down before me and I felt his fingers forcing their way inside my anus alongside the sliding yangchu of the Hungmao. He was stroking his own yangchu back to thickness with his other hand, and for a brief moment I panicked at the sure knowledge that he intended his yangchu to join that of the Hungmao's inside me.

But the Hungmao spoke gruffly to the golden one, and he pulled his fingers from me and stood and moved toward the door. I knew from what he was saying that he was telling the Hungmao it was time for them to return to the vessel in the lagoon.

I tightened my internal muscles on the Hungmao's yangchu inside me and turned his lips to mine and gave him lip-to-lip attention for the first time in our clouds and rain. He reacted with surprise and pleasure, and then I took his head and buried his lips into my shoulder, where there still was some enticement powder lingering. He was lost to me then.

He and the golden Kueilo exchanged hurried and angry words. As they spoke, I performed the fan movement of the clouds and rain. In one deft, lithe movement, I turned on the Hungmao's yangchu to where I was facing him and, at the same time, pushed him down onto his back, with his muscle-bulging hairy legs now stretched out toward the lagoon.

With the golden Kueilo still angrily talking and gesturing and the Hungmao groaning loudly in ecstasy and his pale-blue eyes revolving wildly in their sockets, I began to ride his yangchu hard with revolving hips and rippling internal muscles. The golden one gave up in disgust and departed, while his captain writhed in deep lust under me. The Hungmao flooded me with his essence soon thereafter.

He drifted off to sleep hours later after the third clouds and rain, in which I lay on my back, my hips raised by red silk pillows, my legs flared out wide, and the Hungmao on his knees on the red pallet between my legs, looking out at the now-furled sails of his vessel riding quietly in the lagoon and moving his hips back and forth, rhythmically and forever while I sighed and moaned for him, letting him know he was the most masterful jen in the Central Kingdom. Holding him enthralled with every trick I had learned. I looked again down at the water, rewarded by glimpses of other, more familiar sails of ships pulling into positions in coves between the Kueilo vessel and the open sea, but out of the view of the Hungmao's ship.

I performed clouds and rain, each time in a different position and ever more intricately, holding the Hungmao's total attention between replenishment meals supplied by a delighted Chujen, for the next three days and nights.

When the Hungmao finally descended to his vessel, stiff legged and humming, on the fourth day, I was at the edge of the veranda of the Vermilion Pavilion, only slightly happy to see him go. He had a yangchu such as I would never again ride, a yangchu that the Chujen would have expertly measured in length and thickness in his mind and in his handling during the clouds and rain ointment application and would record on my record of capability. But it wasn't just the size of him, which enhanced my value to the House of the Green Dragon; as my clouds and rain became more inventive, he had become more and more gentle and lost to me. If the Shengchang had instructed that he be held here forever, I could have managed that—and would have been content doing it.

I could part from him with the knowledge that my fortune and legend was now made, not just in the house of the Green Dragon, but beyond the pleasure resort of Xinzhou—perhaps even beyond the province of Hainan. I could dream of being lionized to the emperor himself. Perhaps I could dream of serving the yangchu needs and desires of the Son of Heaven himself.

But as much as I had come to enjoy the Hungmao's horse yangchu churning inside me, I was Chungkuojen to the very fiber of me. I sensed that these Kueilo, these foreign ghosts, were devils to be avoided and kept away from the purity of my land. At least I could rest in the knowledge that my four days of delay had given the Shengchang the time he needed to devise plans to eradicate this threat—to ensure that no Kueilo ghost ships would enter Xinzhou's lagoon or the bays of any other city in the Central Kingdom ever again.

Marking Territory

It was when I threw a match in the third round of the U.S. Open that I fully realized I was obsessed by him. I wasn't afraid of going up against the young Miguel Herrera—the heartthrob of the tennis world groupies they had nicknamed the Argentine Firecracker. I had beaten him all three times we had met on the pro circuit the last two years. It was because I knew I was aging out of the circuit just as he was coming into his own here that I had thrown that match. We were both winning and might meet in the fourth round, and I couldn't have that. I couldn't be sure I'd win this time.

He was gorgeous, and I could tell that he was becoming available. Until now, he had been sequestered by his coaches—his parents—since he was a child. They'd brought him to the States, to Bolettieri in Florida, at a very young age, and had always been there, watching him like eagles, homeschooling him, keeping him away from everyone not inside his tight circle, focusing him completely on developing his tennis and his lovely body. Even between matches, in the locker rooms, his body may have been on display, and he certainly had the opportunity to see mine—I made sure that was so—but even then his father was at his side, protecting him from everyone buzzing around the wonder child.

Miguel had been headstrong. He had rebelled and acted out on the tennis court, and he had filed emancipation papers a year earlier, but all that had done was to make judges side with his parents long enough that when he finally got free of them, he had only exchanged their watchfulness for that of a court-appointed guardian. But he would finally get free of that as well, tomorrow, on his eighteenth birthday.

I knew he, the hard- tanned-bodied Latin honey with the sultry looks and the shock of black curly hair dipping down into his eyes, was interested in men. I could see it in his eyes in the locker room, and I could see it in his face and his body movements when he faced me and others on the tennis court. But he hadn't had the opportunity. And obstinate rebel that he was, I knew that the smothering he had received contributed to his willingness to be bold and wild. My worry was that all of the other men I knew who might be interested, were, indeed, interested in Miguel. It was just a matter of who could get to him first.

I had to have him, and I had to master him before I ever lost a match to him. I had to have him not only on the tennis court, but in bed as well. I had to fuck him and—most important—I had to be the first one who fucked him. I had to mark my territory on the new generation of tennis stars before my own star faded away.

I made my move when he stopped by the players' lounge to commiserate with me on my third round match loss. Ironically, he had lost too. But there was no time for regrets on having thrown my match unnecessarily. I quickly suggested that we play a match of our own on his hotel court the next day—the day he turned eighteen—and he accepted. I was worried enough that he would lose his virginity before I could get to him that I asked whether he wanted to go out that evening, but he flashed me a look of regret, tinged with a sultry come-hither look, pointed to the middle-aged child protection official plastered to his side, and said that, regrettably, he was still under wraps until the morning.

"We will just have to wait for tomorrow," he said. And he left me wondering whether that thought excited him half as much as it did me.

I met him in the lobby of the hotel, both of us dressed for tennis, bright and early the next morning. He turned toward the corridor out to the courts, but I touched him at the waist to get his attention, and said I had a better idea. That I had a limo waiting out front and thought we could go for a ride to some courts up the Hudson River near Hyde Park.

"You want me to take a ride with you?" he asked, a little confused.

I increased the pressure of my hand at his waist.

"More explicitly, I want to ride you," I said, volleying right for the point. "I've seen the way you've been eyeing me, and unless I'm mistaken, you are willing. I want to be the first one to ride you. Would I be?"

"Yes," Miguel responded in a weak voice. And I could feel him trembling under the pressure of my hand.

"Yes to which," I asked.

"To both," he murmured.

I moved the other one to his waist, holding him up with both of my strong hands, making sure his knees wouldn't give out.

"Not here. I booked out at the tennis court, and—" Miguel mumbled.

"I have a car waiting outside. I didn't come for tennis," I said, crowding him, not giving him room to think it out, to come up with objections. "You need someone experienced for the first," I said, reasoning with him. "You're a young stallion. Everyone will want you. You have a brilliant career ahead of you, and I don't just mean on the tennis court. You need to be broken in right. I can do that for you. Come with me. Out of the hotel. Into the car. Into my arms. Let me be the first."

He put his hand on my arm and looked at the door to the street with hungry eyes, and I knew he was mine.

The limo, with its darkly smoked windows, was being driven by a friend of mine, an occasional fuck buddy who had agreed to cruise up the Hudson on parkways and back roads for as long as I wanted him to.

I handed Miguel into the back seat of the limo, and I had my tennis shirt pulled over my head as I entered behind him and my shorts stripped off before my butt hit the seat. I wasn't wearing anything under them. I had wanted to be ready for action.

I went to Miguel immediately, wrapping an arm around him, finding his lips with mine, forcing his hand into my lap so he could see how much I wanted him, how much I had to give him. I didn't want him to have time to rethink this. I captured his eyes with mine. His showed a fierce fight between fright and uncertainty on the one side and desire and wonder on the other. I let loose of his lips and buried my lips and teeth in his neck, while my hand went to measuring and weighing his cock and balls through the fabric of his tennis shorts. He gasped in surprise, and I grunted in appreciation at what I found there. I stopped to strip off his T-shirt, and then my hand went up to his belly and my mouth went back to sucking deeply along his neck below his ear—raising a bruise there, marking my territory for all to see for the week to come. I was here. I was here first.

He was burbling nothings with soft, rhythmic sounds, completely stunned by what was happening and with how fast it was happening. My hand slid down his belly, beyond his waistband, and grabbed his engorging cock and squeezed it hard. And this time it was I who gasped and he who grunted and threw his head back against the padded seat and began making funny little sounds at the back of his throat. I had gasped at the discovery that he hadn't been wearing anything under his tennis shorts either.

I stripped his shorts right off and turned and lifted his lithe body with my hands at his hips and just brought his cock to and into my mouth and drank him into me to the root, my hands now cupping his buttocks to my face. His body just sort of flopped around a bit in that awkward position, his knees hitting about midway up the seat back and his head at first in the back window well, watching the road race by through the rear window, and then, as he arched his back and tried to rise, digging his fingers into my hair, either trying to pull my face off his cock or grind face and pelvis together, I knew not which, and eventually arching his back toward the front of the car, one hand holding onto a leather ceiling strap for leverage and the other scrabbling around, trying to find a grip in the rich velour covering the car's ceiling. At one point I left my attack on his cock to bite him hard enough where his plate-like belly folded into the top of his groin to make him cry out—mostly in surprise, not hard enough to make him scream in pain. He didn't know why I did this, but I knew why. Marking my territory. I was here first.

I moved my palms so that I could get the tips of a finger from each hand into his virginal hole, and Miguel came at the back of my throat quickly in the heavy, strong spurts of the virile, but-as-yet-little-used, youthful cum. I swallowed his sweet juice. He was mine.

I let him just collapse down into my lap then, facing me, his butt in my lap and his hands now spread on the floor of the car, trying to hold his torso up, as I fisted our cocks together and stroked them lightly, captured his eyes with mine, and whispered endearments to him. My other hand was busy exploring his nipples and belly. I raised my legs with my feet buried in the thick cushioning on the backs of the seats in front of it, and Miguel relieved the pressure on his hands by laying his back along my legs.

After his breathing had calmed and he seemed rested, I dragged his hips up my chest, causing his legs to wishbone out wide, his athletic thighs bulging with muscle, as his feet found purchase out wide on the ceiling of the car. And I buried my face in the sweet, honest, youth smell of the rosebud between firm, yet creamy butt cheeks. Miguel moaned and made little gurgling sounds for me while I tongued and then fingered his ass, my fingers wet with the KY I'd had tucked in the seat cushion. He cried out in ecstasy as I slowly opened his ass to me—blowing on his tight rosebud to make him sigh and twitch, tonguing him deeply to make him moan, finger fucking him to make him gasp and grunt.

When he was sufficiently open, I slid my hands under him and sat him, facing me, in my lap again. He was on his haunches, his knees buried in the back of the seat cushion, sitting on my thighs, our cocks once more bunched together. I pulled a condom out from the seat cushions and made him open the packet and sheath my sword. I rubbed that down good with KY and then I lifted him with my hands cupped under his butt and positioned him on my now-throbbing cock.

He was pleading with me to go slowly, and I fully intended to do that, and spent considerable time just lodging the head of my cock inside the opening of his hole, when the car took an inconvenient lurch over a pothole, and I lost grip on his butt cheeks and he slid hard down my pole. He arched his back and screamed in pain. He was beating on my chest and trying to rise off me, but I figured that, since he was already fully skewered, he might as well stay that way, and I just hugged him and held him close in my lap until his sobbing and trembling quieted down. Which it did in short time, and I felt his canal loosening and widening to accommodate me. I wasn't super big, so it wasn't as if he'd been split or anything.

After he had calmed down, we kissed, the tension draining out of him, and I told him to come up a little bit off my lap on his haunches, which he did and he arched his back and head so he was looking up at the ceiling, and grabbed his ankles with his hands. I fucked up into him slowly and deeply then and came before too long. I was nervous and highly aroused myself at my victory, and I couldn't hold off any longer. But I wasn't finished with him, and we were far up the Hudson River parkway, not even ready to turn back for the hotel yet.

I pulled him off me and set him back down on my lap and then rolled the used condom off my still half-hard cock and threw it on the floor. I rubbed my cum-slathered rod around his tender inner thighs until the cock was dry. Marking my territory.

I held Miguel there, his chest arched away from me, while I played with his nipples with my tongue and pulled on his cock. I buried my face in each of his pits in turn and inhaled the pungent-sweet aromas of the pure sweat of youth. He came a second time under the attention my hands were giving him while I tongued his pits and chest.

Then, hard again now myself, I made him roll another condom on my cock and I turned him to where he was sitting in the seat, his legs thrown out, one foot once more dug into the ceiling of the car and the other on the headrest for the driver's seat, and I knelt between his legs and fucked him again, my eyes holding his in thrall, watching his pain turn to desire, to lust, to ecstasy, the Argentine Firecracker meeting my thrusts with those of his own pelvis, fully into the fuck, fully mine.

When I'd come again, I rose up on my knees on the car seat, my knees straddling his thighs, and pulled off the condom and threw it on the floor of the car. I went up on my feet, hovering over him then, keeping him imprisoned with my body, and rubbed my cum-wet cock over his nipples and chest and into his pits. He registered surprise, but he didn't fight me. He didn't even fight me when I forced my still-hard cock between his lips and made him suck off the rest of my semen. Semen I'd spilt between his legs. His first semen from a lover. His first cocksucking. Marking my territory; laying claim to yet another one of his firsts.

I tore open a condom packet and sheathed his cock then and came down on it in his lap, our bare chest chafing against each other as mine slid up and down his. Riding his cock now. Riding him long and hard. Making him grunt and groan and call out endearments and my name and his never-before-imagined love for fucking.

By the time he shot off up into me with the hot, strong fountaining of healthy youth—his first fucking and ejaculation inside a man's ass canal; my ass canal; me first—I was hard again. Another condom on my cock and I was fucking him again, his head now buried in the seat cushions, his knees fighting for purchase on the edge of the seat, and me behind him, fucking him hard, furiously, deep from behind. Shooting off. Sliding condom off and slapping my cock dry on the small of his back and on his tender butt cheeks. Marking my territory.

Another condom and the youthful, athletic Miguel suspended in air in the back seat of the limo. Fists wrapped around straps above the back seat doors on either side, heels dug into headrests of the front seats, head buried into the middle of the top of the back seat. Me hunched over in a half-standing position, between Miguel's outstretched legs and facing him, butt to the back of the middle of the front seat, my hands supporting the small of his back where it rose to his hips—suspending his body there, between the floor and the ceiling of the car, me stroking his hips back and forth on my cock. And just before I ejaculated, me bringing my mouth down to his nipple and biting him there. Marking my territory.

The limo now gliding back into New York City, the towers of the city visible now, if we had been looking for them. But we weren't looking for them. Athletes in our prime, even if an era apart, a last condom and me stroking him from behind in a side split, his leg waving in the air, and us stretched along the back seat of the car. Whispering endearments to each other. Making plans for meetings at future tournaments, although I knew in my heart that there weren't many more future tournaments for me. No matter. I had marked my territory in the next generation of tennis champions.

Later, I gathered up condoms strewn across the floor of the limousine—trophies for me to keep; better for me now than a U.S. Open trophy—even as Miguel would have internal trophies of my marking of my territory even if the more visible markings wouldn't last a week. No matter there, either. I knew it wouldn't be long before someone else was at him. Surely shorter than a week. And they would see and know that they weren't the first. As I gathered up the condoms, I smiled and gave a little laugh—remembering what Miguel whispered to me during our last coupling when I asked him about not having any underwear on. He had told me that I was so anxious to get him into the limo that I hadn't let him finish explaining. He had had no intention of playing tennis that morning either. He had booked a cabana at the hotel's sports center. He had already chosen me for his first.

Iced Flip Side

If I didn't get a good fuck in before tomorrow evening, Tonya and I would be out of the medals for sure. We'd come to the Paris Grand Prix with good hopes of standing on the platform, but my timing was all off in the twists and throws we'd attempted in our practice session tonight, and I knew it was because I was so jittery from not getting my rocks off since we'd been at Skate Canada a couple of weeks ago. I'd hunted all over the skating rink yesterday and today, but none of my usual fuck buddies were here, and I had no idea where to cruise for a quickie in Paris.

I sent Tonya off the ice before our practice time was up, telling her I was just off this evening and there was no use taking a chance on her getting hurt during a botched throw. I told her I'd continue practicing jumps on my own, trying to get rid of the jitters so I'd be straightened out before our short program competition tomorrow night. That's what I needed to be, straightened out and then drained of cum before tomorrow night. But I couldn't tell Tonya that. She knew I swung that way, of course, but she didn't know how much I depended on sex to keep my strength and timing up.

So, Tonya skated off to the locker rooms, and I continued practicing all alone in the gloomy practice rink. I had

93

no idea who had the practice time following mine, but I could have shouted for joy when I saw the French silver medal holder, Andre Larreau, skate out onto the ice and start his warm-ups. A sweet little piece of blond ass, Andre had turned eighteen a few weeks ago, which now made him free game. My fuck buddies and I had even speculated on who was going to get the first crack at him, and now here he was, gliding his tight little butt cheeks around on the ice in this deserted practice ice rink and batting his long eyelashes at me in invitation, and me in a bad way for sex, the very definition of the lighted match meeting the can of petrol.

Wasting no time, I stripped off my practice T and skated back into the center of the ice. I was in great shape and my skintight practice leotard basket showed off not only my great length and thickness but also my immediate need, so I knew if Andre was at all serious underneath that teasing that had driven several of us crazy for the two years he'd been skating professionally, he'd take the bait.

And take the bait he did. We started out pretending at least to be into our individual practice regimes, but our eyes were glued to each other in an undeniable mating dance. Andre skated over to the boards and stripped off his practice T, feigning that the heat was getting to him, but we both knew that I and my magnificent body and obvious need were getting to him. When he glided back onto the ice, our routines came into synch and drew together into ever tighter circles, until, in a cloud of ice shavings, we both stopped dead, facing each other, very close. Both of our chests were heaving from the intensity of the syncopated ice dance. I leaned my head down to the much shorter, more compact solo skater, and he tilted his head up, meeting my lips with his. Our tongues entwined, and I found he had a knob-headed stud in his tongue. I thrilled in anticipation of how I would make use of the stud and laughed to myself at the similar surprise the French youngster was in for.

With one hand on his butt and the other on the small of his back, I arched Andre's torso back and attacked his pert little erect nipples with my lips and teeth, leaving him in no doubt about my need and my intention to ravish his body. He was giving little yips of pleasure and pain and buried his fingers in my hair, giving at least token indication of trying to pull me off him. But his fingers slipped away, as I lifted him off the ice and slid his body up mine while moving my lips and teeth down to his belly and navel, which was pierced with a gold ring that got a workout from my tongue, teeth, and lips.

I let him slide down my body onto the ice and pulled his face into my crotch.

"Suck me," I said, "And then I'm going to fuck you." I had no idea whether or not he understood the English I'd used, knowing for certain he wouldn't understand Russian, but he must have gotten my drift, because he pulled my leotard down to below my pelvis and gasped when he saw my surprise. I had a silver ring with a round knob on it pierced into the helmet of my dick. I felt him shudder as he began to work on my cock, mesmerized not only by the opportunities the cock piercing offered but also by the quickly engorging length and thickness of me.

I didn't give him much time to think about what was happening, though, because my main goal was to get my rocks off and win a medal at the Paris Grand Prix. As it was, I let him work my cock in his mouth longer than I had intended, because that stud on his tongue running along the underside of my cock was sending chills up and down my spine. However, in short order, I had pulled Andre back up to where I could lock my mouth onto his. He wrapped his legs around me above my hips, and I skated over to where the boards broke to accommodate a judges' table.

Flipping Andre around, I laid him on the table chest down, pulled his leotard down to his knees, and went for his asshole with my tongue. With one hand on the small of Andre's back, I held him down on the table. The other hand explored his cock and balls and gave them some appreciated attention.

Quickly, though, I had Andre's ass wetted with my tongue and widened with my roaming fingers, and I crouched up and over him and got the helmet of my cock into his ass opening. Andre whimpered and complained under me as I worked to gain entry, and the whimpers increased to gasps of pain and objection as I pushed into him a few inches. I stopped, giving his ass canal a chance to adjust to the size of my cock, and then, punctuated by his exclamations in French, I pushed on in to the hilt. The objections turned to moans and sighs and more accommodating French phrases, as his tight little ass opened to me and I began to slowly pump him.

I dug my hands into his pecs and pulled him up to me. He turned his head, and we kissed. He looked at me in a dreamy expression and spoke for the first time in a thick English.

"The cock stud," he said. "The feeling."

"You like?" I asked.

"Yes, I like very much," he said. "Please. Can you fuck harder?"

"Sure," I said, although I didn't respond immediately. I twisted his torso so that I could get my teeth at one of his nipples, and he gasped and moaned at the attention I gave him there.

After a few minutes, I let his torso descend back onto the table top. I wanted to twist him around and fuck him from the front. In my urgency and realizing that I wouldn't be able to strip off Andre's practice leotard over his skates, I lifted my own skate-clad foot and neatly and carefully sliced through the crotch of his pants, freeing his legs. I slowly spun him around on the table top then on my buried cock, turn him on his back and lifting his legs in the air with my hands. His hands fluttered up my torso, and I began to deep fuck him. He was letting out little yelps of pleasure and whispering sweet nothings to me in French. He began jerking himself off, which was just as well, because this was all about sexual release for me to bring my performance on the ice to its peak, not about any need he had.

When I was about to come, I pulled out of him and shot off across his belly and up into his pecs. I buried a fist into his long, blond hair, lifted his head to mine, and gave him what I had intended to be one last, deep, brutal kiss. But, while we kissed, Andre's hands went to my cock and pulled me back into him. His hands went to my butt cheeks, holding me inside him, and he writhed under me and his lips flew over my chest and into my pits. He was nipping me and rolling that tongue stud over my flesh. He wrapped his strong legs around me, below my buttocks, and I felt my cock coming to life again. I had the brief

96

fear of his skate edges slicing into my tender butt cheeks, but Andre carefully held them away from my body.

I had thought I was finished, but Andre thought that I had more to give, and Andre proved to be right. This time, he wrapped the strong fingers of a hand around my balls and rolled and pulled them and held me to his pelvis until, many long minutes later, with Andre fucking himself on my cock with the rhythm of his strong leg muscles, I had cum again deep inside him.

I took this as Andre's statement that I hadn't done anything to him that he didn't want done. But this time when I pulled out and away from him, I left him laying there, spread-eagled on the judges' table and skated back out to the center of the ice, where I performed a perfect triple salchow jump. After showing the French youngster what else I could do well, I skated over to the boards, snatched up my athlete T, and skated back to the exit to the locker rooms, not looking back to the blond French skater at all.

I knew now that I'd be in prime condition for the double's short program tomorrow evening. The Frenchee's ass canal was so tight and I was so big and long, however, that I wondered if he would be able to unbow his legs and fight through the ass pain for his own men's short program the following evening. But I didn't care one way or the other. He wasn't competing in the doubles. Regardless of the damage I might already have done to him, I reminded myself that I'd have to check the practice session schedules running up to the long programs to see if Andre would be available for another private workout session before the long programs. None of my regular fuck buddies had come to this competition.

* * * *

I had had my eye on Aleksey since the skating season began. He was the new partner for Tonya in the ice pairs division, and he was sheer sex on ice. He was all dark, brooding good looks; muscle and power and with curly black hair on his arms and legs and swirling around his pecs and diving in a wide path down into the waistband of his leotard. He wore his jet black hair long, in a pony tail, with a few strands loose across his face, only seeming to hide his piercing eyes and sensual mouth, making them all the more desirable.

The public was able to see the loop ring through one ear, but only those of us who saw him in practice and in the showers knew of the ring through a nipple and the other, maddeningly intriguing one down below, in the helmet of his cock.

All season long, I had agonized over the thought of that cock ring running up and down my ass canal, but Aleksey had hardly spoken to me at all, let alone given me a tumble. The lack of attention and interminable waiting only made me love and want him more.

I knew he fucked men. I was well aware of his ritual of having a good fuck the day before competitions, but he'd always had his own friends around him to accommodate him for that— at least until now. None of his usual male friends were in this competition, and he was so on edge that I could tell he hadn't emptied his ball sack since Skate Canada, two weeks previously. I'd watched him just now in practice, and he was so unsettled that his timing was off. I was afraid he was going to drop Tonya to the ice during one of their lifts. He must have been afraid of this as well, as I saw him send her off the ice and start to furiously skim the ice on his own, practicing his moves, trying to get them under control.

I wanted Aleksey to love me, and in order for that to happen, I had to maneuver him into making love to me. No time seemed to be better than the present, so I glided out onto the ice and started some practice warm-ups for my singles routine, hoping to attract his attention.

My timing had been right. I could see instantly that he was watching me. And I could see the desire building in his eyes and his groin coming to life. You can't hide much in an ice skater's practice leotard, and Aleksey was so mammoth down there to start with that any building of sexual energy there was impossible to keep a secret. For performances, he wore a cup that kept his manhood reasonably within bounds, without disguising it to a point of disappointing the women spectators— and a good many of the men spectators as well. But in practice, he didn't bother with a cup, and I could see him lengthen and thicken as I skimmed across the ice.

He skated over to the boards and pulled off his practice T-shirt and came back out to center ice and did some magnificent spins that were not part of his current pairs routine. He was doing them for me. My heart began to pound.

I skated over to the boards and removed my T as well. My smooth, lithe blondness complimented his dark, hairy muscle pack perfectly. I was a youthful yang to his older, experienced yin; I was compliant, soft, seeking bottom to his urgently needy, hard top.

We started to skate in relationship to each other, our glides and spins and jumps coming into a shared rhythm and into a complimentary pattern. We also skated in ever-tighter circles, in toward each other until, in a cloud of ice shavings, we both stopped dead, facing each other, very close. Both of our chests were heaving from the intensity of the syncopated ice dance. He leaned his head down to me as I tilted my head up, meeting his lips with mine. Our tongues entwined, and I felt a flash of recognition and pleasure zip through his body as he discovered I had a knob-headed stud in my tongue. I could feel the wheels turning in his head concerning the pleasure I could give his cock with that stud, just as I was melting in anticipation of what his cock ring could do in my ass.

With one hand on my butt and the other on the small of my back, Aleksey arched my torso back and attacked erect nipples with his lips and teeth, leaving me in no doubt about his need and his intention to ravish my body. I rewarded the hot attention he was giving my body with little yips of pleasure and pain and buried my fingers first in the curls of his chest and then in the hair on his head, giving at least token indication of trying to pull him off me, but only effecting my real goal of releasing his long black hair from the pony tail to flutter across my face, shoulders, and chest, giving me more points of pleasure. My fingers slipped away from his hair and fell limply at my side, as he lifted me off the ice and slid my body up his while moving his lips and teeth down to my belly and navel, which was pierced with a gold ring that got a workout from his tongue, teeth, and lips.

99

He then let me slide down his body onto my knees on the ice and pushed my face into his crotch.

"Suck me," he said in English, which I understood well enough, "And then I'm going to fuck you." I thrilled at hearing those words, which I had longed to hear for months. Without hesitation, I pulled his leotard down to below his pelvis and began working his cock with my mouth. He gasped at what I was able to do with that stud in my tongue. I had barely gotten him hardened up, however, when he pulled me back up to where he could lock his mouth onto mine. I wrapped my legs around him above his hips, and he skated over to where the boards broke to accommodate a judges' table. The urgency of his need was apparent. He seemed like a wild animal in heat now, focused only on his own sex urge. I had envisioned romance and a lover, and I was getting overpowered by a fucking machine.

Flipping me around, Aleksey laid me on the table chest down, pulled my leotard down to my knees, and went for my asshole with his tongue. With one hand on the small of my back, Aleksey held me down on the table. The other hand explored my cock and balls and gave them attention that drove me wild in anticipation.

Quickly, though, he had my ass wetted with his tongue and widened with his roaming fingers, and he crouched up and over me and got the helmet of his cock into my ass opening. I could feel the coldness of the ring. I whimpered and complained under him as he worked to gain entry. I wanted love; I wanted him to make slow, sensual love to me, not just to ravish me. His cock was huge, and my whimpers increased to gasps of pain and objection as he pushed insistently into me a few inches. He stopped the assault, giving my ass canal a chance to adjust to the size of his cock, and then, punctuated by my exclamations in French, obviously not caring about how he was using me, he thrust into me to the hilt. The cock ring caused my ass walls to ripple and tremble as it drove up my canal.

But this was what I wanted. And as my ass accommodated his billy club, the pain subsided and the pleasure flowed in. My objections turned to moans and sighs and more accommodating French phrases, as my tight little ass opened to him. He began to slowly pump me.

He dug his hands into my pecs and pulled me up to his hairy chest. The silkiness of his hair on my smooth back was sensual. Acknowledging my sighs, He turned my head to his, and we kissed. I looked at him with a dreamy expression and searched for the English that would express what I was experiencing; I certainly couldn't express myself in Russian.

"The cock stud," I said. "The feeling."

"You like?" he asked.

"Yes, I like very much," I said. "Please. Can you fuck harder?"

"Sure," he said, although he didn't respond immediately. He twisted my torso so that he could get his teeth at one of my nipples, and I gasped and moaned at the attention he gave me there.

After a few minutes, he let my torso descend back onto the table top. But then he was trying to turn me onto my back on the table. In his urgency and realizing that he wouldn't be able to strip off my practice leotard over my skates, he lifted his own skate-clad foot and sliced through the crotch of my pants, freeing my legs. Then he slowly spun me around on the table top on the spit of his still-buried cock, turned me on my back, and lifting my legs in the air with his hands. My hands fluttered up his torso, following the silk trail of the hair, and he began to deep fuck me. I was letting out little yelps of pleasure and whispering sweet nothings to him in French. He seemed not to be listening to me, to only be tuning in on his own cock. I then began jerking myself off, pushed by the need, but disappointed that he was only thinking of himself and his own needs. I was beginning to cry. This wasn't the romance I had expected from my long-anticipated lover.

When he was about to come, he pulled out of me and shot off across my belly and up into my pecs. He buried a fist in my long, blond hair, lifted his head to mine, and gave me what he obviously intended to be one last, deep, brutal, good-bye kiss. But, while we kissed, I took his cock in my hands and pulled his still-hard dick back into me. I was desperately trying to get him to focus on me; to give me some love, not just a fuck that would relieve his own pressure, enhance his own performance on the ice.

I grabbed his butt cheeks, holding him inside me, and writhed under him, my lips flying through his curly chest hairs and into his pits. I was doing everything I could to arouse him again, to make him want me. I nipped his nipples and rolled my tongue stud over the flesh of his torso. I wrapped my strong legs around him, below his buttocks, and I felt his cock coming to life again.

He had thought we were finished, but I thought he had more to give, more to give me, and I proved to be right. This time, I wrapped the strong fingers of a hand around his balls and rolled and pulled them and held him to my pelvis until, many long minutes later, with me fucking myself on Aleksey's cock with the rhythm of my strong leg muscles, Aleksey had come deep inside me once more.

I just knew I had him now, that now he would become my tender lover, just the way I had envisioned. But I was wrong. All he had wanted was sexual release so that he could perform well in tomorrow's competition. Without further endearments, he just pulled out and away from me and left me laying there, spread-eagled on the judges' table. He skated back out to the center of the ice, performing a perfect triple salchow jump to show me that I had only been part of his routine. Then he skated over to the boards at the other side of the rink, snatched up his athlete T, and skated back to the exit to the locker rooms, not looking back to me at all.

I lay there on the table, sobbing my disappointment and my feeling of being used.

I saw movement in the stands, and my coach rose from a seat and slowly descended the rows of empty stadium seats to the table where I lay. He was bundled up in a long coat to counter the cold air lifting off the ice into the stands. I had no idea how long he'd been sitting in the rink or how much of my encounter with Aleksey he'd seen.

He sat down on the table beside me, his hands deep in the pockets of his coat, and let out a long sigh. He was clucking endearments to me, telling me not to cry. That Aleksey was a pig who had a well-earned reputation of using other skaters to solely serve his needs.

I wiped my eyes, trying to stop the crying, struggled to get back up on my skates at the edge of the judges' table, and started to pull at the tattered fabric of my leotards. Suddenly I felt the need to be covered.

But the hands came out of my coach's coat, and he pulled me toward him, whispering encouragement and comfort to me. He opened his coat and pulled me up into his lap, my back to his chest. He was naked inside the coat, and his cock was fully erect and standing at attention. He gently lifted me with arms around my chest, and lowered my ass onto his cock, penetrating me easily and pulling me down until my butt cheeks felt his wiry pubic hair. He enveloped me in his warm coat and nuzzled his lips into the side my neck and rocked me back and forth in a gentle in and out motion of his cock under the power of his undulating hips that continued long after he had flooded my insides with his cum. This was just what I had wanted from Aleksey. But even now, I knew it was just my coach in a long line of men who would use me.

Best in Show

It was raining hard in Newport. Otherwise Sandy wouldn't have come to his club to do his running that morning. Sandy taught sailing at the nearby U.S. Naval War College, and at his age—he was pushing forty-eight hard—he had to work extra hours to keep in shape. So far, running ten miles a day had helped keep him hard, but Rhode Island wasn't the best place to assume dry days. So, he'd joined a club that had its own indoor track, and that's why he was here this day. It was raining hard outside and it was time for him to run.

But when he arrived at the club, he found the track was covered with little furry things on leashes. He had turned back to the men's dressing room in disgust, thinking hard on where he was going to go for exercise now. He wondered if going back to the war college campus and fucking that young naval lieutenant's brains out for two hours would off-set a ten-mile run. It was at least worth a try.

While he was changing back into his street clothes and feeling mad at the world and sorry for himself, he overheard the conversation between two of the guys who were just returning from swimming laps in the club's indoor pool.

"So, what's going down on the indoor track?" asked one.

"Dog show," answered the other.

"Oh, that sissy stuff," responded the one. "Owners besotted with their dogs and looking just like them. Total waste."

"Not completely so," answered the other. "Clive Bailey owns last year's champion—probably this year's champion too. And he's no dog face; he's a real looker, and I understand he's the most delicious bottom in Rhode Island. He's got one of those fluffy little things that win so many dog shows—his dog, I mean, not his ass. I think it's a Japanese . . . no, it's a Chinese Crested. A very oriental name his has: Da Mei Yang. It was in this morning's paper. But that Clive, now he's got the most talented ass on the East coast."

The two laughed as they went off to the showers. Nicest ass on the East Coast was what translated to Sandy. Sandy collected the nicest asses. And he couldn't resist the challenge of having one that others said was the nicest to be had. Speaking of nice asses, though, there was that young naval lieutenant very ripe and just ready for plucking over at the naval college. Sandy dug out his cell phone and started dialing.

He'd had the naval lieutenant meet him down at the boathouse, where he kept a full range of small sailing boats that he used to train these guys in the basics—these guys who'd forgotten all they knew about the basics of sailing because for the last ten years they'd been driving big ships that did everything but wipe their butts for them on automatic pilot.

Sandy had taken the young lieutenant into a lifeboat hanging off the back end of one of the larger sailing boats, and the nice, young, firm piece of tail was bent over the center wooden seat on his belly and was grabbing the gunwales with white-knuckled fists and was throwing his head back and screaming his satisfied lust as a crouching and covering Sandy split him from behind with the biggest cock in New England.

With each thrust Sandy first thought just how nice and tight this young sailor's ass was and, second, wondered how it compared with the one those guys in the locker room were declaring was the nicest ass to be had in this region. Long after the naval lieutenant had whimpered his surrender and Sandy's digging cock had delivered the coup de grace, Sandy was resolving he was going to get to the bottom of this Clive Bailey guy—to the bottom and then into the bottom and a good ten and half thick inches farther than that.

He turned the young naval lieutenant on his back on the centerboard and held his ankles up and out and fucked him again. The guy would be begging for another private sailing lesson again the next day. They all did.

Sandy returned to his Brenton Cove cottage after having stopped at a convenience store and bought the morning paper. His cottage wasn't the most luxurious house on the cove—not by a long shot—in fact, its low profile and small size, nestled up to his own private dock but hidden from the road by heavy foliage, rendered it almost invisible. But he liked it that way. And in its own way it was more distinctive than any of the hulking wooden waterfront mansions around it. Sandy was quite certain that more future admirals had lost their male cherries and been fucked three ways from Thursday in his bedroom than any of the other houses on the cove could boast.

He settled down in his favorite overstuffed chair, with its wide view of the Newport harbor beyond a bank of sun porch windows, and leafed slowly through the newspaper. There was the report on the dog show and a picture of the champion, Da Mei Yang, but that was the only picture. Not a bad-looking mutt. Sandy read the article very closely; it revealed that Da Mei Yang was being used as a stud for the Bailey Kennels.

A week later, after the submission of voluminous forms and the writing of a hefty check, Sandy answered his door. The man standing on the threshold looked very young—much too young to have already acquired a reputation as a champion bottom—but Sandy had to admit that he was gorgeous and compelling. He could feel that his cock thought that too. He hoped he wasn't being too obvious. All he had on were a pair of running shorts and shoes.

The young man gave him a wondrous smile. He looked like a young Greek god. Dark and heavy tanned and muscled and all white teeth and tumbling black, curly locks of hair. The little ball of fluff he held under his arm that was the celebrated Da Mei Yang was all smiles too. He'd been told why he was here. Sandy was happy to see that his groomer was smiling even though he didn't yet realize he was here for a similar experience.

"Admiral Thompson?" the young Greek god asked with a luminous smile.

"Yes," Sandy answered with a warm, inviting smile of his own. "Here, come through here to the backyard. The bitch is back here. I have her penned and ready for you already."

The Chinese Crested perked up his ears and began to pant in anticipation. Sandy was more than pleased himself with this Greek god Clive, and he was fairly panting himself as he led the groomer and stud through the bungalow and to the backyard.

There was a small, newly improvised dog pen just beyond the lattice-covered and grape-vine bedecked patio off the sun porch, on a short grassy area between the house and the start of the pier out into Newport Harbor.

A dog looking somewhat like a Chinese Crested was bounding around the pen and yapping its silly little head off.

With little fanfare, the young man lifted Da Mei Yang over the lip of the pen, and the champion stud bounded out of his arms and into the enclosure. There was little doubt that the immaculately groomed Chinese Crested knew exactly why he was there.

As Da Mei Yang stood solidly in the middle of the pen and stared down Sandy's pooch, Sandy saddled up close behind the dog groomer. The sounds from Sandy's dog turned from ridiculous but noisy yapping to uncertain yipping to whining, and its head descended lower and lower as Da Mei Yang stood there, majestically, staring the other dog down.

Similarly, Sandy had come in very close to the back of the dog groomer as he stood at the edge of the covered patio, but well in the shadows. The young dog groomer felt Sandy's hand on his arm and the older man's hot breath on his neck. He had been attracted to the retired admiral's handsome, square-cut looks and hard, well-taken-care of body from his first look at the jib of the man. He was graying, but only at the temples, and on him it looked good. He had the torso of a mature man, but one who was still solid muscle and who took pride in and much effort on his form. And the dog groomer hadn't missed the bulge in the admiral's basket and the curly salt and pepper hair that cascade up out of the front waistband of his low-rise running shorts when he had opened the door.

The young man felt paralyzed as a hand came around and fiddled with his belt buckle. He didn't move, although he was trembling from the feel of those strong fingers on his arm and the hot breath on his neck, as his belt gave why and he heard and felt the unzipping of his jeans.

He had come here to witness the breeding of the admiral's dog by Da Mei Yang. Visual witnessing of the breeding was necessary for the contract to be valid and a fee paid whether or not the admiral's bitch littered. He couldn't miss this. It meant the better part of a k note, which the kennel wouldn't see if the bitch didn't have puppies and no one was there to attest the breeding.

The dog groomer was nonplused with what the bitch's owner was doing to him. He certainly hadn't expected the attention he was getting, but he was being played so expertly and the admiral was so good looking and arousing that the dog groomer was confused—and he was paralyzed. Did he even want this to stop? He had no idea. He was just so surprised and the admiral was such a dominating force. But . . . But . . .

"Uh, Sir. What—?"

"Shush, shush," The older man was whispering. "Just watch the dogs. You must attest. The contract says—"

"Yes, but—"

The man had pulled down the back of the dog groomer's jeans and briefs, and he had the most gigantic of cocks rubbing up and down between the young man's butt cheeks.

"Ah . . . Ah . . . ," the young man was murmuring. The cock was huge and it was tantalizing. The young man felt his legs trembling and his knees going weak at the movement of the underside of the cock up and down on his hole.

"Watch the dogs," Sandy whispered. "Attest to the breeding—"

Sandy's dog was hugging the ground on its belly. It was looking up with it muzzle and it had its teeth bared and was giving a weak growl. But Da Mei Yang wasn't fooled. Da Mei Yang's muzzle was above that of Sandy's dog and the Chinese Crested stud was still staring the other dog down. And his teeth were more strongly bared, and his growl was much more authoritative than that of the other dog. Da Mei Yang was slowly, one step at a time, moving around the side of the other dog. Sandy's dog had to move its head to maintain eye contact, but it did so. It was being mesmerized. Its growls were turning to whimpering.

Sandy had one palm on the young man's belly now and the other one on his throat, pulling his head back. Sandy was kissing the young man on the neck, and the young man was just standing there, his arms drooping at his side, paralyzed by the admiral's power. And he was whimpering too. Just like Sandy's dog, the young man was whimpering softly, lost in the dance of domination—losing the dance of domination.

Da Mei Yang was behind Sandy's dog now, and Sandy's dog was lifting its hind quarters. It was still whimpering, but the instinctive response of its body was totally out of its control. The palm of Sandy's hand had left the young man's belly, and the dog groomer felt wet fingers at his asshole. His ass was being prepared. He whimpered and he involuntarily, instinctively lifted his butt toward the invading fingers.

Da Mei Yang was moving over the hindquarters of Sandy's dog, covering the back half of its body with his chest and belly. Sandy's dog was whining, beaten, bested. The head of Sandy's cock was now at the rear door of the young dog groomer, who was sighing quietly to himself, beaten, bested.

Sandy's dog yelped and writhed under the encasing champion Chinese Crested as it was invaded by a champion cock, while at the same time, the young dog groomer, still standing, but held in the embrace of the older man, felt his ass being entered and conquered and invaded by a master cock. He too yelped and writhed within the embrace of the stronger, dominating breeder. Being split and plowed by a hard, thick, long cock.

The yelps of Sandy's dog turned to whimpers, and its tongue lolled out of its mouth, and its eyes blazed wildly, and Da Mei Yang thrust and thrust and thrust.

"I speak Mandarin," Sandy whispered in the young dog groomer's ear as he thrust and thrust and thrust. "Do you?"

"No," the young man answered through clinched teeth. "Ohhhh, ahhhh, oh my GAWD. Why—? What—?"

"It's your dog," Sandy whispered and then laughed. "Do you even know what Da Mei Yang means in Mandarin?" Thrust, thrust, thrust.

"Ohhhhahhhhhh. Oh, Noooo. Yes! No, no, I don't know what it means." The young man was panting. His knees gave way, and Sandy turned him to a picnic table and laid him down on his back, spread his legs, and thrust inside him again.

Da Mei Yang was having his way with Sandy's dog too. The dog just huddled there, trembling, its eyes begging both for mercy and for more, swimming already in the champion Chinese Crested's millionaire-dollar cum.

"Da Mei Yang means 'big beautiful cock.' Whoever bred your dog knew its worth. And do I have a big beautiful cock too, Clive? Am I the best in show too?"

"Oh Gawd yes, oh gawd yes." But then he continued. "My dog? Clive? It's not my dog. I'm not Clive Bailey. I'm just his groomer. He sent me because he was busy today."

Sandy laughed a deep, lustful laugh. Not at all put off. The young guy was luscious. Worth every bit of what he'd had to pay for a stud fee. He dove deep again, throbbing cock plowing undulating ass walls, deep, down, down, down. And the young man yelped and cried for more.

"That's OK," Sandy said, and then laughed again at the totality of the joke. "This isn't my dog, either. I got it at the pound. I even think it's a male. But it's enjoying itself anyway."

And both the dogs and the men fucked on, with Sandy already scheming how he was going to track down and breed the elusive and legendary Mr. Clive Bailey.

Trail "Doctor"

I had never tried to seduce another guy before, but Dale was just there at the right time and place. We were both runners—he because he was on the college football team and running up and down the Pine Mountain trail helped keep him in shape and I because I wasn't that long out of college myself and I was doing the best I could to keep my fine form in shape.

We had passed each other a couple of times going up and down the trail that morning. It was a hot one, and as I was coming down the mountain, I saw that Dale had his sweaty shirt off, as well as his shoes and socks, and he was just standing under the shower by the maintenance hut, letting the water cascade down his beautiful body. He was a square-cut blond, with great pecs going down into washboard abs and a small waist. He had his heavily muscled arms over his head, and all of the muscles of his torso were stretched out to perfection. His calf and thigh muscles showed that he was both a football player and a serious runner. I just stood there and watched him in awe for a few minutes. The shower was sticking his running shorts to his legs and I could see that he had a pretty fine basket confined by his jock. He turned the water off as I was approaching and gave me a shy smile.

"Hi, Jack. It's just too damn hot out here. I couldn't wait to get cooled down."

"I'm right with you, Dale. There's a picnic table over behind those bushes. Let me shower too, and I'll come over, and we can jaw a bit while we both dry off."

"Sounds good," Dale said, and he headed for the picnic table. After making a short instinctive visit to the car for a tube of lubricant, which I plopped in my pocket, I returned and stood under the shower for a couple of minutes. This was crazy, I thought. There would be no way I was going to pull this off. But, just maybe so. I had seen Dale look me over on the trail before, and if he was at all inclined, there just might be some fun to be had here.

When I sauntered around the bushes, I saw that Dale was sitting about two thirds down the bench, his back to the table, and his legs V-ed out at a good angle. He seemed to be wincing.

"What's the matter, Dale?" I asked, as I sat down beside him.

"You don't wanna know," he said morosely.

"Sure I do. You look like you're in pain."

"Yes, I guess I am a bit."

"What's the problem?"

"There are two problems—and you probably don't want to hear them."

"Now you have me interested. Shoot."

"That's the main problem. I can't shoot. And my girl, Cheryl Ann, and this here tight jock are the main problems."

"Now, I'm intrigued; spill."

"I can't," he answered with a little grin. "As I said, that's the problem. I have the hots for my girl, Cheryl Ann, and she won't put out. I've got all this stuff built up, and this tight jock is driving me crazy this morning."

"Well," I laughed, "I can't do anything about Cheryl Ann, but you're out here alone this morning and you've finished your run. There's no reason you can't just take your jock off and hang free."

"Hey, I guess you're right," Dale said with a chuckle. He stood and turned his back to me, pulled his shorts down, pulled

114

his jock down and off, pulled his shorts back up, and sat back down in the same stance he'd been in. I hadn't seen his package, but his bulbous butt cheeks had been mighty interesting. I took a peek and saw that his shorts were tented up real nice now. I could actually make out a huge knob against the wet material.

"There, is that better?" I asked.

"A little, but not much," Dale said sadly.

We sat there for a few minutes.

"You know that guys have a way to take care of that themselves," I ventured.

"Yeah, I know, but that doesn't really do it for me. I apparently build up a lot and fast, and it just never seems complete when I do it myself."

Another short pause.

"And you know that sometimes guys let other guys help them with that when it's really bad. I mean it isn't a queer thing or anything. Just playing around and releasing some tension when their girls won't put out. It's really unhealthy to just let it build, you know. It might hurt performance later."

"Really? I hadn't heard that." Dale sounded a little scared and a lot skeptical.

"Yes, really. I'm a doctor, and I'd do something about this if I were you. You wouldn't want to ruin yourself for later, when you and your girlfriend have finally hooked up."

Dale looked both dubious and scared now. And he was still wincing.

"Go ahead and do yourself, Dale. You obviously need some release right now. No one else is here. I'm a doctor, and I've seen it all. Just pull your pants on down and give yourself some relief while we talk."

Dale hesitated, but the tension must really have been getting to him, because he lowered his shorts to his thighs and took a very nice, erect cock in his left hand and began to slowly jack off.

I could hardly keep my hands and eyes off him, but, beyond a few glances when he was looking away, I kept off him. I could feel my own cock hardening and giving me some of the same jock problem he'd had.

"You said I should do something about it. What could I do?"

"Well, guys come to me all the time for this sort of relief. There's something we can do called prostate massage. It's all medical, of course, not a gay thing. It's just that some guys have to be what we call 'milked' manually regularly because they can't get enough sexual release otherwise. It isn't a sign that you like guys; it just means that you are extra virile. It's usually young guys like you who have this problem."

"It's all medical? Is there much pain in the procedure?"

"Sure it's medical, and, on the contrary, there's the same or more pleasure you'd get from penetration sex. It's just a medical procedure to alleviate a normal medical problem. The pleasure is just a bonus. And you'd lose that tension and pain you've got for a couple of days at least," I said, making it up as I went along and hoping this sounded reasonable. And before he could raise more doubts about this, I steamed on. "You've heard about the prostate, haven't you?"

"Yes, guys get testicle cancer from that, don't they?"

"Well, yes, they can, and that can be an added risk for someone like you who doesn't take care of the problem at this stage. The prostate is a gland behind the testicles. It's where all that semen is being manufactured that you can't get rid of fast enough. Surely you've had a prostate exam during a medical checkup before."

"Oh, yeah, that's where the doctor put his finger up my ass."

"Did it hurt?"

"Naw. It felt a little tight and strange down there, but it didn't hurt."

"Well, in that exam, the doctor was just checking to see if your prostate was enlarging, which would be sign of trouble. In prostate massage, the doctor massages the prostate from inside your anal canal for several minutes, which milks the built-up semen out of you more effectively than jerking off does and also gives you more pleasure than jerking off can. I hope you can follow what I'm saying; I'm trying to use words that you would understand rather than the fancy medical terms for all this. In extreme cases like yours, the doctor milks the penis at the same time."

"It sounds . . . interesting, Doc. And you say I can get this done by going to a doctor?"

"Yes, certainly."

"And could you recommend such a doctor for me?"

"I can do better than that, Dale. It doesn't require sterile surroundings. I can save you the money and give you immediate relief by showing you how it's done right here and now."

"Right here and now?"

"Absolutely. You're already in a good initial position, and I just happen to have a tube of lubricant with me, which is all we need. Just strip those shorts off. I'll need you fully erect, so I'll have to do some preliminary work on you, and, with your serious condition, I'd better take charge of the penis for a while."

Dale pulled his shorts off and put both beefy arms back on the table.

"There, that's right; arch your back for me." I put my left leg over the bench and under the picnic table so that I was facing his side. I tentatively wrapped my left hand loosely around his cock, which made him twitch. "Okay?" I asked. "Any problems?"

"No," he answered, although not really sure. I continued quickly, not wanting to give him too much time to think about this.

"Okay now, I'll do some preliminary rubbing of your pecs and nipples until I feel your penis fully engorge, and then we can begin. Okay with that?"

A muffled affirmative; my right hand went up to his chest and I lightly ran it around his pecs and nipples, slowly increasing the pressure and taking a few nips and squeezes of his nipples. I could tell he was stifling some grunts.

"Our goal is to release the tension here, Dale, not compound it. Just let those grunts and moans out. There's no reason not to enjoy this medical procedure."

"But it's so . . . weird. I mean it doesn't seem right."

"Would it seem right to have sex with Cheryl Ann, if she'd let you, Dale? Of course it would. Why would it be wrong to take care of a medical condition and still have sexual pleasure out of it? Everything's just fine, Dale. Ah, there, your penis seems to be ready. I'm going to be manipulating your penis now with one hand and doing some checking and preparing for the prostate massage with the other one now. We'll move slowly, and I'll tell you what is happening as we go along." I was slowly pumping his cock now, and he was beginning to pant and moan.

"There, yes, that's good. Just go with the flow of your feelings, Dale. We're alone out here, and this is just a medical procedure. Be natural." I took his balls in my right hand and weighed and teased them, rolling them around gently. Dale flinched.

"This is the testicular part of the procedure. I have to examine your testicles to make sure everything is okay there. And it does seem to be. And you were right; you seem to have a lot of semen backed up in here. We'll see what we can do about getting all of that cleared out. I'm now going on down toward your anus, Dale. Don't be alarmed, I won't enter the short way I have to go for this procedure without having you well lubricated. So, there will be only pleasure, no pain."

Dale tensed up a bit as I put the heel of my hand under his balls and ran my finger to the rim of his ass. I would have liked to have gotten my mouth on that asshole too, but I couldn't think of any medical excuse to do that. So, I just left my finger there on his hole, applying a little pressure, while I took the fingers of my left hand up to the glans on his cock.

"Any problem with the glans, Dale?"

"The glans? What's a glans?"

"The head, the knob, on your penis. It seems a little distended. But that might be because of how long you've gone without fixing this problem."

Dale answered with a moaning, "No, I don't think I've had a problem there."

"Well, I'll have to put some lubricant on it to examine it well. Here this will feel cool." I rubbed a small glob of lubricant on his dick head and swirled it down and around the rim. Dale flinched and moaned. I squeezed the spongy bulb and watched his slit open up. I moved my index finger there and pushed it open farther.

"Oh, oh," Dale moaned, and he brought a hand down to mine.

"No, hands up, Dale, this has to stay medical. There, I guess all is in order with you there; just lubricating up for the massage now." I lubricated the fingers of my right hand well and took an added glop to start lathering up around his asshole. My left hand went back to stroking his cock, but I didn't do this too vigorously, because I didn't really want him to release yet.

I did a lot of work on his entry, making it large enough for what I was planning. I made a few forays farther in, just to let him know I was continuing the procedure. When he had relaxed and his hole opening had loosened up, I slid my middle finger in to the sphincter. He gave a little lurch and yelp when the sphincter picked up the finger and sucked it into place at his prostate.

"There, can you feel that?" I asked.

"Yes," he moaned through pants.

"It will take time to build the sensation up, but this should give you release." I started a gentle massaging of the prostate, and Dale slowly started to writhe and moan and grind his pelvis.

"Here, this isn't the best position now, because you are naturally going to be moving around in response to the procedure. Here. Get up and move around to the end of the table here. Perch up on the end. There, that's right. Now lay back on the table and wrap your arms around the other end to give you support. There, that's right. This is now more like the table in the examination room. Now, we don't have stirrups. So, can you get your left foot on the edge of the bench there and keep a wide stance with that leg. Good. And now, your right leg, I guess will have to go over my left shoulder so that I have you open enough down there to proceed with the massage. There, that's good. Now I'm entering again." I gently slid my index finger in to the prostate again and restarted the massage. Dale went back to panting and moaning and gyrating his pelvis slightly. His pants came louder and more quickly together, and my left finger on his glans felt some precum dribbling out.

"There, is that feeling better, Dale? The milk is beginning to show."

"Aw, shit yes, Man. That feels great—waves and waves of great."

"Here, I can increase that and quicken the flow. I'll use my thumb rather than my finger. Just stick with me here, Dale, I've got a large thumb." I quickly slipped my shorts and jock off with my right hand and lathered up my cock with lubricant. I put my dick head up against his now-open asshole and slowly pushed in.

"Oh, God, that's big," Dale yelped. I had gotten it in to the prostate, and was manipulating my cock head against his prostate. "Oh, but it feels so good," Dale continued.

"Yes, big thumb. Just the right thing to get you off when you need it."

"Oh, oh, oh, Gawd Damn!" And Dale was spurting several weeks of backup cum into the air and back down on his chest. He arched his torso up and then thumped it back down on the table. The last time he thumped it down, I slid my cock past the prostate and right on in.

"What the fuck?" Dale screamed, and thrashed about on the table. He grabbed for me with his arms, but I got his legs in both of mine and lifted them up and out, bringing his butt up to a more open position. I pulled out nearly to the end and then stroked all the way back in to the root.

"Still workin' the prostate here, Dale. Want me to stop?"

"YES!" I gyrated my hips in a rotating motion while fully encased. "Oh, gawd. No, no."

"No what, Dale?" I asked, pumping and pumping and pumping.

"No, don't stop. Don't stop," Dale whimpered. And he began to move his hips in syncopation with my thrusts, and dug his fingers into my chest hair and nipples. We came—he for the second time within a few short minutes—at nearly the same time. I released his legs, which just flopped down beyond the table, and I ran my hands up his abs to his pecs and collapsed on him. We looked each other in the eye and both leaned into a long, lingering kiss. I started to withdraw from him, but he moved his hands to my butt cheeks and kept me in place.

When our lips parted, he looked into my eyes with a satisfied smile and said, "You aren't really a doctor, are you?"

"Yes, of course I am," I answered. "I wouldn't lie to you. I have a doctorate in geology, which means I'm eminently qualified to get your rocks off. I'm not a medical doctor, but I can do a prostate massage for free, and a medical doctor will charge you $100, and it won't be half the fun I can give you. You'll need another good milking in a couple of days, if Cheryl Ann keeps holding out."

Another kiss, after which he responded. "Good. I'll stick with the doctor I've got. . . . and who's Cheryl Ann?"

"That's my boy."

Locker Room Revelation

It wasn't a regular day of practice; only Hank and I had come in, and we'd worked out in the gym after we'd done laps on the field. I could tell he was steamed about something, but I didn't ask about what. He had finished first, and it looked like I had the locker room to myself when I came in from the gym. I took a quick shower and pulled on my briefs and some baggy shorts and an athletic T, and there he was, right at my locker before I had gotten around to pulling my sneakers on. There was fire in his eyes, and he slammed my locker closed with his fist.

"What's the matter, Hank?" I didn't want to have Hank upset at me. He was a real hunk of a man and could probably break me in two without raising a sweat.

"I saw you in Hardesties the other night, didn't I?"

Oh God, I was sure I wouldn't be seen going into that gay bar.

"Oh, shit," I said. "Okay, I admit I was there. But you don't have to tell anyone, do you? I was just—" If this got out of control and was talked around, I'd be out of a job.

"Tell anyone?" Hank yelled at me. "Don't you get it, I saw in you Hardesties. That means I was in Hardesties. I've wanted you for two years, and I just now find out that you are cruising."

I just stood there, giving him a blank look. And just as I got it, he was on me.

"Hank, I'm not—" I started to say, but I got nothing else out, because he came right up to me, wrapped his left hand around the back of my head, and pulled me in to a hungry, almost brutal kiss. He had my lips parted with his and was sucking face for all his might. Meanwhile, his right hand had gone to my basket, and he was feeling me through the two thin layers of clothing, finding my cock, measuring the whole length of It, and ending by grabbing my balls and almost lifting me off the ground. I groaned, and my cock began to engorge at the assault. While still holding me in a lip lock, his hand traveled up to my belly and then under the rim of my shorts and briefs and dove for my cock. Skin on skin now, and I found I was getting as excited as he was. I lost control. My hands strayed to the hem of his T-shirt, and I let my hands slide under and then up his fantastic abs to his bulging pecs.

His hands flew to work. He reached down for the hem of my T and pulled it off me and threw it to the side, and in the very next motion, he did the same thing with his. Then he jerked off his shorts, and there he stood, erect and magnificent, and not a little frightening. He jerked my shorts and briefs down in one swift move, going down in front of me, banging me up against my locker and attacking my hardening cock with his mouth.

"Oh, God, you have no idea how I've longed to suck this big prick," he said between licks and swallows. And, he was right. I'd had no idea.

"Straddle the bench with your legs and sit down," he commanded. I did so, rather numbly. I still hadn't gotten adjusted to the sudden assault. He sat down facing me. His big dick running along the bench seat, pointed at me. He scooted up to me, so his knees were pushing mine out and away from the bench, put a big mitt on my chest and said, "Lay back."

I laid back as his hand pushed me down. He leaned in over me, his dick running up beside mine, and I gave a little shudder as his mouth went to my nipples. First the right one and then the left. He sucked and nipped and bit, and I squirmed. Not knowing what else to do with them, my hands went to his shoulder and back muscles and I massaged them. He didn't stay at my nipples long with his mouth. He didn't seem to be staying anywhere very long. His tongue and sucking kisses moved to my sternum and then descended as his hands covered my pecs and held me pinned flat to the bench. He was sliding away from me now, and I lost touch with his prick. He was at my navel, tonguing and sucking and then on my flat belly, tonguing through my pubic hair, and he had my rod in his mouth again. He spent a little longer there, as I did some squirming and bucking and trying to reason with him.

"Umm, Hank. Don't you think we should be going slower on this—and maybe somewhere else, if at all?"

"Shut up, stud," was his reply. "I've been building this up for you for two years and I never knew I had a chance. I think I'm going to explode, and when I do, I want it to be in you." That sounded rather ominous, and I started to try to get up, but he pushed me back with his strong arms and latched onto my prick with his teeth. I was hard and panting when he left my rod and moved to my balls. He swallowed those whole and then popped them out and gave them some nibbles. The last few minutes he had my cock in his mouth, he had brought his right hand down and was fingering my asshole. Directly from my balls, he moved to my asshole with his lips and tongue and slobbered me up pretty good down there. I was afraid he was going to make do just with that; I knew from his grunting and groaning sounds that he wasn't going to wait long to split me, but he reached down and came up with a little tube of lubricant. He had come prepared. He quickly lathered up my hole and stuck his finger in it, pushing on in past the sphincter and being drawn to my prostate, which he firmly pressed, causing me to almost piss, but quickly making me moan and leak cum.

He rose up on his feet, his erection standing straight out from his body, and lathered his tool up as I watched in awe and fear. He was a wild man. I knew it would be useless even to try to stop him or slow him down.

"Turn over on the bench," he said. And then when I didn't react fast enough. "Turn over, I said," and he reached down and pulled me up and flipped me over. My hard cock was painful lying between my body and the hard, cold bench, but Hank wasn't to be denied. His lubricated fingers went back to

125

my ass, and he inserted them and forced the hole more open, all the time rotating and flipping them up and down, driving me crazy. Then he had his hands on my hips and pulled my butt up in the air.

"Stand where I put you," he directed, and he moved me up to the level of his cock, where he was standing behind me.

"Umm, Hank, I've never really—"

His answer was a slap across one of my butt cheeks. While holding his left hand to my left hip to show what level he wanted me to maintain, his right hand guided his cock to my hole and he pushed in to the rim of the glans.

"God, Hank, just hold on a minute!" He did hold there several seconds, but then was pushing again. He had trouble getting farther in and commanded, "Widen your legs. Give me a bigger hole." I wondered really how I was going to manage that, but I did widen my stance. I had one arm between my head and the bench to protect my brains from being banged to death and the other arm was wrapped around the bench to keep me steady. Hank was now using both hands to pull my butt cheeks as far apart as possible. With a grunt, his dong went past the sphincter, which pulled him in a few more inches.

"Ahh," he intoned, as he held there for a few seconds. But then, with another grunt he was pushing right on in. I screamed in pain, but my sobs subsided as the pleasure of being wanted this much by another man and of being so intimately stuffed to the fullest turned the pain to pleasure. And then he was pumping, taking slow, long strokes to begin with. Fully encased, He stood, bringing me up with him. He buried his mouth in the side of my neck, finding the throbbing artery there in gentle teething, and driving me wild with ecstasy. I arched my chest, pulling my butt up to give him full, close access, and I laced my hands behind his neck, drawing my torso taut. He had his hands on my chest, rubbing my nipples with his thumbs.

But then he lost himself and pushed me back down on the bench, planted a strong hand in the middle of the small of my back, and just pumped wildly away, until with a scream of satisfaction and fulfilled fantasies, he shot his load deep inside me.

Hank collapsed on top of me then, wrapping his arms around me and nuzzling in my neck. "That was the greatest, Baby," he cooed in my ear. "You are just the fuck that I imagined."

"Hank," I whispered. "Could I say something now?"

"Shoot."

"When you saw me in Hardesties, I was just trying to pull my kid brother out of there. I'm not really gay. I've never done it with a guy before."

"Oh, my so sorry," Hank responded, all embarrassed. He started to pull out of me and stand up.

But, I whipped both of my hands back to his butt cheeks and pulled him back into me. "No apologies necessary, Hank. Could you fuck me again, please—just like that last one?"

Big Boy Curious

We'd met in passing on a porn Web site and had given each other a couple of satisfying private chat cyber fucks. Without openly asking for it, he increasingly pushed our cyber play to the kinky and S&M. His site moniker was Bigboy and mine was Viper, and it didn't take me long to figure out that he turned on to bottom and domination, which was just fine with me. I could also tell that he was very curious, if a little shy and hesitant. Chances were good he'd never gone beyond the cyber but was drawn like a moth to the whole concept of what we were cybering.

His site profile was scanty—an artist in California, claiming to be bi—but the location opened up a wealth of possibilities for me.

[Viper] Located in California, bb? North, South, Central?

[Bigboy] Central.

[Viper] Ah, profile says u're an artist. frisco then?

[Bigboy] No, farther south. even more artsy. Coast.

[Viper] must be monterey then.

(Pause)

[Viper] santa cruz myself.

(Pause)

[Bigboy] Interesting.

129

[Viper] yes, interesting. interested, yes?

(Pause)

[Viper] u've said u wanted to see my basement room.

(Pause for three minutes, and Bigboy signed off chat)

Three days later I was cruising the chat room, and he invited me for a private chat. I was beginning to think he wouldn't contact me again, but all the time the moth was fluttering around my flame.

[Bigboy] Maybe. But here in Monterey. Out on the pier.

[Viper] no. must be something u want. u have to come to me in santa cruz.

He signed off again then, and I didn't enter the chat room at all the next evening. Toward midnight, he IMed me, eagerly agreeing to come to Santa Cruz that weekend. I put him off, telling him I couldn't make it until the following weekend, although I didn't really have anything else to do. Just stringing him out; giving him line to either slither away or hook himself. He agreed to meet, and I picked out a gay biker's bar in the rough part of town, telling him what the bar was, giving him plenty of room to cut and run.

On the designated night, I tricked myself out in my leathers and black net muscle shirt that stopped short of my belly button, showing off my abs real good, and biked my Harley over to the bar. Chances were that he wouldn't show, but I'd have me a fine evening anyway.

Surprise, surprise, though. He showed. I easily picked up on him when he entered. Nice looking; good, trim, muscled bod, but nervous as hell. He saw me when I waved at him, and I saw his eyes get all big. I didn't think he was dissatisfied, just hyperventilating at the whole concept. I figured him right there for first time.

He came over and sat, and after establishing we were who we thought we were, we tried some small talk. From time to time, he looked like he wanted to bolt for it, and each time I asked him if he wanted to leave alone, but he set his jaw and said no. He told me that his life had become just so boring in the sex department and he needed to give it a jolt start. I told him I could do that—and he had no idea how close to reality my plans were to do that—but that where we could go from here wasn't

130

going to be for the fainthearted. He swallowed hard and asked me if I was going to show him my basement. I told him, no, not this time—and his body seemed to deflate as if he'd worked himself up for nothing. But I went on to say that I thought he might like to see my garage instead tonight. Asked him if doing it tied up and on my Harley appealed to him, and I felt his thigh tremble under my hand.

Out in the parking lot, he climbed onto the bike behind me. When we started off, he was sitting well behind me and having a hard time figuring out where to put his hands, but I upped my speed, and his pelvis was soon plastered tight against mine and he had to wrap his arms around my bare, steely midsection to keep from flying off the bike. I could tell he was excited by what I could feel snaking up the small of my back and getting harder as it rubbed up against me.

We sped through the town and back out into a more disserted area in the dust- and sagebrush-covered hills and pulled up short in front of the large corrugated, isolated garage building I kept to work on my cars and bikes. I zapped the high entry door open, and then zapped it closed again when we had driven into the building. The same zapping turned on the industrial-strength lights hanging from the rafters well above our heads. I ran the cycle right up to a clearing in the middle, under some gymnastic arm rings suspended from an overhead beam. I stopped the bike there and knocked down the kick stand with my boot as I hopped off. Bigboy, who I had learned was really named Roy—or at least had chosen for me to know him by this name—sat on the cycle, scoping out the surroundings in the brightly lit garage, as I went over to the side and picked up a pile of leather material and tossed it at him.

"Here. Strip and put these on," I directed, using a voice of authority both to keep him focused and because I had discerned that was what he wanted from me.

He stripped, and I was pleased to see that he had gotten the Web moniker "Bigboy" honestly. His new costume was composed of a leather harness crisscrossing his chest, leather chaps, leather boots, and thick leather wristbands lined with fleece. No pants. He seemed pleased with the outfit, and his cock was rising to attention, clearly anticipating having a good time.

"Come over here and get back on the cycle; turned facing the back, your back on the handlebars," I commanded.

When he'd done that, and after showing him what I was holding in my hands and giving him an opportunity to object, which he didn't do, I quickly attached a long chain to his right wristband, threw the chain through one of the gymnast rings overhead, and attached the other end to his left wristband. There was some give in the chain, but he couldn't bring his hands and arms to in front of him now. I then attached shorter chains through rings in the ankles of his boots to something in the wheel of the motorcycle on either side. He wasn't going anywhere for a while.

He watched me, all wide eyed, as I then stripped my own pants and muscle shirt off, and stood there only in my leather boots—and those busy tattoos and all those metal rings piercing my body, including the big, thick silver ring in the head of my penis. I already had quite a hard-on, one to rival what he was showing me. His cock was something to whistle at, but I was bigger and thicker than he was. I could see that he was panting at the sight of me. Starting to sweat, and his well-muscled pecs were twitching.

I took out a camera and snapped "memory" shots of him astride my cycle and in restraints, which I promised to share only with him. I expected him to object to that, but he was licking his lips, obviously aroused at the prospect of being able to see this real-life encounter on replay. I promised to break out the video when the scene heated up.

I brought out a tube of ointment and started lathering up Roy's ass, while pumping his cock with my other hand. He was already writhing under my touch. When I had him all lathered and pumped up, I took out the camera again and took some "hard-on" shots of my new Harley decoration. Then I set up video cameras on pods that zeroed in on the bike and the now-glistening-with-anticipation Roy from three different directions, turned up the lights on the "set," turned on the video cameras, and came back to the bike. I threw my leg over the bike and was sitting on the seat, facing Roy. He was trembling all over, and his skin sizzled where I touched it. The video cameras were running, as I ran my hands over Roy's torso and thighs and lathered up and stroked my own cock until it was hard and slick enough for me.

I told Roy what I was going to do to him then, and he invited me in—hesitatingly, but I could see the lust in his eyes. There was no way his libido was going to let his body back out of this now. Then I tilted his ass up with my hands on his butt cheeks and entered him, slowly but fully. He was in fine shape and was very vocal for the cameras—and so was I.

All the way in and pumping in short strokes deep. "Nice tight ass, and nice tits, Hot Shot. Gonna fuck you until your eyeballs are swimming in spunk." I was using the language of our cyber fucks now, language that turned him on for real as much as it had hard the Internet. It certainly was keeping him aroused now.

"There, you want me. Not just in the chat room. You want my cock throbbing inside you. I'm in and you're pulling me farther in. Can't get enough of me, can you? Been wanting me for weeks, haven't you? Ah, made you moan, made you flinch, made you pant. You haven't had a man until you've had me, have you?"

His "yes" answers were inserted weakly, but with determination, between moans and groans and pain cut by pleasure outcries.

He managed to pant out that my penis ring was driving his ass walls to distraction deep inside him, and I pulled my cock toward the surface until he could feel the ring dragging back and forth across his prostate. He threw back his head and screamed in ecstasy, the reality obviously living up to what he'd imagined and was seeking.

And I pumped and pumped and pumped, showing off for the cameras—covering his torso and thighs with my searching hands and brutalizing his nipples and armpits with my teeth. When I was about to blow, I withdrew, stood up, and sent my cream flying all over his chest and belly, good footage for the cameras.

I then got up and switched off the cameras. I went back to the cycle with a damp cloth and wiped Roy down and then I

133

wiped myself down. I did this all in silence, listening to Roy's panting and groaning as he rattled the chains holding him on the back of the Harley and came to grips with his fantasy turning into reality. He probably wondered if it was over, but I wasn't ready to let him go yet—not by a long shot.

I glided around the garage in fluid motions, with Roy's lust-filled eyes following my every move, working myself up for what he'd learn was a grand finale, recharging my load.

After several minutes, I went back over to Roy and wrapped a studded leather ring around the base of his cock, ensuring that he would remain hard for the cameras when he got hard again. Then he watched me as I encased my own cock in a special sort of sheath and strapped an apparatus around my head and over my mouth, that, when it was in place, made me look like I had big, thick, black lips. I moved my new set of lips up and down, making sure that the device moved with me properly. Then I turned the video cameras back on and went back to the bike, once more throwing my leg over the saddle and facing Roy. I didn't make him wait long to learn what my new lips were for.

The lip device was electrically charged, with batteries and emitted a low-level current that registered at just above the tingle stage. It did have an electrical zap feel to it, but only just at the threshold of being painful.

My torso muscles rippled for the cameras and Roy screamed out in agony and ecstasy, as I started to kiss him with those lips from his neck to his pits and biceps, across his chest to his nipples, and down his sternum to his belly, navel, pubic region, thighs, and cock and balls, sending slight electric shocks into him wherever they touched. Pleasure mixed with shock, causing Roy to jerk slightly for the cameras with each touch of the lips. Electric pinpricks to his tender inner thighs, on his butt cheeks, across his perineum, on his balls, and firmly applied to the rim of his asshole. He jerked and jumped and cried out with each touch.

Then Roy found out about that sheath covering my cock. I tilted up his ass with hands under his butt. My cock slid into him again, and he found that the sheath was electrified too. But the voltage here was higher. I was manually operating the jolts, applying the first one as I slid my penis ring over his prostate, causing his whole torso to lift off the bike handles in shock and arousal and sending him into spasms that had barely subsided when the second jolt hit him, all along the ass canal some five inches down; another half inch and another jolt. My lips went to his nipples and held onto them, one after another, sending electrical shocks into him there. Six and half inches of my cock's journey up his canal and another, stronger, more prolonged jolt. It lifted his torso off the bike and took me with him.

He was bucking like a rodeo stallion now. I wrapped my arms around his waist and rode with him, giving the muffled shout through my electrified lips, "Whooeee! Ride 'em, Cowboy!"

Seven inches in and a jolt that made him spew his hot lead all over my belly, and seven and a half inches in, I filled him with even hotter lead of my own.

We lay there, arms and legs entwined, astride the Harley, panting and moaning and coming down off our electric high. I removed the apparatus from my head and nuzzled my own lips into the sweat-drenched hollow of his neck.

"So, how does the real thing stack up to the cyber fucking?" I whispered in his ear.

"Amazing. Can I see what you've got waiting for me in your basement now?" he croaked back at me between heavy pants.

Substitute

Cliff took me for granted. For some reason he thought I was safe. Once I overheard him tell one of those guys he brought home that he wanted only straight roommates, guys who wouldn't hit on him, because he only wanted to fuck when he was in the mood. Well, he had been in the mood a lot these past several weeks. And he also didn't know me worth spit. I only stayed around here and waited on him and cleaned up after him like I did because I wanted him.

I wanted him so bad.

I'd stay awake nights waiting to hear the scrape of the key in the lock. Then I'd hold my breath and close my eyes tight in case he checked on me before he took his pick of the night to his room. I'd wait until I started to hear the moaning, and then I'd quietly leave my bed and steal across to the dark living room, right there in the darker shadow of the TV cabinet, where I could get a good view of the bed in his room. He never shut the door. It was almost as if he expected me to watch . . . but I'm sure he didn't, because he sure didn't show any interest in me when we were alone.

Sometimes Cliff was the top and sometimes he was the bottom. I only really got into the scene when he was the top, though. I wanted him to top me. I'd never done it with a guy before, but I knew from the first time I saw him fucking one of those guys he'd brought home late at night that I wanted him to fuck me. I'd watch them sucking each other off, building up to grappling on the bed, building up their moaning, and my hand went to the front of my sleeping shorts, and I'd start going numb everywhere but the very center of me.

I'd see Cliff's cock thicken and lengthen, and my butt would twitch from the fantasy of him preparing himself for me. The legs would open wide, and the little cry and the arching of the receiver's back as he was being entered and filled would have me swaying and moaning and pulling my dong out into the open. Then my eyes would slit and I'd focus on the contracting and rhythm of Cliff's butt cheeks as he either possessed or was stroked by his lover of the night.

God, I wanted to palm my hands on those butt cheeks as Cliff worked inside me.

From that point I was lost, wanting to move with the figures on the bed, to become one with them. And as time went on, I learned the signals of approaching release, and I was able to time my ejaculations closely with theirs.

Then I would retreat back to my bed, as quietly as I could. I never knew where they would go from there. Sometimes the other man would leave immediately and sometimes they would come out to the living area and raid the refrigerator. But sometimes, there would be a short period of silence and then the moaning would start again. And I'd then leave my bed again and move to my observation nook beside the TV cabinet and watch and stroke to the renewed mating.

The next day, Cliff would act like nothing at all had happened. I don't know how many times I wanted to say that I wanted it to be me he brought into his room one of those nights. But I just couldn't bring myself to do it.

I probably would have remained a pining virgin for months only to finally move out of the apartment in frustration from unrequited need for Cliff, leaving him scratching his head about what had gone wrong in what he thought was a perfect roommate setup, if he hadn't gotten dead drunk that night after our university football team unexpectedly won the Gator Bowl game.

Cliff was half looped on a combination of Bud and vodka and euphoria over the game win even before he flipped off the TV, dressed and grabbed up his jacket, and headed out into the night. We watched the game together and he seemed to enjoy my company. He even flicked me with his towel off and on during the second half as our team piled touchdown on touchdown in what became a rout. He'd taken a shower during halftime and padded out with just the towel around him. I'd stripped off my T myself, hoping that his euphoria might at last turn into arousal for me. But nada. I was just his roommate; someone else in the room. Someone who would clean up the empty bottles and cardboard pizza boxes after he'd left. Someone safe.

"Whooeee, gotta get me some," was all he said as time ran out on the field. And then he padded back to his room and pulled on a pair of jeans and a T and was out the door in a flash. He didn't put on any briefs, so I knew he was going out on the prowl and would be back with some stud in tow a couple of hours later. I could have cried. He didn't have to go anywhere to find someone for the night.

So, what did I do after Cliff left? I started picking up empty bottles and pizza boxes, of course, and making the place presentable for whoever Cliff came home with. But all the time I was doing it, I was muttering to myself that one of these days I was going to pull on my jeans without any briefs under them, just like Cliff did, and tug on the tightest T I could find . . . my body was just as well developed as Cliff's was . . . and I'd go out into the night and find someone of my own to bring home too.

Who was I kidding, though? It was Cliff I wanted, not any of those guys he brought home.

That night was different from any of the others. Cliff didn't slip quietly into the apartment with his one night stand that night. Cliff was drunker than a skunk when he came home, and he was making a whole lot of noise.

I decided he had struck out at the pickup bars and had some sort of homing device inside him that managed to get him back in spite of being plastered. My first thought as I heard him muttering incoherently to himself and stumbling through the living room and to his bedroom was intense relief that he hadn't had a car wreck. But then, when the sound just abruptly stopped, I held my breath for the longest time. Was he OK? Did he need help?

He'd never come home this drunk before. Maybe he was choking on his own vomit or something. I had no experience in this. Was it good or bad that he'd just gone silent? I knew I had to check on him. I had no idea what to do if he was seriously in need of help, but I had to at least check to see what was what.

I got out of bed, clad only in my droopy sleeping shorts, and padded through the living room and toward the light in his bedroom. I could see Cliff as I approached. He was huddled on the bed, his chest buried in the bedspread, his arms flung out wide, and his knees drawn up so that his bare butt was jutting up at me. My cock gave a lurch at the sight of those rounded orbs that fascinated and aroused me so. His face was turned to me and he was blowing bubbles and snorting and snoring quietly. And he had the most angelic expression on his handsome face.

I ached for him. I didn't even think of wondering why he was bare-assed. He did have his T-shirt on still. I was drawn to that luscious ass of his. I approached the bed in faulting steps. He certainly didn't look like he was in any danger. But he also looked like he was totally oblivious to the world and that nothing short of a four alarm fire would rouse him for hours.

I couldn't resist. I reached out a hand, ever so tentatively. My fingers were on the flesh of his glutes. The skin felt firm and soft and warm and cool all at the same time. And just the contact made by the pads of my fingers sent little chills up my arms. I heard myself moan, and then, not having any control over myself, I felt my palm stretch out over the curve of his buttock.

At that instant, though, I heard the sound of rustling from the closet corner of the room, and I snatched my hand away and turned and looked there with a little cry of shock and surprise.

He laughed out loud. There was a big, hulking dude in the room with us. A biker type. All tricked out in leather and tattoos. Not fat; heavily muscled. A good face, if a little hard looking; and a great body; the impression of dark curly hair here and about.

He was holding Cliff's jeans in front of him, and I'd swear he had a hand in one of the back pockets. Taking advantage of the situation.

"Who the hell are you?" he said, as if I was the intruder and this was his room.

"I live here; I'm Cliff's roommate," I retorted, rising anger overcoming the surprise. I was in shape, but not in shape like this guy was . . . and certainly not nearly as big . . . so I wasn't thinking too well to go belligerent on him.

"This Cliff?" he asked, pointing to the bubbling angel on the bed.

"Yeah," I said. "And this is our apartment. What . . . ?"

"They call me Horse," the biker-type said as he tossed Cliff's jeans on the floor behind his back, almost daring me to ask him what he was doing with them. "You can guess why they call me that," he went on. A sneery sort of smile was spreading across his face.

With the jeans out of the way, I got a good look at him. No shirt . . . none required really; he was clothed in red, blue, and black tattooing in an intricate floral design with flowing vines . . . black leather vest, tight black leather pants with a big bulge at the crotch, black leather boots, and a black leather baseball cap peeking out over black curly locks of hair. He was darkish; probably at least part Hispanic.

"Well, Horse," I said, trying, unsuccessfully, to keep a stammer out of my voice, "thanks for getting Cliff home. Now I guess you'd better be—"

"I don't think so," Horse said, that sneery smile of his unfaltering.

"What . . . ?"

"Your roomie here brought me clear across town for a fuck."

"Well, you can see he's in no shape to—" I responded, indigence involuntarily creeping into my voice, not able to say that word.

"Yes, I see that," Horse answered in a throaty voice. "Looks like it's substitute time, then."

"Oh, no. No," I said, taking a faltering step away. "I don't . . . I'm not."

141

"I saw you stroke his ass," Horse said. "Don't tell me you two aren't fucking like bunnies."

"No. I've never. . . . You need to leave." My words came out choked, and I turned and fled the room.

But he was faster than I was. And bigger and stronger. I was only half way across the living room when he tackled me to the floor. I don't know where he got the leather thongs from, but he had me belly down to the carpet, fully covering my body with his, and he held me flat there while he bound my hands together at the wrists above my head. I saw him effortless lift a heavy recliner and bring it back down so that one of the legs came down between my forearms, entrapping my hands under the heavy chair and making sure I couldn't slither away from him.

I lay there, immobilized by shock, fear, surprise, and his heavy body, whimpering and hyperventilating, too numb from it all to yell out or to demonstrate any form of objection or resistance.

His hands were flying all over my body, and he literally ripped my sleeping shorts off me. He had also stripped himself, because I now felt skin on skin. The hardness and power of him was overwhelming. He had his face buried in the back of my neck, and he was nipping me there and making little animal noises. His chest was rubbing against my shoulder blades. I could feel cold metal rubbing against me there; I was dumbly thinking he must have body piercings and, my mind racing to defend my senses from the reality that was happening to me, I was musing about how many rings and such he had about his body. I knew of one for sure. His hips were moving against my buttocks, and there was little doubt that he had a penis ring of some thickness.

The Horse lifted his weight from my back, but still encased my sides closely with his knees, and he flipped me over. I barely had time to focus on the determined sneer on and lust in his face before he was straddling my chest, pulling my head up roughly by the hair, and forcing his ring-pierced cock head between my lips.

I gagged as he took possession of me and quickly filled my mouth with his manhood to the edge of choking. My eyes were watering and I whimpering and thrashing about, trying to escape him. But he was too strong for me.

"Take it," He muttered darkly. He was stabbing down into my mouth with short, quick strokes. "Suck it proper," he said. "Open. Take it."

I was doing my best, but I had no idea what to do, and this all was moving just too fast for me. I was still in shock.

The Horse slammed my head back on the carpet in disgust. And then I saw the expression on his face change. He was regaining control. He had been operating out of animal instinct. The hunt.

"You really haven't done this before, have you?" he asked, his voice full of wonder.

"No, I haven't," I stammered. I suddenly was ashamed. I was twenty and I'd wanted to do this for years. I hadn't done it because I was a lump. A scared lump. I certainly wanted to do it with Cliff.

"Could of fooled me," the Horse muttered. "You're hard enough. Your cock tells me you want it." He was stroking my cock with a hand thrown back behind him. And I couldn't deny that I was reacting to that like I wanted sex.

"I saw you with that dude in the bedroom. You wanted him, didn't you?"

It was a struggle to admit it, but I let it out in almost a wail. "Yes. Yes, I want him."

I had no chance to say more, because he brought his face down to mine, and he possessed my lips with his. He was stretched across my body again. His body, his full body tattoo undulating provocatively, was covering mine and moving on mine.

My body was taking over my decision making. He was stroking my cock and moving his body on mine and kissing me deeply. The tension began to drain out of my body to be replaced with a motion that matched his and sighing and moaning that more than matched his. I closed my eyes tightly and imagined that this was Cliff who was making love to me.

But that wasn't working. When I tried to surface the image of Cliff in my mind, the reality of this nut-brown, muscular body, covered with tattoos and piercings and danger and erotic exoticness fought for recognition. And won. I wasn't writhing in arousal with Cliff. There was no substituting the elusive, aloof . . . and drunk on his tail in the other room . . . Cliff for the strong, powerful, arousing man who was making love to me in reality here on the living room carpet.

He waited for the moment when he no longer was kissing me, but when I was kissing him. And then he broke the kiss and lifted his face from mine and gave me a broad smile.

"Do you want me to stop?" he asked simply.

"No." I managed to say, surprised at myself that the decision had come so easily. "No. No, don't stop. But—"

"Shhh," he said, moving the hand from my cock to brush against my lips. "I can be gentle. If I'm the first, I can control myself."

"Ohhh," I whimpered. The reality of what was about to happen was becoming more and more real for the first time. "Ohhh. Please," I whimpered.

"Please stop?" he asked.

"No. No. Please. I want it. Just. You know."

"Do you want me to untie you? Shall we move to your bed."

I chomped on that for a few seconds. What did I want? If this was going to happen, did I want it half way? What was the thrill of this man for me? The danger. The power he had over my powerlessness. The whole rough, swarthy, tattooed and body-pierced aspect of him aroused me. I had to admit that the rougher the one night stand that Cliff brought home, the more of a thrill it was for me. The surprise. The forceful taking. I wanted it all.

"No, please. Take me here, like this."

"Right. Good," he said, the lust-filled smile returning to his face. "Shall we start from the beginning?"

"What do you mean. I don't—"

But the Horse had already started showing me what he meant. He moved to astride my chest again, with his knees encasing my side and he has pushing the head of his ring-pierced cock head at my lips again. this time I opened wide to him, and he slowly stroked against my inner cheeks, moving my head up and down on his rod with hands buried in the hair at the back of my head. He was murmuring instructions. Taking it slow, but filling me to capacity again. Pulling back when I gagged and choked, but relentlessly arousing himself, bringing his cock to gigantic proportions in the warmth of my mouth.

I could feel him trembling above me, but he didn't take this the full way. He withdrew from me and moved his pelvis down to mine. He was rhythmically moving his hips against mine, and I returned the favor, in coordinating rhythm. Our cocks were rubbing against each other and up and down on each other's bellies. We were both writhing and trembling now. His chest was rocking up and down just inches above my face, and he brought my lips to a ring-tipped nipple with his hands.

I needed no encouragement but started licking and kissing from one hard nipple to the other and then I was tonguing farther afield, following the curls of his chest hair and the vining of the floral tattooing across his torso with my tongue. He raised his arms, one after the other, and I buried my face in his pits, tonguing the profusion of black, curly hair there and drinking in the lusty man scent of him hungrily.

His hard, horse-hung cock was slapping against my belly, and I could tell from the increasing rapid rate of the movement of his hips that his needs were becoming more and more insistent.

Well, so were mine.

He was on the move. His face came down to my chest and he was tonguing and nipping at my nipples. Slowly moving down my torso with exploring lips and tongue and wandering hands. I arched my back and gave a little cry as his mouth opened over the head of my throbbing cock and he took me in. And in and in and in.

I ejaculated almost immediately within the close warmth of his mouth, and he swallowed me down with a low guttural humming sound.

He pulled away from me and his knees no longer were encasing my thighs.

"Open to me," he said in an insistent throaty voice. "Your legs. Open them."

I opened my legs wide as he pulled a cushion off the nearby sofa. He lifted my pelvis with one hand and pushed the

145

cushion under my hips with the other. My butt was elevated over my head. But he wanted me elevated even farther. He was on his knees below me and between my legs. He gripped the backs of my thighs in strong hands and pushed my torso up so that my weight was borne on my shoulder blades. The sofa cushion was pushing against the small of my back.

I gave a little cry and arched up again as I felt his tongue run between my butt cheeks and brush across my asshole. He continued on up my perineum and was swallowing and working my balls. I was starting to go hard again and I was barely able to control the trembling of my body. The tongue worked its way back to my hole, and he was rimming and then tongue-fucking me. I sighed and moaned while he spent several minutes working me with his tongue, making me open to him. The first opening of those gates to the possession of man.

"Rubber. I need a rubber . . . and some lube. God, you are tight. A rubber."

"I don't. I don't know . . . I . . . Cliff's nightstand. He's sure to have them there."

I was left alone, ass over head, hands trapped under a recliner, beginning to have doubts and to hyperventilate again. But, thankfully, only briefly. The Horse had found what he needed and was back.

He stood over me, between my spread thighs, letting me watch him open the condom packet and roll the thin latex on that monster of a cock he had. God, his body was beautiful. Dark, swarthy, covered with a profusion of tattoos. Black, curly hair. A lusty smile. And at the very center of him. Demanding my full attention. Making me fearful and anxious at the same time. That magnificent cock. Soon to be inside me. Could I take it? Surely I couldn't take it all in.

But I could. And I did.

He went slowly and was as gently as he could be . . . at least at first. It seemed like hours ticked slowly away as he took his time entering me, fucking down into my hole from a crouched stance below and above me, with my butt high above my head.

And I watched every inch disappear into me. And I screamed, first in pain, but eventually in ecstasy. And I sweated and strained and cursed and cried out against it and cried for more of it.

When it was all buried inside me and his pubic hair was brushing against my tender inner thighs and I was still gulping and groaning and moaning, he at last lost control and started pumping me long and hard and deeply. My body thrashed about involuntarily, but he kept a firm grip in my upper thighs with those strong hands of his, holding my pelvis firmly against his while he fucked me in rapid strokes and to completion.

I ejaculated again up his belly as he went rigid for a brief second, stroked hard three more times, and then went rigid again, gave a deep, animal sound in his throat and collapsed onto my body.

He remained inside me, as he lay on top of me, his sweat slick and musky-sweet to the senses. And I felt him soften, contracting in my canal, and I almost felt a pang of loss as he did so. I was sore and at the edge of exhaustion from the exertion and release of the pent up emotions. The awe of the memory of the straining, flexing muscles of his body as he worked inside me, the undulating garden tattooing. All of that to possess me. Me bringing out that need and lust in him.

It was done. And it was more than I had imagined it would be. Could Cliff had done better? I would never know. The first time could not be repeated.

But the act itself could be repeated.

After only a few moments, the Horse rose up off me and stood over me, a look of satisfaction and possession in his face. A slight return of the sneer. He'd had me. And he'd been the first one to have me. That was something I couldn't give any other man. Another notch on his belt, but probably a special notch for him. I doubted that he got to fuck too many virgins.

I watched him roll the spent condom, its bulbous head ballooned with his prodigious semen, off his reawakening cock. And then he gave me a wicked smile and I watched him open another condom packet, roll it onto his cock, and stroke himself bigger while he dribbled more lube along his shaft.

"Roll over." It wasn't a request.

This time he took me more roughly, my hips on the sofa pillow again, and him on his knees behind me and stroking hard and long into me. He had his hands buried in the hair on my head and had my torso arched back and taunt as he gave me what was probably his usual long, hard, rough fuck.

After this time, I just lay there on the floor, exhausted and moaning and whimpering. Loving it, but hoping to hell he wasn't going to do it again . . . at least for a while.

And he didn't.

I watched his lithe figure move around the apartment with authority and familiarity, just like he owned the place. Just like he owned my body now. He moved like a cat, completely comfortable with his beautiful nakedness.

He raided the refrigerator. He quickly drank off a beer. He burped and then he farted.

And then he moved to Cliff's room and I watched, stretched out on the floor, while he fucked the passed-out Cliff quickly and brutally from the rear, a repeat of how he had just fucked me. I watched every stroke, remembering and reliving it as he had done it to me. Savoring it. Loving it. Almost wanting it again. Almost.

After the Horse was finished with Cliff, he went in and took a shower, leaving the door to the bathroom open so that I could watch the entire process. Then he dried himself in the doorway and gave me a full shot of stretching his leathers back on his beautiful body.

He leaned down and whispered something in my ear as he untied my hands. Then he pocketed the leather restraints, sauntered slowly over to the door, and was gone into the night.

"Wow, look at you," Cliff was saying the next evening as he leaned on the frame of my bedroom door and watched me pull a pair of tight jeans over my naked hips. "Lookin' good, man."

Cliff had just showered and a towel was fighting very hard to hold place around his hips and was about to lose the fight. I could tell from the bulge in front that he was interested in something. I couldn't remember that he'd shown any interest like this around me ever before.

He'd been eyeing me all through dinner and even had made some comments about me being different somehow. And I could swear that he seemed to be flirting with me.

"Goin' out?" He asked.

"Yeah, I think so," I answered, pulling a tight T-shirt down over my torso.

"'Cause, ya know, I thought we might stay in tonight and watch a movie, or somethin' . . . or somethin'," Cliff said. And he was giving me "that" look. I couldn't remember him giving me that look before.

"Sorry, can't," I said. "Got a date." At least I hoped I had. I hoped I'd remembered the name of the bar the Horse had whispered in my ear before he left.

I was humming when I walked out the door to the apartment and shut it behind me, leaving Cliff standing alone in the middle of the living room . . . right on the spot where I had learned I liked danger and a little rough fucking.

Patience Rewarded

I knew the moment the cute little blond twink strolled into my storefront gym that I was going to have him, but by the way he shrank away from me and trembled a bit when I approached him, I also knew I would have to prepare for that moment well.

"Hi, I'm Rod." I said pleasantly. "I run this place and act as personal trainer. And who are you and what are you interested in?"

I had hoped that he'd say right out that he wanted to be fucked by a horse-hung muscle stud like me, but he didn't respond to that innuendo.

"Hi, Rod. I'm Craig. I'm tired of everyone thinking I'm too young to buy beer. I want to bulk up."

"You mean something like this?" I said, and I pulled my gym T over my head. I could hear Craig gasp when he saw my massive, well-cut torso.

"Y-e-s-s," he stammered out, "something like that . . . if that's possible."

"Well, let's see what we have to work with," I said pleasantly. "Off with that T-shirt."

He stripped his T off, and I could tell right off that he wouldn't bulk up very much, although we could do something with those pecs and abs. But I also saw that I wouldn't want him to bulk up too much. He was one beautiful twink. It set my cock to twitching just to see him.

But I told him that I could help him if he came in twice a week. And he did that for the next two months, during which time I unfolded my plan to have my cock pulsating inside his cute little ass. I gave him a lot of personal attention, telling him that I wanted him to go shirtless in his workouts so I could see what was being worked out and how well in the exercises and that I would go shirtless as well so he could see what muscles should be worked with the exercises. And I gave him plenty of muscle work to see during the workouts—all except for the one muscle I really wanted him to see. I took care of that by hitting the showers whenever he did and giving him a full display.

For the first couple of weeks he remained ultrasensitive to my touching him or even coming close, but I was persistent in needing to put my hands on him to show him how to do the exercises properly, and slowly but surely he let me touch him and, with time and confidence, let my hands linger on the curves and folds of his torso and legs during the exercises. And he was lingering longer in the shower as well. One evening after two months of preparation, I began to slowly stroke out my cock while we were in the shower, and I was sure he was ogling me sideways. His eyes bugged out and he dropped the soap. When he bent over to pick it up, I almost took him then, but I didn't. Others were in the gym. I needed to wait a bit longer, and needed him to signal his willingness.

On his next visit, I decided to bring this to a new level. We were over in the corner of the room, away from the storefront picture window and everyone else working out was focused on their own exercising. I had Craig laying down on his back, bench pressing a barbell.

"No, no, Craig," I said. "You're putting too much leg in it. Here, let me show you how to get the power into your shoulders and pecs, which is what you want to be developing here."

I squatted down on the bench, facing him, and pushed my knees under his thighs, pushing his legs over mine and out. I spread the palms of my hands on his tender inner thighs. "There, try it like that."

He huffed and puffed for a few minutes, barely getting the barbell up, concentrating hard. But then I started to gently stroke his inner thighs with my fingers and he was suddenly concentrating on something else. He started to tremble all over and he couldn't get the barbell fully extended.

"No, you're trying to get the power from your stomach, Craig. It must be from your chest and shoulders. Don't arch your back. Here, now try it." I moved one of my hands to his flat little belly and held him down on the board. He was trying his best to raise the barbell, but not having much luck.

"It's no use, Rod," he whimpered. "I can't get it up."

"It doesn't look to me like you are having trouble getting it up, Craig," I said, as my hand slid down to his basket. I admit that I was a little surprised myself. In the shower he had present a pert little prick, like a chaste Greek statue, but now he was filling out nicely in that department.

Craig sat up in panic. "Please, don't, Rod. I can't do it." His body was shaking like a leaf, and he couldn't look me in the face. His gaze was glued to my hand cupping his basket.

I took one of his hands in mine and guided it to my own basket. He gasped and tried to pull away but I didn't let him. "Well, when you can do it, this is what is waiting for you, Craig."

He jerked his hand away, jumped off the bench, and bustled back to the dressing room. He was back in a moment with his clothes hurriedly stuffed in his gym bag, not even having showered, and escaped out the door.

All the next day, I wondered if I had acted too quickly, but right before closing time, there he was again. He'd never come two days in a row and never this late. He stayed over to the side, well away from me, working out with hand weights until the last of the other patrons had left.

"We're closing now," I said as I picked up my duffel bag and walked by him on the way to the door.

"I think I can do it now," was all he said, in a small, distant voice. He looked so vulnerably twinky even after all those weeks of working out.

I continued on to the door and locked it from the inside, and then I returned and took his hand and led him to the hallway leading to the dressing rooms, where we couldn't be seen through the storefront window.

I pushed his back against the wall, while I stripped off my T and shorts. I then pushed him down on his knees and leaned close into him at the wall, holding him prisoner there with my strong thighs. I pushed my engorging cock past his lips and made him work me up big. He was gagging and choking, but he did a good, fast job of it. Then I pulled him back up to his feet, flipped him around, belly to the wall, and covered his soft little twinky body with my hard muscled one. My cock was running up the small of his back, and I stroked it up and down his back while my hands groped his body in a frenzy. He was moaning and sighing and hiccupping, his body all atremble. I went down on my knees behind him and pushed my tongue between his pert little butt cheeks. I pushed his legs apart while I flicked my tongue in his sweet little asshole. I stroked his inner thighs with my fingers, which he enjoyed immensely, and reached through and milked his cock from delicately small to presentably hard; after he'd hardened, he came almost immediately in my hand with a twitch and a lurch.

Then I opened my bag and took out a tube of lube and a condom packet. lubed his ass and fingered his hole, working on opening him to me, while my teeth nipped at his now-rosy butt cheeks. Then I rolled the condom on my huge tool and started working my way into his ass, full of lust now, not giving it enough time. He screamed and cried, but declined all offers for me to stop or slow down. I allowed him to widen his stance and arch his back, my hands going to his pecs and nipples, but entry was still being difficult. I couldn't wait.

I kicked the duffel bag over to the middle of the hall, and took Craig's lithe little body in my hands by his hips and turned him and pushed his pelvis down onto the duffel. His cute little butt was pointed up in the air now, and I came down between his legs and into him. Entry was easier now, and I filled him to the limit and rocked him back and forth on duffel as my pulsating cock rode his ass hard in six long strokes that were crowned with repeated gushes of man juice, my cry of fulfilled patience mingling with his screams of realized ecstasy. Months of preparation for no more than fifteen minutes of frenzied quickie fuck from first feel to gush.

All of the waiting and preparation were well worth the reward, though, and now that I had won the prize, I could savor it. I covered Craig's trembling body with mine, pulled his legs in with mine to tighten his already-tight ass, and rocked my pelvis back and forth on his buttocks. We cuddled and whispered sweet nothings to each other as I reloaded. And when I had filled him out again with my battering ram, I fucked him there astride the duffel bag on the hall carpet a second time and then a third time in long, lingering strokes, accompanied by the music of his falsetto purring.

When I was done, Craig was acting like a zombie. I asked him what was wrong, but he didn't respond and didn't seem able to look me in the eye. He gathered up his shorts and T, quickly slipped them on, and fled the room. When I walked out onto the main exercise floor, he was gone. I wondered if I'd gone too far.

But while I was closing up the next night, there was Craig, appearing from out of the darkness.

"Can we do it in the showers this time?" he murmured as he slipped past me and into the gym. "Some time ago, I thought you'd do me when we were in the showers and I bent over for the soap. But you didn't, and I haven't been able to get that out of my mind since then."

I was, of course, more than happy to oblige.

Seizing the Moment

The news of Ted Robertson's auto accident, relayed to us just before we were closing up the gym for the night, was a crushing blow to Daren. I had been watching Daren work out alone for the past hour and had even spent more time than usual with him in my capacity of the trainer on duty, and I could tell that he was in a dither. Ted Robertson, a good twenty years older than Daren, had become Daren's spotting partner at the gym in support of Daren's post-high school bulking up program in preparation for taking up his football scholarship at a prestigious university. And Ted hadn't shown up tonight.

To most, Daren's near-total collapse in response both to Ted's absence when Daren expected to be working out with him and to the news that Ted had had an auto accident would seem an overreaction. Ted had not suffered life-threatening injuries and had been taken to the hospital in time to ensure a full recovery. But I knew what most didn't and what Daren didn't know I knew. I knew that Ted had finally convinced Daren to go home with him after the workout tonight and let Ted make love to him. Ted and I had both been cultivating the handsome young man for a couple of months, and Ted had not been able to resist gloating to me that he had won in the "deflower Daren" contest.

As the last of the clients were getting their gear together and preparing to leave the gym, I walked over to Daren, who was just sitting on a weight-lifting bench with a deer-in-the-headlights look of confusion and dismay about him.

"Daren, buddy. He's going to be all right. The hospital said it will just take him some time to recover. Why don't you hit the showers and then work out that tension for the shock in the hot tub?"

"But you're closing," Daren muttered. "I should go on home. Or I should go over to the hospital and check on him. Or . . . I just don't know. It's just such a shock."

"I don't have anywhere I need to be this evening, Daren," I said in the best soothing voice I had. "No problem with staying open for you for a while. I don't really think you should be driving home or even over to the hospital until the shock wears off anyway."

"Well."

"Tell you what. I've got a bottle of wine in the fridge here. I think a little bit of alcohol will help calm your nerves. And I'll hit the hot tub too. We can talk it out. I feel you need to talk about it to get your bearings."

"Well, OK," Daren said, and he stood and shuffled almost zombie style toward the shower—or at least as zombie style as a hot young blond bulking up for a college football scholarship could look.

I hurried and opened the wine and got two glasses and stripped down and entered the hot tub before Daren had finished showering. He came out in a pretty skimpy Speedo that started my juices to boiling.

When Daren entered the water and sat down across from me in the tub, I poured him a glass of wine and then another while we luxuriated in the hot, swirling waters. When I thought the moment was right, I opened up my campaign.

"You're taking Ted's accident a little hard," I began. "Tell me what you're feeling about that."

"I don't know. I don't know why it's hit me like this," Daren said. And I heard the catch in his voice. He was on the edge of control. I poured him another glass—and not really to steady his nerves as I claimed to him but to bring him closer to that edge.

"Maybe it's that immortality thing," I suggested gently.

"That immortality thing?"

"Yes, guys your age are just coming out of the phase where they assume they are invulnerable. That they'll live forever and never have to think about death. And then, wham, sometime a long about now, when you are approaching twenty and facing the world on your own, things start to happen to upset that apple cart. Ted could have died. One moment you expect him to be coming through the door and doing a gym routine with you and then the next moment, poof, he's gone. Is that what has you so choked up over this?"

"Yeah, I guess," Daren answered. "Well most of it . . . maybe in part. It's just that—"

But he couldn't go on. The wine was loosening him up, tearing down his defenses, and he hunched over in the hot tub, staring at the water, not at me. Unable to complete his thought . . . to tell me what was bothering him the most. Not knowing that I already knew. I seized the moment and scooted around the seating platform rim of the tub and came in close beside him. I then put my arm around him and hugged him tight into my side.

"And you had plans this evening—with Ted—didn't you? No need to deny it. I saw it in your faces, as the need and willingness developed over the last couple of weeks."

He gave a little sob and tried to turn away from me, but I held him in a strong grip within my arms.

"There, there," I whispered. "It will be fine. I'll take care of you. You still have that need, don't you?"

He looked up into my eyes, his face questioning, not having any idea how I knew, not sure what I was suggesting. Seizing the moment again, I brought the hand of the arm I was using to hug him and put it on his cheek and turned his head to mine. I brushed my lips to his and felt him stiffen, but before he could recover from the shock of that, I pressed my lips to his more insistently. My other arm circled around his chest and held him there, squirming slightly—but only slightly—against me, his eyes all bulgy and shocked, staring into mine.

He finally managed to pull away and sputter, "God, Lance, what . . .?"

He maybe was bulking up nicely, but I was way stronger than he was. I picked him up, the buoyancy of the water helping me, and moved him over to where he was sitting in my lap. I held him in a tight hug while he fought me, trying to escape my embracing, not managing to do so.

"Lance! Let me—"

"Shush, shush," I was saying over his protests in my most soothing voice.

"Oh, God, Lance. You're not wearing a suit. Your cock . . . it's . . . it's—"

And indeed my cock was engorging and was plastered to the small of his back, running up toward his shoulder blades.

"There, there. Don't fight me. Just calm down. I know, I know, Daren."

"You know what?" It was a panicked, plaintive question—thrown out while he was renewing his struggle to be free.

"I know what you're not telling me about why Ted's failure to show up tonight was such a shock to you."

"You know? What could you know?" Daren fairly screeched out in frustration.

"I know this was the night that Ted was going to make love to you. I know that you'd agreed to let Ted fuck you. Your first fuck."

"Oh, God," Daren cried out with a sob. And it was just as if he were a balloon that had been popped. He just collapsed, spent, against me, held firmly in my lap. I took advantage of his collapse to move a hand down to cup his basket. I had my chin on his shoulder and was making soothing clucking sounds in his ear. He was like a thoroughbred race horse I was working to break, all atremble and ready to break away from me at a moment's notice, but calming, losing his will to fight me.

"Oh, God, oh, God," he was sobbing.

"I know how hard this decision was in coming, Daren," I whispered. "I know how keyed up you were this evening in anticipation of something you've thought about long and hard. Ted's not able to be here, though. And he won't be here for several months to come. It will be months before he can come to you. Don't lose the moment. I can be your Ted. Let me be your Ted. Let me be your first fuck."

"Oh, God, oh, God," was all Daren could say. But his whimpering changed to strangled moaning as I traced the growing thickness of his young cock through the material of the Speedo. And he lifted his hips for me when I pulled his suit off of him and down his legs.

I settled him back into my lap, having pushed my cock down to where it ran under him and served as a platform for the underside of his own cock when he had settled in my lap. I wrapped a hand around both of the cocks and squeezed and pulled at them. His moaning and sighing increased in response. My other hand was exploring all of the creases and curves of his torso. I spent a long time preparing him and arousing him, and his trembling slowly decreased. When I felt his hand on top of mine as it was wrapped around our cocks, I turned my face to his, and this time his lips met mine half way and opened to my deep, exploring kiss.

At length, I stood up in the tub, bringing him with me and turned him on his back on the tiles outside the tub. I lowered my mouth to his engorged cock and sucked him off. He came quickly, excited at the strangeness of the male blow job, although I could tell in his responses that he'd probably been sucked off by a girlfriend or two before.

I spread his legs and went for his sweet, puckered hole with my tongue then. He was emitting little yip, yip sounds and groaning heavily. I was reasonably sure no girlfriend had done this for him before. While I was gently but fully eating out his tender and luscious ass, I was opening a small bag that had been lying beside the wine bottle and took out a small bottle of KY and a condom packet. I managed to get the bottle open and the condom rolled onto my cock without losing purchase on his hole with my tongue. And then he rolled his nicely rounded butt cheeks around the rim of the hot tub and arched his back and gave appreciative little gruntings while I fingered KY into him, widened his hole with my searching fingers, and lathered up my sheathed tool.

I turned him on his belly and spread his legs. My sheathed cock went to his asshole, and I held his hips firmly in place with my hands while I slowly worked my way into his tight hole.

"Ahhhhh! Oh, God, oh God. It hurts so bad!" he was screaming. He was fighting my grip in his hips, arching his back up and trying to writhe his ass away from my assault.

"Do you want me to stop?" I asked. "You know Ted is longer and thicker than I am. If you wait for him, it's going to hurt more. If you manage the initial pain with me, you'll be ready for Ted when he's ready. So, do you want me to stop?"

Silence for a few seconds, as I held myself there, my cock just an inch inside him, waiting for him to make up his mind, willing him to let me continue.

"Oh shit," he whimpered. "No, don't stop. But go slow. p-l-e-a-s-e! You promise it will stop hurting?"

"Yes, just moments from now you'll be in heaven. And then when Ted's well, you'll be able to take him with only pleasure. Think of Ted fucking you. That's all you've been thinking about for weeks, isn't it. We're just getting you ready for Ted."

Daren whimpered and sobbed then while I slowly plowed to the hilt and held there, waiting for him to accommodate me. He had grabbed at the legs of a nearby wrought-iron table and was hanging on for dear life with white-knuckled fists. He also was all tensed up and hadn't taken a breath for I don't know how long.

"Relax, Daren," I said in my soothing voice. I'm all in now, it's all pleasure from now—but only if you relax and let the tension out. And breathe. Breathe normally. I let loose of his hips and started rubbing his back, helping him to relax, which, at length he did. then I started to slowly pump him, and he did, indeed, start moaning and sighing like I was taking him to heaven. And shortly before I came deep inside him, he was meeting my thrusts with thrusts of his own.

When I had shot off, I collapsed onto his back and gathered body to me in a close embrace.

"So, how was that for your first time?" I whispered in his ear.

162

"Oh, God, oh God," he was whimpering again, but this time his voice had an entirely different, satisfied and lust-laced tone to it.

When we had rested, I changed to a fresh condom and we sank back into the hot tub, he again in my lap, but facing me this time, and we kissed deeply as he slowly pumped his ass up and down on my cock.

All during this second fuck I was trying to hold my triumphant thoughts in check. The first thing tomorrow I'd be at the hospital, with flowers and candy for Ted—and with a gloating description of how I had seized the opportunity to take advantage of his months of cultivation of Daren to sweep in and usurp his deflowering campaign.

Ranger Guided

I didn't go to the gym to work out after my class as I'd told my roommate, Trent, I was going to do. I don't really know why I didn't do that. I was just so nervous and frustrated and jumpy that a good workout was probably just what I needed, but my mind wasn't on that sort of workout. My mind was on Trent, and I was just so embarrassed and confused and, yes, scared about this that I didn't know what to do. Although I had avoided the thought for weeks, I was beginning to accept that I was in love, or at least in lust, with my college roommate.

I'd never had these feelings for another man before I'd arrived at this university, but I hadn't been rooming with Trent more than a week before the feelings of desire began to build up in my body. It was all I could do not to let him see the physical evidence of his effect on me. I was sure that he'd be disgusted; he'd probably scream my infatuation throughout the dorm, and I'd be marked and laughed off campus.

Maybe it was forgetfulness that caused me to return to the room earlier than Trent thought I would rather than going to the gym. But maybe it was some sort of fate. I was deep in thought when I opened the door to the room. I could see that the shades were drawn and it was dark in the room, so I moved quietly, assuming that Trent was taking a nap on his bed. And at first I thought that was exactly what he was doing. He was stretched out on the bed on his belly, naked as usual. He always slept in the nude, which had been part of what had driven me crazy with lust. He had a deeply tanned, perfect body.

But when I looked closer, I could see that he wasn't asleep. He was moving. And he wasn't belly to the mattress either. There was another deeply tanned, male body under his. Trent was stretched out over another man, who also was belly to mattress under him, and Trent's arms stretched up and out wide with the other man's, the fingers of their hands entwined; their legs also were entwined. Trent's chest was close into the other man's shoulder blades, and his chin was hooked on the crook of the man's shoulder. The two faces were glued at the lips. The movement I'd discerned was focused on the hips of both men. Trent's cock was buried to the hilt in the other man's ass, and both were moving at the hips, Trent in a slow circular motion and the man underneath him in an equally languid rising and falling motion. I could see the underside of the hard cock of the skewered man rubbing back and forth against the bed sheet. As I stopped breathing, the shock of what was happening sinking in, sinking in to the very center of me where I felt my own cock coming to life, I could hear their soft moaning and sighing.

I turned and fled the room, quietly clicking the door behind me; walked swiftly to my car; and sat there trying to compose myself. Although I'd lusted after Trent in a way that was new and frightening to me, I'd had no inkling that he fucked other men. I was being consumed with a combination of joy at the possibilities and a visceral desire to be the man under Trent, being fucked by Trent, and of self-disgust at having these feelings and a horror of what sort of edge I was walking along here.

I had to get away. I had to think and reason this out. And, I had to fight with my instincts, fight not to go over that edge. The edge scared me. My whole life would change if I went over that edge. I couldn't just walk into our room and tell my roommate I wanted him to fuck me, could I? And, then what, even if I did? I had no idea what to do and how it would feel. I just knew that when I saw those two together just now, I ached to be the man writhing under Trent.

I needed to get away to some place entirely not here. I needed to think this out. I turned the key in the ignition and drove away from the university toward the outskirts of the college town. There was a historical house on a hill overlooking the town, and it had a mile-long hiking trail up to it in a national park area from the bottom, where there was a parking lot. I woke up from something of a trance to find myself parked in that lot. I'd never visited the historical house, and I knew I could use the hike up through the woods to it, so I got out of the car and started walking. I was wearing shorts, a T-shirt, and good sturdy running shoes, as I had intended on going to the gym after class; I hoped they'd let me in to the house tour. However, I was a college student, so I guess they'd become accustomed to young guys dressed like this.

I couldn't get the image of Trent so closely and intimately fucking that other guy out of my mind as I hiked up the hill, and it was giving me a raging hard-on. About half way up the hill, I slipped off the trail and far enough into the woods that I couldn't be seen from the trail. I leaned up against a tree, pulled my cock out over my waistband, and began stroking myself off. I closed my eyes and tried to imagine Trent's lovely cock entering me and pumping me. But the image had no sensation to it, and I was cooling off. My cock was not engorging; this wasn't giving me any relief or release. I thought I heard a sound nearby in the underbrush, and I quickly pushed my cock back inside my shorts and turned back to the trail. The frustration was absorbing me. I didn't want to cross the edge, but I wanted Trent to fuck me. The idea of that was driving me wild, but I was numb from having absolutely no experience in what males did with males.

Two thirds of the way up the trail, I heard a noise behind me and turned to see that there was a man in khaki uniform and a wide-brimmed hat pacing my walk up the mountain. As I turned, he took his hat off and wiped his arm across his face and then put the hat back on. He was tall, thin, and sinewy looking, with powerful-looking arms. He had a buzz cut, and my first impression was of a former marine who kept up with his routine. He kept his pace gauged to mine, and he didn't pass me by until

I reached the building where tickets were sold to tour the house and gardens.

When I entered the house and gave my ticket to the guide, I saw that the man from the trail was standing there with her and talking in friendly tones with another guide. I could see now that he was a park ranger. He turned hazel eyes and a friendly smile to me, and I felt myself turning red for some reason. It seemed like he was looking right into my mind, discerning that I was all messed up, and why.

Without thinking, I gave him a shy smile and quickly turned and entered the house's parlor, where I joined five or six others who were on the same tour.

Three rooms later I was standing at the back of the group, lost in an explanation on eighteenth-century life in the house of a Revolutionary War notable when I realized that someone was touching me. It wasn't just that someone had brushed by me; someone had a hand firmly on one of my butt cheeks and was definitely copping a feel. I quickly pulled away and moved to another part of the group, no longer on the back row. When I looked around, I saw that the park ranger was now with the group. He gave me another one of those smiles, and my cheeks burned. I don't know if it was because of what I was going through, but I hadn't been repelled by the encounter. I had enjoyed it. But, again, I was frustrated by not knowing what it meant or where it might be headed, or how it might get there.

Shortly thereafter we found ourselves in the dimly lit kitchen in the slaves' quarters area in the gardens away from the main house. We were all packed pretty close together, and once again I found myself on the back row listening to the guide's description of the kitchen and how activity here fit into the rhythm of the plantation life.

The hand was on my butt again. I didn't move away this time, even when the hand had squeezed my butt cheek. And then I felt the hand come up and go under the waistband and squeeze the butt cheek, skin on skin. It moved over, centered on the small of my back, and I felt a long, strong finger slowly pushing down into my crack. This scared me, and my knees began to tremble uncontrollably as it ran across my asshole. I did move away this time, moving around the edge of the group and then swirling out of the kitchen door with them, into the sunlight, as the tour ended.

I didn't follow the others into the garden but stumbled quickly in the direction of the entrance—toward the path back down the hillside. This was all just too overwhelming. I'd teetered there on the edge, and it had disturbed me deeply; I hadn't had any idea where to go from there.

I was moving quickly, blindly down the path. I heard him behind me. The park ranger was following me down the path, moving more quickly than I was.

"Stop," he yelled in a deep, hoarse voice. "Just stop."

I stopped dead in my tracks. His was a voice not to be challenged. But I was trembling all over when he reached me and turned me around, facing him.

He held me out from him with strong hands on my upper arms. I looked down at his hands and wrists. He was wiry, but his fingers were long, strong, and sensuous. Blue veins stood out on his hands and ran up his wrists into the cuffs of his khaki shirt.

"What are you running from, son? Why did you leave so quickly?"

"I don't know," I said. "Excuse me, but I've got to—"

"I don't think you know what you've 'got to' do, son. I think you're all mixed up about something. Is that right?"

"Maybe," I said in a weak voice. "But, but . . . please, I've got to go."

"Here, we need to get off this path," he was saying. He dropped one hand, but he kept a hold on my arm with the other one and pulled me off the side of the path into the trees and to a little glen, where some trees had recently fallen. There were fresh tree stumps and big chunks of tree sections scattered around, sunlit in the dappled rays thrusting in, invading the glen. I didn't feel there was any chance of breaking away and running back down the path because the grip of his single hand was overwhelmingly powerful. His grip on me was as much emotional and psychological as physical. There wasn't anything happening to me here that I didn't want to happen. I just didn't know how to go about my role. I was standing on the edge, looking down into the abyss.

When we reached the edge of the sunlit area, he turned me around to face him. He'd unbuttoned his shirt en route and pulled the tail out of his pants. As I had imagined, he had a long, lithe chest with heavily muscled pecs and thick, blue veins running around through patches of curly hair outlining his pecs and meeting to travel down his flat belly and under his belt buckle. He pulled me into his chest, thrusting my T-shirt up and off my body in the process. He had one strong arm wrapped around my back and the hand of the other arm palmed out over the small of my back. My nipples were rubbing against his skin below his pecs, and his nipples were rubbing against my upper chest. The sensation was new and very pleasant to me. I was breathing heavily and beginning to tremble again.

"I think that your problem is that your body wants one thing and your mind and emotions haven't quite caught up with that yet. Am I missing my guess here?"

"I don't know," I murmured. "No, maybe not."

I felt his hand go under my waistband, palm out over my buttocks, and that long, sensuous finger pushing down into my crack again.

"You enjoyed this up at the house, didn't you?"

"Yes," I whispered. And then I gasped, as his finger found my asshole. I involuntarily went up on my toes, raising my ass up to him, and he took advantage of that to enter me with his finger. I gasped again.

"Then I'm right," he said. "This is what your body is telling you it wants. I want you to bring your hand around and feel my cock through my pants now."

I did so. His prick was long and hard. I groaned and he kissed me then. And then, without losing his finger hold in my ass, he brought his lips and tongue down my neck and to my nipples, arching my torso back.

"Does my cock scare you?" he whispered at the level of my nipple.

"Yes," I whimpered.

"But do you want it in you? Do you want me to fuck you?"

"Yes," I whimpered again.

"Then do you have a problem with getting on with it?"

170

"I . . . I don't know what to do," I murmured. I was close to tears.

"You don't have to do anything," he said. "I'll do it all. And I'll be gentle. You've never done this before, have you?"

"No."

"But you want to do this now?"

"Yes, oh yes."

He stripped off my shorts and picked the shorts and T-shirt up and walked me over to one of the big, broad tree stumps. He removed his shirt and spread this and my shorts and T on top of the stump. He looked down at me and I looked up at him. His arms were strongly muscled and his thick veins rolled around as he moved them. The potential of his power still frightened me. He unbuckled his pants and dropped them to the ground. He could see my eyes blaze with fear and uncertainty, and he grinned a big grin for me. His cock was long but not unusually thick. It was almost fully engorged and curled slightly up toward his stomach. He dropped on his knees below me out of sight, but I knew exactly where he was because he was sucking my cock and had his fingers back working at my asshole. He'd lubricated them and was greasing my hole and a good three inches up my shunt. The pad of a finger found my prostate, which caused a whole new realm of flash-point sensations for me. I felt like I was going to piss and come at the same time, but the latter won out as his tongue and lips caused me to shoot my load down his throat. His lips and tongue moved on to my asshole, and I writhed in pleasure as he rimmed and tongue fucked me.

"Do you want me now?" I heard him ask huskily.

"Yes, yes, yes," I replied. "But . . . please. I've never—"

"Trust me," he said, as he stood up. "I'm from the government and I'm here to protect you." He gave me a reassuring smile, telling me that it was a joke to cut through all of the tension.

I laughed weakly as I watched him split open a condom packet and roll the translucent sheath onto his cock. I felt his cock head at my hole, and then I felt the pain of him entering me to the rim of his head. He took my hips in his strong hands and rotated me around, opening me to him, and slowly entering

171

me. I groaned and grunted and several times was on the edge of screaming for him to make it stop, but this is what I wanted. After this it would be easier with Trent. I knew that. Trent was thicker than the ranger was. Not as long, but thicker. Doing it with the ranger would help me to do it with Trent. I knew that, and I wanted Trent to do me.

Once his cock had purchase inside me, the ranger let my hips drop back onto the tree stump and he took my legs by the ankles and wishboned them. This opened me more, helping me to accommodate him, as he began to pump me deeply. There was pain, but there was pleasure too, and I was exhilarated at the thought of that long cock buried in me, and of a strongly muscled stranger fucking me. It would be much easier to approach Trent now. While he was pumping me, I imagined it was Trent inside me, and this time I could feel all of the sensations of being fucked by Trent. I could hardly wait.

* * * *

Was it possible that Trent didn't know what effect he had on me? He was driving me crazy. He'd been doing this since we were thrown together as college roommates two months earlier.

I was sitting at my desk, trying to concentrate on my calculus homework, when the door to our room opened and Trent padded in straight from the shower, dripping wet. He stood there on the carpet, within clear sight of me, and whipped the towel off from around his waist and started to dry himself down. He was whistling and chatting at me, apparently oblivious to the fact that I couldn't catch my breath well enough to answer him.

He was beautiful. He had a lithe, deeply tanned athlete's body. Everything was perfectly proportioned, from his shiny white teeth down to his size nine and a half feet. Everything, that is, except for his outsized cock and low-hanging balls.

He slept in the nude, and this evening he showed every sign that he wasn't going to dress up now just to have to prepare for bed a little later. He moved around the room like a dancer—no, like a big cat stalking its prey—with his heavy cock swaying back and forth. I tried to bury my face in my math problems, but I just couldn't ignore him. I was glad my knees were under the desk, because I would have been very embarrassed for him to see the hard-on he was giving me.

At length, he stretched out on his bed and read a sports magazine. His free hand was gliding along the contours of his torso and occasionally down to his cock, and I watched him from the corner of my eye, aching to run my hands where his were going.

"Gotta sleep the sleep of the dead tonight," he said as he sat up, scoffed down a couple of pills, and drank from a cup on the table beside his bed. "Important lacrosse game tomorrow." He turned out his light and pulled a sheet over his beautiful body and lay there on his back with his eyes closed tight.

"I'll have the lights off in a few minutes," I said.

"No problem," he said, already yawning. "When I take these pills, you could set off a bomb on my stomach and I'd never notice."

And he was right about that. When Trent took his sleeping pills, you'd lost him for at least six hours.

I turned my desk chair around and sat there and watched him as his breath became regular. And I pined for him. I wondered what he'd do if he knew how much I wanted him inside me. This sinful feeling had only been accentuated earlier in the day when I'd come back to the room early and found him fucking another guy in his bed. I'd been quiet and they'd been very absorbed in what they were doing, so he hadn't noticed that I'd seen him. I was wild for him now that I knew he fucked guys. Before it had only been a remote dream; now it seemed like a possibility. If only he'd notice me, give me some sign.

He fidgeted in the bed, and one leg came out from under the sheet. I fixated on that deeply tanned leg, with its heavily muscled calf and thigh. And on his feet, not too big, but with long, sensuous toes. I tried to turn back to my studies, but my eyes were drawn to him. He snorted in his sleep, and an edge of the sheet came off one side of his chest as well. I stared at his well-defined chest and at the nipple peeking out just at the side of the sheet—dark brown, round, and full. Now I was physically drawn to him. He'd get cold, I was telling myself. He should be covered.

I rose and moved to the bed and sat down beside his leg. I lifted the sheet to pull it back onto his body, but I found myself moving it off the rest of his body instead and folding it over toward the wall. He was stretched out on his back on the bed beside me, his arms raised above his head. Beauty in repose. His breathing was regular, and his magnificent chest was rising and falling in a rhythm that was making my blood run hot.

I gently placed the palm of my hand on his flat belly. If he awoke, I could still say I was trying to reach for the sheet to cover him. But he didn't wake. He sighed for me instead, an innocuous little response that sent a shock through my cock and down into my balls.

I let my hands roam on his torso then just as he had done to himself earlier while I was stealing glances at him. He sighed and moaned quietly for me; I no doubt was causing him to have a pleasant dream. It was not only the sighing and moaning that told me this was the case. His cock was beginning to engorge. I gently encased it with one of my hands and lightly stroked him. His cock got bigger and his mouth opened and he was licking his lips.

I rose and came around to the foot of the bed. Crouching down, I wove my arms under his thighs and brought both hands up onto his belly and took his tool into my mouth. I teased his cock head with my tongue and lips, and he engorged further. I sucked cock, trying to get as much of him into me as possible, keeping the strokes slow and gentle so as not to break into his dream. He moaned more deeply for me and began to weakly grind his pelvis into my face. I moved my hands up to his nipples, which were erect and hard. I briefly moved my tongue and lips to his now-tight balls. He had a musky smell that I found intoxicating. After a few minutes, I returned my lips and tongue to his cock.

I had him as big as I'd ever seen him now. I was wondering if I could make him ejaculate down my throat without him awakening. If I could, I'd at least have that. He'd never have to know we'd even had sex.

"If you make me come now, it will be at least twenty minutes before we can fuck."

I sat up in total shock. He was wide awake, his arms folded behind his head and giving me a big grin.

"Oh, God, Trent. I was just. . . . Oh, God, I'm so sorry."

"You were doing just what, Hugh? Looks to me like you were just giving me great head."

"But, but. . . . You were asleep. You took those pills."

"No, I didn't take those pills. I pretended to take those pills. I was going to slip those pills in that cup of water you take every night before going to bed. It was my last-ditch effort to jump your bones."

"Jump my bones?" I asked incredulously.

"I can hardly see you way down there. Can you come up here, please?"

I was in shock, but I slid up the bed until I was laying on my side beside him. He encircled me in his arms and kissed me on the lips. I was dumbfounded.

"So, what are we going to do now, Hugh?" he asked when we came out of the kiss. "From my perspective, we have two choices. I can fuck you hard, or you can finish sucking me off. I'm a resolute top, so it's down to those two choices. Which shall we do?"

My mind raced back to the scene earlier where I'd seen him fucking another guy in this bed, and there was no question in my mind what I wanted.

"Fuck me," I answered in a small voice. "I want you to fuck me. I've wanted you to fuck me for weeks."

"And I've wanted to fuck you for that long, too," Trent murmured. "I wonder why we took so long to get around to this." His hand glided down my bare chest and under the waistband of my sleeping shorts. He possessed my cock now, and it lengthened and thickened under his attention.

"Sort of too bad I don't do bottom," he whispered. "You have very nice equipment. But, here, I'll get up over you and I want you to lay on your belly." My mind raced back to how I'd found him earlier today. Yes, I wanted it just the same way. Me on my belly and him covering me close from above, churning his cock in my canal by rotating his hips, while I

175

stroked up into him and rubbed my dick on the sheet. But when I was stretched out and he moved over me, it wasn't like the position that had been burned into my mind when I had found him fucking that other guy earlier today. Instead, he lowered his body on mine, head to toe, with his strong legs running up and closely encasing my torso and his head between my wide-spread thighs. His cock was running up and pressing in me between my shoulder blades. I grabbed the brass headboard slats above my head and hung on for dear life as he pulled my dick back between my legs and alternated between sucking on that from above and tonguing my asshole. I ground my body into the mattress under him in ecstasy. If this had been part of the routine he'd gone through earlier in the day, I had arrived too late for this scene. But I certainly enjoyed it.

He had brought a tube of lubricant down with him when he'd straddled me, and after he tongued my ass, he lubed it and worked it with his fingers.

"Nice tight ass," he murmured. "Am I the first?"

"Not quite," I answered in a lust-choked voice. "But close enough."

I felt his weight come off me. I looked up and he was standing on the floor beside me, holding out a condom packet.

"Would you like to do the honors?" he asked.

With trembling hands, I clumsily got the packet open and the condom extracted and rolled it onto his gigantic cock.

"Well done," he said, with a laugh. "You're sure you want to do this?"

"Yes, oh yes."

"Well, then prepare to be totally fucked. You really turn me on. Up on your knees, legs spread."

I did as he asked, and he was back up on the bed on his knees behind me now, moving like a cat. I moaned and groaned when I felt his cock head at my hole and grunted and yelped as he pushed it into me. I was tight, and he was rotating his tool around, trying to get it inside me. He pulled my butt cheeks apart with the palms of his hands, and he was in a couple of inches. He had a bulbous cock head, so this was the roughest part of the ordeal—at least in the thickness department. I panted and moaned and groaned and thought the trembling in my legs and knees would cause me to collapse.

"Too much?" he asked. "Do you want me to stop?"

"No, no, do me," I gasped.

I cried out as he pushed on into me then, stretching my canal to the limit, filling me up to what seemed to be the depth of a mile. My knees did collapse then, which I was very happy to have happen, because then Trent came down on to me just as I had seen him do to that other guy earlier in the day and just as I had fanaticized about ever since. His chest dug into my shoulder blades and his hands glided up my own arms and grabbed me by the wrists. They moved on then to my hands, and he entwined his fingers in mine around the brass headboard slats. His thighs and calves overlay mine, out wide, and my ass canal tightly held his throbbing cock. We lay there for a few minutes, as my waves of pain slowly morphed into waves of pleasure, my ass canal starting to undulate around his throbbing dick. I felt his chin hook onto my shoulder, and I turned my head and lips to him. As his tongue pushed its way between my lips, his hips started their motion.

First he pumped in and out of me in both long and short strokes, and then, as my own hips started to answer in a raised and lower rhythm, his hips started to rotate in a circular motion, moving his cock around in my ass canal. My ass walls started to tremble and undulate again. I was panting and moaning, and so was he.

"It's so nice," he was whispering in my ear. "So tight and so sweet, and so, so nice."

My hips were off the bed now, and my reengorged cock was dragging its head back and forth on the sheet, fucking the bed.

Suddenly, he had dug his knees into the bed again, released my hands, and brought me up to my knees in front of him. We were both up on our knees on the bed, and my back was arched so that only my shoulder blades touched his shoulders. he had the nails of one hand dug in around one of my aureoles now, and I could feel the pain, but I didn't care. I didn't want it to stop. And he was furiously jacking me off with the other hand. He was pumping his cock up into me from below now, with long, fast, and deep thrusts.

We came almost simultaneously and fell back onto the bed, he still stretched out on my back.

"I'm sorry," he whispered in my ear. "I don't know what came over me. I lost it. You are just so tight and sexy. I couldn't control myself."

"It was great," I answered. "You can do that again anytime you want."

"How about as soon as I can reload?" he asked with a low laugh.

"You're on," I answered.

So, we lay there, while we cooled off and his cock contracted inside my asshole. He still filled me in tumescence, and he didn't lose purchase when he rolled us over onto our sides. His body was cupped around mine. After a few minutes, we started to kiss again and to relight the fire. His hands roamed around my torso and played with my nipples. I could feel his cock reawakening.

"I'm clean," I whispered to him. "Never been barebacked. If you know you're clean too—"

Trent's answer was an intake of breath and a deep kiss, while he pulled his dick out of me. When he slid back in, I could tell that it was skin on skin. This gave me an extra thrill, and I wiggled my butt at him. Trent responded by lifting my leg in the air, getting his pelvis close in under my buttocks, filling me to the hilt with his delicious sausage, and side-splitting me in fast and furious thrusts for a good twenty minutes until I felt his spasms of semen flooding my insides. Our cries of ecstasy mingled as I rejoiced at the thought that I could have this for almost every night for the rest of the school year if I wanted. But why did I think "if"?

The Caregiver

Perhaps I gave in so easily because Lenny embodied the best of two worlds. First, he was a wonderful, gentle caregiver. He had been coming to my house twice a day for several weeks to take care of my bed-bound grandmother, who was recovering from a broken hip. Second, he was drop-dead gorgeous. All blond Swedish muscle with a shy smile to accompany his sensuous mouth.

I'd had a rough week trying to take care of my grandmother's needs when he came to change her bedding and to give her a massage that Thursday evening. He found me in the kitchen at the table when he was finished getting her ready.

"There," he said, "I think she will go right to sleep. My massages usually take all of the tension out and she goes out like a light."

"Here, sit and have a cup of coffee before you go, Lenny," I told him. "I envy her." Lenny sat across the table from me, filling out the chair and bulging chest and leg muscles stretching his T-shirt and shorts.

"You envy her sleep, her release of tension, or her massage, you mean? Surely you don't envy her age and her pain." He gave me a smile that made me ache.

"Well, the release of tension and the massage, at least," I admitted. "It's been a rough week so far."

"Yes, I could tell. You do look like you could use a good massage. I'm off duty now; I could release that tension for you."

"I don't know, Lenny," I said. "I've never had a massage before."

"I do a great full-body massage, Tim," he said, not taking his eyes from mine. "I sense that's exactly what you need."

"A full-body massage? I don't think I know what that entails."

"Well, the best way to explain it is to do it. Come on, I'll give you a very good free massage. I can get rid of any sort of tension you might have."

I began to suspect what he was proposing, but I was too afraid and hesitant to ask. I could fanaticize, though. I had been dying to be touched by him for weeks, which was a sensation I'd had before but always repressed. "Well, OK, what do I need to do?"

"That sounds great, Tim. I've been thinking about your building tension and wanting to give you a massage for some time now. This can be such a difficult time for everyone involved, not just the patient. I care about the whole family. And I like you. I think you've got a hot body, and I enjoy massaging hot bodies."

Lenny cared about me. Great, he thinks I have a hot body. Even greater.

"So, I've noticed you have plenty of room in your bedroom for me to set up my massage table. Why don't you take a shower and wrap yourself in a towel and I'll go out to the car and get my table."

When I came out of the bathroom, Lenny had already gotten the massage table back out of his van and set up and had stripped off his T-shirt. What a beautiful bod.

"Up on the table, on your back," he commanded. "Strip the towel, and I'll put it over your privates."

I did as he asked and thought he took a bit longer than necessary before draping the towel over me. I wasn't sure how this was going to work out, as I already felt I was losing control over my cock.

He came around to above my head and started working on rubbing my temples and my head. I looked up and the view from under his bulging and moving pecs was very interesting. He raised my head and massaged my neck muscles. I could clearly see the tenting of the towel over my loins. He worked my shoulder and upper arms muscles and then moved both hands down to my pecs, where he massaged my nipples just as much as he worked on my muscles there. I could feel my rod rising. His massaging worked its way down my abs and to my belly. I sighed and moaned in appreciation. Then he came around beside me and whipped the towel off. I knew it. I had a Grade A hard-on.

I was embarrassed, but Lenny didn't seem to mind at all. He moved down to below my feet. I looked down and was surprised to see that now his shorts were off and he was barely encased in a thong that didn't hide a thing. My cock hardened even more at the sight. Lenny saw my response to what I'd seen and just gave me a shy smile with those sensuous thick lips.

He worked on my toes and feet and then lifted my legs one at a time and did my calves and lower thighs.

"Flip over," he said, and I did. He came back to above me and did my back and shoulder muscles and then the muscles of each arm in turn. Then, starting with my calf muscles, he worked his way up. He did a good job on my lower thighs and pulled my legs a bit apart as he worked higher and higher. He was at my inner thighs now, way up next to my groin. His sensuous fingers touched my balls as he massaged. I couldn't help letting out a little moan of pleasure.

He moved his hands, moistened with oil, onto my butt cheeks, which he kneaded and rolled in a sensuous motion. My cock came alive, and before I knew it I was grinding away with my pelvis, fucking the towel under me on the surface of the massage table. Lenny was helping me with the movement, lifting my hips a bit and revolving my pelvis around and helping me pump. The underside of my engorged cock was sliding along the surface of the table, stroking up and back, and before I knew it I spouted off up my belly and into the cleavage of my chest. All the time, Lenny was murmuring how well I was doing, what I nice big cock I had, and how nice my butt cheeks were.

After I had shot off, Lenny turned me back over on the table. He was below me again and lifting one of my feet. But now he was bringing the foot up to his mouth. He sucked my toes, first one foot and then the other, while he held my eyes captive with his. As he held the heel of the foot of each leg with one hand, he let the other glide up and down on the inner calf and thigh of that leg. I was hardening and sighing for him again. He could do anything he wanted with me now.

Lenny turned me on my belly again and gently pulled my legs down off the end of table to where I could stand on the floor with my still-heaving chest on the surface of the board. I felt my butt cheeks being spread, and a cool mouth and tongue found my asshole. Lenny licked and sucked and tongued me there, as I groaned and moaned and sighed. After several minutes of this, his tongue slurped out of my hole, and he stood and placed his left hand firmly in the small of my back, holding my torso down on the table. The fingers of a well-oiled right hand went to my hole, and Lenny ever-more-intensely finger fucked me, getting the oil well up into my ass passage and opening me up and helping me to relax my ass muscles.

The fingers were pulled out, and I felt the big helmet of his cock at the hole. He pushed the helmet in to its rim and stopped there briefly.

"Are you ready for the internal part of the massage, Tim?" he asked in a breathy voice. "I won't go further unless you want the whole massage."

"Yes, yes," I whispered. "Do me. Just be gentle. You're not too big are you?"

"Just seven and half inches hard," he replied and then gave a little throaty laugh. "But we'll go slowly and I won't go deeper than you can take."

I groaned, "Seven and a half inches! God, I've never done this before. Be—"

I jerked as he pushed in past the sphincter muscle. And then his helmet was at my prostate, rubbing it and causing little sparks of pleasure to fly through my body.

"So, is that a 'yes,' Tim? Do you want me to fuck you deeper?" He was dragging his helmet back and forth across my prostate and had taken his hand and was rotating his well-oiled

182

cock around in the canal, giving my ass channel walls special attention.

I gasped and moaned and was rotating my pelvis, wanting to feel all of the big cock everywhere at once. "Yes, yes," I managed between gasps, "Fuck me, deep and thick. Fill me up, you beautiful Swedish stud."

And then he slid up into me, deep. I arched my back, breaking the pressure of his hand on the small of my back and rose up, throwing an arm around his neck and bringing his lips to mine in a deep kiss. He grabbed my hips with his hands and pumped me slowly with his cock, in long oil-slicked slides in to where his helmet dragged back across my prostate and then deep glides, loving and churning and stretching my channel walls.

He broke the kiss, laughed, and pushed my chest back down on the table. Then he started pumping me in earnest, in long, gliding motions.

"Ahh, Ahhhh, Ahhhh," I cried. "Give it to me, Lenny, shoot off inside me. Deep, like this."

"Deep like this?" Lenny asked, the amusement in his voice dancing. "I haven't gone deep yet, Lover. This is me going deep."

And he pushed my legs out wider with a slap of his feet, grabbed my butt cheeks and pulled them wide apart, and plunged his oiled rod a good two and half inches deeper than he'd gone up me before.

"No . . . No!" I screamed. "It hurts. I don't think I can . . . Ugh . . . Ahhh . . . Yes. Oh, yes, Lenny. Lenny! Lenny!!! Give it to me. I want it all. Just like that! Pump me, Man. Fill my stomach with your sweet cum."

He was deep fucking me wildly now. Staying deep, but pumping in and out. Then he stopped and rotated me around and pushing me up on the massage table, until I was facing him, still able to stay deep. He buried his hands in my chest and massaged my nipples. I wrapped my legs around the small of his back, wanting to keep him in me forever, and I stroked my cock vigorously. And he stroked and he stroked and he stroked; hard and deep.

I came before he did, shooting my load off on his chest and up mine. He gave a little yelp of delight then as he ejaculated

183

in heavy bursts deep inside me. Then he collapsed on top of me, nuzzling his face into the hollow of my neck, savoring the moment. I kept my legs firmly wrapped around his waist, holding him in me, feeling that long, thick cock soften and retreat, but not all that far.

"God, to think I've had seven and a half inches in me," I whispered, pride and awe spilling over in my voice.

"Sorry, I lied," Lenny responded, with a little laugh. "I'm a good eight and half inches hard; didn't want to scare you. Wasn't sure how much I could stuff in you. But you took it all. You're a fucking amazing screw."

Silence for a few minutes, while I thought that over.

"So, do you want a massage now?" I then asked. "I'm wondering how much of that dick I can get in my mouth."

"Not tonight, Tim, as tempting as that thought is. I'm wasted. I come back to give your grandmother some more care tomorrow. How about tomorrow then? But rest up. There are some other tricks to a good Swedish massage."

"Can't wait."

I Only Wanted to Watch

Brandon had told me that if I wasn't going to move to a new, all-the-way level with him, he was going to a gay bar and would bring someone back to the dorm with him. He said he couldn't take the frustration any longer. I thought he had been joking, that he was as scared about this as I was. But there they were, entering the door from the street and moving toward Brandon's room at the other end of the suite in the middle of the night, having awakened me from a light sleep when Brandon's friend knocked over a lamp and exclaimed a four-letter word.

I had only been dozing, because I had been aroused by Brandon's plan, even though I hadn't really believed he was going to go through with it, and I hadn't been able to keep my hands off my own cock and couldn't go to sleep when I was that hard. I wasn't any less frustrated at the nonmovement in our relationship than Brandon was. If he had been here, we would have just jacked off together, but I just couldn't bring myself to do certain things yet. I was more of a watcher than a doer still.

I thus was quickly out of my bed at the sound of their arrival, and when I'd opened my door a crack and peeked out, I could see that Brandon had brought back a four-letter-word kind of guy. He was decked out in black—black leather vest over a tight black muscle shirt and black jeans, shredded at the knees and also tight on well-muscled legs. He had a square-jawed face, covered in a couple of day's growth of black stubble. His hair was long and tied off in a ponytail, and I wouldn't have doubted a claim that he was a gang banger straight off his motorcycle.

Brandon's friend had almost fallen when he'd run into the lamp, and when Brandon instinctively put out his arms to keep his friend from going down, the friend came up hugging Brandon tight. He was kissing Brandon on the lips and arching him over backward in a possessive stance.

When he broke away from this, I could hear Brandon whisper that they needed to wait until they got in his room, because he didn't want to wake any of his suite mates. And then they were out of my sight and down the hall toward where Brandon's room was.

My dick went hard and I thought I was going to hyperventilate. Brandon had done it. He had said he was so horny for a guy that he was going to go out and pick one up, and he'd done it. I'd thought that was all talk.

I scurried down the hall as quietly as I could and came up real close to Brandon's door. He hadn't gotten the door shut tight, and I pushed it open a smidgen, giving me a full view of the bed in the glaring light of the overhead bulb.

They were both sitting on the opposite side of the bed from me, next to and close to each other. Their shirts were already off, and Brandon's friend had Brandon's smooth, cut torso arched back, with one arm wrapped under Brandon's shoulder blades. The guy's lips were already on Brandon's nipples, and I could tell from the angle of the guy's other arm that he had a hand on Brandon's basket. The expression on Brandon's face told me a lot. I could see apprehension and a little fear, but an overwhelming helping of desire and excitement that were overpowering the other two emotions.

Brandon's friend came up for air from nibbling at Brandon's nipples and loosened the hold of the arm around Brandon's back, permitting Brandon to slowly lower himself on the bed. The friend's torso was turned toward me now, and I could see it clearly. Where Brandon was the blond, smooth-bodied college jock, his visitor was a dark, hirsute gypsy—lithe and sinewy, with a hairy chest and arms, and a look of danger about him. This impression was only enhanced by the two silver rings in his nipples, the stud in one ear, and the crown-of-thorns tattoos around both bulging biceps. Even the expression on his face contrasted perfectly with Brandon's hesitancy and indecision at this point. Full confidence; full control. He conveyed that he knew exactly what he wanted and that he was going to get it.

He placed his thumbs under Brandon's pecs and his fingers around his sides and pushed the blond's body up until it was fully on the bed. And then he came down, full length, on top of Brandon, pecs to pecs, belly to belly, and basket to basket. They were only in their jeans now. They had removed both their shoes and their socks. They kissed deeply, and then the gypsy put his arms on Brandon's upper arms, pinning him to the bed, and raised his chest up, putting the weight of his body on his hips and pelvis.

He proceeded to grind his basket into Brandon's while he possessed Brandon's eyes with his own, focusing Brandon on what was happening, forcing Brandon to acknowledge what was going to happen, no matter what simpler, less dangerous ideas Brandon might have had when he brought the man back to the dorm with him. The gypsy reached around and undid his ponytail, and long, silky black hair cascaded down to his shoulders.

Uncertainty and a bit of fear were fighting the lust in Brandon's eyes—and slowly losing the battle. The gypsy had his knees between Brandon's legs, and Brandon slowly opened his stance and then, in resignation, brought his legs around and placed the backs of his calves over those of his new-found friend. The gypsy raised up on his knees then and unbuckled Brandon's jeans, pulled the zipper down, fanned out the two sides of the material, pushed the band on his briefs down to below his balls, and brought out Brandon's rod. Brandon had a very nice dick, rather thin, but of good length. I had admired it often when we were showering. I instinctively pushed my sleeping shorts down to below my own respectable cock and lightly fingered what had already hardened nicely.

Then I almost audibly gasped when the gypsy proceeded to undo his own belt buckle, unzip himself, and fan out the waist of his jeans. He hadn't been wearing anything under the jeans, and his cock was mammoth—both long and thick, truly horse hung. The head of his dick was a dark red and bulbous, and a silver ring piercing it caught the light of the overhead fixture. I could feel my own cock beginning to form precum.

The gypsy came down onto Brandon again and mashed his pelvis into Brandon's, introducing the cocks to each other. Brandon's hands had gone to the slats of the headboard above him, and I could see the whiteness of his knuckles as he held onto the iron rods. The muscles of his arms were bulging under the strain, as the gypsy ground his hot cock into Brandon's pubes. The gypsy was holding Brandon firmly by the wrists with his hands, and he had his lips and teeth buried in the hollow of Brandon's neck. Brandon's back was slightly bowed back, and his head was arched back at even a greater angle. His eyes were wildly searching the ceiling, as if he was on the brink of trying to bolt from the room.

But there was no bolting. The gypsy was firmly in control, both physically and psychologically. He was the older of the two by a good ten years, but there appeared to be limitless strength in his body, and he had the manner of a man who knew exactly how to get what he wanted. Brandon was a soft, spoiled college student in comparison, no matter how well built he was. He was probably thinking now that this obsessive lark of his hadn't been such a great idea, but the two were well beyond just calling it a night and going their separate ways.

The gypsy was so fast in stripping them both of the rest of their clothes that I hardly noticed it had been done. My attention was arrested by that blunderbuss of a cock curved up from between the gypsy's legs as he rose up over Brandon. I'd certainly never seen anything this formidable in the dorm shower room. The first I noticed, he was up with his knees on either side of Brandon's pecs, and, while still holding Brandon's wrists at the headboard slats, he was forcing his cock between Brandon's lips and pumping his face slowly. I was getting all of this in a side view, and I couldn't help but start stroking my own cock as the gypsy's seven or eight inches started working their way down Brandon's throat.

Brandon's knuckles were even whiter than before from the pressure on the iron rods of his headboard, and I saw his knees come up and his heels dig into the bedspread under the strain. The muscles of his calves and thighs were popping out, and I could hear him moaning and groaning and gagging under the assault. I tried to see his eyes, but he had them shut tight.

I could almost hear the audible sigh of relief from across the room, as the gypsy pulled out of Brandon's mouth and turned him around until he was laying across the width of the bed on his back, with his butt cheeks at the edge of the bed.

The gypsy was giving Brandon head now. Although I was watching from the angle of the top of Brandon's head, I was standing at the door and looking slightly down on the tableau on the bed, so I could look down Brandon's trembling torso and see the gypsy's head bobbing above his pelvis. The gypsy was running one hand up to Brandon's nipples and then down fanning out over his flat, pulsating belly. And the other hand was between Brandon's thighs somewhere, probably doing something lustful with Brandon's balls.

Brandon had his head arched back between his arms, which were bent at the elbows close to each side of his head, with his hands bunching up the bedspread above and to the sides of his head. I could tell by the rhythmic bunching of Brandon's fists in the bedspread and the bouncing of his hips that the gypsy was stroking him deeply and fully with his mouth. He was probably an expert at this. I found myself matching the rhythm with the stroking of my own cock, and I was beginning to begrudge Brandon his adventure. He had such a look of pleasure and abandon in his eyes that I envied him that. We had talked about the pleasure of getting good head, and even had done some fumbling experimentation with each other, but I could tell from the expression on Brandon's face that we had never even come close to the real thing.

I realized then that Brandon could see me. His eyes were piercing mine. I could almost tell that he was trying to convey that this could be us—that it might very well be us on another night, if I could suspend my inhibitions as he now had. My cock

189

gave a lurch, and I moved my free hand up and glided up my taut stomach and pecs and squeezed my nipples. I returned his look of expectation and desire as best I could, sealing the unspoken agreement. He seemed almost to be telling me that this whole episode had been constructed to bring me out fully, to make me acknowledge that I wanted him and was willing to go the distance. I lifted my cock and pointed it at him, and he gave me a kissing gesture with his mouth. The agreement was ratified.

I now could see Brandon's cock bouncing on his belly. The gypsy had moved on—and down—with his lips. Brandon sighed and then moaned and then gave little yipping sounds and beat his fists against the bed in ecstasy as the gypsy expertly worked his asshole with his lips and tongue. Brandon raised his legs and then pulled them down onto his chest with his hands under his knees, giving the gypsy the deepest, widest possible access to his ass. All the time, Brandon was holding my eyes with his, conveying the most intense sense of pleasure and desire that he could across the room to me.

With a little cry, Brandon unfolded his legs wide, dug his heels into the edge of the bed. He then wrapped both of his hands around his long, engorged cock and stroked himself to ejaculation. I found that I had been stroking myself along with him, and we shot off together. I had cried out myself upon release, but the gypsy showed no sign of having heard me.

This might have been because he was changing position now. I saw the look of elation on Brandon's face at the prodigious release of his cum up his belly change almost instantly to surprise, pain, and fear upon the realization that his new-found master had come up and had his bludgeon at Brandon's back door. There was little warning and no mercy as the gypsy pushed his humongous cock into Brandon's ass. Brandon first arched back, his heels scrabbling for purchase at the edge of the bed, and showed me a face of deeply wounded pain, his mouth open in a big "O" that somehow couldn't muster a sound, and his eyes rolling back into his head so that about all I could see were the whites. He was clawing at the air with his hands at first. Then he raised his shoulders, and reached for the gypsy, trying to put an end to the relentless plowing up his ass canal. But the gypsy just laughed and pushed Brandon down onto his back on the bed with a strong hand in the sternum.

Brandon's hips were briefly rolled up and the gypsy came up onto the edge of the bed with his knees, and I now could see the impossible thickness of his cock buried under Brandon's balls. He was fucking down into Brandon, with a good four inches of dark cock root still showing against the paleness of Brandon's thighs. I held my breath and pulled at my own, reawakening cock, as I watched those last four, thick inches bury themselves in my classmate. Then the gypsy emitted an evil laugh. The cock came out almost the whole way, and, as Brandon cried out, it slowly started to disappear inside him once more.

The gypsy came back off the bed and onto his feet between Brandon's legs, and the horse-hung cock continued its second, less hampered journey to the center of Brandon, during which Brandon writhed under the gypsy's hand and gulped and gasped for air. Then I could see from my vantage point black silky pubic hair meeting and mingling with the blond down on Brandon's balls again, and the world held still. Brandon's gulping turned to panting and then to just quiet moaning, as his body slowly decreased its trembling and twitching and he accommodated himself to having been so thickly and deeply skewered.

After a short while, the gypsy removed his hand from Brandon's chest and took Brandon's legs in his hands at the ankles and spread-eagled them up and out. I saw the gypsy's hips go into a slight in and out stroking motion. He looked down into Brandon's face and gave him a big, appreciative smile. I couldn't see that Brandon was smiling back, but I could see that the tension had gone out of his body, and his own hips were moving slightly now, in rhythm with the man who was fucking him, the stranger who he had brought back to the dorm, the mysterious gypsy who now had seven or eight inches of pulsating cock up Brandon's undulating ass canal.

I could feel the strain going out of my body now too. I had seen the unknown and it could be conquered. If Brandon could adjust to seven or eight thick, horse-hung inches, I surely could manage Brandon, and he me. Brandon had arched his head back and he was watching me again, his eyes glued to my face, telling me that it was all right; that the pain had been worth the pleasure.

And then his eyes took on a look of pure ecstasy, as the gypsy started pumping him fast and deep. He was rotating his hips as he pumped and his undulating torso was glistening with sweat in the overhead light. I found his hairiness, with the silver nipple rings and bicep tattoos, mesmerizing in their exotic dance of lust. His head was moving, and his hair was flipping around in the air. Brandon's hips were meeting his gyrations, the younger man's legs were now propped on the older man's shoulders, and their arms were entwined with the firm grips of their fingers on each other's elbows. They were one now, one pulsating, pumping, fucking machine. One part blond, smooth and all-American; one part dark, hairy, and mysterious—but both united as one, at the pelvis, exchanging pleasure, moans, sighs, and body fluids.

I thought the dance had gone on longer than it actually had. They had stopped before I noticed it, with no sign of the gypsy's release. And they were both looking up, at the door, at me, suspended in time. Waiting for me to realize that there were three of us in this, not just two. Brandon wasn't the only one who had seen me in the shadows just beyond the door.

I have no idea when the gypsy had realized that I was there. But it had been long enough for him to decide what he wanted to do about that.

Through the fog of discovery, I heard him mutter, "Next." And before I knew what was happening, he had me over at the bed, bent over, my legs spread wide, and that big juicy cock of his was probing beyond my protesting sphincter and then, with a bursting of the dam inside me, being pulled in by my undulating ass muscles and making its journey up my ass canal from behind. He had his fingers digging into my nipples, and his cold, nipple rings were sliding around on my shoulder blades. I was writhing and struggling, my fists buried in the bedspread and mounding that up just as I had seen Brandon do under the same circumstances. I had my mouth open to scream, but as with Brandon, my lungs were in shock and I couldn't form the sounds.

Brandon came to my rescue then. He had his knees under me, at my belly. He helped me stretch my arms around him and cup his butt cheeks in my hands for leverage and for some place to put them, and he was gently pushing his rehardened dick between my lips, giving me something pleasant to concentrate on while the gypsy stretched and plowed me deeply from behind, giving me that education I could use for the rest of the semester with Brandon.

The two of them found each other above me with their lips, and I heard Brandon whisper a thank you to the masterful stranger. It occurred to me then that this had all been Brandon's plan, all of it, from the start.

Pen Pal

Paul first saw him in the prison library. His name was Dexter, and Paul helped him find a book. An adventure book with words that weren't too difficult to comprehend. Paul felt a chill go up his spine when their hands brushed against each other—and he knew.

Dexter was an indescribable mix of races that pretty much resolved itself into overpowering and "mean." Skin that came across as deeply tanned without having taken the effort to go outside, a montage of tattoos that screamed brutality, and a physique that revealed he'd been penned up for years with little better to do than work out and work at working off angry aggression.

Paul couldn't believe—couldn't hope—that Dexter would ever be in a position to leave the penitentiary, but after months of exchanging pen pal letters, it looked like that might be the case.

While he waited, Paul, who worked a couple of volunteer hours a week in the prison library, dutifully went to his accountant's job in a medium-sized cubicle in an unending bank of cubicles on the third floor of a mammoth insurance agency and quietly and innocuously put in his time. After working into the early evening hours, he'd stop at a modest grocery store on his way home and pick up his canned or quick-frozen supper. And then he'd enter his sixth-floor, one-bedroom apartment without a view in a medium-rise, thirty-year-old apartment block and sit and eat his meal with a television show going in the background that he never watched or listened to.

While Paul ate, he'd concentrate on dredging up and continually replaying the last short, seemingly innocuous conversation he had with Dexter in the prison library. When he was finished eating his meal, he'd wash his dishes and stack them back in the cupboard. Then he'd walk over and turn off the television, take a shower, and then, naked, lie on his bed and masturbate to the rereading of the letters from Dexter and the imaginings of being fucked by Dexter, being Dexter's cellmate and being taken by Dexter without his consent. Then spent and satisfied, Paul would turn off his night light and sleep until it was time to start the cycle all over again.

When he learned that Dexter was being paroled, Paul broke out into a sweat and his hands trembled so badly that he could neither finish his evening meal nor his nightly masturbation. It was only then that he realized that perhaps the reason he had focused on Dexter was that he seemingly was unattainable. Safe. Probably never going to see the outside of the prison.

But Dexter was paroled. And on the day Dexter walked out of the prison, Paul was standing on the pavement outside the gates, as he had agreed he would be, waiting for Dexter.

"You got a room?" was the first thing a miraculously free Dexter said at the prison gate.

"Yes," Paul said meekly. And, indeed, he did. It wasn't his apartment, of course. It was a room at a good motel. And he'd prepaid for a week. He'd promised Dexter the room would be clean and his—for a week.

"Clothes first. I gotta get out of these shitty rags. And money. You said you'd give me a thou."

"Yes, here's the money," Paul murmured. He couldn't look at Dexter. He was all atremble. Scared and aroused at the same time. Being alone in his apartment with the letters and Dexter behind bars was one thing. Dexter here in the flesh out on the street and the content of those letters zinging through

196

Paul's brain were something else altogether. He was half expecting, half wanting, for Dexter to just blow him off at that point—take the money and find out where the prepaid motel was and tell him to take a hike. Then Paul will have brushed against his hidden desires but escaped them as well.

But Dexter just stood there, looking at Paul, expectantly.

Paul sighed and said, "My car's over here. I'll take you to a good clothes store."

"Think they'll have something to go over these pecs and biceps," Dexter asked with pride in his voice. He flexed and made the tattoos running down his arm jiggle.

"Yes, sure, we'll find something," Paul responded. A whole other world, he was thinking. There was absolutely nothing that Dexter's world had in common with Paul's. But then Paul's life wasn't all that hot, he thought. This gave Paul a little thrill, and he felt himself going hard. Maybe this would be OK.

"A bar. After the clothes, then a bar. Then that room." Dexter gave Paul a look—that look—and he smacked his lips and sucked his teeth in.

Paul looked down and blushed.

"Hey, you really want this?" Dexter asked. "You know the money, clothes, and room will do me if you don't. I can find someone else to screw. That ain't no problem."

"No . . . no. The clothes, a bar, and then . . . the room. It's what I want."

Later, in the motel room, blinds drawn, and a underamped light bulb in a bedside lamp sending shadows into the corners of the room.

"What you said in the letters . . . what you described . . . did you really . . .?" Paul couldn't complete the sentence. He was hunched down in the chair, Dexter towering over him, naked and aglow from a shower now except for his newly purchased briefs, having wanted to wash every hint of prison from his body the first thing after they'd entered the room.

"Yeah, it's true. It's what I do. It's rough in there. And when you don't got no power in one way, it sorta shows in other ways. You either do or you get done. And if you do, you make sure everyone knows you can do."

Paul trembling a bit now. And aroused. On the edge. Those letters . . . they were quite graphic. And, as the correspondence had progressed, they had increasingly become focused on Paul. Paul knew it probably was only because of what he promised to do for Dexter—the transition from prison. But . . .

Paul looked up at Dexter, at the rippling muscles of his chest, the constantly rippling tattoo display, the barrel chest tapering down to the thin waist. The broken nose, the mean, screaming gash across his cheek. The ropy muscles with the veins popping out, the rock-solid meat inside giving them no place else to go.

The thought of what was there under the prison uniform, plus what was in those letters, had sustained Paul for months of solitary masturbation. Now, in the flesh. . . . Paul felt himself turning to jelly. He suddenly longed for this to be fantasy. It *had* all been a fantasy. Hadn't it? He attempted to transport himself back to his cubicle, among all of those other cubicles, soft, nondescript music in the background, crunching numbers as he listened to two guys down the corridor discuss the previous night's basketball game.

But there was no transporting himself to the "other side"—to safety.

"Did you mean what you put in the letters?" Dexter asked gruffly. "Do you want this?"

He dropped his briefs. He was ready. Long and thick and throbbing and ready.

"Yes," Paul murmured quietly. He hadn't meant to say that. But someone in the room other than Dexter had said it, so Paul guessed it had been him. Paul didn't want to look at Dexter's mammoth cock. But he couldn't look anywhere else.

"And you want it prison style, like you said in your letters?"

"Yes." Whispered. Surely by someone else. Paul wouldn't have said that.

"Like a virgin? First night in my cell? Guards pissy at the new pretty boy in my cell, needing to be taken down a notch. Everyone lookin' the other way?"

"Yes."

"Are you that, Paul? Are you a virgin?"

"That way. That way, yes,"

Dexter was smiling. He also was stroking his cock—which was growing in size, although Paul hadn't thought that was possible.

"You bring rubbers?"

"Yes. There. There, in my briefcase."

"Lots?"

"Yes."

"Tonight. Tonight, you understand. Then that's it. I get the money and the clothes and this room for a week. And you get lost. And no calling the cops, no matter what, Right?"

"Right. Yes, it's what we agreed."

"Cause if you call in the cops, I got friends that'll do you good and forever, understand?"

"Yes."

"After it starts, no stoppin' it, you understand? Otherwise it ain't real. Not like in my prison cell. Not like fresh meat thrown into my cell."

"Yes." Close to tears now. The last yes whimpered. Hanging out over the edge. He wasn't safely tucked away in his cubicle now.

Paul's head snapped to the side in pain and shock as Dexter took two strides toward him and backhanded him across the cheek. An evil grin on his face. Wanting and intending to take. Brutally.

This pushed all of the air out Paul's lungs, and he was given scant chance of replacing that. Dexter grabbed Paul's head between his hands and had the head of his cock forcing its way between Paul's lips.

"Treat it right, baby, or you'll regret it."

Paul, trapped in the chair by Dexter's hulking body hunched over his, gagged and fought for breath as Dexter filled him to the back of his throat and, grabbing Paul's hair in his hands, began moving Paul's head back and forth, back and forth on his rod.

This was only the beginning. And Dexter saved himself, wanting the virginal ass—and sooner rather than later. When he released Paul from the face fuck and turned to fish condoms out of the brief case, Paul made a struggling lurch out of the chair and for the door. This definitely wasn't fantasy. This was overload.

But Dexter turned and tackled Paul down to the floor. He held Paul down with one strong hand holding the accountant's arm twisted, painfully behind his back, Paul's face buried in the carpet, while the erstwhile inmate jerked off Paul's pants and briefs. Then, crowned, but without lubricant or any other preparation, Dexter pulled Paul up to his hands and knees, hunched over his pelvis, and brutally thrust his dick at Paul's hole again and again and again, until he was in, past the sphincter, into the tight, previously unused channel.

Paul was gasping and crying out to the ceiling and writhing. Dexter was laughing and pounding away. Having a good old time. When Paul's knees gave way, Dexter just rode him down to the carpet, and kept thrusting away.

Later, Paul laying on his back on the bed, exhausted and brutalized. Dexter, sitting, still naked, in the chair facing the foot of the bed. Swigging one of the beers they had brought back to the room.

"Stroke it," Dexter said in a guttural voice. "Stroke yourself."

"What? Why?" Paul said, his voice spent and trembling.

"Just do it. I want to see how big it gets."

After a bit.

"Ah. Good. Nice size. Keep it up. I want to see the cream. Think of the letters. You said you did it to the letters."

Heavy breathing, from both bed and chair. At last an "Ahhh," and Paul let his head drop back, spent, dribbles of cum on his flat belly.

"Spread 'em."

"N-o-o," wheedling, weakly voiced. "Please, no."

"I said spread 'em for me. I'm in a fuckin' mood again. Your jackoff put me in a fuckin' mood."

Dexter was already at the end of the bed, pulling Paul down to the edge with a fist wrapped around his ankle.

"Nooo," Paul whimpered, trying to come up in a sitting position. He started to say something else, but this was cut off by a backhand across his face that sent his head reeling back onto the bedspread.

"Here, hold this," Dexter said as he thrust his half-empty beer bottle into Paul's hand. "Don't lose none."

As Paul meekly took hold of the beer bottle, fighting to keep it upright, Dexter fisted Paul's calves and pulled them wide apart. Then he grabbed one of the bed pillows and stuffed that under Paul's hips, raising his pelvis. Dexter took the beer bottle back in one hand and pinned Paul's sternum to the bed surface with the other. Paul didn't have a chance. Dexter was twice as big and three times bulkier than Paul.

Paul cried out in surprise and pain as he felt the cold glass of the beer bottle neck being pushed into his ass. He started to struggle, but Dexter lifted his hand long enough to backhand Paul's cheek again and then returned it to his sternum.

"The more you struggle, the worse it will feel," Dexter said, giving his prey a cruel grin. "Thought we'd do it this time with some lube."

The cold beer felt strangely soothing as it spread and sloshed around inside Paul's stretched and bruised channel, and Paul just laid back and took it. Again.

Soon the thrusting bottle was replaced with a hard, thrusting, insistent cock.

Dexter was in high heat. Who knows how long it had been since he'd gotten his rocks off—years at least since he had been able to enjoy it without keeping one eye and ear cocked to the cell door in case a guard was passing by—assuming that it would be one of the few guards who cared what he was doing with and to his cellmate.

While he fucked, Dexter took Paul's cock in one hand and treated it like it was the stick shift in a drag race. He grunted and lowered his lips and teeth to Paul's nipples and neck and licked and kissed and bit and chewed, while Paul panted and moaned and groaned and moved in waves of his own new-found passion and lust under the attentions of a man who fucked brutally and roughly—and completely.

Hours later a bruised and whimpering Paul was dumped unceremoniously outside the motel door, on the balcony overlooking the parking lot and a Pizza Hut, and the door to what was now wholly Dexter's room was shut firmly and locked. It was several more minutes before Paul was able to rise and drag himself down to his car . . .

. . . and back to his life.

Paul saw him for the first time three weeks later, in the prison library. His name was Digger, or at least that was the name he went by in prison, and Paul helped him find a book. An adventure book with words that weren't too difficult to comprehend. Paul felt a chill go up his spine when their hands brushed against each other—and he knew.

Interruptus Completus

I really wanted to get into that particular fraternity. It was said to be the coolest one on campus, and I didn't know if there was anything I wouldn't do to get in. And I finally got an invitation to one of their after-game parties, a game our university had unexpectedly won. This victory was the first time we'd beaten our traditional rival in three years, a rival that ranked well above us in the predictions. The unexpectedness of all of this had probably been why the party got wild enough that the police had shown up to shut it down.

The frat house had quickly gotten on overload. The music was loud, and people were hanging from the ceiling and pressed up against each other so that even the dancers couldn't do much more than sway their hips without bruising someone else. I thought I'd hit the jackpot on my chances of getting a bid when a senior, Greg, who I knew to be the pledge chairman, was thrown up against me in a stuffed back hall. We were practically belly to belly, with me backed to the wall and he facing me, his arm stiff out above my shoulder to the wall, keeping those trying to muscle past us from crushing his body into mine.

I was trying to impress him with my family's prominence and the good grade average and community service record I could bring to the fraternity, but all he seemed to be interested in talking about was sex on campus and how free everyone here was to experiment before they had to settle down in life. He'd given me a beer, which I really wasn't supposed to have, and we swigged as best we could between trying to make ourselves heard to each other over the loud music and the silly screaming around us.

He seemed to be getting crushed closer and closer into me, and I was feeling a little intimidated by the bulk of him and his bulging muscles pressing up against me, but in a titillating way I couldn't quite get a grip on. Then we heard the sirens.

I heard him say, "Oh, shit," and he grabbed the half-finished bottle of beer out of my hand and disappeared farther down the hall. But as he left me, I heard a distinct, "You. You and me later, dude," thrown at me in his wake.

This seemed great news. If I impressed the pledge chairman, I'd likely get into the fraternity; if I didn't, my chances weren't good. I couldn't sleep very well that night, and when I did get to sleep, I had strange dreams about that close encounter with Greg, which had been interrupted just when I thought I'd been making an impression on him. When I woke, I discovered I'd had a wet dream incident. But there wasn't anything strange about that for a healthy college freshman, so I didn't really think anything of it.

I found I wasn't being able to study in the noisy dorm the next afternoon, and, without giving it much consideration, I took my books and papers to a picnic table at a little park across the street from the fraternity house I was trying to pledge. I think subconsciously I must have reasoned that maybe I'd be noticed by someone with clout in the fraternity and could do some politicking.

I thought that the view into the park was obscured from across the street, but when I sat down; I saw that I had a straight line of vision to the front of the fraternity house. I had been studying pretty intensely for nearly an hour, though, when I realized that the sound of running water was intruding into my mind. I looked over toward the fraternity house, and, to my consternation and slight exhilaration, I saw Greg, the house's pledge chairman.

He had his classic red Thunderbird convertible out in the circular drive in front of the fraternity house, and he was washing it with a bucket of soapy water and a garden house. I tried to return to my studies, but he was mesmerizing. His personal attraction, no matter his power position in the fraternity, could not be denied. He was stripped down to tight, low-cut latex biker's shorts and was barefoot. It was undeniable that he had a great body and fluid motions, just what a competing wrestler needed—and I knew he was a champion wrestler in his division. As he ran a sponge over the car hood and the canvas top, his muscles rippled. I watched as he stood up and pushed a blond curl back from his face. I think he must have seen me then.

He smiled invitingly, but I pretended I didn't see him. I don't know why; if I was honest with myself, I'd have realized that I came here explicitly to renew our talk about my pledge possibilities. He moved around to the other side of the car and did some more sponge work. He seemed to be flexing his muscles and doing stretches to loosen up his back more than was required to be washing a car. I felt something stirring below my belt. It couldn't be. I wasn't thinking about Greg in that way, was I? I just wanted his heavily weighted vote. But it occurred to me then that maybe I'd been fooling myself. Without even thinking about what I was doing, I put my hand in my lap and stroked myself through the silky basketball shorts I was wearing.

Greg came around to this side of his car. He leaned over the hood and shimmied his rear end as he rubbed the sponge over the car. His butt cheeks were well defined in the rider's shorts, and they were nicely rounded. He turned full toward me, lifted the hose over his head, arched his back, and just let the water stream over his blond hair and down across his solid, well-cut torso. I could see he was laughing. He threw the hose down, went out of sight briefly, presumably to cut off the water, and returned with a hand towel. He tossed his head back and forth to fling off the excess water and then slowly toweled himself down. He dropped the towel and languidly ran his hand over his pecs and his six pack and his belly and down to his basket. He stood stroking himself there, just as I was stroking myself where I sat, and then I saw him laugh and walk straight in my direction.

I was glued to the spot by the shock that he was coming to me; I should have gotten up and hurriedly left in the other direction, but I just sat there, watching him come to me.

Greg sauntered up to the table and around to my side and leaned his butt into the edge of the table right next to me.

"Well, hello there, stud. We didn't really get very far with our talk yesterday, did we? Glad you came by. If you hadn't, I'd have come looking for you."

"Why would you be looking for me?" I asked dumbly. I wasn't any brighter than any other college freshman. But I was pleased. He had remembered me well enough from the previous day to go looking for me. My chances of joining the fraternity seemed to be improving immensely.

"I felt we didn't really get to know each other yesterday before the cops broke up the party. And I would really like to get to know you better. I don't even remember your name. What's your name?"

I told him in a faltering voice. It was true that he couldn't very well champion my membership if he hadn't even remembered my name.

"You would agree that it would be nice for us to know each other better?"

"Yes, of course," I answered. Absolutely, I thought. That's exactly what I'm after here.

"And I have a special reason to want to get to know you better," Greg said with a grin.

"A special reason?" Greg was beginning to lose me here.

"Yes, look. Here, look here." He had his hand on his basket. His cock was standing almost straight out, trying to get out of the confining tight latex. "Doesn't this explain why I'd want to get to know you better. You're one hot dude, and that cock of yours looks like it's a champion."

Wow! My mind exploded, and my brain went numb and into overdrive all at the same time. Boy were we ever on a different frequency. But then Greg showed me that maybe we weren't.

"And you want to get to know me better too, don't you? This is the fraternity you want to join, isn't it?" he said, all big smile and bulging basket. "What's your name again? Could it be

Peter? See, Peter is wanting to know me better." And he reach down and tweaked the tented fabric in my lap. There was no doubt that he was having an effect on me. And, dumb me, I had been the last one to know about it.

"I . . . I think I'd better go," I squeaked out and started to gather up my books and rise from the bench. But Greg was too fast for me. He quickly and fluidly swiveled behind me and swung his left leg around me; sitting right behind me, with me scooted up to the front edge of the bench and him barely on the back edge. I was trapped with him behind and on either side of me and the picnic table digging into my belly. He wrapped his arms around me and gave a sigh. I could feel his insistent cock trapped between his body and the small of my back.

"Listen, Greg. I'm not really—"

"You want to get into this fraternity, don't you? As I told you yesterday, this is a pretty freewheeling campus, and our fraternity is the best one here, the one with the best men. In every way, if you know what I mean. If you want to get along here, you're going to need to go along. Besides, you can't hide your interest in me. I can see it there in your shorts."

"Look, Greg. Yes I want to get into your fraternity and would do almost anything to do so, but I've never. . . . I've had no experience in—"

"Screw experience. Experience can be overrated. I like you just the way you are, fresh and ripe—and with a big cock." He wasn't wasting time; his right hand drifted down the front of my T-shirt, went between my belly and the waistband of my shorts, found my cock, and started teasing and stroking it.

"Greg. I'm not going to—"

"Sure you are," Greg said in a steely voice. "Sure you are, but I'd much rather it was because you wanted to." With his left hand he pushed my shorts down in the back so that they were half-way down my butt cheeks, and he released his cock from his latex biker's shorts and let it run itself up the top of my butt crack and onto the small of my back. Then, with his left hand, he reached around and gently pushed my face to the side.

"Kiss me. We didn't get to kiss yesterday, and it's been driving me crazy wondering how you taste."

"No, Greg, I don't want—"

207

"Hey, haven't you had the basic logic course here yet? How do you know you don't want to until you've tried it? It's just logic." Then he laughed and gave me a million-dollar smile, which moved to my lips. He started with a sweet lips-only kiss but moved into a more open, deeply probing kiss. He was still stroking my cock, and I put my hand over his there, on the outer side of the material and moved with him. He was stroking his hardened cock up and down along my butt crack in back, dry fucking me there. He brought his hand out of my crotch and, with both hands, pulled my T-shirt up and off my torso and threw it to the side. His hands were flying all over my arm muscles, my pits, pecs, nipples, navel, belly, and back down to stroking my cock. With a sigh, I lifted my butt a bit more, and he pulled my pants down further, and continued dry fucking up my crack and onto the small of my back, this time with more cleavage to stroke in. I must admit I expected him to try to enter me from that position, both fearing and getting a little thrill from the anticipation. I was, however, marshaling my strength to try to fight him off, but before he could get around to that, he had come up the small of my back in a jerk and jack off that probably surprised him as much as me.

"See what you do to me?" he whispered in my ear while he was nibbling it. "You are delicious. The best bod I've seen on this campus in some time. I've never gotten off with just a dry fuck before."

Then he was up like a jack rabbit. "On the table. Get up there and lay down on the table."

"That's enough Greg. You got your rocks off. I've got to study."

"On the table—now, pledge! Listen to that. If you want into the fraternity, you're going to have to respond immediately to a demand like this from the pledge chairman." He swept my books off the top of the picnic table, grabbed me by the elbow and hurried me along. I lay down the length of the table, trying to be careful not to get my ass anywhere near an edge. When I was lying down, he stripped off my shorts and then his own. He had quite a formidable cock, if not either as long or thick as mine, I must say. All in all, he had a beautiful body, and, in spite of my misgivings, I now ached for him.

208

He knelt on the bench beside my hips and gave me suck while letting his hands roam around the rest of my body. I moaned and squirmed under his attention. Without my really realizing it, my hand sought out his cock, and I stroked him. In answer, he rose off the bench and positioned himself in a 69 position, and, for the first time in my life, I found myself kissing, licking, and sucking another man's dick. He tasted salty and had a strong male smell, but I didn't find this unpleasant. I started to mimic doing to his cock what he was doing to mine. After a while, he moved so that I was presented with his asshole rather than his cock, and, instinctively, I moistened him up there and explored him with my lips and my tongue. He writhed above me, giving deep sighs and moans.

When I had him moistened up real well, he rose and turned and straddled me from above. With one hand holding my cock in place, he lifted his hips and then slowly came down on me, impaling his own ass with my cock. In, in I went. It was somewhat like with a woman's channel, but it seemed tighter. He buried his hands in my chest hair, finding and working my nipples, while he slowly pumped himself. I found I was joining his rhythm, and then he lifted his hips off me a good six inches.

"You pump," he said, "you fuck me. Fuck me hard and deep."

I took over the pelvis action, sending my engorged dick up into him as far as it would go and then withdrawing half way and plunging up again. He moaned and groaned and we both went into a wild pumping action. I had one hand wrapped around his cock and was pumping that in rhythm to the wild tune we were playing in his ass. We came almost simultaneously. Me, pulling out of him and shooting up his belly and he shooting off up mine. He collapsed on top of me, taking my arms above my head with my wrists in his strong grasp. He kissed me long and deep and arched up a bit to permit him to kiss and nibble his way down my neck and to my nipples.

When I was truly relaxed and close to drifting off to sleep, he came off me and the picnic table top. With a laugh, he pulled his biking shorts back on.

"That was what I wanted, sport. Thanks. Don't, worry, with a dick like that, you shouldn't have any trouble getting a bid from the fraternity. Of course, you would enhance your chances if you helped finish washing my T-bird over there. And then, maybe later today, I'll show you what my other bird can do inside you. If you pledge our fraternity, your ass is mine. And both you and I know there'll be a next time. Ciao, Baby."

And he turned and strutted back to his red Thunderbird and his fraternity house, leaving me there, stretched out on the top of the picnic table, alone, and wondering just how much of "almost anything" I'd really do to get into this fraternity.

Rest Stop

We were tooling down the highway in the early evening at a pretty good clip in my BMW Z4 Roadster when Perry started to get frisky. Perry was this hulking blond roommate of mine who also was on the football team, but who was a couple of years older than I was and played first-string tailback. I'd just started college this year and was still warming the bench, although I'd impressed the coach pretty much with my catching and running ability.

I was headed home for spring break, and I really needed a break. Between the studies, trying to keep my football scholarship, and my part-time job as a model for men's wear catalogs, I was really zonked out and needed time away.

Perry had asked me for a ride to the house of a friend of his in a town near mine, and, fool that I was, I had agreed. He was a cocky bastard--always on the move and exercising his mouth and topping any of the guys who appealed to him. The coach never said anything about this, because he was topping Perry. With Perry's status on the football team, and his hunky good looks, he didn't have too much trouble getting his cock in his ass of choice. But thus far I had held off all of his advances myself. I'd fooled around with guys in high school, but not all that seriously—just some mutual cock handling—and I just didn't want Perry to have any power over me.

I guess my stonewalling had only increased his determination to get into my pants, though, because he admitted to me as we tooled down the highway that he'd only asked for this ride because he wanted to do me. If I'd known that, I wouldn't have been wearing the comfortable sweat shorts and T-shirt I had on for the journey.

"Hey, I like you in that T-shirt, man," he turned and said to me, "Sets off your pecs and biceps real well. You're turning me on, Dale. Let's have the shirt off. See, mine is off."

"Cool it, Perry. Just sit back and relax. We're still several hours from home."

"Can't cool it, Dale. You're making me hot." He ran his hand up under my T and slowly worked his way up from my belly to one of my nipples. I slapped at the hand with one of mine, causing the car to swerve a bit on the pavement.

"Whoa. Hold steady, Dale. Look, you've got me excited."

I instinctively looked down in his lap, and, sure enough, his pants were tenting at the crotch, which was quite a feat, considering how tight his jeans were. I already knew he had an oversized package, because he had been careful to show it to me several times in the locker room shower.

"Knock it off, Perry." I didn't give you this ride just so you could proposition me again.

"Yes you did, sport. I didn't need this ride. I've got a car of my own. I assumed you knew that and were game. I asked for the ride because I'm dying to fuck you."

"Well, it isn't going to happen," I answered with irritation. "And put that hand somewhere else."

"Of course, anything you say, Dale," Perry answered with a laugh. His hand slowly moved back down my torso and across my belly and under the waistband of my shorts.

"Ah, very nice," he was saying as his hand got the measure of my cock.

"Stop That! We're going to crash," I yelled. And, indeed, the car was weaving in the lane. I pulled over to the slow lane and brought the car down to the speed limit.

"OK, OK," Perry answered. "That's not what I'm really interested in anyway." And with that, his fingers went under my balls and glided across the perineum in search of my asshole.

"I said stop."

"Open your legs to me," Perry commanded in a husky voice. The fingers of his other hand got entwined in my hair, and his lips went to the side of my neck. He was tracing my carotid with his tongue. For some reason, I responded to his command. I shifted my left leg over to where it was touching the door, and widened the stance on my right knee as well as I could while still keeping my foot on the accelerator. His middle finger found my asshole and pushed in up to the knuckle. I gasped and felt like my legs were turning to jelly.

"No, don't. Perry," I pleaded in a suddenly hoarse voice. "I'm trying to drive."

But he paid me no heed. His mouth traveled down my torso and swallowed my cock, which was engorging under his attention. My pelvis instinctively tilted up to meet his mouth, and he was able to get a second, and then a third finger into my asshole and to push them deeper. I felt him rubbing on my prostate. I was melting.

"God, at least let me pull over somewhere," I pleaded. Luckily I saw the sign for a turnoff into a rest area in the next mile, because he just kept on sucking and rotating his fingers in my ass.

The car was barely creeping along and I was fighting to keep it between the lines as we took the exit to the rest stop. I bypassed the well-lit car park and pulled behind the building into the truck parking lot and over to an area that was as far away from the trucks parked there as I could get.

The top was down on the roadster, and I propped my left leg up on the top of the windshield and just lay my head back on the head rest while Perry finished blowing me off and playing with his fingers in my ass. After I'd come and he'd licked me off, he brought his lips to mine and gave me a deep kiss. The fingers of his left hand were still entwined in my hair and he was holding my head back on the armrest in a hair lock. His heel of his right hand was still lodged under my balls, and his fingers were up my ass.

213

"Climb over here on my lap," he commanded in that husky voice of his. "I'm going to fuck you now."

"No, you're not," I responded in a strong voice. "Not here and not now. Possibly not ever! I have to piss, so I'm going into the men's room, and then we're going on and you're not touching me again. Or I can bail you out right here." Without waiting for a response, I brought my left leg down, threw open the door, adjusted my shorts, and marched off to the building with the rest rooms.

I was standing at a urinal, pissing, when a hulking, dark-haired dude, very hairy, but handsome in a sultry Spanish sort of way, came into the rest room. I'd seen him moving in my direction from a group of trucks across the lot as I headed for the facilities, so I assumed he was one of the truckers putting in here for a rest. He smiled at me when he entered the rest room and then moved over to the urinal at the end of the row and unzipped his pants. He rolled out a thick, but not unusually long, pecker, and held it and showed it to me before turning to toward the urinal. I got a good look at him but shifted my eyes to the tiles in front of me to let him know I wasn't interested.

Then Perry entered the rest room and unzipped himself and pulled his long cock out before he'd come anywhere close to the urinal. He took the urinal right beside me and made sexually insinuating comments all of the time our cocks were streaming. I could have died from the embarrassment.

He was finished before I was and, without unzipping, came in back of me, kissed me on the neck, and rubbed his cock on the small of my back.

"Sure you don't want some of this, honey?" he asked sweetly. "You got me worked up, and I'm dying to get my nuts off."

"Just stop, Perry. You're embarrassing yourself as much as you're embarrassing me."

A stall door banged open across the room, and both Perry and I jumped in surprise. The dark trucker at the end of the line of urinals didn't flinch, however, so he must have known someone was in that stall.

I quickly pulled my shorts up as I turned to see a mountain of a man sitting stark naked on a toilet in the stall and pulling at one of the most enormous cocks I'd ever seen. He was all muscle, with flaming red hair, worn long, in a pony tail.

"If cutie there don't want you, Blondie, come over here. I'll give you a blow job you won't forget for some time. God, look at you. You work out most of the day?"

"First-string college tailback," Perry responded with pride.

"Figures; come over here and give me a taste of that. I could tell you what a tailback is good for."

"Sure, any port in a storm."

I looked on with fascination and horror as the man mountain pulled Perry into the stall at his side and went down on his cock expertly, getting Perry to moan and gasp with ecstasy within seconds.

The guy at the end of the urinals watched for only a minute and then made like he was coming over to do the same to me, but I waved him away and stepped back. Taking the hint, he left the rest room.

"At least close the door in case someone else comes in," I said, as I pushed the stall door closed. Upon reflection, I decided that Perry getting his rocks off this way was better than continuing to hit on me for the rest of the trip, so I finally shouted at him over the door, "I'll give you fifteen minutes and then I'm pulling the car around to the car lot. If you're not back out in twenty minutes, I'm tossing your bag out and leaving you here."

I took the hoarse mumble I got back as agreement. So, I marched out of the restroom facility and back to the car and sat there for fifteen minutes. I noticed that the Spanish-looking guy from the men's room was sitting on a picnic table nearby and watching me. After the fifteen minutes, I turned the key in the ignition, planning to drive around to the front of the facility. But nothing happened. The car didn't start. The engine didn't even attempt to turn over. I tried it several times—nothing.

The Spanish-looking truck driver strolled over to the car, put his hand on the window ledge, and looked down at the dash board with a concerned look on his face, as if maybe he could tell from a dark dash what the problem might be.

"Got a problem?" he asked.

"Yeah, it won't start," I answered. "Guess I'll have to look under the hood."

"Sounds like that would be a waste of time. I think you need a mechanic."

"Yeah, you're probably right. Guess I'll have to call AAA."

"Doubt they'll be out here too fast," the trucker said. "And this might not be a good place for you and your friend to be after dark. It'll get dark soon."

I had to admit he was right. The truckers I'd seen here had been pretty direct about what they wanted to do with Perry and me.

"I'll tell you what, though," he said. "I know of a mechanic living nearby. I know that he works on Bimmers too. I can drive you there and back, and he can get this baby fixed quick like."

"Hmmmm, I don't know. Maybe."

"All I'd ask is for the same consideration your friend was giving that trucker back in the men's room."

"What? I don't—"

"Just let me suck you off, like's happening with your friend, and I'll help you get this car fixed up."

I was pretty scared now. "I don't think I can leave my friend like that. In fact, I think I'd better go over and check with him before making any decisions about getting the car fixed."

"Oh, I don't think he's in any mood to be going anywhere for the moment. We have plenty of time to connect and get your car fixed before he'll be ready to go, I think."

"What do you mean?"

"Get out of the car, and come on over here, and I'll show you what I mean."

I got out of the car and followed the Spanish-looking trucker over to where a group of trucks were parked together. Beyond their trucks, shielded from the rest facilities, there was a picnic area, with tables, and I saw what the trucker meant. I saw Perry stretched out on a picnic table, totally nude. A beefy black guy with flowing dreadlocks who I'd never seen before was standing over Perry's head, his torso arched over Perry's and his mouth working Perry's cock. Perry's mouth, in turn, was

216

working the black guy's cock. Perry's legs were splayed out, in the grip of the redheaded monster from the toilet stall, who had his dick up Perry's asshole and who was pumping away at Perry's channel. I thought idiotically for a second that Perry was being shown the redhead's definition of a tailback.

I stood there in horror and fascination—watching Perry get sucked and plowed at both ends.

The Spanish-looking trucker stood close behind me. I felt his arms go around me. He pulled my T-shirt off, and he had his big, beefy hands covering my pecs. I could feel the hardness of his cock at the small of my back.

"It looks like your friend is used to this," the man whispered in my ear. "But I'm willing to bet you aren't ready to party like that. Come with me. I'll blow you in the privacy of my truck's sleeper cabin, where none of the rest of them can see us. And they we'll go get your car fixed and you and your friend can get out of here. How about it? If you won't come with me, there's no telling what will happen to you out here."

One of his hands had traveled down below my waistband and to my crotch, and he was gently pulling my cock. Between that sensation and what I could see going on on the picnic table, I was hardening and lengthening pretty solidly. I felt trapped, wondering what would be the lesser of the evils of this situation. I made my decision as I watched the huge cock of the redhead stroke in and out of Perry's asshole. Perry was used to this; I certainly wasn't.

"Okay, I guess that would be best," I whispered, as my eyes went back to the brooding line of Trucks and I wondered what lay in wait for me in one of those foreboding cabs.

"My truck's just over here," the trucker said. He led me over to a huge semi with a large cabin behind the driving compartment. He opened the door to this cabin, and I saw that there was a short-lengthened twin-sized bed in it along with some shelves, a compact toilet, and a small refrigerator and cooking unit. The bed was covered with pillows and there were shiny hold bars on the cabin wall at either end of the bed.

"There, stretch yourself up on those pillows and get comfortable," he said in a friendly voice. I laid down, with my legs sort of dangling off to the side, and he pulled off my shorts and briefs and knelt between my legs. I tensed up as he gently took me by the balls and the root of my cock with his mouth and ran his tongue over and around my cock helmet. I could see him tracing a thick vein running up the side of my cock with his tongue.

He took his mouth away and said, "Easy there, we'll go slowly. You have a beautiful cock. In fact everything about your body is beautiful." He went back to running his tongue around my helmet and then down the sides of my cock, while his free hand went to my belly and then on up my torso, tracing my muscles lightly, stroking me into relaxation. He surprised me. He was a trucker, but his attentions were a lot less rough and insistent than Perry's blow job had been.

He slid his mouth over my cock, and I began to moan and sigh softly for him. His free hand went between my thighs, and I opened my stance for him, as he gently massaged my leg muscles and stroked my inner thighs. I groaned and arched my back. But when the tip of one of his fingers went to my asshole, I tensed again.

"A blow job; we agreed on just a blow job," I said with alarm.

"OK, OK. I was just trying to add extra pleasure to it." His mouth slid over my cock and just kept sliding until I felt his lips at my root. He had deep throated me and I felt warmth and pressure at all points on my cock. I gasped and grabbed his head with both of my hands. He was cupping my butt cheeks with his hands and pumping me with his mouth now in long, relentless strokes. I writhed under him, alternately struggling against him and meeting his rhythm, until I felt like I was going to explode.

He had a finger at my asshole again, and I no longer cared. He held it there for nearly a minute, just covering my hole, and then I felt him moving around the rim in a circular motion, rubbing me, and then he moved it back to the center. All the time his mouth was going up and down on my cock and his tongue was at my piss slit, the tip pushing its way in.

He didn't have to penetrate my ass with his now well-lubricated finger. I pushed my butt cheeks down on him, pulling his finger in myself, all the way to where the pad of his finger rubbed up against my prostate gland. I moaned loudly, and tensed, ready to shoot my load.

But then his mouth came off my cock and he held me there, very still, until my breathing became normal again and I had passed the urge to ejaculate.

I looked at him with a question mark written all over my face. The deal was that I would let him suck me off, but when he'd brought me to the brink, he hadn't collected on the deal. I needed to get this over with, get my car fixed, and get back on the road.

"What . . .?" I started to ask.

"Shush," he said. "I don't want you to come yet. I want you to come inside me. I want you to fuck me."

"That wasn't the deal," I objected, as I tried to struggle up from the bed and head for the door. But then he got serious with me. He backhanded me across the mouth to stun me, and then he produced a pair of handcuffs connected with a good three feet of chain, and cuffed one of my hands, drew the chain through the slot in the hold bar on the side of the truck at the head of the bed and then cuffed my other hand. He whipped out a black rubber gag with a mouthpiece that looked like a thick, four-inch cock with a bulbous head and stuffed the dildo in my mouth and tied the gag at the back of my head.

Then he opened a drawer, took out a handful of condoms, and opened one packet and rolled the condom on my dick. He climbed up astride my lap and tried to sit on my cock. I fought him, though, not allowing him to get my cock into his hole. In frustration, he pushed his hairy torso down onto my chest, put his mouth very close to my ear, and pinched my nostrils together with his fingers. I couldn't breathe. The gag completely filled my mouth, and I had to keep my nostrils open to be able to breathe.

"Now relax and don't fight me on this or I'm going to snuff you," he whispered in my ear. "Nod your head to let me know you're going to cooperate."

I held out for as long as I could, but when I felt my lungs were going to burst, I nodded my head and he released his hold on my nose.

I was still pumping air into my lungs when I felt my cock at his hole and being slowly encased in the clinging warmth of his canal. I just lay there, letting him do the pumping, but increasingly enjoying the friction of my cock against his ass walls. He had one hand pulling at my balls when he could get to them in a pumping down stroke and the other hand planted on my sternum, with one thumb squarely pushing and rubbing on one of my nipples. He was riding me like he'd ride a bull in arena, letting me know that he liked my length and thickness just fine.

This went on for several minutes before I heard the door to the truck open and a jumble of arms and legs and engorged dicks filling the sleeper behind the cab. Perry and his redheaded and black monster friends were joining the party. They'd all been tossing off beers.

"What?" I heard Perry bellow. "That was my lay. I was going to be the first to fuck Dale."

"Well, you can still be the first," my Spanish assaulter tossed amicably over his shoulder. "I've got him fucking me now. I haven't had more than one finger in his ass yet. Here, here are some condoms. His hole ain't busy."

I stared, aghast, as Perry laughed and opened a condom packet with his teeth. He rolled the sheath on his big cock, and I lost sight of him behind the bouncing torso of the Spaniard. But then the Spaniard was being pitched forward again onto my chest, and I could see a grinning Perry beyond him. The redheaded guy and the black guy were at either side of me, each with one of my legs in a beefy hand, and they too were grinning at me as they wishboned my legs up and out.

Perry's head disappeared right before I felt a wet tongue penetrating my asshole, pushing it open and making it wet. This didn't go on too long before I saw Perry's head come up again and felt the palm of a hand under my tailbone, lifting my butt. All the time this was going on, my Spaniard continued to ride my cock like a rodeo star.

I bit down on the mouthpiece, trying to scream, as I felt the big head of Perry's cock at the entrance of my hole. And then he was pushing into me. Searing pain at first, but when he was a good five inches in, he went still and waited for me to adjust to him. The last two or three inches of penetration was more pleasurable than painful, and after he was in to the hilt, Perry started to stroke me, at first deep and shallow and then with longer strokes, almost exiting altogether before he slid back in to the hilt.

At some point I felt the truck began to move, and both the Spaniard and Perry matched their rhythm to the rhythm of the tires on the pavement.

I heard Perry exclaim with pleasure as the black guy got behind him and appeared to be fucking him from behind. But minutes later, I heard Perry exclaim more in anger and fear as I saw the redheaded guy trying to throw his leg up and between Perry's back and the black guy's belly.

"No, no doubling," Perry was screaming.

"But you've got the hole for it," The redhead was saying. "I know you've done it before."

"Oh, all right," Perry tossed off. "This is your luck day. Have a ball."

In a flurry of activity announced with a slurping sound, I felt Perry being pulled out of me. The redhead and the black guy were manhandling him, and I saw him being handcuffed to the hold bar at the other end of the bed and gagged just as I was. The black dude was under him, penetrating Perry's asshole from behind, and the redhead's belly was sliding against Perry's, and his cock was snaking in, with some difficulty, on top of the black guy's dick in Perry's hole. Perry was writhing and throwing his body about between them, but they had him double skewered and handcuffed and gagged, and it was quite clear that they intended to play him like a pump organ.

I would have felt sorry for him, but he had invited all of this and got me involved in my own predicament as well.

Watching the two muscle-bound truckers double Perry was more than I could take. I ballooned out the head of my condom, shooting my load deep inside the Spaniard. He sat back on his haunches, letting my cock go soft inside him. His eyes were locked on mine, and I could see that his eyes were swimming in desire. His cock was engorged. And I became aware that he hadn't come yet himself.

I watched him anxiously as he slowly reached over and picked up a condom packet, opened it, and rolled the sheath onto his cock.

He rose off me and turned me around on my belly.

"On your feet," he commanded, "No, chest still on the bed. And spread those legs. You'll want to." I did as he ordered, and I felt his cock sliding into my ass canal, which had already been widened and lubricated by Perry. He arched his chest down over my back, and I felt his chest hair tickling my shoulder blades. As he pumped me, he had his hands over my pecs for a while, playing with my erect nipples. At length, one hand went down to my cock and balls. He rolled the used condom off my dick and milked me. I came for the second time, and he for the first, almost simultaneously.

Not long after that, I felt the truck stop and then the door to the sleeper cabin open. A guy I'd never seen before, short, middle-aged, and a bit paunchy stood at the door.

"Thanks for rolling us around so we didn't get noticed," Jake, the Spaniard chimed up. "I'll take the wheel now, and you can take your pick of one of these studs."

As Jake was sizing the situation up and the Spaniard was dressing and leaving the sleeper, I looked over at Perry. He seemed to be unconscious, although there was a sloppy grin on his face, and the two monster truckers still had their cocks buried deep in his hole, although their languid looks and the deep kissing they were engaged in with each other told me that they had both flooded Perry's insides and essentially were done with him now. I hadn't seen that either had taken the time to use condoms.

I guess both Jake and I realized that this meant he was going to pick me. He grinned at me and took his time taking his clothes off. I hunched up the best I could in the back corner of the sleeper, folding my thigh over my privates.

He wasn't in all that bad shape for an old guy, even with the beer belly he sported. Most notably, though, he was a true bear, furry from head to toe and sporting a full beard and shoulder-length hair. He'd been dark-haired at one time, but much of that had gone to gray. I thought it had been the beer belly that caused me not to be able to see his cock, but after he was undressed and was fiddling with a condom, I saw that his cock appeared to be stubby in repose, but it had a gigantic girth of almost three inches. Fascinatingly enough, also, the bulbous helmet was pierced with a gold stud.

He lost patience with the condom packet and threw it aside. Then he reached out and grasped my ankles and opened my legs up. He came down on his knees between my legs, and let one of his hands roam around on my body while he pumped himself up with the other hand.

Miracle of miracles, his dick was reaching a prodigious length while retaining its ass-splitting width, and I started to moan in mixed fear and anticipation.

I thought about objecting, but I was still struggling with trepidation versus desire when he bunched up some pillows under the small of my back, lifted one of my legs and wedged it against the edge of the side window in the sleeper, and entered my ass with his ram in a side split.

It immediately became obvious that he'd been doing this for a whole lot longer and with a whole lot more skill than either Perry or the Spaniard who had plowed me earlier, because he had me interested and working with him almost from the beginning. The stud in his dick helmet played my prostate so well and so long that I was spewing precum in greater quantities and pleasure than when I had ejaculated. Then he dragged his stud along my ass walls, sending ripples of pleasure through my body. He could feel that I was enjoying this fuck, and he released the gag from my mouth, and we kissed deeply. I lowered my mouth in search of his nipples, but I couldn't reach them, so he released my hands as well, and pulled his dick out of me and allowed me to work my tongue and mouth down his hairy torso and down to his cock and balls, where I gave him head for several minutes. At length, he lifted my body and turned to where he was sitting on the edge of the bed and then he brought me back down on his dick, with me facing him. I arched my back as his hands guided my pelvis up and down and his lips played on my torso.

The truck had stopped again, and the redhead and black dudes had extricated themselves from Perry, unbound him, and left him in a heap in the other corner of the bed, when Jake was finally finished with me and had bathed my insides with his man cum.

The Spaniard returned to the sleeper and he and Jake scouted up Perry's clothes and redressed him while I painfully dressed myself. When I emerged from the semi sleeper, I saw that we were back at the rest stop, parked right next to my Bimmer.

"You can go now," the Spaniard said, as he and Jake moved Perry's unconscious body to the passenger seat of my car. "Just don't tell anyone about what happened or you'll be regretting it. And, for Chris' sake don't pull into the truck area of a rest stop in the evening unless you are looking to get fucked. Not that I wouldn't welcome having you visit me at a truck stop again real soon."

"But my car," I said. "You were going to help get a mechanic."

"There was nothing wrong with your car that didn't get fixed by another visit under the hood," the Spaniard said with a laugh. "As I said, don't go messing around in areas like this at night unless you are looking for the kind of ride you don't get in a car."

Then he and Jake climbed up into the semi and drove away. As far as I could see, the other two guys who had done us weren't anywhere around. But I didn't take any chances; I revved up the Bimmer, roared out of the rest stop, and took the first turn I could find off of the Interstate and on to a secondary road that was heading toward home.

I was one sore dude for several days, and, I'm glad to say, that once Perry woke up, he was pretty quiet and didn't try to hit on me again for several weeks.

I do regret that I didn't get a number or anything for that old guy, Jake. As long as I kept my eyes closed, he reached my itch better and longer than anyone who has tried since that night at the rest stop.

Nailed by Obsession

He had become obsessed with me. The party was large and boisterous, and our eyes met across the room and he gave me a brilliant smile. A short time later, he sat down beside me with people swirling all around us and put his hand on my thigh and gave me that brilliant smile again. I tipped my glass to show I needed a refill and glided away from him, not wanting to make a scene. Not long after that, he trapped me in an alcove and kissed me on the lips and put a hand on my crotch. He managed to whisper "I want you; I want you now. I want to feel my cock inside you," before I broke away and put as much distance as I could between him and me. As soon as I could make my way to the door, I left, and walked back upstairs to my own apartment.

His obsession had disturbed me greatly. I'd been propositioned by men before, but never so blatantly or persistently. It had been a party of stage actors, and artists, and models—narcissism abounding—so I knew there would be offers. Just nothing that insistent and demanding—and open.

I showered, opened the widow onto the terrace to take advantage of the breeze wafting across the top of the city, and lay down on my bed, naked. I was drowsy, a little drunk—and disturbed. I couldn't get the man's handsome face and brilliant smile out of my mind. What could he have seen in me to have

225

formed such an obsession? I wasn't that way; I didn't go around advertising myself.

The breeze from the terrace caressed my body, and I found myself gliding one hand around my torso and pinching at my nipples, while slowly stroking my cock with the other hand. Hardening my cock and relaxing myself in my own way as I drifted off to sleep, as I often did on these breezy nights in the city.

I heard a sigh and moan and my eyes popped open. He was standing there in the moonlight from the open terrace door. He was naked, and he was beautiful. And he was fully aroused; the obsessed man from the party. His eyes were captured by the sight of my hand stroking up and down on my cock.

He came down on the bed below me and wrapped a hand around my engorged cock and covered the end of it with his mouth. He rotated my cock in his mouth while his tongue slid over and around its helmet and sucked it with his tongue flicking the slit at the end of the bulb. Then he swallowed me down to the root and applied even pressure all up and down my cock. In shock, I let him do this to me. And when I recovered and put my hand down to his head to pull him away from me, he took my hands in his and slid them out to each side of the silken bedspread, while he started to pump my cock slowly with his mouth.

I don't know why, but neither one of us spoke. I had been so close to sleep that I couldn't be fully sure this wasn't just a dream, just an extension of my masturbating myself to sleep after having encountered a man who claimed to want me, to want his cock inside me. A sensation I'd never had and that sent a chill of fear and anticipation through me.

He took my right hand in his and guided it to my cock. I felt powerless and just let him take the lead. He entwined his fingers in mine and then wrapped both hands around my cock, his hand guiding me in stroking myself. His eyes glittered as he watched me masturbating under his guidance. I sighed and arched my back, feeling so much more aroused than if I had been doing this solo. I or, rather, we brought my throbbing tool close to ejaculation, and when he let go of my hand, I was too near to climax to fight him for what he obviously wanted from me.

His mouth once more slid down over my cock. My hands went to entwine themselves in his beautiful blond hair, and his hands slid up my sides and buried themselves in my chest hair. He was rubbing and rolling my nipples when I shot off down his throat, in three strong and satisfying spasms.

He sucked me clean and then sent his lips and tongue on a journey up across my belly and my abs and onto my pecs and nipples and then into the hollow of my neck and, at last to my mouth. He enveloped me in his arms, there in the dark, the breeze caressing both of our bodies, and our dicks entwined between our bellies. Mine was soft but quickly reloading and his was hard as a rock and gigantic and pushing insistently up my belly, reaching for the cleft between my pecs.

I was struggling to get free, but he was too strong for me. We rolled in the bed, limbs and cocks entwined and dueling, until I was exhausted. He then turned me on my belly and kissed and tongued his way down from my shoulders to the small of my back. He pulled my butt cheeks apart with strong, wide hands, and his tongue and lips went to my tight virgin asshole. A hand snaked up between my thighs, and I rose my hips a bit while he rolled and gently squeezed and pulled on my balls. My cock was coming alive again, and he pulled that on through between my thighs and alternated kissing and tonguing my hole with kissing and tonguing the helmet on my cock.

His full attention went back to my asshole. His hands were kneading and rolling my butt cheeks, and I found I was grinding my cock into the bedspread, fucking the bedspread. His hands encased my pelvis and he helped me with the grinding. Then he was only helping me with one strong hand, which had had run between my legs and fanned out over my lower belly, using his elbow to help hold my pelvis up from the surface of the bedspread to help me stroke the underside of my cock along the silken cloth.

He started inserting fingers into my moistened and loosened hole. He managed to insert two fingers to where my sphincter muscle picked them up and drew the index finger to my prostate gland. When he'd rubbed across that a couple of times, I came again, for a second time and collapsed onto my belly. His fingers had maintained hold, however, and he continued to finger fuck me for several minutes, the big palm of his other hand firmly planted in the small of my back, symbolically asserting his control, his possession of me.

I don't know why, but I just laid there, letting him have his way with me. He was dominating me in silence. Still neither of us had spoken.

He turned me on my left side, as he stretched his body up behind me. His left arm went under me and wrapped around and he cupped my right breast with his left hand. I raised my right arm over my head and my left hand lowered to languidly play with my recovering cock and my balls.

He rose up enough over me to give me a deep kiss and then he settled down below me, his pelvis nestled under my butt cheeks. His alarmingly long cock had pierced its way through my thighs and the head had come out under my balls. I managed to reach and fingered the helmet of his cock, working up precum and sliding it around on the sensitive knob, until he moaned and I could felt him quivering. He stroked my cock and cuddled my balls for a short while and then brought his fingers to mine on the head of his cock and helped me excite him there.

He sank his face into the hollow of my neck and found the throbbing carotid artery there and sucked and kissed at that, while he raised my right leg in the air and I felt the head of his cock at my asshole. I moved to escape him and lurched a bit as the helmet went in up to its rim. I cried out then, the first time that the silence had been broken. He buried his left hand into my chest, holding me firmly there, and his teeth pressed firmly into the hollow of my neck, as he forced his cock in a good five inches. I jerked and shuddered as the helmet of his cock dragged across my prostate.

I was panting from the feeling of being stuffed and from the initial pain. He held there as the pain slowly subsided and whispered endearments in my ear. "Ah, it will be fine; the pain will go away. You're so fine, such a beautiful body. I've been obsessed with you all evening. A nice tender, tight ass; I love the feeling of my cock up this sweet ass."

When he felt me relaxing a bit, he pushed in another couple of inches and then started pumping me in short strokes, never coming back more than a couple of inches. He lowered my right leg down and back, which made my canal all that much tighter, and he spread his right hand across my belly.

He must have stroked me like this for a good ten minutes, whispering encouragement and voicing how much he loved being in my body all the while.

It was like I'd been hypnotized. I just lay there enveloped in his embrace, letting him do what no man had ever done to me before.

I thought that it was long past when he should have come and left me, but his stamina was amazing and I wasn't anywhere close to end of this ravishment. He had grown a couple of inches and now was at least seven and a half inches into me.

Before I knew it, he had pulled out of me, and I started to rise, thinking this was over, but he just laughed and slapped me on the butt and rose from the end of the bed on his feet. He flipped me over on my belly and pulled my hips back to the end of the bed and entered my asshole with that big rod again. He had his hands on my hips and he just brought me back onto his skewer. He went in at least seven inches this time and then pushed to eight or more and deep stroked me. He stopped occasionally and rotated his cock around inside me, giving special attention to the walls of my canal.

After an eternity, he turned me again, this time onto my back and without losing purchase with his cock and he seemed to attain even more depth. He was churning around inside me nine inches or more deep, and I was holding him to me, seeking as much intimacy as I could get. His pelvis was riding up on my buttocks. We were belly to belly, heaving chest to heaving chest. His arms held me fast to the surface of the bed, his hands cupping my head, his mouth kissing me wherever it could reach. I held his chest close to me in my enveloping arms and had my legs tightly wrapped around the small of his back. My cock was being stroked between our bellies by the rocking and churning of his pelvis, and I came for the third time just before he shot his load deep inside me.

He slid both of us up onto the bed and collapsed on top of me, enveloping my body once more with his arms and searching for my mouth with his. When his mouth had dropped to the hollow of my neck, I looked over toward the terrace door and saw that dawn was near.

We slept, and when I awoke the day was bright and full—and I was alone. I padded through the apartment to both the foyer and service doors and found that they both were still bolted from the inside. I looked out on the terrace, but knew even when I did so that my nineteenth-floor terrace connected with no other.

I lay back down on my bed and started to languidly masturbate while my mind searched for clues on how my obsessive lover got to me wondering now if I even could be quite sure that wishful thinking had been my lover in a drunken dream. I closed my eyes; arched my back; imagined a strong hand on mine, guiding the stroking of my throbbing cock; and gave a little cry of pleasure as release flowed up through me and fountained onto my belly and thighs.

The Dog Groomer

Right off the top, I'll make quite clear that I'm not a dog person. I'm a cat person. You don't have to walk cats and they can be on their own for a weekend without chewing up the new sofa. But my wife thought we needed a dog—because we lived in a "ripe for ripping the rich folk off" golf club community, she said. But I know it was really because Libby next door got an Irish Setter, so naturally we had to have a Wolfhound.

Well, Wolfhounds are high maintenance, and I made quite clear to my wife from the get go that this was her dog. In retaliation, she decided that the dog would substitute for me everywhere except in her vagina. She still made quite clear that my cock was top dog in that kennel.

And when Angie gets involved in a project, she goes the whole distance.

This is just a preamble to bringing the dog groomer on the scene. Which is what Angie did two sessions into taking Grrr (her name for the dog, not mine) to an expensive dog obedience and grooming "college." After listening to all of the introductions on how to acclimate our high-strung purebred to his home environment (presumably so he doesn't start gifting us with pungent symbols of dissatisfaction and disdain on the floor of the front foyer), Angie decided that our home had to be evaluated as to its suitability to Grrr's needs and for advice on how to bring our 4,000-square foot, $2 million hovel up to dog code. So, she paid the extra fee for the dog groomer to make a home visit and inspection.

On the appointed day, I retired to poolside in disgust, separating myself entirely from anything to do with Grrr—or my wife concerning her current project. I heard them in the house and I hit the pool and did enough laps that I thought I'd toned up so well on the spot that I'd just slide out of my Speedo. Then I pulled myself across the pool tiles and collapsed on the lounger and promptly went to sleep.

I woke to voices under the patio table umbrella nearby. Angie and the dog groomer had come out to the pool area to discuss the grim details of our home's deficiencies as a dog safe haven.

When I opened my eyes, I saw that he was staring at me—talking to Angie, but having as much attention as he could muster plastered to me as I lay there in my skimpy Speedo. I knew that look. He was interested.

I slipped my dark sunglasses on and gave him a look back. Very presentable he was. Not a pretty boy or a muscle stud by any means. But very presentable. And he had a shy look about him, which probably went over as well with the dog owners as it did with the pooches. He wasn't a limp wrister either, despite anything I would have assumed or because I had caught him checking my assets out, which, if I don't mind saying, were a whole bank vault full.

I watched him as he talked to Angie and I liked his look and his manner. I could see how he'd be good at handling dogs. He showed every evidence of being good at handling people too. And the longer I watched him the more I became interested in being handled by him and handling him in turn.

Who knows who we are attracted to, what alignment of the stars and circumstance makes us want someone. I don't know and I don't care. I just know that, from that brief look at Cliff Marsden, the dog groomer, I wanted him.

And I soon could see that he felt the same way about me. He took a sudden interest in Grrr that went way beyond even Angie's interest and almost bordered on the unhealthy, I thought.

For three weeks Cliff found every form of excuse he could to drop by the house to give us this or that little thing that Grrr needed before their next grooming session or to consult with Angie on Grrr's progress (which was almost nonexistent as far as I could determine). And each time, as I saw him walking up the driveway, I found an excuse to be minimally dressed and just walking through the house wherever they were consulting. I made more trips to the front foyer in those weeks than I ever had before—and not just to clean of the inevitable present from Grrr that I usually found there. Angie, I'm sure, thought Cliff was interested in her, and she was mildly flattered. But I knew those looks he had given me. I knew when a man was interested in me.

This couldn't go on forever I thought, and Cliff was certainly playing out as the shy kind. There was nothing shy about me, though. So, I took the dog by the collar, so to speak, and made the first move myself. I set up an end-of-the-day appointment for a grooming of Grrr with Cliff. He was grooming the dogs at his home, in a downstairs room that obviously served as mud room, winter storage of the outside furniture, and laundry room—in addition to his dog work room. It was white tiled, floor, wall, and ceiling, and it looked somewhat like an operating room, with a sloping floor and drain in the center and everything. I'm sure it was ideal for whatever he had to do with the dogs, none of which I really had any interest in hearing about. I was a cat person.

"Oh, hi, Mr. Blade," he said when I arrived. "I'm surprised you came instead of Mrs. Blade. And where's Grrr?"

I just bet he was surprised to see me instead of Angie, I thought. He probably had been able to tell right off the bat, as I stretched out in feline fashion on my pool lounger that first day, that I was a cat person.

"I made the appointment, Cliff," I said as I moved into the room, making him retreat before me toward the alcove with the washer and dryer. "And Grrr won't be joining us either," I said.

"I don't understand. What . . .?"

233

"I think you'd agree that Grrr is the nervous type," I said, and then I added, a bit more maliciously than I intended, "And I think that Angie might be a bit too high strung to watch us fucking too."

"Excuse me, Mr.—" He was too shocked for words. But I was the very direct variety.

"You need no excuse, Cliff. You look just fine. And that basket of yours looks nice and bulgy too. I've seen how you look at me. Don't you think it time for you to stop making house calls and for us just to do it?"

I had him backed up against the washing machine now, and with one hand I was working the buttons on his shirt and with the other I was unbuttoning the fly to his shorts. He was stammering and yammering. But he wasn't stopping me.

I went into a lip lock while my hands ran across his body, exposing more flesh and rubbing it and gliding from one sensitive spot to another. I had him pushed into the washing machine. He was rigid at first in his confusion and not believing that this was happening so fast; not believing it was happening to him at all. But he warmed up fast enough, and soon his hands were opening up and peeling away my clothing and gliding along my body as searchingly as I what I was doing to him. He thawed completely to me and was devouring my mouth and making loud, animal-like sounds.

His yammering served to summon forth a small collection of pooches, who trotted out to the grooming room from all parts of his house and politely formed a semicircle around us, making up an attentive, appreciative audience. I don't know if Cliff minded the audience, but I thought it was kind of cute. I almost wished they'd brought their wallets so I could charge admission.

We were both naked as the dogs now, if not as furry—although Cliff did have that nice chest pelt playing ring-around-a-rosy with his pert nipples, one with a silver ring in it, and trailing down his torso into his bush. I lifted him up and slammed his nicely rounded butt cheeks down on top of the washing machine and started my lips on a journey down that trail.

"Mind the machine," Cliff managed with a gasp. "It's about broke as it is."

"Oh?" I asked, suddenly quite interested. "In what way?"

"It bucks and rumbles. Practically moves across the floor."

That was good to know.

Then I continued on my tonguing journey down into the bush. Cliff gasped again when I possessed him fully with my mouth, and he made little urping sounds that had the dogs perking their ears up as I worked his cock with my lips and tongue.

All shyness was gone and he was fully into the experience now, so I pushed his back against the machine's control panel and came up on top of the machine with my knees on either side of his thighs, grasped a pipe running along the ceiling above the machine with my fists, and pushed my pelvis toward his face. Cliff got the drift of where I was going with this and worked my cock big and moist with a very soft and inviting mouth. The dogs wagged their tails and had their hinies thumping against the white tiles of the floor and were licking their chops in empathy with the work we were doing on the washing machine. I remembered to be ever so thankful that none of them were attack dogs—Dobermans or Rottweilers— with a protective instinct for their daddy, because I was surely worrying his mouth with my poker.

When I'd worked up a good stroking rhythm of my own, I took one of my hands off the pipe and punched the washing machine button, turning it on. As Cliff had promised, it began to rumble and buck—and it added a good bounce to my fucking of his face.

He was gasping and screaming between swallows and gagging for me to fuck him for real, so I went back on my haunches a bit, pulled his legs around my hips, and drew his pelvis in toward mine. I glided inside him easily enough, which told me that this all wasn't exactly new to him and more or less assured me that he really had been signaling his want of me and was just too shy to be more direct about it. Shyness wasn't one of my problems, however.

The machine reached a particularly rumbling cycle as I bottomed out inside him, and we both had quite a long and wild ride before our own little show for the canines was over, with me spilling my seed deep inside him and him flicking his all across my belly and the top of the washing machine. I had his head flapping back and forth and his eyes wildly revolving around the grooming room and his howling setting off a chorus from our audience. All very satisfying for performers and onlookers alike.

After that I hauled him upstairs to his bedroom and laid him out on his bed on his belly and then laid him extra specially well and hard and deep and long. The dogs joined us on the bed, and, although they didn't exactly participate in my debauching of Cliff for a second time, they certainly sat around panting as much as he did and looked on very sympathetically, probably thinking that he was in some sort of painful fix as much yelping as he was doing.

I went away with a lip-smacking appreciating for the charms of Cliff and an agreement on a time for a repeat breeding session. I made but one request—that he not get his washing machine fixed for a while. I wanted to take both it and him for a ride again soon. The dogs were a good audience. But, as nice and polite and attentive as they were, I think I'm still a cat person.

Joggered

"Open to me. Open to Daddy."

And I spread my legs for him.

Before that, he had pushed me back gently onto the thick carpet on the moss covering the little sun-spackled glen. He had me kneel before him and take his beautiful, huge cock into my mouth, where I worked it up to over eight inches of hardness to the sounds of the birds twittering in the trees and the other jogger emitting little sighs and moans of pleasure.

It had been that big, beautiful cock that had melted my defenses and inhibitions and that opened me to him. I had been jogging the wooded river trail three days a week for several months, drawn there by the need to release tensions from my graduate school studies, by the waterside park's beauty and isolation, and by ever seeking to lose that last pound and bring pure definition to that last muscle. I was usually all alone out on the trail in the early afternoon. But in the previous week my schedule had coincided with that of another jogger, someone who also attended the same gym I did. We had never spoken to each other, but he had always had a ready smile for me, and I always took pleasure in seeing him work out. His body was the one that I sought. He was nearly two decades older than I was,

was probably pushing forty-five hard, and was graying at the temples already. But he was handsome and had a body to die for.

I have no idea how we wound up on the same jogging trail at the same time, but one day, there he was. We'd pass each other going and coming from the two ends of the trail, and he'd give me that wondrous, mature, experienced man-of-the-world smile, which I would return with a smile of my own and a wave of my hand.

Then on the fourth day that our runs overlapped, he made his move. At the half-way mark in the three-mile jogging course, a sturdy wooden picnic bench was positioned right beside the trail where joggers could take a rest. As I ran the trail the first time that day, he was sprawled out on the picnic table, cooling down from his run. He'd taken off his T, and his perfectly cut torso muscles glistened in the sun. We exchanged our customary smiles. When I jogged back on the return stretch, he was still sprawled on the top of the table, his feet up on the bench toward the trail, but now he was fully naked. I stopped dead in my tracks, as surely he intended me to, and his eyes willed mine to go to his pelvis, which I couldn't have avoided doing even if I'd really wanted to. There, dangling between his legs, was a magnificent long, thick cock, half hard and uncut. I gasped, and he smiled and pointed his hands at his manhood, making me an offer. But I was too shocked to respond. I just smiled weakly at him, resumed my jog, and quickly got in my car and drove off when I'd reached the parking lot.

If I wasn't tempted—at least subconsciously—I would have changed my jogging trail—or at least have changed my running schedule. But I didn't. The next day of my normal routine, I was back on the jogging trail, doing my regular run. It was my routine to stop at the picnic table in the middle of my return run and to use the picnic table to do some stretches.

I was doing a leg stretch with my right heel on the rim of the table, when the jogger came up behind me and wrapped his arms around me. One of his hands went up under my T-shirt and latched onto one of my nipples, while the other palmed across my naked belly for a moment, savoring my intake of breath and trembling, and then moved on down to cover my basket, tracing my engorging cock through the fabric of my running shorts. His pelvis was pushed into my butt and I could feel the power and urgency of his manhood. His lips went to the side of my neck.

I should have said something, made some countermove, pushed him away and run off. But I did none of these things. I just threw my head back and enjoyed what this rock-solid, experienced older man was doing to my body, arousing my senses, making me very, very horny in a very, very short time. These were all new sensations to me; I'd never done this before.

I turned my face toward his, and we went into a long, wet kiss. I could feel the tension draining out of my body, and so could he. He could sense me becoming compliant to his wishes and needs, bowing to his confidence and domination. The hand at my basket withdrew, and he must have pulled his shorts down in front, because I suddenly could feel his ram rod coming up between my thighs, and he began dry humping me between my butt cheeks. The hand came back, but this time, it went beneath my waistband and encircled my cock, bringing me to life there.

We disengaged from the kiss, and I found my voice at last. "No, we shouldn't. Someone could come along and find us. And I've never . . . with one that big," I croaked.

The jogger's response was to virtually frog march me back behind the table, through a wooded area, and to a small glen carpeted with moss. He gently pushed me down on my knees in front of him, stepped out of his shorts, and rubbed his cock against my closed lips. His foreskin was pulled slightly back from his huge cock helmet, and I could see a small dab of precum on his piss slit.

I opened my lips slightly to him, and he opened them wider by pushing the helmet of his cock into my mouth. I used the inside edge of my lips to push his foreskin back behind the rim of his helmet, and he grunted for me in pleasure, putting his hands on my head and helping me to work his dick into my mouth. I let my cheeks glide down the sides of his cock, taking him a bit farther into me with each slow stroke. It was very awkward at first and I did a lot of gagging, but I soon got some sense of the technique and rhythm. His cock moistly encased, I cupped his well-rounded butt cheeks in my hands, and we became an efficient face-fucking machine.

The stroking picked up in rhythm, and I was having increasing difficulty accommodating his length at the back of my throat. Before he became fully engorged, however, I had deep throated him to the point where my lips were being tickled by his pubic hair, and I just held there for a long moment, while the jogger trembled and groaned his approval. When he was fully engorged, however, there no longer was any hope of deep-throating him, and I took him at the root in one hand and ran my tongue up and down the sides of his cock, tracing bulging veins, while the other hand rolled and pulled at his low-hanging ball sack. I alternated the side tonguing with brief passes of my tongue over his piss slit to collect the precum bubbling up there and an occasional intake of the upper half of his cock into my mouth and vigorous stroking that slid his loose cock skin up and down.

When the jogger couldn't take this anymore, he pulled my T-shirt off and gently pushed me onto my back in front of him onto the moss. He pulled my shorts off and threw them to the side and stood there, hovering over me, his smiling face peering at me above the gigantic battering ram of his. I smiled back weakly, both fearing and anxious for what was likely to come.

"Open to me. Open to Daddy."

And I spread my legs for him. I was his. He came down on his knees between my legs and started running his hands over my torso, belly, and thighs. He was murmuring to me. "Sweet boy; Such a sweet boy. Daddy's going to be good to you."

One of his hands went to my cock and encircled it and began to gently stroke it. My cock answered by quickly engorging.

"Ahh, sweet cock; big, luscious cock," the jogger whispered, and I saw his head dip down and felt his lips part over my cock and travel on down to my root. I felt warm and wet down there, and I lurched and gasped as his soft mouth ran up and down my cock. After a while, my cock came out of his mouth and he encircled my dick with his hand and gently squeezed and stroked it as his tongue went to my balls. I felt my balls, in turn, drawn into his mouth with a sucking sound and sensation, and I moaned and sighed my pleasure.

I turned my head and took in all of the life of nature around me, as I enjoyed being sucked off and used my hands to travel up and down my own torso and to pinch and pull at my nipples. My hands were pushed aside by the jogger's tongue, though, as he moved his head up to my chest and tongued my torso and nipples, slowly working his way down to my belly and navel and then back to my cock very briefly.

This time when his mouth left my cock, though, he said in a very hoarse voice, "Open your legs wider. Open to me."

I lifted my legs and opened them as wide as I could, holding them open with hands under thighs. His lips and tongue went to my asshole now, and he was wetting me down there and opening me up. At length his tongue was joined—and then replaced—first with one finger and then with more. They were going deeper and deeper, and pushing my canal walls apart more and more. The pad of a finger found my prostate, and I trembled and grunted, as I felt the precum bubble up and over in my cock. I had never felt such sexual pleasure before.

"It's time. It's time for Daddy to do his little boy."

"No," I whimpered, remembering the size of that cock of his.

"You want me to stop right now?" the jogger asked in a low voice. "You want me to just get up and walk away right now?"

"Yes . . . No. Oh, no. Do it, but slowly, please. I don't know if I can—"

"Well, I know I can," the jogger answered. And then the three fingers in my ass passage spread the opening wide, and that bulbous helmet of his cock was at my asshole, rotating around and sinking deeper in the space widened by the fingers, with each revolution. I cried out in pain, and he stopped momentarily, waiting for me to open further to him. And as I did, his fingers retracted and his cock, alone now, pushed in deeper and deeper. Until eventually he was all the way in, and I was gasping for breath, cock stuffed to the very edge of my endurance.

"There, you see that you can, don't you? Oh, that's nice," he whispered to me, "Such a nice, tight ass. I could hold it in this sweet ass forever." Although there still was pain, it now was being mostly masked with the pleasure of being filled with that big, beautiful cock.

The jogger started to pump me deep in short, slow strokes. He took my legs in his own hands, as I was trembling too much to keep them spread myself, and stroked away inside me. I felt his loose foreskin sliding up and down my ass canal, giving me added pleasure—a loose membrane working back and forth over a thick, long, solid rod. His knees must have gotten tired, because, after a short time he pulled out of me and told me to come up on my hands and feet and turn my back to him, and he entered me from behind, and unrolled that long, thick hose of his to the very center of me. Now he was taking longer and quicker strokes, and I was widening to accommodate him to the point where all I felt was the pleasure of being fucked deep and fully. He reached a depth I'd never yielded before, and he tarried there, his dick motionless in stroking but throbbing in a rhythm that matched the throbbing of my heart. His hands went to my pecs, and he pulled my torso up to his chest. I turned my face to his, and we engaged in another long, wet, tongue-probing kiss as he held his dick still, deep, throbbing inside me. One of his hands went to my cock, and he stroked me off. My ejaculate arched out over the green moss in front of us.

He pulled me down to the ground after that, not losing purchase of his cock up my ass, and gently side-split me, one hand holding one of my legs up in the air to allow a close fit of his groin against my butt and the other hand wandering all over my body. He came deep inside me with three separate floods of warm, lubricating semen, and then we just lay there, drowsily listening to the wind in the trees and the birds on the fly.

I slept, and when I awoke he was gone. I lay there for several minutes, savoring the totally fulfilling fuck, calculating when my next scheduled jog was, and wondering if the jogger, that amazingly experienced daddy, would return then as well.

Marine's Choice

Mitch was a lot older than the rest of us in the college program. He was an ex-Marine. Back from a second tour in Iraq, catching up with his life. He would be a natural leader among the students even if his playing skills didn't shine brightly above the rest of ours in all of the intramural sports we played to let off steam. Even in choosing sides and getting anything going, we'd all hem and haw and throw out suggestions, until, at some point, in a few, not-to-be-questioned, barked-out words, Mitch would tell us what we'd do. And we'd do it.

Even though he was graying at the temples now, which was barely discernible with that buzz cut he maintained, and had some tested-by-life lines in his handsome, square-cut face, he was still every inch the in-control Marine. When I'd go down to the basement of the intramural gym to swim my laps early in the morning before classes started, he'd be there in the weight room, stripped down to gym shorts, lifting weights and doing push-ups and pull-ups a couple of hundred reps at a time. Not an ounce of flab on him, all steel and muscle, with his veins popping out on his arms and legs and along his torso because there wasn't any fat for them to run through under the skin.

Other than the gym and the class and the pickup sports games out on the basketball and tennis courts and intramural football field in the afternoons, he didn't really fraternize with the college students much at all. He was a man of few words and of hard, serious stares that made you feel compelled to pay attention to him, to make him approve of what you were saying and doing. He never talked about what he'd done in life, what he'd done in combat, or what combat had done to him, but the bearing and intensity he approached everything with, whether it was classroom work, the pickup games, or those solitary morning gym workouts, made you want to accept whatever he said as basic truth the rare times he said anything.

He had the exact same effect on our professors that he had on the students. If there was a discussion or argument going on in class, all Mitch had to do was to start a sentence, and by the end of just one sentence, the discussion had been decided and the room was quiet.

He really was reclusive and totally apart from the other students, something that went way beyond the difference in our ages, life experiences, and his manner of being above any argument or discussion rather in it, of being the last, authoritative word. He didn't live in the dorms with the other students; he had a small house out on the edge of the college town. At one time it probably had been the gatehouse of some estate, although the bigger house was no longer there.

That's where he held his study sessions with a select set of students.

The study sessions became somewhat of a mystery that students whispered about but never reached any conclusion on about exactly what they entailed and how much of a help they were in passing tests and completing winning papers. No one even could—or would—say for sure who was in the study group, or had been at one time. The only common denominator in the names tossed out were that you had to be a serious student, not into the party scene, good looking—and male.

Mitch did spend a fair amount of time studying at the library in the late evening. That's where I'd see him the most. We shared a few classes; we'd been in a couple of afternoon pickup basketball games, where he'd chosen me for the skins side and we'd shared wins; and I'd occasionally see him standing at the weight room door, panting in shallow, controlled breaths between his marathon one-armed push-up sessions, watching me come out of the gym pool some mornings. But it was really seeing him at a nearby table at the library that caught my attention the most—probably because in the most recent weeks it seemed like he wasn't really studying much there at the library; he seemed more sitting there and watching me study.

It should have made me uncomfortable, I suppose. But it didn't. I found it flattering. Mitch was taking an interest in me. Mitch, the natural leader, the one with all of the answers, all of the experience. Mitch, who already had met life head on and who had his own house and camouflage-painted Hummer H2 that made all the heads snap whenever it floated across campus. Mitch, the man of the world, who even the professors listened to and obeyed.

Chuck Albert stopped me on the quad one day. He pulled away from a group of guys he was joking with as I passed by and said he wanted to tell me something in private. Chuck, the college team's quarterback, a guy I wouldn't have thought even knew I existed. Quiet Chuck, the guy who aced all of his tests, had a solid-gold passing arm, and who I assumed could pop the cherry of any coed on campus just with one of his sultry gazes.

"Big test coming up in calculus," he said to me when we had withdrawn to the verge of the quad's tree line.

"Yeah," I said. "I've already started studying."

"But you'd like help and would be willing to contribute, wouldn't you?" Chuck asked. He was looking at me with a hard stare. He seemed a little more serious than the test was worth.

"Yeah, I guess so. I usually study alone, but . . . it's a big test, and—"

"Mitch wants me to invite you to his study group. Seven next Tuesday, at his place. You know where it is?"

"Mitch's group?" I was practically speechless. The mystery group. Something like a golden ticket. Of course I couldn't say no. Especially to Chuck. "Um, yes. Yeah, sure. I'm sure I can make it. Out at the end of Pine, right?"

"Right. Seven on Tuesday. I can tell him you'll be there, then?"

"Yeah. Yes, I'll be there."

Chuck gave me a hard look and then he turned and was gone.

Tuesday night, almost exactly at seven, I pulled into the asphalted area at the side of Mitch's cottage. The house was right off the road, but there was such a thick fringe of trees and bushes between it and the road that you'd never know a house even was there if you didn't know it was there and if you didn't see the mailbox at the edge of the drive.

Mitch's Hummer was there and just one other car, a BMW convertible I thought belonged to Bud Howard. That figured. Bud was one of our math brains in addition to being a star basketball player. No other cars, though. I looked at my watch. No, I wasn't early. I would have thought that anyone invited to be in Mitch's study group would be prompt. I'd think they would know that much about Marines. Well, maybe I'd rack up points with him for being on time.

The front door was ajar when I got to it, and there was a note taped to the knocker to come on back to the back of the house, so I didn't knock or ring the bell. I entered directly into the living room, which was sparsely furnished, but all of the furniture looked like it was good quality. And the place was neat as a pin. Another Marine trait, I assumed. The living room was only dimly lit, but a hallway running off it toward the back of the cottage was brightly lit, so I just moved on back. I could hear the murmuring of voices from somewhere in the back of the house.

A door was open as far back down the hallway as I could go, and a light was on in that room, so that's where I headed.

And I stopped dead in my tracks, in shock, as soon as I walked through the door.

I was in a sparsely furnished bedroom. A double bed against the wall to my left. A straight chair immediately to my left beside the door, with a wooden bureau beyond that.

And directly in front of me, in front of a draped window, under a pole light, the only light in the room, in a straight chair set at a three-quarters angle to me—Bud and Mitch.

Bud was the first one I identified, because Mitch was behind and below him in the chair. Both were nude. Tall, lithe, almost gangling, sandy-haired, ruddy skinned Bud, sitting on Mitch's lap, facing me, his long, thin legs hooked over Mitch's

246

muscular, widespread legs. The balls of Bud's feet planted on the carpet, giving him leverage for his rising and falling hips. Bud's chest was arched out, and Mitch's arms were wrapped around him, his hands palmed on Bud's pecs, Mitch's thumbs and forefingers playing Bud's nipples.

Bud's face had a mixed expression of pain and ecstasy and wonder and panic all at once. Bud was the one who I heard murmuring. He was panting and moaning and making little gurgling sounds. He was the one doing most of the moving as he rose and fell on Mitch's thick cock. On the rise I could see a good three inches of condom-sheathed cock appear above the short, curly pubic hairs at Mitch's crotch. And then the three inches would slowly disappear as Bud descended on it. Bud was also doing most of the huffing and puffing. Mitch was more or less just sitting under him, solid as a rock. Muscles taut, bulging. A slight smile on his face—slight, but more expression than I usually saw from him. The only movement from him those thumbs and forefingers rolling Bud's nipples and a slight undulation of his pelvis as he rolled, almost imperceptibly, in countermovement to Bud's rising and falling, moving back as Bud rose, and forward to meet Bud's downward thrusts.

When he noticed me standing, dumbstruck, unable to move from the doorway, to retreat from the shocking sight, Bud looked surprised and more than a little embarrassed. But he just kept on pumping, his eyes searching mine, seeking understanding and acceptance.

"Sit in the chair." It was Mitch's voice, clearly Mitch's voice, although it had a guttural edge to it. The voice of the Mitch who was to be obeyed.

I stumbled to my left and fell more than sat in the chair.

"Faster." The voice again. I was confused. Faster what? But then I saw that the command wasn't for me. Bud dutifully picked up the rhythm of his rising and falling. Bud was moaning louder now, his eyes still on me, but I could not hold the gaze. I was watching that three inches of hard, thick, condom-crowned cock disappearing and reappearing. I'd never seen anything like this before. Shock, dismay, interest, arousal.

"Unzip." I sat there, hearing him but not comprehending him.

"Unzip your pants. Pull it out." The voice was for me. I realized that now. No, I certainly wouldn't do anything like that. I would stand up right now and leave the house. Never speak to either one of them again. Transfer. Put this all behind me.

All the time I was thinking that, I was unzipping my pants and fishing my cock out. It was half hard already. Gawd, why was that? I couldn't find this arousing. Could I? I'd never . . .

"Thought so. Stroke it." The voice that was to be obeyed.

"Rotate." The commanding voice again. But this time for Bud. Bud moved his hands back to cup the back of Mitch's head and, leveraging off the balls of his feet, began to rotate his hips back and forth and in a circular motion. Mitch moved his hands to Bud's small waist and helped control the movement. Moans in harmony now, Bud's tenor and Mitch's bass. Bud's louder than Mitch's, but Mitch was softly grunting and groaning now too. And I could see his muscles straining and the veins popping out on his ropy forearms.

My cock was hard already, rising to my involuntary stroking. I moved my other hand up under the hem of my T-shirt and up to a nipple. Three-part harmony in the moaning now. Bud's tenor, Mitch's bass, my baritone.

"Up on your feet." Who was that for? Must be Bud, although he didn't seem to fully comprehend.

"Up on your feet. Now!" Mitch brought Bud up out of his lap with the grip he had on the basketball player's waist. Bud stood, but still crouch over Mitch's lap. I saw a good five inches of the condomed cock now, but the head was still embedded in Bud's ass.

Mitch's pelvis came up off the chair and he thrust up into Bud's ass, again and again and again. Six, seven inches sliding out and then disappearing in a quick upward jab. Bud lurching and twisting and gasping and yelping. Muscles rolling, bulging, straining. Both straining and breathing heavily.

Bud's legs were trembling uncontrollably and his knees gave way and he fell back into Mitch's lap, fully impaled. Mitch snaked a hand around and fisted Bud's engorged cock in a steel grip and started pumping, slowly but relentlessly. Bud was trembling and writhing under his grip. Mitch had his lips buried in Bud's neck. Loud oohs and ahhs and gruntings and groanings now. All tenor, all Bud.

Bud cried out in a shooting of cum and collapsed like a rag doll in Mitch's lap. Mitch's pelvis was still slowly churning. He wasn't finished, although Bud certainly was.

Bud raised his head and searched out my eyes with his. He had a languid, well-taken expression on his face. I don't know why, but I somehow knew this had been his first taking and that he was lost to the Marine now. Whatever Mitch, still churning inside him, wanted, he would do. And there was another look in his eyes. A message for me. A "you're next" warning.

I gathered strength and fled the room and the house.

Another week and nothing. I spoke to neither Mitch nor Bud, nor Chuck, for that matter, during that time. I went to a college basketball game on the Friday following that Tuesday and Bud was there and was the star of the game. He was all smiles and fluid movement and jazzed-up energy. So, no crushing experience for him there then.

After a week, I stopped trying to avoid seeing any of the three and started looking for them. In the meantime, I found I was jacking myself off at every opportunity. I was embarrassed and ashamed, but that didn't stop me from doing it and from thinking about what I'd seen in Mitch's house.

A week and two days later, there he was. I was studying in the library and looked up, almost in expectation, and there Mitch was, at the next table, a book open in front of him, but his eyes glued to me. Trembling, I pulled my books together and stumbled out of the library.

The next night I returned to the same table in the library. He already was there, sitting sideways to the table, his muscular legs spread. He knew I'd come back. It was the last thing I planned to do, but here I was. I opened my books, but my eyes were on him. His eyes were on me. He moved one of those strong, sensuous hands to his crotch and let it just sit there, cupping his power through the material of his jeans. I couldn't take my eyes from him.

A slight imperceptible smile, and then he uncoiled from the chair in one fluid, graceful moment. As he passed my table, he leaned down and whispered in my ear, "Tomorrow, six thirty, my place."

"Nooo," I moaned softly back to him. But he already was gone.

* * * *

"Strip and lay on your back on the bed." The voice to be obeyed.

When I was laying back on the sheeted mattress, Mitch stood at the foot of the bed and slowly stripped himself. He was just as strong and powerful all over as I knew he'd be. Thick and long, ball sacs full and hanging low. Every muscle fully developed and taunt and bulgy. Every muscle.

"Stroke yourself." I wrapped my hand around my half-hard cock and started doing what I'd done at least daily ever since I last was in this bedroom.

He was standing over me, stroking his own cock. Within moments we were both hard. he leaned over me and wrapped his hands around the underside of my thighs and pulled my butt to the foot of the bed.

"Sit up. Suck me." I sat up, my face right at the level of his hard-on. But I was at a loss of what to do now. I'd never done this before. I had no intention of doing anything here. I shouldn't be here at all. I wasn't staying here. I, in fact, wasn't here. This was all fantasy. I was in the library studying.

"Kiss it." He touched his bulging dick head to my lips. Moist, salty taste. And then I was gagging slightly and having trouble breathing, as his moist bulb pushed my lips open and he was inside me, moving it from cheek to cheek, sliding back over tongue. My eyes were tearing and I tried to move my head back, off the invading tool. But strong hands fisted my hair at the back of my head and held me to him. Held there for several moments and then I felt my lips sliding along veiny, smooth skin of thick, warm cylinder, and my jaw was aching to open wide enough and my throat was clogging. I wrapped my hands around his hard, bulging thighs and started to go with the rhythm he was setting.

I heard sighing, in that bass voice. I was pleasing the Marine. Mitch was pleased.

"Lay back." It seemed to have been an eternity that I had that thick cock inside my mouth, but it surely was only moments. As he drew it out, I closed my lips tightly over the rim of the glans and gave a little extra suck, flicking the piss slit with the tip of my tongue. I felt Mitch shudder. Good. At least I had retained that much control.

Mitch moved away from the bed. When he returned, he had a big black dildo in his hand and a tube of lube. He extracted a big glob of lube and then tossed the tube to me.

"Lube your ass."

"Nooo." I don't know if my whimper was audible to him, but he got the hint of rebellion.

"Do it, Now! You'll be glad later you did."

Back in full control. Any sign of resistance evaporated. While I worked the cool lubricant into my tight, virginal ass, Mitch lubed up the dildo. He was going to fuck me with the dildo!

But, no he wasn't. He handed it to me.

"Fuck yourself with this. Slowly, shallow at first. But you'll want to open to a good eight inches of it. You'll want to be stretched."

This was the most painful part of all. I slowly worked myself with the dildo, as Mitch stood between my spread legs, stroking his cock and pulling on his ball sacs.

"Stroke yourself. It will help." My fist went back to my hard cock.

Mitch disappeared from my vision.

"Come over here and sit on it."

He was in the chair I'd seen him in the previous time I'd been here. The only light on in the room was the pole lamp, its beam of light trained on the chair. Mitch was rolling a condom on his huge cock.

I cried out in first taking, in pain, and wonder, and awe, and arousal, and ecstasy, as my ass channel descended on his possessing cock, my channel stretching as best it could, caressing his cock, feeling every veiny contour of it as it moved up inside me. I was faced away from him, my legs spread wide on either

251

side of his thighs, the balls of my feet dug into the carpet, ready to leverage my rise and fall on his impaling cock. I arched my back, and Mitch reached around me with his sinewy arms and covered my pecs with his palms; his thumbs and forefingers went to my nipples, and I grunted and sighed as he started to pinch and roll them. I could feel his hot breath between my shoulder blades.

"Fuck yourself. Up and down on my shaft." The voice that must be obeyed, thick now with lust.

Leveraging off the balls of my feet, I began to rise and fall on his cock. All of my senses going to that thick rod running up inside me, electrifying my walls, stuffing me, fully possessing me to the quick. Up, down. Groan, moan, sigh. Up, down.

I sensed more than heard the other presence in the room. Then the heavy release of breath that wasn't mine or the Marine's. A slight gurgling noise.

"Sit in the chair." Mitch's voice. But not speaking to me.

I looked up in time to see a dark, chocolate brown, trim figure collapse into the chair by the door. The shocked look on his face. I'd seen him before. Tennis team, I think, and in a couple of my classes. Smart. Achingly handsome. Confused now, torn.

I sought his eyes out with mine. Not a warning. Warnings already useless. A sense of sharing, of inevitability. "You're next," my eyes said.

"Faster." I picked up speed in the rising and falling. Overwhelming ecstasy. Taking it deeper. Moaning.

"Unzip yourself. Pull it out." Familiar, but not meant for me.

Gasping at the depth and stretching of it. Pinching of nipples overwhelming. Up, up, and away. A feel of a sudden twitching and further engorging of the hot poker inside me, constriction of Mitch's thigh muscles under me.

"Ah, I thought so. Stroke it—"

Late Night Workout

I had been going to Gabe and Steve's Gym for a couple of months, and I was quite pleased with the results. I could tell that Gabe and Steve were pleased too, because they'd both been giving me the eye when I was in the shower. I didn't mind all that much; it was a free world and looks didn't cost me anything—or so I thought at the time. I knew that Gabe and Steve were a couple, but that didn't mean much to me either. Somewhat of an odd couple. Both were handsome and well built, to be sure, but Gabe was a bulging Nordic god, while Steve was the lithe and hirsute Mediterranean type.

Everything was going fine until that evening when I'd worked late and didn't arrive at the gym until near closing. No problem, Gabe had said. I could continue working out after they closed, as Steve had to do some paperwork anyway. Gabe could spot me, if I liked for my barbell set. While he was talking to me, he stripped off his shirt. His bulging chest muscles tapering down to washboard abs and strong stomach muscles were an inspiration for me to work harder on my own routines. He was well tanned and hairless; I knew that he shaved all over regularly, as he appeared in many local bodybuilding contests.

When I got around to doing my barbell lifts, I started to settle on my usual bench, when Gabe suggested I try the new bench in the back room. It was a strange contraption, raised higher than the normal bench off the ground and with stirrups for the feet. Gabe told me this was an improvement in two ways, as it prevented the lifter from using his feet so much for traction and put the barbells at a better height for the spotter to work with. I knew little about such things, so I didn't ask any questions and jumped up on the bench and flopped down on my back.

Gabe called Steve in from the office and asked him to help get me settled on the bench. Steve must have been on his way to the showers when Gabe called, because when he entered the room, all he had around him was a skimpy towel. Incongruously, though, he was carrying a big pair of scissors. He was deeply tanned and covered in curly black hair that spiraled down the front of him to where the towel was knotted. His muscles didn't bulge like Gabe's, but he was still well muscled and lean, a regular Apollo. He sauntered over to us, gave me a big toothy smile and, flipping my right foot out of my sneaker, began strapping my foot into one of the stirrups. When I was lying flat on the bench, my legs didn't reach the ground, but the stirrups, which were attached to the bench by long leather straps could be adjusted to my leg length. They really were quite comfortable when Steve had gotten my feet strapped into them.

Gabe put a set of bells on the stand, and I took hold of the bar. He wrapped his big fists around mine but let me provide all of the power in the lifts. I had done a couple of lifts before I even noticed that Steve had his hands on my knees, and I probably wouldn't have noticed even then if he hadn't been working his hands up my thighs.

"What?" I said as I looked up sharply. Steve was still smiling that smile, but he had lost the towel and his prick was standing at attention. I started to lurch up, but Gabe swiftly tied my hands to the ends of the barbell rack with leather straps I hadn't noticed being there before.

Steve's hand went up into the legs of my shorts and stroked my dong through my jock strap. I started to curse them both in a loud voice, but Gabe just laughed and told me to go ahead and yell. No one would hear. I looked back down at Steve, whose hands had withdrawn from my shorts, and my eyes opened wide as I saw him coming at me with that pair of scissors.

"Be still, or you'll get hurt," he said, as he snipped at the hems of my shorts and gym shirt. Then, in almost simultaneous motion, he ripped off my shorts and, after cutting the bands on my jock strap, ripped that off as well, as Gabe reached down, took the hem of my gym shirt, and just ripped that off my body.

"Hmmm, nice, Steve, said, as he took my now-naked and quivering body in." I gasped, as he took my dick into his mouth, He swallowed it all the way to the root in one gulp, and, I couldn't help myself, it started to engorge.

"There, that's good," Steve said, as he withdrew. "We'll have this stiffened up in no time." He licked down to the root on one side and then back up the head, which he took into his mouth. He rimmed the underside of this with his tongue and then moved the tip of his tongue to my piss slit, which he flicked and forth while I moaned quietly in guilty ecstasy. His hand went to my balls, which he rolled and pulled gently.

I felt something hard and moist strike my cheek, and I looked up to see, to my horror, Gabe's huge dick and balls suspended above me. He took my head between his two big mitts and positioned my mouth under his dick and commanded me to suck him. I refused indignantly, and suddenly I felt an excruciating pain in my balls, which Steve was crushing.

"Do as he says," Steve commanded, so I started tentatively giving Gabe head. Meanwhile, I felt my legs being pulled apart and up by some unseen adjustment Steve had made to the stirrups. Steve took hold of me by the hips and slid me until my butt cheeks were off the end of the bench. The next thing I felt down there was Steve's tongue. He started rimming my ass with his wet tongue and flicking his tongue in and out of my ass. I tightened up down there initially, but as his tongue probed deeper, I felt myself loosening and my ass passage relaxing and widening. I was enjoying this now. I could continue to fight it, but I knew I was beginning to want this.

Gabe took his dong from my mouth and moved around the bench, straddling me above my chest and coming at me again with that big cock of his.

"Rim it," he commanded, and I took the knob of his cock into my mouth again and ran my tongue around where the glans met skin.

"Open wider," he said, and as I did, he pushed his cock farther into my mouth, and I almost gagged on the load.

"Don't fight it," he said. "Stay relaxed and open and you'll manage just fine. This is all quite natural; it just takes some experience."

I tried to do as he said, and I found that I could, indeed, manage the slow pumping action Gabe had set up. After a few minutes, I found, also that, if I brought my tongue into play around his glans, he spent more time right at the entrance of my mouth and less time probing the back of my throat.

Meanwhile, Steve had taken some cool salve of some sort and slapped it on my asshole and was slowly working his fingers into my ass; first one finger and then two, and eventually three. I jerked as he found my prostate. A jolt of sexual arousal and pleasure shot through me.

Gabe reversed above me, taking my cock in his mouth and presenting his cock, balls, and asshole for me to lick and suck.

I gasped and lurched again when Steve entered me. He held his dick just inside my hole until I had adjusted and then just drilled it in deep and plowed me. I began to buck against him in a passionate response to the action of his dick.

All of this was just too much for me, and I shot off in Gabe's mouth, my cum bubbling out of his mouth and down onto my belly. Gabe cleaned me off and then got off me and went behind Steve, where he entered him, and fucked Steve in rhythm with Steve fucking me.

When they had both come, they released me and told me to go off to the showers and then I could dress and leave. They were laughing and joking and saying we'd all gotten a good late-night workout. They acted like they'd done nothing wrong and that I had no reason to be upset. And I went along with them; I certainly didn't want to make them angry. They had the cheapest gym in this part of town, and there was a long waiting list for members. They were nice enough to tell me they'd take the cost of the shredded gym top and shorts off my monthly bill.

But my indignation was all just rationalization on my part. Three nights later I appeared again at closing and they didn't even have to tie me down this time when they ravished me.

My Lover's Stepfather

This must be it; this must be when Shawn finally takes me.

That thought raced through my mind as Shawn brutally attacked my lips with his. We were stretched out on my dorm bed, me on my back and him covering my body with his. His tanned and muscular body, a gymnast's perfectly chiseled body, was undulating full length on mine. He held my arms above my head, his strong hands wrapped around my wrists, as I gripped the slats of the headboard and arched my pelvis up to him, willing his hard cock, stroking across my belly, to move down between my legs. I wanted him inside me so badly. I moaned for him and was begging for him to take me at last when he shut off my pleas with his lips and searching tongue.

His tongue invaded my mouth just as his hard, thick cock had done before he pushed me back on the bed.

I had never done this with anyone before. He was my lover. My first. He had come after me. I'd been reluctant at first. But he was just too beautiful, too persistent, too arousing. He had told me we wouldn't go all of the way—him fucking me— until he knew that I really wanted it.

Well, I had really wanted it for weeks now. I had told him so; I had done everything I could to show him it was what I wanted. But it hadn't happened.

Maybe it would happen now, though. I had brought him to the brink when I had given him suck. I could tell that he was about to explode. But he didn't. He withdrew and pushed me down full length on the bed on my back and made full-body love to me. I was the one about to explode now.

Shawn rose off me and turned me on my stomach, and he held me close, still trapping my arms above my head with the strong grip of his hands holding my wrists. I felt his cock move down the small of my back. I cried out for joy and turned my face to his, and he was deep kissing me again. His hard cock was between my ass cheeks, in my crack, rubbing across my hole as he stroked up and down across my hole.

I lifted my pelvis to him, willing the cock to enter me on an upward thrust. Not caring that I wasn't prepared to receive him, not caring that he was barebacking me. Beyond caring for anything but for that last barrier to be crossed, for my lover to totally possess me.

I felt him shudder, and I felt the wetness of his ejaculate spinning up the small of my back. He collapsed on me with a long sigh of satisfaction. His lips went to the hollow of my neck, as my hopes collapsed in another night of "almost," and not quite enough.

Shawn sucked on my neck, marking me as his—to take whenever he wanted, but not before—while I tried to suppress my own shudder. Mine not the product of release but of frustration and disappointment. When I was able to control myself, not wanting to whine or start an argument, or in any way move back from the brink we had almost crossed, I whispered the question I knew he'd understand, because I had asked it before.

"Why? Why not, Shawn? I've said I was ready."

"Not here, baby," Shawn whispered back. "Not here in this room. I want the first time to be special. Don't you?"

"The first time will be special, Shawn. I've told you that. All it needs to be special is that it needs to be you. You've overcome all my inhibitions. I surrender. But to you; only to you."

"Soon, love. Just not here. Not in a college dorm room. The place needs to be memorable—and separate from our everyday lives. Soon. Very soon. Give us a kiss."

* * * *

Soon came three weeks later, at spring break. Most of the guys were going to Daytona Beach. But Shawn and I were going to his family's remote house near Oriental, North Carolina, on the inland waterway inside the Carolina Outer Banks. It really wasn't all that far a drive for Shawn and me down Route 17 from Old Dominion University in Norfolk in his new Thunderbird, but his family was coming down from New York and Boston. Oriental was really remote, far out on a peninsula with only one road in from New Bern. Shawn said they had the house there because of the good duck hunting in the marshlands on the fringes of the Pamlico Peninsula.

"My stepfather is an avid game hunter," Shawn said. "Nothing he likes better than bagging fresh game."

"Your stepfather?" I asked. "Your father, then, is—"

"Dead, yes," Shawn said. "He shot himself right after my mother divorced my stepfather. I don't see much of her. She lives in Europe somewhere or in South America. Who knows from moment to moment?"

"Your father shot himself after your mother divorced his replacement?"

"Yeah," Shawn said. "It's not all that complicated. My father and stepfather were in business together. Their company builds skyscrapers across the Northeast. My mother went from one to the other—to my father's best friend and partner, and my father didn't get around to making a statement about that until after my mother dumped my stepfather."

"And you stuck with your stepfather rather than your mother?"

"He's the one with the money. So, of course I did," Shawn said with a mischievous smile. "Now, enough of that. You haven't noticed that Willy is taking in the sights."

261

Actually, I had noticed that Shawn had pulled his dick out of his pants and was driving down Route 17 with one hand on the wheel and the other stroking his cock.

"I really shouldn't be driving with one hand, Gabe. Help me out so we don't get a ticket." And with a grin, he pulled my face down to his lap, and I gave him head at 60 miles an hour down the Mid-Atlantic Coast.

"Take good care of it now, and it will take especially good care of you tonight, Gabe."

At last, I thought, as I took very special care of him in the North Carolina sunshine while cruising down Route 17.

* * * *

The Morton's house just a couple of miles outside Oriental must have been the seat of an early plantation on the inland waterway. The main house was an imposing, if not an oversized, wooden structure with a southern colonial portico and six thick white-plastered columns holding up a full-length porch over the front veranda. The room Shawn led me to was large and grand, one of the corner rooms with French doors out to the second-floor porch. From these I could see down to the water and could make out pleasure craft taking the inland passage back up the coast from Florida to summer quarters in New England.

The bed was a huge, dark-wood four poster, whose highly polished corner columns were crowned with wooden pineapples, which Shawn was quick to tell me was the southern symbol of hospitality.

"I've wrangled you one of the best rooms, Gabe," he said, brushing the back of his hand up and down my arm and giving me goose bumps of arousal. "This is where your desires will be fulfilled, if you are as welcoming as these pineapples symbolize."

"Of course," I whispered in a hoarse, desire-filled voice. "Now?"

"No, not now. Joe wants us to picnic with him down by the water now. He's in the mood to bag some game and wants company before he sets forth. This room is for later. For you to experience an initiation beyond your wildest dreams. Now, isn't this better than our dingy little dorm room?"

"Yes," I answered in a small, thick voice. "But, Joe?"

"Oh, Joe's my stepfather. The others aren't getting here until late this afternoon."

"Others?"

"Yes. His three brothers. The rest of the firm of Morton and Stabler. The Morton brothers. I'm afraid I have to hold up the Stabler part all on my own now."

"Hey, you comin' or not?"

The voice coming up from the lawn below was gruff, deep, an edge of impatience. A voice not to be denied. Shawn had a hand on my arm, and I felt him give a little shudder. There was something in his face, something that I couldn't categorize. Just the sound of the voice appeared to have subdued him, changed him somehow. He wasn't as brash and expressive as he had always been in my presence.

"Stepfather Joe calls. Ours is to obey," Shawn said with a sigh. He took my arm and pulled me out through the French doors and to the edge of the porch.

We looked down onto the front lawn of the house, and I saw him.

Joe Morton was obviously a formidable man. A king of industries who went straight for what he wanted and usually got what he went for. He was wearing camouflaged hunting gear with high rubber wading boots, obviously prepared to chase down whatever game he shot down over the marshlands. A heavy shotgun rested comfortably in the crook of a brawny arm that handled the weight with ease.

He was a good six and a half feet tall and was, by no means, a small-boned man. Plenty of meat on this man, most of it gristle. It was obvious that he didn't run his empire from behind a desk but with constant supervision at the top of unfinished skyscrapers. He had a rough-looking, squarish, florid face that probably had seen more of its share of barroom brawls, and he was bald, although the thick, dark hair on his forearms suggested that only his head was hairless.

"You comin' or not? Is that him then?" Joe Morton had turned his gaze on me, and I felt myself shuddering at the power in his voice and gaze.

"Yes, Joe. We'll be right out as soon as I swing by the kitchen and get the cooler. And yes, this is Gabe. I told you I'd bring him. Gabe, my stepfather, Joe. It's all fine, Joe. It's a go, we'll be right down."

I helped Shawn carry the cooler, which was pretty heavy with beer bottles in addition to a picnic lunch, down to the water. Joe had picked out a grassy place under trees with broadly reaching branches overhanging the water, where there was little verge between land and water, just a drop of a couple of inches. Not much in the way of sea vegetation on the margin right here either, although not far in either direction, tall grasses and cattails marked a transition zone of marshy land. There was a pier going a good fifty feet out into the water from here too, with a fair-sized boat house at the end, so it appeared that this was where the family moored their boats and they probably periodically had the water dredged in this strip of land. We were just around a bend of trees from a line of sight from the house.

We might as well have been the only three people on earth in this isolated spot on the remote Pamlico Peninsula. It was the height of the afternoon, and I could see sails far out in the Pamlico Sound, but certainly no one was able to see us.

We were shaded here under the low branches of the trees. The ground was mossy and soft. Shawn threw out a large blanket, plunked the large cooler in the middle of that, and started pulling out sandwiches and beer. The sandwiches were great, but the free-flowing beer was even better. Shawn and Joe were drinking Bud, but Shawn insisted that I drink my favorite, Corona, which he said he'd brought especially for me.

Eventually, Joe went off to do his hunting, and Shawn and I began to make out on the blanket.

The beer was going to my head. I must have drunk more of them than I thought I was. It wasn't long before I was pretty woozy and everything seemed to be happening in slow motion and in a blue haze.

Shawn was being unusually amorous, and I did nothing to stop him. He'd said we'd finally fuck for the first time in my room in the house, but if he took me here and now, that certainly was fine with me.

We were naked and Shawn was sitting on the blanket, facing the water. He had pulled me down to where I was sitting, facing him, on his thighs, with my legs straddling his hips. We were kissing and he had a hand wrapped around both of our dicks, holding them together, and was stroking them slowly. We were both hard as a rock, and I was panting for him, pining for him to take me at long last.

We'd never done this before, and I loved it. I loved it even more when he pushed me down on my back along his legs and lifted my pelvis up to his face and was giving me head. I moaned and groaned for him, and he kept playing my cock until I spouted for him too. We'd certainly never done that before.

I was in a daze. I had no idea how we had changed position so that I was bent over the cooler on my belly, my buttocks presenting, ready for the plowing, but there we were. And Shawn was on his knees behind me, and his hands were spreading my cheeks and his tongue was at my asshole.

I writhed and sighed and grunted for him. He was going to do it. He finally was going to take me. I only wished I wasn't so drunk. Why was I so out of it? I'd never gotten this drunk before in my life. I was at the moment of fully coupling with my lover, and I was too drunk to do anything but lay there and take whatever he gave me.

Shawn moved around to in front of me. He went down on his knees and took my head in his hands and guided my lips to his cock and slowly slid into my mouth.

But what was that? Shawn was at my head, but I also had hands on my hips. Big, strong, callused hands.

I was almost lifted off the cooler in shock and surprise and pain, as I felt a bulbous pressure at my asshole—a club pushing to enter my virginal ass. I tried to retreat from the assault, but the hands were holding me fast at the hips and Shawn was now pinning my biceps in a vice grip, holding me down, belly plastered to the plastic top of the cooler, butt waving in the air.

I wildly pulled my head away from Shawn's cock and looked around to behind me, as best I could. I opened my mouth in a primeval cry that caused a flutter in the cattails nearby, and a covey of ducks took to the air, as Stepfather Joe's thick cock breached my sphincter and rose inside me, grabbing for the very center of me, possessing me, taking my virginity.

He was still wearing his camouflage vest and those high-topped rubber boots, but he was otherwise naked. Big, heavily muscled, hairy, powerful, filling and stretching me to the limit.

And unrelenting in his deflowering of me. Together, the two men were just too strong for me, and I was too far gone from the beer—and not just from the beer, I groggily realized, but also from whatever they had put in the beer.

Joe was virile and strong and long-lasting and hard and thick and long. He fucked and fucked, while I weakly writhed and took him long and deep in relentless thrustings. It wasn't long before I gave over to the pleasure enveloping the pain. What was gone was gone. At this point, any release from the frustration was freeing. I still wanted Shawn; it would just now have to be later rather than sooner. Shawn pulled my face back down to his cock and I sucked him to completion, trying to convey to him that he still was my lover, and had spilled my seed myself before Joe was finished with me.

The haze overpowered me before Joe had withdrawn, but when next I returned to some semblance of consciousness, I was stretched out on my belly on the moss beside the blanket and Joe now was fucking Shawn. Shawn was on his back, with his legs spread, and Joe was crouched between Shawn's legs and pumping away inside his hole. Now that I could see the power of what Joe had between his legs, I almost swooned at what I had taken from him. Shawn's head was lolled to the side, facing me, and I could tell by the expression on his face that he loved this congress with his stepfather. Even in my groggy state, the truth of who was whose lover here and why Shawn hadn't taken me before now seeped into my brain.

After they were finished, Shawn helped me up to the house and upstairs and sat me down on the bed. He brought out another Corona and forced the cool beer down my throat. I was zoning out again as he took my head in his hands and guided my mouth to his invading cock, face fucking me to his completion.

He stretched me out on the bed on my back and was tying off my wrists above my head at the headboard.

Then he turned and walked out of the room. Still not taking me properly and fully.

My mind swam around with no focused thoughts until I fixated on the sensation of being penetrated again. I opened my eyes, or at least thought I did, and all was dark. Still, I thought I got some sense of being in that large bedroom on the second floor of the Oriental house. My legs were being spread by brawny hands, and I could make out a big, barrel chest hovering over me. Neither Shawn's young, sculpted muscles, nor Joe's hairy chest. Definitely not Joe—a full head of hair. Older than Shawn. I was being plowed, filled and pumped. I whimpered and protested, but I was too weak and groggy to put up any sort of resistance and I was bound. I heard a groan and felt a shudder and then relief as the pressure in my bowels lessened.

I drifted off to sleep only to partially awaken, on my side this time, to being encased by strong arms by a body stretched behind me. My leg was being lifted, and I almost was startled into full consciousness as a club thrust itself into my channel and began churning away. I started to scream out in indignation and surprise and pain, but a hand went over my mouth and pinched my nose, and I couldn't breathe. I was fighting for breath and unsuccessfully trying to pull away from the hot rod rising up my channel, only serving to pull a throbbing tool deeper inside me, when I blacked out.

The dream was so vivid that I could have sworn I was completely awake while I was being fucked a third time in that dark room. This time I was on my belly, apparently turned and retied at the headboard, and there was a heavy weight on my hips and hands holding down my upper arms, as again a hard tool was plowing my channel in long, deep strokes.

* * * *

The click of the bedroom door woke me the next morning. I was stretched out on the bed, naked and sore. Sore of muscles, but mostly sore inside my channel. I had no illusion that I had finally been fucked. But everything was hazy. Had

Shawn and I made love? It seemed like I had been fucked repeatedly, but somehow I didn't feel Shawn had been doing any of it. I was confused. But I no longer was tense from the frustration of not being fucked, because I definitely could feel that it had happened.

I looked over to where there was a wing-back chair in front of a fireplace. There was a small side table next to the chair and a breakfast tray on top of the table. I decided that was why I had heard the door click. I'd received breakfast.

I had to admit I was hungry. I painfully pulled myself off the bed, took a pair of jeans from my suitcase, pulled them gingerly on, and went over to the tray. I was pouring a cup of coffee, when I heard the braying of more than one dog out on the front lawn. Taking the coffee with me, and sipping as I went, I went out on the porch and over to the railing.

I arrived there just in time to see five men striding down the lawn toward the water, with three hounds nipping merrily at their heels. Four of the men were dressed as Joe was the previous day, prepared for a day of hunting. One of them was Joe Morton and three of them were almost carbon copies of him—undoubtedly the remaining Morton brothers. The head of hair on one of them brought back a painful memory. They must have arrived yesterday while Joe was fucking me down by the pier. I wasn't all that dumb. The "nightmare" of the previous night was getting a lot less hazy. I'd been drugged and bagged by the Morton brothers. It wasn't only ducks they hunted down on the remote Pamlico Peninsula.

The fifth figure, dressed in khaki slacks and a red T, was Shawn. Shawn, my erstwhile lover. A procurer of virgins for Joe and his brothers. Joe his real lover. Shawn broke away from the other four and headed around to the side of the house as the four brothers jauntily walked toward the marshlands, their shotguns slung over their broad shoulders, ready to continue bagging game.

I ate and dressed and slowly descended the broad staircase to the first floor, bowlegged and fighting the pains deep inside me that screamed at each step—pains not only inside me but also in my conflicted emotions. I should be angry and indignant, but I had wanted to be fucked—and now I certainly had been.

An elderly black man, dressed in a black suit, was waiting for me at the bottom of the stairs.

"Good morning, sir," he said. "Mr. Morton told me to drive you back to Norfolk this morning, sir. He and the other gentlemen will be out hunting all day."

"But Shawn—" I started to say. I had quite a bit to say to my college roomy.

"Young Mr. Stabler is already gone, sir. He drove out just a few minutes ago."

Gone? Shawn gone? "But I came down here with him. We came together." I was having trouble processing. This was all just too much for me to process.

"Mr. Stabler isn't going back to Norfolk, sir. He's transferred elsewhere. He won't be going back to Old Dominion."

So much for all of my dreams of a first time with Shawn.

Neighbor's Hot Tub

My wife was off to see her mother, and for the first time since he'd gotten it, my neighbor, Marty, had invited me for an evening in the hot tub he had put in. His house backed onto my side yard, and he'd done a whole lot of nice renovation on his property since he had moved in. Marty was divorced and probably was in his early fifties, judging from his graying hair, but he had kept himself quite fit. He was a businessman, and I could tell he was doing well at that because of all of the money he must be spending on fixing his house up.

His fitness probably was a result of the many hours he spent at the gym. He had a good gym in his basement, but he still frequently went to a big fitness center in town. Marty said he went there for the people he met; he had already had a string of subtenants pass through in the two years he'd been here who he said he'd met at the gym. He said he could use the company and that it was always good to have someone at home to take care of his dog when he traveled.

I had deduced for myself, of course, what the real reason for the string of young, buffed male tenants was. For this reason, I had contemplated and planned what I was going to say if he ever asked me to visit his hot tub. I had noticed him eyeing me when I was doing yard work with my shirt stripped off. And when he did ask me over, I was prepared, although I wondered if the minimalist Speedo I had bought and not yet worn would give too obvious of a signal to him. I had always been curious about, and, if truth be known, attracted to that lifestyle.

It was dusk when I walked around my fence and into his yard, with both a T and some shorts on over my Speedo, so as not to arouse the other neighbors, and a big towel draped over my shoulder. My wife had gone the day before, and I had called her shortly before making the trip next door to assure myself she had arrived at a destination a good five-hour drive away.

Marty was already in the tub, and his CD player was set on some music that had a real good steady beat to it and at a volume that would not impede discussion in the tub but would keep it to the near vicinity of the tub. The tub itself was quite large, more than eight feet in diameter—and a good thing too, because Marty wasn't the only one in the tub. Across from him was his most recent tenant, Seth, I think his name was. He was a big, black handsome dude, with Mulatto features, a massive chest that I could see above the water line, and a blue, intricate tattoo following the curve of his left chest muscle and wrapping up around his left biceps and down his arm to just above his elbow. I must admit that his presence was a little intimidating, but I'd waited for several months in anticipation of a new experience, so I gave him a friendly wave back in answer to the welcoming gestures from both of them.

"Come on in, neighbor," Marty invited. "The water's great and is bubbling up just fine. You've met Seth, haven't you?"

"Hi, Seth," I said. "We haven't actually met yet," I said, "but I've seen you around."

"And I've seen you gardening too," Seth said with a big, friendly grin. "Strip down and come on in."

I pulled my T over my head, glad just now that I'd put so much work into my own physique, pulled my shorts down, taking my loafers with them, and stepped down into the tub. The water was warm and swirled around my legs with a pretty forceful pressure.

"Here, over by me," Marty said. "Here's a beer."

I pushed my way over near Marty and took the beer gratefully. I downed a swig to calm myself, hoping that neither Marty nor Seth could see my hand shaking, and settled down on the bench ringing the inside of the tub.

Marty spread his arms around the rim of the tub, and his left arm was draped loosely behind me. We chit chatted for a short while before I took the initiative that I had planned to take. We were talking about the placement of Marty's hot tub, and I said, "You know, Marty, that I can see your whole tub from my study window. I don't think it can be seen from anywhere else, but I can see it."

"Yes, I know," Marty said. "I've sensed that you were up there looking down here on occasion." There was a short silence, and Marty added, "And I'll bet you know I don't bring young men home from the gym because I need the rent money, don't you?"

"Yes," I said quietly and took another long swig of beer. "I figured that out some time ago."

"And that doesn't bother you, as a neighbor?" Marty asked.

I turned and looked into his baby blue eyes and said, "No, not particularly. Live and let live, I say."

"So, and still you accepted my invitation to try out my hot tub while your wife was away? Why, might I ask?"

A long swig at the beer. "Curious, I guess," I answered, "just curious."

"Have you ever been . . . curious . . . before?"

"No, not actually. No, no . . . never before." Another nervous swig at the beer. It was beginning to give me a buzz.

"But you're . . . curious . . . now?"

"Yes, I guess so."

"Just how curious?"

"Very curious, I guess. I've had a long time to think about it."

With that, Marty moved in until we were touching sides, and the arm he had extended around me wrapped more snuggly and he draped his left hand over my shoulder. His fingers touched my chest lightly, but to me they felt heavy and to be marking a point of no return.

"Curious enough to try a kiss?" Marty asked.

"Yes, I guess so. But I won't be good at it. As I've said, I've never done this before."

His left hand lifted to the side of my head and he turned my face to his. He brought his lips to mine. First a light kiss on the lips, but the one that followed was more firm and he opened my lips with his. He tasted sweet and I hoped I did as well. His right hand went to my lower belly, and I gave a nervous twitch. But he held me there and I settled back down. He pulled his lips away and, in a low voice, said, "I thought that was nice. Are you OK?"

"Yes," I whispered. "I thought that was nice too." All of my attention was on that hand on my belly, however. He had moved his index finger to my navel and had pushed it in ever so slightly. He brought his lips back to mine; again a light kiss and then a deeper one. This time he took my lower lip between his and ran his tongue over my lip. My right arm was pretty much pinned against his side, but I instinctively raised my left hand up to cup his head and to hold him to me. His upper lip pushed up, opening my mouth to his tongue. I returned the pressure of the kiss for the first time. I liked this. I had had no idea whether I would, but I did, and I'm afraid that my cock liked it as well. I could feel myself grow. Marty must have known that this should be happening about now, because the hand that was on my belly moved downward and explored the basket of my Speedo until he was able to outline the bulge down there. I first felt him get the measure of my cock, which I was pleased gave him a little shudder, and then he outlined where my balls were. But he returned to my cock and was gently rubbing it.

He broke away from the kiss. "Ah, I can see that you are curious," he said, "Very nice."

"Thank you, I guess," I answered, nervously.

"Yes, very nice, indeed," he said. While stroking and rubbing below with his right hand, he gently encased his left hand in the hair at the back of my head and pulled my head back. He then buried his lips in my neck, finding an artery pumping blood there. His lips on that artery caused my cock to lurch. He squeezed with his right hand and kept nibbling at my neck, and my cock swelled further.

"Yes, very, very nice indeed," he mewed. His kisses traveled around to the other side of my neck, and his right hand came back up onto my belly, but only long enough to push under the rim of my Speedo and to gently pull my cock free. I moaned and closed my eyes.

"Here's where you can feel me too, if you'd like," Marty instructed. I tentatively moved my free hand to his chest and ran it from nipple to nipple. He had a good chest. I then ran my hand down to his washboard stomach. Very nice shape for his age. Marty's lips ran through my chest hair and went to my right nipple, where he applied suction. His right hand went down to cup my balls, pulling the Speedo down farther.

"Am I moving too fast for you?" he asked. "Everything still all right?"

"Yes, thanks. That feels nice."

"Here, let's get these off," Marty said, and I raised my butt so that he could pushed the Speedo down and off my feet, and he then flipped it away from the tub. While he was doing this, I looked over at Seth. He had pulled himself up on the edge of the tub and had a beefy mitt wrapped around one of the fattest and blackest—far blacker than his own skin—pricks I'd ever seen. He had a look of languid pleasure in his eyes as he watched Marty perform at our side of the tub.

When Marty came back around, he twisted his torso so we were face to face, chest to chest, and gave me a deep kiss. My right arm went around his back, my hand at his waist, and my left hand slid back down his chest to his belly and then, tentatively on down. I gasped as I realized that he hadn't been wearing any trunks at all. His pubic hair was thick, but not anywhere near as thick and long as the dong my hand found. I gave out little gasps again, and Marty registered his pleasure with his mouth, as I encased the root lightly in my hand and then slowly explored every inch of his tool.

Marty leaned over, fiddled with something on the rim of the hot tub and came back with a big gob of goo in his hand.

"Lubricant, a special kind," he whispered in my ear, as his hand went under the water and he started lathering up my cock with it. "But we still have to be fairly quick," he whispered again, "or the hot water would eventually dry it out and wash it away." We kissed while he slowly hand pumped me up, the lubricant providing additional pleasurable friction. Within a few minutes I was pretty well pumped up. He swung up and around me, suspended over me with his knees on the bench facing me and me between his legs.

"Here, scoot out on the bench a bit," Marty directed. I did so, beginning to understand what he had in mind, and feeling a little thrill running through my body. This was what I had been most curious about. Marty's hand went to my cock, and I felt its head being positioned at his asshole.

"But, but, don't you need something, too?" I asked.

"Oh, I'm well oiled down there already," Marty said. "Seth and I got started before you arrived."

I could feel my cock go into his ass up to the rim of the helmet. Anxiously, I started pushing up.

"Easy, there, big fellow," Marty said. "And I do mean big fellow. Give us a minute."

But in far less than that, I felt I was beyond the first tight area, and his sphincter muscle pulled me on in. Marty did a few up and down pumps while he was skewering himself on me, but, in large, it was a quick slide down my pole. It felt tight and bumpy, not at all what I had expected. Marty winked at me and asked, "How do you like my new sleeve? The first half of the channel you just went up has a sleeve with silicon bumps in it, both inside and out, to give your cock and my hole a ride I bet you haven't gotten from your women." And with that he reached out and grabbed the rim of the hot tub with both hands and I grabbed his hips with both of my hands, and he began pumping up and down, short and long, slow and fast, until we were both panting and I felt like I was going to explode. He was right; I'd never gotten this kind of ride from a woman before, and I'll have to admit that I've been up a few women's asses. I was about to shoot, when Marty rose off me and plopped down beside me again. He took my cock in his hand and held it still. I tried to hand fuck him to completion, but he held me still until the urge subsided.

"Not yet, good neighbor," he whispered in my ear. "Too early for your first load."

After I had calmed down, Marty took another glob of ointment in his right hand and slid it down my belly and along my upper thigh to my crotch. He put the heel of his hand under my balls, made me spread my legs with the pressure from his fingers, and found my asshole with his index finger. He held the tip of the finger on the rim for a moment, but then pushed it and some of the ointment ever slightly into the hole. I flinched and tightened up.

"No? Not yet? Too fast?" he whispered, as he came out of the kiss.

"No." I said. "Yes, I mean too fast. In fact, I'm not sure—"

"Nothing you're not sure about," He whispered. "We won't do anything you're not sure about until you are sure. Don't worry." His hand came back up to my cock. He took the dick helmet in his fingers. I found I had been holding his the same way without quite knowing what else to do with it.

"Here, follow my lead," he said. He wrapped his hand around my cock and slid it down to the root. I did the same to his dick. Applying pressure, he gently, but steadily pumped my cock for about a dozen beats. I did the same in rhythm, and both of our cocks grew. He then slid back up to the helmet, and so did I. Taking that in his fingers, he ran his fingers lightly around the rim of the helmet. I did so as well, and we both gave a low moan, although mine perhaps was deeper and more surprised than his. He put his thumb on the slit at the top of the helmet, and I returned the favor. He brought another finger up and squeezed so that that hole opened more. I began to squirm, but Marty remained rock solid—and I mean rock solid. All the time, he had my lips in his and was deep kissing me. I looked at Seth. He was stroking himself with one hand and pinching at the nipples on his gigantic chest with the other.

I pulled away from Marty's lips and said. "Umm, maybe we'd better cool it a minute again, Marty. This might be getting a little critical with me."

"Not to worry, neighbor," Marty answered with a little laugh. "I think you can come now. You're a young, virile guy. I'm sure you have fast enough reloads if we need them. In fact, I think it's time for a little change." With that, he pulled away, knelt beside me on the hot tub seat, put his hands under my butt cheeks and raised me up. To my surprise and somewhat consternation, Seth was there behind me, kneeling with his knees behind my waist, my butt hanging just below the rim of the hot tub, and supporting my back along the incline of his torso. I could feel his huge dick running up my spine, which, I must admit, was not the least pleasurable feeling I've ever had. He wrapped his arms around me and placed his hands over my chest, where he did some subtle work on my nipples and chest muscles. From time to time, he buried his face in my neck and gave my arteries there a sensual sucking.

Marty, his knees in the hot tub and on the bench, facing me, was between my legs. His hands were encasing and squeezing my butt cheeks. "Gawd, what a nice butt you have," he said, with admiration. "And that prick. Get a load of that prick, Seth." Indeed, I must admit that my cock was very much on display, sticking straight up there in the air.

Marty brought his lips down to my navel, and he kissed and tongued me there, as I squirmed a little and did some sighing and moaning.

"This okay?" he asked.

"Yes, fine," I answered.

"This okay?" he asked, as he moved his lips farther down and kissed and tongued along my pubic hair line.

"Yes," I answered weakly. He ran his tongue down along my crotch and around my dick until he got to my balls. He tongued and kissed those. "And this, this OK?" he asked.

"Yes," I moaned. Then he popped one of my balls into his mouth and extended it out.

"No, no . . . yes," I volunteered. He took the other testicle in his mouth. He now had one in each cheek. Again he extended them out and down and applied a little sucking pressure.

I couldn't say anything at this point. I was holding as still as possible and was beginning to pant. Seth ran a hand down across my belly and encased my cock and squeezed.

"Oh, oh," I moaned. And then, "Yes, oh yes," as Marty popped my balls out of his mouth and was fed my cock by Seth, who was holding it upright. Marty treated it like a Popsicle briefly, running his tongue down to Seth's hand and then around to the other side and then up. He took just the helmet in his mouth and ran his tongue over it and around the rim and into the slit and then sucked it. What a sensation. I'd never felt this during sex before. Then he started deep-throating me, first soft and slow strokes and then faster and deeper, with the beat of the music of his CD.

I was writhing under Seth's bonds, moaning and whimpering, and murmuring that we needed to stop and cool down a bit. It was then that I noticed that Marty had worked his way along and inside my butt cheeks and now had two fingers, one from each hand on the rim of my asshole and slowly pulling the opening apart. I could feel more of the cool ointment.

"No, no, Marty," I said, as I tried to slap at him with my hands. "Get away from my ass."

Seth put me in a headlock that threw my arms over my head, but Marty did move his hands higher on my butt cheeks without losing a beat of his pumping action on my cock.

"Oh, oh, I'm going to come, Marty. Pull off, I can't hold it much longer."

"No problem," Seth whispered in my ear." Marty can take it. He likes it." And take it he did, three jolts of wad, down his throat. Then he relaxed and looked up at me with a smile.

"There, that was lovely," Marty whispered as he came up for air after swallowing my jism. I just lay there in Seth's grasp, panting from my first male cocksucking. "You have one of the nicest packages I've ever had," he went on to say.

I thought that Seth would let me go then, but he didn't. What he did do was drag me farther out of the hot tub, so that my butt was on the rim. I could barely reach the seat with my feet.

Marty rose up on his knees and said, "What I can't understand is your fear for your ass. All I want to do is what a doctor can do. Didn't you know the prostate was the men's G-spot? All you heteros don't know the pleasure you are missing. It's just a little ways in; I just want to show you what a pleasure a prostrate massage can be."

"I . . . I don't know," I answered uncertainly.

279

"You came for adventure, didn't you?" Marty asked. "Why leave without knowing just how much pleasure you even could be getting with your wife. She could be doing this just as easily as I can. But obviously she hasn't been. You've been missing out. I'll bet you make sure you service her G-spot."

Again, "I just don't know."

"Well, let me start and you can always let me know when to stop. I've done that before, haven't I?"

"Well, I suppose." I couldn't think of a better answer. And without waiting for a further answer, Marty pushed my legs apart and was lightly kissing my asshole. It did feel pleasurable. Seth lowered my arms again and again wrapped his hands around my chest and played in my chest hair and with my nipples. I turned my head and we kissed. His lips were bigger than Marty's had been, and his kiss was more bruising and insistent, but the taste was just as sweet. I could feel his hot sausage-like prick on my back, and I snaked my hands behind me in search of it. Seth lowered his shoulders to take the weight off mine and pushed my torso up so that I could reach his rod with both of my hands. I wrapped my hands around it covered from top to bottom without the hands overlapping.

"Raise your legs when I push them up," Marty commanded in a husky voice. I did so, and he got his hands where my thighs met my buttocks and pushed my legs apart. He had his fingers dug into my butt cheeks, and he used them to pull them apart to give maximum access to my asshole. He kissed my puckering hole again and rimmed me with his wet tongue. It felt strange but tingly. I felt his tongue enter my channel and I gave a little gasp.

"Okay, so far?" he asked. I broke away from the kiss with Seth to give a hesitant affirmative response.

"This will feel cold, but it will make it more comfortable for my finger to reach the proper position," he said reassuringly. With that, he draped my left leg over his shoulder and came up with another large dab of ointment. This time I felt the cool moisture pushed farther into my asshole than he had done earlier. Marty spent some time working this in, and I could feel my asshole loosen up and expand.

"My, my, my," I heard him cluck.

280

"What?" I asked.

"Oh, just my, my, my. This is going to be better than I hoped. Opening right up." Not bothering to pursue that point farther, I relaxed a bit under his ministrations to the point that I no more than flinched when I felt a finger at the rim and tentatively push up to the first knuckle into the hole.

"There, does that hurt?" Marty asked.

"N-o-o," I said with an edge of doubt in my voice. "Huh," I said with a gulp, as I felt the finger push further in. I felt my sphincter muscle catch it and draw it even further in. And then I felt the pad of the finger on my prostate. Marty could feel he'd found the spot too, even though I gave him notice by flinching and giving a little gasp. Marty applied gentle pressure and began to rub.

"Here, this will take a few minutes," Marty said. Seth pushed the full length of his torso into me again, trapped my hands between him and me and slid his right hand down to my cock again. As Marty rubbed, I felt almost as if I had to piss, and I could feel a few dabs of cum involuntarily dribble up and out of my cock, but, oh what a sensual and relaxing feeling it was. I almost thought I'd begin to purr. I'm glad I found out about this. Seth rubbed the precum around my cock with his finger. He had propped me up so I could look down the whole length of my body and see him playing with my cock and Marty there between my legs. The pleasure from watching what was going on and the pressure on my prostate began to grow, and along with it my cock began to engorge again.

And then Marty's finger was out of my hole and he standing on the floor of the hot tub. I could see his erect phallus, and it was leaning its way in, toward my butt.

My intense pleasure flipped to fear, "No! I half yelled. No, I don't want—" My voice was muffled by Seth's big mitt coming up and covering my mouth.

"Hey, you came to find out what this is all about. This is part of what this is all about," Marty said with a husky voice. "You came here. Who are you going to complain to? Who in the neighborhood wants to know what you are a part of now? Your wife maybe? Don't worry; I'll make it a good experience. No, I'll make it a great experience; I can tell from your reaction that it's already gone beyond a good experience. And your hole has opened up incredibly. I've never seen this happen the first time. I bet you could take me and Seth both." I moaned and writhed at the thought. I didn't want to admit that I'd played dildo games with my women partners for years.

He still had my left leg over his shoulder, so he lathered up his dick with ointment and positioned its head up against my asshole with his right hand and pushed in just enough to get the helmet in and to have purchased. Then he grabbed both of my legs at the ankles and split me up and out like a wishbone. I saw him slowly entering me and I began to buck my pelvis, which only increased the pain, so I stopped. What I didn't want to admit, even to myself, was that this felt a whole lot better than the dildos I'd taken up there. Marty held still, while Seth reached over and turned up the music and did a quick turnaround on me. He had my hands by the wrists and was kneeling with my chest between his knees.

"You can scream if you want," he told me. "But I'm going to get rough if you do. And I'm going to get rough if you don't pay some attention to me now." There was little doubt what attention Seth had in mind. From where he was positioned, the moist head of his long dong was touching my cheek.

"Seth's right," Marty said from below me. "I can either give this to you within your tolerances, or I can give it to you really hard. If you service Seth, I'll be as gentle as possible."

"I don't think I'm ready for this," I screamed. I had barely gotten this out, though, when Marty pushed a good five inches up my ass in one slide. I thought I was going to be ripped apart.

"What was that you said?" Marty asked.

I didn't answer, but I opened my mouth and turned it toward Seth's dick and took the bulbous head in. I licked and sucked, and Seth gave little whimpers of pleasure. "Get your tongue under it," he said, and I complied. He entered me about three inches and I thought I'd gag. "Don't think gag," he directed. "Lift your chin to give it a straight shot and push your tongue and under it as far as it can go. And open wide, very wide. Loosen your jawbone. You can do it." I did so, and he slid in a little farther. Then me began to slowly pump in and out,

282

fucking my face but not trying to give me more than I could manage.

Meanwhile, down below, Marty had withdrawn his prick most of the way and was pushing back in. He reached my prostate again with his cock and he was rubbing up against that and giving me a not-unpleasurable sensation. Other than the one painful punishment thrust, he hadn't been doing more than slowly working his way in at this point, holding for me to stretch to be able to accommodate him. After he had gotten past the sphincter, I no longer felt great pain and the sensation of being stuffed beyond limits, and shortly I could feel I had loosened and relaxed and a felt the whole length of him glide on in. I could feel his pubic hair mashing down on mine.

"There," he grunted, "you did it. You did fine. You've got one sweet, big ass channel." He didn't do any pumping at that point, but he did move his pelvis around, rotating his cock inside me. My prostate liked that just fine, and it served to loosen and widen the canal some more. He came back up on the hot tub seat with his knees, so that now me was hunched over me. He pushed my legs down toward the deck at an almost impossible angle, so that now we was hovering over me, with his ramrod almost on the vertical.

It was then that Seth jerked out of my mouth with a grunt and spurted cum all over my chest, and as that happened, Marty began his pumping action in my ass. In and out, short strokes and then long strokes. Wiggling his pelvis and rotating his dick around, stretching and filling me. Seth changed positions again, without me being able to escape. He turned around on me, putting my head firmly between his knees and kneeling there. His hands went to my dick and my balls. He played with the balls for a while and then got hold of the cock and started stroking and pumping it. He and Marty did some kissing without letting it interfere with their other activities. And then I felt lips on the tip of my cock, and Seth took me on to the root in one slide, showing me that, indeed, it could be done. In turn, I showed him I wasn't taking any of this passively. I pulled his butt cheeks apart and started tonguing and rimming his asshole. I then fisted a hand and started pushing the knuckles at his hole, and, to my surprise, they started working their way in. Seth's only response was to wiggle his ass in pleasure, which I increased by taking his dick in my other hand and starting to milk him.

Marty, Seth, and I came at just about the same time, and, with a combined scream of release, followed by a sigh of relief, we all were back in the hot tub, soaking away body fluids. I wasn't really in any condition to look where I was going, however, because when I went to sit down on the hot tub ledge, Seth was under me. I struggled and objected, but he had only of those beefy arms around me and the other was on his dong, which he guided to my newly plowed asshole as I came down. I managed to stop, at first, when helmet of his cock was just at my entrance. But Seth held me there steadfastly and slowly, ever so slowly, my leg muscles gave way and I descended down his gigantic tool, feeling every inch in both length and diameter as I was skewered until my butt was nestled up against his upper thighs. I panted and moaned, while Seth clucked sweet nothings in my ear and nibbled at my neck.

"Oh, gawd, no, Seth. You're too big. Let me go," I whined.

"You've already taken me in, Glen. From here, just take it and enjoy it. You now know there isn't anyone you can't take. I'm more than eight inches long and mighty thick, Glen. There aren't many bigger than that. Just relax. That ointment we used is good stuff, and, as Marty said, you've got one incredible ass canal."

When I had stopped panting and groaning, Seth pulled my knees up and into my chest and began gently rocking from front to back. His rock-hard, yet flexible dong was rubbing my prostate and other nooks and crannies up my ass channel in a way that gave me a whole new sensation, and I found that I could accommodate him without pain now. I was lulled into a sense of relaxation, but the two weren't finished with me yet.

I had about dozed off in exhaustion, when I felt Seth standing up. He still had me folded into his chest by the knees, and he bore my weight as if I were a rag doll. He didn't go far, however, he just moved up to where he was perched on the rim of the hot tub. That's when Marty came back into view. Seth leaned back so that my butt was lifted in the air and there Marty was, with more ointment, and spreading it around my now-occupied asshole. I don't know how he was doing it, but he was managing to get a few fingers into the hole above Seth's buried dong.

"What are you doing?" I cried. "Oh, no, not that."

"Such a sweet hole and channel, Glen," Marty cooed. "And so flexible. It opened right up. More than I thought possible for a first time. Have you and your wife been playing rear-entry games? Don't do anything rash, Glen. Just hold very still there, for me . . . and for your sake."

And then he did it. I felt the head of his cock at my hole above Seth's rod and slowly, ever so slowly, he was entering me as well. He was half way in when he slowly pulled out again and then in, a little farther than the first time, and then slowly out and slowly back in. Seth was giving little yelps of pleasure at the friction Marty was bringing to bear on his buried cock between kisses he was enjoying with Marty. His cock began to do some involuntary pumping as well. I zoned out before they were finished.

No More Evening Shifts

There were four of them who entered the store close to closing time, all muscled punks decked out in black leather. I owned the small convenience store but found myself behind the counter this evening because my regular night clerk called in sick.

The hunkiest of the four came up to the counter, puckered his lips. and tossed me an air kiss. He asked me where Jake, my regular evening clerk, was. When I answered, telling him Jake was sick tonight, he told me that I was cuter than Jake and that I turned him on. He asked if I wanted to join the group for a good time after closing. I knew Jake swung that way, which had never bothered me, but I told this guy as politely as I could that I didn't. But he kept right on sweet talking me. I figuring he was just trying to keep my attention while the other three picked out some presents for themselves, and this assumption proved to be correct.

I looked past the guy who was harassing me and saw one of his friends, a big black dude, heading for the door with a six pack of beer.

I brought my handgun up from under the counter where everyone could see it and, as confidently as I could, said in a loud voice, "I think you might want to put that back unless you are going to pay for it. And I have to close up now, so perhaps you guys need to go on to your party."

They left, but not without giving me meaningful looks and a few sniggers. Their bikes were gone from in front when I locked up and walked around to the back of the store to my car, and my mind was so full of business matters that I wasn't even thinking about them. But as I got out my keys to open my car door, there they were—all four of them.

Two of them had me in their powerful grip as the blond hunk who had harassed me and the black dude who had tried to make off with the beer stripped down. They both had strongly muscled bodies and were horse hung. They pulled at their cocks as the other two roughly stripped off my clothes.

The blond broadcasted that he liked what he saw—better than the Jake he had expected to find here this evening. One of the guys who had stripped me waved my key ring in the air, and the blond hunk told him to go back into the store and get that beer they had wanted.

The other guy and the black dude slammed me down on my back onto the hood of my car, and the black dude mounted my chest. He was holding my arms against the hood of the car with his knees, and he pulled my head up by the hair so that my mouth was touching the big glob of penis helmet dangling from his loins. He directed me to suck him and to be good at it, or I'd regret it. I took his dick into my mouth and did what I thought would please him with my tongue on his glans and piss slit, and he did indeed seem to be pleased. His dick began to thicken and harden. I could hardly get it into my mouth.

Meanwhile, the blond dude had gotten his hand under my butt and was assailing my ass with his fingers. First one, then two, and then three. And he was finger fucking me. I couldn't help it; he was turning me on. My own dick began to harden, and the third guy swallowed it and began sucking me off as he rolled my balls with his fingers.

The fourth guy returned with several six packs of cold beer and a handful of condoms, and they all paused to drink a bottle off. I was in no position to say anything, though, as the black dude was rotating his cock around in my mouth, rubbing his helmet against the inside of one cheek and then moving it to the other.

The blond hunk took one of the condom packets, opened it, and slowly rolled the condom onto his huge cock.

"Sure hope you stand behind your products," he said with a laugh. "Cause I'm going to stand behind you and test this fucker out. You'd better hope your goods hold up to the test."

He then opened a bottle of beer, held it up, and said, "Think I'll try both of your products out on you." He passed out of my view behind me and gave a command, and the other two guys were grabbing my ankles and wishboning my legs. I felt the cold neck of a beer bottle being pushed into my ass, and then, at another command from the blond hunk, my legs were being pulled up toward the windshield, my ass was rotating up toward the sky, the bottle was tilting up, and cold beer was gushing down my insides. I heard the blond hunk and his cohorts laughing at this trick. And then the blond hunk's mouth was at my asshole. He was slurping beer and pushing his tongue into my channel.

The black dude was right over my face now, pushing his dick deeper into my mouth. I felt cold beer being sloshed over my chest, belly, and cock and balls, and one of the other guys, whose hands were still holding my leg up at the thigh, was tonguing the beer off me. He was driving me wild with his nipping and sucking at my nipples.

The blond hunk stopped slurping and tonguing my ass, and I felt his bulbous cock head at my hole. He entered me and I lurched, forcing the black dude's cock down my throat and causing me to gag. The blond guy kept his cock helmet just inside my ass opening for a few minutes, rotating it around, encouraging me to open to him—which, luckily for me, I was doing. When he was satisfied, he started to slowly but relentlessly feed his long, thick hose into me, stretching me to the edge of endurance.

The pain and sense of being filled to the limit was excruciating, but I couldn't scream, as the black dude was now face fucking me deeply, and it was all I could do to keep from gagging and to try to catch my breath. I could moan, though, and I was doing plenty of that. And the blond dude said he loved my moaning and that I should do it louder for him. He also said he loved my tight ass, and that he knew the others would love it to. The others? I moaned louder.

The fourth guy swallowed my cock with his mouth, and my cock betrayed me, showing that it enjoyed the attention.

The blond hunk was in to the root now, and he started a slow, steady pumping action, which started off deep and shallow and slowly lengthened. The pain was subsiding, and, as it did, I found a sense of pleasure increasing. My cock felt like it was going to explode. And then it did, and the guy who was giving me head took the full wad and licked me off before pulling away. Shortly thereafter, the blond hunk pulled out of me and shot his jism up my belly.

In a loud voice, he proclaimed it was the black dude's turn, and my jaws were given relief as the black dude withdrew from me, still kneeling above me, although his knees were now off my arms. He barked a command, and one of the guys threw him a condom packet, which he neatly pulled out of the air.

"Cap me, stud," the black dude said, as he put the condom packet in my hand.

My hands trembled as I fumbled with getting the packet open and then rolling it onto his giant tool. He then pulled my mouth back up to his dick, and forced himself back into my mouth.

"Get it nice and wet," he commanded, and I felt the acrid taste of latex in my mouth. When he was satisfied, he hopped off my chest. The other two guys let loose of my legs and the black dude had me flipped onto my belly and his cock moving up my ass chute before I had time to react. He was holding my torso down on the hood of the car with one beefy arm. His efforts to bury his enormous dick in me were causing him to grunt with frustration, and he commanded me to widen my legs. I did, and this helped him bury himself to the hilt.

He got his big mitts under my chest and grabbed me by the pecs and arched my back up to him. He had me in a lip lock, and his tongue was now deeply probing my mouth just as his dick had been doing shortly before. He pumped his cock in and out of me like a piston and soon came in a big gush of semen that filled the head of the condom and made me pray that the latex would hold. He then let me fall in an exhausted heap on the hood of the car and pulled away from me.

I lay there, panting, unable to move, as the blond dude signaled to the other two guys and they stripped. They were both thinner and wirier than the blond and black guys, but they quite clearly were strongly muscled as well. They also didn't have the monster cocks of their cohorts. They weren't all that thick, but both were long and one had an unusual crook in it that brought the head up toward the guy's belly when it was erect. Both cocks were very much erect. The blond flipped them a couple of condoms, and they took their time, standing very close together and facing each other, in getting a condom rolled onto the other's cock.

The blond pointed to one guy and said "bottom" and to the other and said "top," and the bottom, the one with the straighter cock, came over to me, pulled me up off the hood of the car, got behind me, and pulled me back down on top of him. He got his feet on the inside of my ankles and pulled my legs wide apart. And his powerful arms held me in a full nelson hold, with my arms above my head. Thereupon, the top guy walked between my legs, spread my aching asshole with two fingers and helped the bottom insert his cock and run it up my canal.

I twitched and grunted, but this cock didn't compare to what I'd already taken in, so I wasn't all that much alarmed. But then alarm started to set in, as the "top" moved into me and started to push his own dick in above that of the bottom. I suddenly realized what the bottom and top business was all about. I was being sandwiched.

I screamed as my ass canal was being stretched and nearly split, and the blond and black dudes answered with gales of laughter as they finished off another round of beer.

The top, the one with the crooked cock, pushed into where the helmet of his cock was positioned directly on top of my prostate, and he rubbed me there until I myself was in a sexual frenzy and my cock was oozing precum once more. Then he pushed right on in, and the two of them started a counterpiston action that played my ass passage like a calliope. The hands of the top were wandering all over the bodies of both the bottom and me, and all three of us were alternating kisses.

The top's mouth went to my nipples while I was in the lip lock with the bottom, and I just relaxed and gave up my inhibitions. I became adjusted to the action and went with the flow. My cock was rubbing up and down the top's belly, and all three of us came almost in succession—and my cry of enthusiasm was no less heartfelt than theirs.

The top and bottom disentangled themselves, and the black dude picked up my clothes and threw them at me, while the blond hunk opened the driver's door of my car and waved me in.

Relieved that they weren't going to do worse with me, I headed for the car door. I wouldn't stop to put my clothes back on; I'd wait until I had driven out of danger before I did that. As I got to the door, however, the blond hunk roughly pushed me down on my side across the seat and center console with his hand, lifted my leg over his shoulder, and fucked me in a side split one last time. Skin on skin. No condom this time. Deep strokes, in which he fully withdrew and then power-drove back into me and up to the hilt. I was moaning and sobbing, which he seemed to be enjoying a lot. And then I was enjoying it too. I had to admit to myself that I loved this hunk's cock up my ass. I started to go with his rhythm, and the blond sensed that I had given in to him at last.

"What do you think now, stud? Want me to pull out of you now?"

"No," I reluctantly moaned, "Don't stop now. I think I'm going to come."

"Tell me you like it," he commanded after a particularly long stroke that had me gasping.

"Oh, god yes. Plow me. Plow me deeper." I felt shame, but the sexual charge had taken me over.

Satisfied, he continued pumping me. He wrapped his hand around my cock and milked me until I came in a splat on the pavement below the door sill. And this time he came in an explosion and a cry of pleasure deep inside me, bathing my insides with his semen.

He leaned over and whispered in my ear. "There, I own you now, you muthafucker—just leaving you a little something to remember me by until the next time. It was a nice party;

thanks for providing both the refreshments and the entertainment."

And then they were gone. I just lay there, until I was sure I was alone. And then I pulled myself out of the car, dressed, went back to make sure the door to the store was locked, and drove on home and took a long shower, ashamed that I had enjoyed much of the evening.

However, this was the last evening shift I ever worked in my store. But it was not because I didn't want to; it was because I couldn't trust myself.

Gotta Keep This Job

I had been summoned to the medical suite at my office at the end of the Friday dayshift of my second week on the job, and I showed up with a great sense of trepidation. It had been hard finding this job, and I just had to keep it. But I'd scored drugs for a short time when I'd been in college, and I knew this company had a strict drug policy. I hoped that they hadn't found out about that—or that they wouldn't find out about it in this surprise appointment.

"Come in here, take off all your clothes, and sit up on that table," a perky young nurse told me. "The doctor will be in to see you in a minute."

"Take off all my clothes?" I asked dubiously.

"Yes. Don't worry. I go off shift now. It will be just you and the doctor."

"Great," I thought, as I followed her direction. I didn't know why I felt self-conscious. I was in great shape and wouldn't have minded the cute little nurse knowing just how great shape I was in and how well hung I was.

But I was in shock when the doctor walked in. It was Larry, my boss, the owner of the company.

"Mr. Sturgis," I stammered. "What . . .?"

"Oh, didn't you know," the handsome young redhead said, "I'm the company doctor too. It saves a lot on the medical bills. Now, let's see what we have here. Everything seems to be in order and in good shape. Yes, in very good shape, I'd say. Here, put this in your mouth and cough for me."

He stuck a wooden tongue depressor in my mouth, and I coughed for him. He ran long, elegant fingers up and down the sides of my neck and prodded around the top of my breast bone. Then, in turn, he lifted my arms, pushed a finger up into my arm pits and gave my arm muscles a good feel.

"OK, very good there," he said. He whipped out a stethoscope and listened to my chest.

"Take deep breaths and hold them," he said. His stethoscope went to one nipple, and he laid his hand over the other one.

"Cough," he commanded. I obliged.

Then after a long time, he reversed the stethoscope and the hand over the other nipple and commanded me to cough again. I obliged again, hoping he hadn't noticed that my nipples were hardening up from the attention.

"Good full chest," he said. "Lungs seem fine. Not a smoker, are you?"

"No," I answered too quickly. That had been another one of my vices in college. But I'd also been on the swim team and had developed a deep chest and lungs.

His hands glided down the sides of my torso, and he put one palm over my belly and left it there for a minute. I had no idea what sort of new examination technique this was, but I was mortified that it was causing me to have a half-hard-on.

He had a hand on my balls, and I flinched as he rolled them.

"Cough," he commanded, and I did so.

"Everything seems in fine shape here," he said. "In fine shape."

He had his hand on my dick and was flopping it around gently. "Get it off regularly?" he asked.

"Uh, yes, regularly enough," I answered. "Uh, Mr. Sturgis. I mean Dr. Sturgis—"

"Would have liked to stick it to that cute little nurse who was just in here, would you?" he continued.

"Well, yes. Wouldn't anyone?" I responded, embarrassed. I was doubly embarrassed, because my cock had thickened and lengthened significantly at this suggestion.

"Sorry about that," he said with a laugh. "I was just checking to see if everything was in working order down here. It sure seems to be. That's good news. Now, I want you to lay back on the table and draw your knees up to your chest. I need to check your prostate."

He was putting a glove on his hand and dipping his fingers into a jar of lubricant.

"But, shouldn't I stand and lean over for . . .?"

"Naw," he answered. "I have my own procedure for this. It's less painful this way."

So, I lay back on the table and drew my knees up to my chest. It seemed like quite a while before I felt anything else, but then there was his cold and wet gloved finger working its way into my asshole. I knew when it had reached my prostate, because he was rubbing me there, sending strokes of pleasure through my balls and dick, and I felt precum forming on my cock helmet. A moan escaped my lips.

He withdrew his finger, but I heard him mutter something about thinking he'd felt something odd in there and needing to probe farther.

And then he was probing farther, but it seemed like he was probing with a bigger finger, and then I realized that he had both hands on my knees, squeezing them.

I lurched up in pain and surprise, but he already had his dick far enough inside me to maintain leverage, and he just kept unwinding his hose up my ass chute. My legs shot down and my torso came up, and I flailed around as his strong hands grabbed my shoulder blades. His long, slender hands wrapped around the sides of my pecs, and his thumbs landed on my nipples. His white doctor's coat was open and he otherwise was naked. He had a good build, and there was fluffy red hair covering his pecs and working its way down his belly.

I cried out in pain and frustration as his cock continued its journey up my ass canal until I felt his pubic hair tickling the insides of my thighs.

"Oh, God. Sturgis. Don't—"

"I already am, Mark. You're already split and filled. Can't go back now. Just calm down and enjoy it."

"Enjoy it?" I screamed. "Get off me, you—"

"Get off you, or what?" Sturgis asked with a heavy laugh. "I'm already in you, and I'm going to fuck you regardless. You can either enjoy it or fight it, but you are already fucked. I've had my eye on you since we interviewed you for the job. Why do you think you got the job over all those others?"

I was fighting him, but he was too strong, and every time I tried to move, his dick went a little deeper into my ass.

"Stop fighting for a minute and listen to me." I stopped moving. He moved his torso into mine, and his chest hair felt silky against my bare skin. My cock was throbbing against his belly. "Do you think you were picked because you were the most qualified? No, you were picked because you were the most desirable. And do you think you were picked only because you are a stud?"

"I don't understand. Why . . .?"

"You were also picked because you had a drug history. You were picked because if you want to keep this job, you are going to let me fuck you now. And you are going to let me fuck you again and again, if I want to. Do you understand?"

"But, but—" I whimpered.

"How badly do you want this job, Mark?"

A long moment of silence and then I whispered, "Badly."

"I didn't hear you, Mark. How badly do you want this job?"

"Badly," I almost screamed back at him. "I gotta keep this job."

"And what do you want me to do to you so you can keep this job, Mark?"

"Whatever you want," I whimpered after a moment of contemplation.

"Tell me you want me to make love to you, Mark."

"I want you to make love to me, Larry."

"Like this?" Sturgis asked, and his lips went to my nipples, which he started to ravish with his tongue and teeth.

"Yes, like that," I moaned.

"And like this?" he asked as he set his cock in action. Stroking me, first shallow and deep and then in longer strokes that brought his cock helmet almost to the rim of my asshole and then glided in again down to the hilt.

My cries of "Oh, god, no, you're splitting me," turned to moans of pleasure and "Yes, yes," as my ass passage calibrated to the size of his rocket and ripples of pleasure ran around my ass walls.

"I asked you if you wanted it like that," he said in a hoarse voice.

"Yes, yes, like that."

"Deeper and harder?" he asked.

"Yes, yes, deeper and harder. Plow me. Fuck me."

I no longer was thinking just of the job. I was thinking of having a piston alive inside me, filling me and stroking me in waves of pleasure.

His lips went to mine, and I opened to his tongue. I was gasping for breath and groaning and moaning. He was completely turned on by my compliance. He turned me on the table and pumped me in a side split while he stroked my cock with his hand. In my excitement and nervousness at the newness of all this, I came quickly, which set off his ejaculation as well.

He pulled out of me, buttoned up his coat, swept his pants off of the floor, and turned toward the door.

"Let's see how well you can do with a blow job tomorrow. Say ten in the morning in my office? We'll see how permanent we can make your job from there. If you can learn to suck as well as you take a fuck, I see a quick promotion in your future."

And then he was gone. I lay there and collected myself and tried to pull the shreds of my pride back together again.

But what was I to do. I gotta keep this job. And truth be known, I was looking forward to my next session with Larry.

Highballing

If the CEO of my company hadn't seen me recently in that gay bar over on 12th and Madison, I don't know how long it would have taken me to get invited to the executive floor. But Pete Peterson had seen me, and there I was, in his conference room, sitting in a second-row position in the weekly executive meeting.

I'd been surprised, but pleasantly so, to see Peterson in the bar. He was one of those young, charging CEOs who took real good care of himself and whose movie-star looks popped out of the eminently eligible bachelor stories in the Sunday paper. I'd seen him working out in the office gym over the past several months and, even though I'd never indulged in that world beyond letting a guy or two blow me in college, I had found him to be quite a tasty package. I'd observed him looking me over at the office gym, too, but until our across-the-room mutual sighting at Rockies, I'd assumed he had been assessing my management potential—or just wondering who the hell I was and where I fit into his business empire. Now, I thought maybe something else had been going through his mind.

It was a long meeting, I had to take a piss pretty badly when it finally broke up. I asked the man next to me where the men's room was on this floor, and, having overheard me,

Peterson chimed in that I was welcome to use the executive rest room just down the hall from the conference room.

This was quite a snazzy room, all brown marble and expensive fixtures, and mirrors everywhere, including over the two urinals. There was even a convenient place for me to hang my suit coat. I did that and then quickly moved over to a urinal, unzipped my tight-fitting pants, pushed my ultra briefs down to under my balls, and sighed a great sigh, as I let loose with a strong and steady stream into the urinal.

I heard the door open and then the click of a lock, which I thought was a little strange, and, although I expected to have one of the executives belly up to the urinal beside me, I was surprised to feel someone right behind me. Before I could turn around, which would have been a little awkward because I was still pissing out a steady stream, in the mirror I saw Pete Peterson's well-chiseled face appear over my shoulder and heard him speak in a low, husky voice. "Here, let me help you with that."

He came up right against me in back and reached around with his right hand and took my dong in his hand. I could feel his intake of breath when he got the measure of me. His left hand came around and rested on my tightening stomach. I felt myself go a little weak in the knees and reached out with both hands to steady myself against the wall. I looked into the mirror and let my eyes be captured by his. He gave me a movie-star smile of assurance.

I had finished my business, and he shook the last drops into the urinal, but he kept his hand wrapped around my penis, which was steadily growing. "Nice," he whispered in my ear, "Very nice. Bigger than I had thought. That's very nice." He reached down with his left hand and cuddled my balls for a brief moment, and then he moved his hand up my stomach, under my shirt, found my right nipple, and played with that and in my chest hair.

I gasped as the fingers of his right hand went to the tip of my dick and he lightly ran them around the rim of my glans and then put a finger over my piss slit and applied a gentle pressure. He was nibbling on my ear, and I pulled my right arm away from the wall and wrapped it around his head so that I

302

could run my fingers into his hair. I turned my head and found his mouth in a searching kiss. He began to stroke my cock, and I felt my knees go weak again. I'd thought often how my first time might be if and when I decided to cross the threshold, and nothing I had imagined came out this good.

His left hand left its exploration of my chest, and I heard the sound of a belt being undone and a zipper being lowered. I then felt my pants and briefs being pulled off my butt, and my pants hit the floor. We were still kissing and he was still stroking my cock, and now his other hand was wandering all over my butt cheeks. He gave a sound of animal pleasure and broke away from the kiss long enough to whisper, "What a great, round butt. I love good, round butts."

I could feel his engorging penis pressing at my butt, working its way into my crack, and I began to spread my legs to receive him, when he pulled back a little and stopped stroking my cock.

"My limo will be down on the street in fifteen minutes to take me to my country home for the night. May I assume you would be willing to be my guest there for tonight?"

That was a good assumption.

A few minutes later, I was down on the street in front of our office building, where I found a stretch limousine and a big, black, bald bodybuilder-type driver holding the back door open. He gave me a smile and motioned toward the door with his head. I only had time enough to register that the back of the limousine was roomy and plush, burgundy velour with wood paneling, and that there were some pretty hefty throw pillows around, when Pete Peterson entered the limo and plopped down beside me. The door closed with a good solid sound, and Peterson informed me, with a proud grin, that we could see out of the smoked windows, but no one could see in—including the window to the driver's compartment—and that the car was quite soundproof.

As the limo moved into traffic, Peterson moved to the jump seat facing me and said, "It's a long drive; more than an hour. So, we might as well go ahead and get comfortable."

He flipped a CD into a machine next to him, which introduced a sensuous sound, with a good beat to it into the compartment. Then he proceeded to do a private strip tease for me. First his coat and his tie, which he folded and placed on the other jump seat, then his shirt and his shoes and socks. He was probably in his late thirties, but he was in superb condition. He had sandy-colored hair, tending toward the red, and hazel-green eyes that held a smile real well. His chest was well developed and the hair on his chest was a fine, blond-red color, descending straight down from his neck, flaring out over his chest muscles and then back down to a thin line stopping above his navel.

He pulled his pants and briefs off, folded them, and placed them on top of his coat and tie, and there he was in all his glory. His pubic hair was even redder than his head hair, and his longer than average, very thick cock stood at attention as if he had not forgotten in the least our recent encounter in the executive men's room. He pointed to a bar between the jump seats and offered me a drink, to which I could only croak a, "Thanks, maybe later."

That caused him to smile broadly, and he went down onto his knees and moved to where I was stretched out in a sitting position at one side of the plush bench seat.

"OK, then we might as well get right to the second round," he said. He tugged at my suit coat, and I slipped it off and gave it to him. He folded it neatly and placed it on top his folded clothes. He loosened my tie, but didn't take it off. Instead, he slowly unbuttoned my shirt and took it off me, adding it to the clothes pile.

"My, my, we're pretty everywhere, aren't we?" he said, and I was happy that he seemed to appreciate someone with darker and more body hair than he had. He leaned in to me and gave me a kiss. My hands went to his waist and then one wandered down and cupped his balls and his dick. He sighed and slowly ran a hand up my thigh and to my crotch, where he found my engorging cock and rubbed it up and down through my pants. He kissed me on the neck and then ran his tongue down through my chest hair to one of my nipples. The nipple puckered right up for him as he tongued and nipped at it. I threw my head back into the seat and moaned quietly, pushing my dick into his hand through the fabric of my pants. I wanted to feel skin on skin there.

"Ah, such nice tits," he whispered, as he slid his tongue over to the other nipple, "and such a sweet, big cock too." He then undid my belt and unzipped my pants and pulled my pants, briefs, shoes, and socks off in one smooth move. He reached over and grabbed a couple of pillows, threw them up to me with a "Here, put these behind your back," and he turned me so I was laying the length of the seat. He took my right leg and placed it along the back of the seat, trapped there by his own body. My left leg jutted out onto the floor of the limo, and there I was, fully open to him. I put the pillows behind me, with my head in the back corner of the limo. I could turn my head and watch the world go by, beyond the smoke glass, while Peterson did me.

And he did do me. Immediately after we had both gotten comfortable, Peterson took my dick in his mouth and started playing with my glans with his tongue. My dick steadily engorged to its full seven inches under his attention. His right hand was running all over my upper body, up and down arms, up to my throat, playing with the hair in my pits, spending extra time on my chest hair and nipples, and trailing down across my washboard abs and into my pubic hair. With the other hand, he massaged my right leg and foot and then my butt cheeks. He pulled away from his sucking long enough to say, "Man, I love your butt. I can't wait to get more of these cheeks." Then we went back to my now-fully stiffened cock and began a rhythm of ever-deeper swallows. I moaned and moved to join his rhythm. My hands went to his head, playing in his hair, and down to massaging his shoulders and reaching down to playing with his nipples.

I was bucking wildly with him now, meeting every deep-throating with a plunge of my own. He had both hands encircling my butt cheeks, and I gasped as his hands pulled the cheeks apart and his thumbs reached for my asshole. He flicked my asshole with both of his thumbs, and I twitched in response, digging my hands in his hair. He was deep-throating me down to the root now.

"Oh, Gawd, I think I'm going to come," I croaked in warning. But he didn't stop pumping me and took the three separate jerking spurts down his throat with ease. I rolled my head back toward the window, and that's when I noticed that the window between the compartments in the limo was down and that the burly limo driver was eyeing the action through the rear-view mirror. All I could think of was that maybe I'd get a piece of that hunk sometime during this adventure as well.

I felt my hips elevating, as Peterson took up another pillow and placed it under my lower back. His hands went back to covering and squeezing my butt cheeks, and his thumbs to gently resting on the rim of my asshole and spreading that entrance. His mouth went to my balls, which he licked and sucked and then gently pulled away from my body and down. I moaned in mixed pleasure and pain. And then his mouth was buried between my butt cheeks, his tongue exploring and moistening my asshole, until I found the hole loosening and opening to him. He came up onto the seat on his knees between my legs, and I felt the head of his cock against the entrance of my hole. I gulped and gasped as he entered me a couple of inches.

He held himself there, into me up to the rim of his glans, giving my canal time to adjust to him. He then took his cock in one hand and rotated it back and forth in my hole, driving me to distraction, and causing me to open even more. Then his big, thick cock then just slid right in until a good seven inches of it was buried in my hole. Once again, he then took his cock in his hand and rotated it within my canal, stretching and adding to the sensation of being properly and fully stuffed. He started a rhythmic pumping action, squeezing my butt cheeks with his hands in syncopation, and it wasn't long until he came with a jerk and collapsed full length on top of me. He found my mouth with his, and we consummated our coupling with a deep-tongued kiss.

I didn't have to wonder what came next. While he still held me in a lip lock, Peterson slowly withdrew from my anus, and brought his knees up on each side of my waist and lifted his chest off of mine. I could feel him wrapping a hand around my still-engorged cock, as he maneuvered over me. I felt the head of my cock sliding across skin and being positioned at Peterson's asshole. He took his mouth from mine and let out a little whimper of pain as he took the head of my cock into his ass. Then he arched his chest back, taking several inches of my cock into him, and grabbed his ankles. I took his waist in my two hands, as he slowly raised and lowered his buttocks, taking more of me in with each downward slide. He pumped away for what seemed like ages, and after I had come for the second time, he gave a little sigh and lowered himself unto my chest. Without pulling himself away from my buried cock, he laid his head on my chest and slowly tongued my nipples and chest hair.

I must have gone to sleep soon thereafter, because the first thing I knew was that the car had stopped, the door had opened, and Peterson had gathered his clothes and was exiting the vehicle. I sat up and started gathering my clothes as well, but as I started to exit, I found the door was blocked by the hulky driver.

"Not so fast, sweet cheeks," the Hulk said to me with a grin, as he pushed me back onto the floor of the limo with a big mitt. "Someone has to pay the taxi fare," he said. "And Mr. Peterson said that someone might as well be you."

I laid there awestruck, as he pulled his shirt out of his pants, quickly unbuttoned it and drew it off his gigantic, barrel chest. He was magnificent, and I sucked in my breath at his hairless, burly beauty. Just as quickly, off came his pants and shoes, and I sucked even harder for air. His rod was a veritable telephone pole. It wasn't hard to imagine that it must reach almost to his knees when it wasn't hard, but just now it certainly was hard.

I made another dash for freedom past him, but he was too quick for me. Grabbing me around the upper arm, he threw me back into the limo, and, with the momentum of that, came through the door himself. I tried to fight him off, but he must have been a professional wrestler, because in no time he had me flipped across one of the jump seats, and, with my leather belt and his own, he had my wrists tied together and laced up to the anchor of one of the front seats with one of the belts and my left ankle attached to one of the anchors of the driver's seat. Wasting no time at all, he pulled my butt cheeks apart and had his tongue buried in my ass. I tried to raise myself, but he just pushed my back down with one of his big mitts and kept on tonguing me with satisfied gurgling and slurping sounds.

His tongue seemed bigger than the dick I'd just taken, and it wasn't long before I was lathered up real good again. I felt his tongue pull out of my ass, but he gave me no time to wonder what came next. The huge knob of his cock was at my asshole, and there was no coyness to his approach at all. He just drilled that telephone pole right on in, spreading my butt cheeks as much as possible. I screamed, and rose up involuntarily, but he only stopped long enough to push me down by the back of the neck.

After he was in a good seven or eight inches, he reached around me with both of his big mitts and started deeply massaging my chest, back, and shoulder muscles while vigorously pumping away, ever deeper and wider up my ass channel. there was pain, to be sure, but the thought of this big, beautiful monster, with what was now nine or more inches of thick black cock stuffed inside me, going wild with lust in my body—and that I was able to take him and give him such a buzz—gave me exquisite pleasure. It wasn't long before I felt him release with a violent jerk, coating my insides with his cum.

Then the lion turned into a lamb. He kissed me on the back of the neck and then returned to slowly and deeply massaging my aching body. One of his huge hands wrapped itself around my cock, and he gave me a slow hand job. After I had come, he continued to massage my body until a slept. When I awoke, I was free of my bonds and lying across the backseat of the limo. The driver had dressed again and was waiting to show me into Peterson's country home. I pulled my briefs, pants, and loafers back on, stuffed my socks in my pockets and put my arms through my shirt. I didn't have time to dress further, though, before the Hulk had taken up my suit coat and tie, picked up my duffel bag, and was heading for the front door of an ostentatious beach house. Not knowing what else to do, I followed along behind him.

We entered a large foyer with two banks of stairs raising two stories. The Hulk started trudging up the stairs to the second floor, with me trailing behind him, gawking at the undoubtedly expensive erotic art on the stairwell walls. We went down a long corridor and entered a large bedroom, decorated for a gentleman in soft leathers and greens and browns and golds. I heard the water running in a side room, and before I could explore there, a Greek god appeared at the door. He was young, couldn't have been twenty yet, and lithe, with a slim waist and hips, although with well-defined musculature; black curly hair, flopping down into his face and gorgeous light-blue eyes. His welcoming smile showed luminous pearly whites. He was wearing form-fitting white T-shirt, and tight gray slacks that showed a respectable basket at the crouch. Fine, curly black hair laced down his forearms and blossomed from the V neck of his T.

"Hello, there, my name is Salvas. You both look exhausted," he said with a grin. "To the showers with both of you."

Both I and the Hulk stripped down again and padded into the bathroom, which boasted a particularly large shower stall. The water was on from two jets, and the Hulk and I entered. I turned and watched the Greek god pull the T over his head and strip off his trousers. He was wearing a silky thong that left little to the imagination, and he was beautiful—slim, lithe, well-muscled through the chest and arms, and covered with curly hair. He winked at me as he stepped out his thong, showing a good six inches of fairly thick, uncircumcised dick, picked up a cake of soap and a wash cloth, and entered the shower.

I was the guest, so Salvas soaked me up first, running his soap and wash cloth around my body in a way that made my cock stand at attention again. During this process, the Hulk leaned back in a corner, watched us, and languidly pulled at his dick.

Having soaped me up, Salvas turned to the Hulk and quickly soaped him up as well. Fascinated by Salvas's pert little butt cheeks, I couldn't help but reach over and run my hands over them and then to continue on around his hips with one hand to explore his cock and through his legs with the other to nuzzle his balls. Salvas stopped his soaping of the Hulk long enough to turn his face to me and part my lips with his. I gasped, as he ran his tongue into my mouth and explored. I ran my fingers down to the tip of his dick and received a little thrill at the feel of the loose skin there as I pulled it back and got my fingers between it and his glans. Salvas shuddered with pleasure,

309

and, leaving the Hulk to wash himself off, put one of his hands over mine, and brought my hand up to encase his engorged cock lightly. I kept my thumb on his piss slit. He wrapped his own hand over mine, and provided the slow pumping action on his dick. With each downward stroke, I could feel foreskin coming back up onto his glans and touching my thumb. This was a new, very interesting sensation for me. Shortly, with a shudder, Salvas came in my hand, and his cum was washed down into the drain. I looked around and the hulk was gone. It was just me and Salvas now.

I got out of the shower and Salvas dried me off with the towel, Making quite sure that all of my private parts were dry and well rubbed. After he finished, he moved around the room, straightening up, but never quite getting around to putting his clothes back on. I sat on the end of the bed and watched him.

"Now, Mr. Peterson told me to tell you that you were expected out on the patio in an hour for drinks with his other guests," Salvas told me as he stood at the door, ready to leave. "He said that dress would be optional, because anything you wore probably wouldn't stay on you very long. Was there anything else before I go?"

"Yes, I think so, I said. Please come over here." He walked over to me and I spun him around and threw him down on the bed. He went down on his side, and I just lifted his leg up and entered him with my engorged cock. He gasped but took me deeply without any trouble. After pumping him that way for several minutes, I turned him on his stomach and gave it to him doggy style. I was determined to get a little of my own back after playing bottom on the road trip here. I felt quite sure that it would be bottom for me again when I went downstairs.

I never did make it downstairs for drinks. But when I was missed, Mr. Peterson and his guests came looking for me and, indeed, I spent the rest of the evening being bottom for a variety of men in a variety of positions. I only hoped Peterson and our company were going to be making a whole lot of sweet deals out of this little gift-giving evening, because I was really putting out for the firm.

Phoned

I should never have been flip when Vincent asked me about that photo of Phil and me I kept on the shelf in my cubicle at work. I didn't really want to talk about Phil. We'd been roommates at the university. He'd been the star athlete and I'd been the quiet, studious geek. Still, we'd gotten along real well. Night and day we were called at school—which was a southern school where that still meant something to some people. But I'd had no trouble with his color and he'd never expressed having trouble with mine. He'd been destined for the NFL, and I'd been teased I'd have made my first million off of some dot-com enterprise before I was twenty-five.

It hadn't happened that way—for either of us. The dot-com revolution collapsed before I could grab my brass ring, and the best I could do was doing "pretty good" as a stockbroker. Phil decided that a tour in Iraq would toughen him for professional football. But all it did was kill him. That's why I had a picture sitting on the shelf in my work cubicle of the two of us, half looped at a frat party, arms draped around each other, and silly grins on our faces. Sort of a shrine to not taking life for granted, for going with the moment, in case there are no more moments.

But when Vincent, the broker in the cubicle next to me, asked, I was flip. I said the other guy in the photo was my boyfriend.

I have no satisfactory idea why I said that. I think mainly it was because Vincent was so crude at the office, always cracking dirty jokes and making with the sexual innuendo—and I didn't want an intrusion like that in the tragedy I saw in my link to Phil. I just wanted to shock Vincent and make him stop asking about the photo. And especially, maybe I told him that because I had a hard time looking at Vincent and not seeing Phil. And then again it was a Freudian thing. Wishful thinking reaching down through the years to grab me.

Vincent was a real good looker, just like Phil had been. He said he was Jamaican. And maybe he was. He had a build just like Phil's, and he was always flashing a winsome smile and was so self-assured, just like Phil had been. All the women in the office ate him up despite what any one of them could claim was sexual harassment, if they'd wanted to—if someone not as hunky as him was doing it, maybe.

But I also might have blurted it out because of the half-way, or subliminal wishful thinking. There had never been anything real between Phil and me, but I'll have to admit that he aroused me and I'd had a crush on him that I never got up the courage to fully acknowledge to myself, let alone to Phil, when he was alive. And now that would never happen. Any possible moment of it happening was gone for good.

From the moment I'd blurted that flippant response out, though, Vincent had turned his innuendo onto me—asking me if I liked him, pointing out that Phil was black too. Asking me if I was especially attracted to black men. Whispering about "you know what they say about black men." And, in time, asking me if Phil and I were still doing it, and, if so, which one of us topped.

Always whispered and in passing, at first covered so that I couldn't tell if he was just joking, trying to get a rise out of me. Maybe baiting me for an office joke. But it continued, and when he moved on to touching me when and as and where he could do it when no one was looking, I knew he wasn't joking. He suggested we go for a drink after work, he complimented me on my clothes, and then on my physique. He even started dropping notes on my desk, asking me to meet him in the men's room, the notes becoming increasingly more explicit. Saying we should compare cocks. Saying he was built especially long and thick, as in "you know what they say about black men." Asking me what Phil was swinging.

I don't know if I could have stopped it. I just know I didn't try. I tried to hold back, but it was arousing. I'd never had attention paid to me like this before. I could have just told him exactly who Phil was and why that photo was on my cubicle shelf. But I didn't.

He got my home phone number somehow and he began calling me—almost always at about the same time in the evening, so I'd know it was him. One phone call after another, progressively more suggestive, more demanding.

"Hey, Jeff, I'm bored. Let's go play some pool."

"Hey, guy, it's me. What'yer doing. Want to do it together?"

"Thinkin' about you, Jeff. What are you wearing right now? Know what I'm wearing? Nothing."

"Hey, guy. I'm all alone and lonely. I've got something for you. It's long and thick and hard, and it wants you."

A phone call entirely of heavy breathing and the whispering of my name.

"You have it out, don't you? You are stroking it, aren't you?" And, of course, I was.

". . . A big black, hard cock churning around in your tight white ass . . ."

It had been weeks. Almost every night. A phone call almost every night at just about the same time. I could have changed numbers, gotten an unlisted one. I could have arranged to be out three evenings in a row and see it if stopped. I didn't. I started clearing everything away so that I could sit by the phone. Waiting for the call. Being disgusted when it came. But disgusted with myself, not with the call. Being frustrated when there was no call that night. Wearing less and less as the calls progressed in suggestiveness. Something loose; something that didn't hinder access.

A Saturday night. Just about that time. Me, sitting by the phone. Naked.

It rang.

"Something special tonight, Jeff. I have Manuel here. Say something, Manuel."

A groan in the background behind Vincent's smooth, velvety, baritone voice.

"Manuel's nice, Jeff. I met Manuel at the gym. He's cut and oh so nice."

Moaning in the background and a distant voice, "Gawd, Vinny. Oh gawd. Ahhh."

"You and Mani have something in common, Jeff. You know what that is, Jeff?"

"No," I whispered down the line. I had rarely responded previously, not after my initial attempts to tell him to stop got nowhere. But I was mesmerized. I already had my hand wrapped around my cock and was stroking. This was way beyond any of the previous calls.

"Mani loves black cock, Jeff. Just like you do. I'm fucking Mani now, Jeff. And he loves it. Listen to Mani, Jeff."

The other voice no longer distant. Heavy panting and groaning, "Oh, fuck, Vinny. Oh gawd. Yes, like that. Harder, deeper. Oh Fuccckkkkk."

The phone voice reverted to Vincent's. "Mani can't stay, Jeff, and I'm still horny. In fact I'm even more horny now. It's time, Jeff; it's time for you to come for your big, black cock. You know where I live."

The phone clicked off. I was stroking, but not anywhere near completion. This was too much. I let out a long sob.

I knew where this was going. I certainly wasn't fooled. I put on just a loose T and baggy gym shorts. Something had to give here, though. Either it was all a big joke and I'd be the laughing stock of the guys at the office Monday morning, or something would explode. But one way or the other, something was going to happen.

I stood at Vincent's door and knocked.

The door opened to a room that was dark except for strobing lights in blue and red and a blast of sound. Some sort of primeval recording resounding around the room; heavy breathing and panting and moans and groans, evoking high heat and lust. Directly across from the door, hung on the far wall, a giant flat-screen TV, screaming out the image of muscle guys fucking. Between the door and the TV some sort of black vinyl cube, not really a chair, not really anything but a waist-high black vinyl cube.

An overwhelming cacophony of sound and sensations of high heat and lust. No time to think, the images and sounds pushing all reason out of my mind, making my heart pound.

And out of the darkness, a big, black, naked Vincent pulled me into the room, and the door closed behind me as if on a spring. Bulging, shiny muscles. Gorgeous musculature. Everything that was boasted of, promised, swinging between his muscular thighs below and full chest V-ing down to a tiny waist overlaid with a hard slab of belly muscle. The spitting image of Phil in all his athletic glory.

Vincent pulled my T-shirt up and off my torso, and, while my arms were lifted for that, another set of arms, behind me, caught me in a full Nelson, trapping my arms above my head.

I flinched and squirmed, trying to pull free.

"Just relax, Jeff," Vincent said in a low, hoarse voice. "It's just Manuel. He decided to stay. Don't fight it. You came to be fucked. You decided. Let's all just enjoy it."

Before I could respond, Vincent had leaned in close and had taken my mouth with his big, thick lips, pushing my lips apart and inserting his tongue. Taking my breath away. The moaning sounds of lust reverberating around me. The flashing lights, the swirling images on the far wall of men fucking.

Vincent's hands were on my hips, insinuating themselves under the waistband of my shorts, hot palms on my hips. Manuel was holding me close from behind. And I knew he was naked too, I could feel the heat of a cock pushing up my lower back, the heavy pectorals against my shoulder blades. His lips and teeth buried in one of my arm pits, licking and nipping and kissing.

Vincent slowly kissed and nipped his way down my chest and belly, and he nibbled in my thatch as he slowly pulled the shorts down until my cock popped out—and into his mouth. In one movement, he stripped off my shorts.

I was overwhelmed with sensations as never before. I had no idea that cock sucking could arouse me this way. Manuel pushed his hardening cock down to between my butt cheeks, and I writhed and whimpered. Both wanting it all and being scared shitless at what was happening to me. The sounds and lights and the sudden sexual stimulation was overpowering.

There were three men fucking on the TV. A black and a white and a Hispanic, the black and Hispanic sandwiching the white. This couldn't be some coincidence. I nearly fainted when I realized that this was no professional movie. The black on the screen was Vincent, there was no doubt. And if the Hispanic was Manuel, he was every inch the hunk that Vincent said he was.

It was all just too much too fast for me. I came in a fountain of semen across Vincent's face. He merely laughed and went down deep on me, sucking me dry.

Manuel had forced my head to turn with pressure from his enslaving bicep and his mouth was now attacking mine, possessing me fully. Big brown eyes. What I could see of the face was chiseled and handsome. Straight, silky dark hair of at least shoulder length. The pressure of his cock between my legs had forced me into a wide stance, and he was dry fucking me rapidly across my perineum, pushing my ball sac and the root of my cock up. Vincent was sucking my balls into his mouth and rolling them around against his inner cheeks.

The sounds of the moaning and groaning from the stereo system were becoming more stereo like. Or so I thought, until I realized that it was me who was adding to the electronic moaning and groaning.

Vincent moved from in front of me, and Manuel frog marched me forward—onto the vinyl cube. I was pushed over onto the cube on my belly, and Manuel released my arms from the full Nelson. But as quick as he did that, Vincent was grabbing my wrists and tying them off on plush-lined leather restraints at each side of the cube. The cube wasn't all that wide, and my knees almost reached the carpet on either side.

On the screen, the white guy was bent over the arm of a sofa. The black guy was on the sofa cushions on his knees and was stuffing his cock into the white guy's mouth. The Hispanic was hunched over the white guy from behind and plowing his ass vigorously.

But that had barely registered with me when my view was blocked by a close up-and-personal of a mammoth black cock, which was forcing itself between my lips. Vincent took my head between his hands and was guiding me on giving his cock a tour of my mouth cavity and the back of my throat.

Manuel was restraining my legs in a wide stance at the base of the back side of the cube, and then I felt the wet roughness of his tongue on the rim of my ass. He was squeezing and lightly slapping my ass cheeks and pulling them apart with his fists and seeing how far, first, his tongue, and eventually, his lubed fingers could get inside my ass.

I was gurgling and sobbing and whimpering at what both of them were doing to me. I was overwhelmed with the surprise and the threat of it. But I also was steeped in the arousal and lust of it all.

I tensed and lifted up on the balls of my feet as much as the restraints on the cube would allow as Manuel started working his cock inside me. He was murmuring to me, though, advising me to relax and go with the fuck, that I'd enjoy it. When I was able to relax, after Vincent had pulled his cock out of my mouth, I found that it was at least somewhat closer to enjoyment than to intense pain.

Manuel was stroking faster and faster and getting noisier and noisier about his enjoyment of my ass canal. Vincent left, leaving me to watch the white guy on the TV get just about the same thing I was receiving—which, I have to admit, I found to be quite hot.

As Manuel was in the last throes of his fucking, however, Vincent came back into my vision. He stood there, purposely in front of me, giving me that "I got you" smile of his, letting me watch as he split open a condom packet and rolled the transparent film onto his tool. It didn't roll back much more than half onto his cock and it was straining at the thickness of him.

"Manuel's real nice, Jeff," he murmured to me. "But, you know, he's no horse like I am. He fucks, but he doesn't FUCK, If you know what I mean. Is your Phil a stud like me, Jeff? Have you had eight thick inches before? Do you know that I fucked a guy for forty-five minutes straight once and that he came twice while I was doing it?"

I heard Manuel cry out and felt his condom bubble out inside me, and he bent over and kissed me on the shoulder blade and mumbled something about a nice, tight ride.

And then Vincent disappeared from view, and I felt Manuel sliding out of me. And I watched the Vincent of the TV video slowly working his cock into the white guy bent over the sofa arm. And I saw the white guy on the TV open his mouth wide and yowl to the ceiling, all of his muscles and veins straining hard at the invasion. And I felt the heaviness and thickness of Vincent's cock head at my entrance, and I opened my mouth wide and yowled to the ceiling, all of my muscles and veins straining hard at the invasion, as a far superior club to Manuel's started its digging into me.

The moaning and groaning of the sound system changed to cries of overstretched taking and groans and heavy panting, begging for release, begging for deeper, faster taking. All of which was matched from the TV screen and the vinyl cube.

At length, at great length, I both sensed and heard Vincent tense and give up the rhythmic plowing and a burst of release. I felt him relax down on my back, covering me close, his chest expanding and contracting close against my back, and his hands running down the length of my restrained arms. He kissed me at the nape of my neck and whispered, "You done good, Jeff. That was worth the investment."

My whimpers subsided into sighs, just as what seemed to be happening on the screen flickering in front of me. I'd done it. I'd thought about doing it. I'd worried about doing it. I had fantasized about it—nothing like this, of course—but about doing it. And I let it possess me and control me. But now it was done. I felt slight embarrassment and triumph. Which was disconcerting. I should feel anger. But I didn't. I sighed, in almost contentment under Vincent's trembling, sheltering body.

I sensed a change in the air; a new sound. The ring of a telephone cut through the other sounds still circling around the room.

I heard Manuel answer it. "Yeah. That's right. OK."

Then he came into view in front of me—and I saw for the first time what a hunk he really was.

"That's the other guys. They're on their way up from the lobby."

The OTHER guys?!

Zonked

I had literally creamed myself almost nightly for Phil's body, but Phil was about as straight as they come—and getting all the female tail he could handle if all the talk around campus was true. I left little doubt with him how I swung, but that didn't seem to faze him—he didn't shun me; he just didn't jump into my bed.

We were both attending the university on athletic scholarships—Phil on a football and baseball scholarship and me on a wrestling scholarship, wrestling being a good way for me to get down and dirty with other hot, sweating, muscular dudes. We roomed in the same suite, athletes being given separate bedrooms in a suite of eight rooms with a communal head and shower. And I had ached for three months into the school year, being able to see Phil's beautiful, cut body in the shower almost daily, but knowing that he would never take interest in another guy as long as he was being worn out by the campus cunts.

And then I got a gift from heaven. We were at lunch, when Phil was telling us about the physical exam he had to take before the baseball season and that they were doing full exams, including MRI's and colonoscopies—the exam where they send a tube with a camera all the way up into your intestines from your asshole to check for cancerous polyps. They were being required this year because some dude had dropped over dead on the baseball diamond last season. It wasn't even anything related to his colon. But they weren't taking any chances anymore—or, I guess, the insurance companies weren't.

Phil was being asked if he feared the colonoscopy, because having some tube running up your ass canal didn't sound to him like anybody's idea of a picnic. I was thinking that the dude just didn't understand what a picnic that really could be when I heard Phil answer that they were trying a new technique on the team. They were testing a fancier camera with a thicker-than-normal tube, and therefore were giving the guys medicine that really opened the canal up before the test and then giving them knockout drops during the test and for the night after the test so that they could sleep through most of the pain that accompanied and followed the procedure.

"So, there will be pain, but there shouldn't be that much left after I've wakened the next morning," Phil was saying. "Personally, I think they only are forcing us to take the exam so they'll have healthy guinea pigs to see how the new equipment and procedure goes."

My tablemates droned on with a scatological discussion of having a thick tube going up your ass, but I tuned them out while my mind quickly formed a plan that would fulfill my dreams without Phil ever knowing what had happened to him.

The night of the day of Phil's exam, I took a long, hot shower while my suite mates were settling in for the night and then waited until four in the morning, breathing heavily, in anticipation of the pleasure that I hoped was to come.

All was quiet as I tiptoed from my room to Phil's. I was wearing my sleeping trunks and would have just sidestepped off into the head if anyone had caught me on the move. When I got to his door, I quickly looked around to make sure I wasn't being observed and then opened his door quietly and slipped in. His blinds were open, and the full moon lit up the room. I found him zonked on his bed, conveniently lying on his back on top of his covers, completely nude. Boy was he a hunk. Built like the quarterback he was. Sturdily constructed, but with muscle. No fat on him, dark curly hair covering his pecs and meeting to descend in a thin line down across his belly and fanning out

322

around his well-hung cock and big balls and then down, weaving around his strong thighs and calves.

I whispered to him, asking if he was awake, prepared with my excuse for waking him up in the middle of the night. Silence. I spoke to him in a louder tone. No response. I came over and sat down on his bed, putting my hand on his arm and speaking to him again, still posed with a good reason for disturbing him in the night if he woke. Nada.

My hand moved up his arm and onto his chest, stopping at one of his nipples, still within the zone of being able to excuse jostling him awake. I jostled him with my hand on his chest. Both hands on arms, I shook him hard. Nothing. He was stone cold out, just as he told us he would be.

I put one hand on his shoulder, almost at his neck and allowed the other hand to travel down his belly and into his pubic hair. Phil sighed in pleasure, but he didn't wake. I kept my eyes glued on his as I encased his dick in my hand and started to play with it. He licked his lips and moaned, but he remained asleep. Probably thought I was someone named Veronica, but not minding the attention I was giving him one bit.

I couldn't resist the lip licking. I put my lips to his, and he opened to my kiss. I stroked his cock as we kissed, and he responded by lengthening and thickening and moving his hips with the rhythm of my hands and giving deep-throated moaning for me. The intensity of his kiss told me that he was enjoying this.

I wondered if the Veronica he was wet dreaming about gave him blow jobs. I decided to find out, knowing, though, that this was pretty much a threshold beyond which I could give no plausible explanations if he suddenly awoke.

But, although his body was fully awake to my touch, Phil was not consciously in the room. I tongued my way around his nipples and down his belly and swallowed his cock whole, letting it engorge in my mouth as my lips pressed on the root of his shaft and my nose took in the welcome, manly smell of his pubes. My finger found his asshole as I stroked his cock off with my mouth, and, as advertised, I found the lasting effects of something that had widened his hole opening for that thick colonoscopy tube—and hopefully now for my thick tube. I hoped he was still feeling the effects of that all up his ass canal, because I didn't want him to feel suspiciously sore in the morning.

He ejaculated deep down my throat, still pleasantly living his wet dream with Veronica.

Time was a wasting, and I wanted to live my own dream before dawn—and certainly before Phil woke up—so I stripped off the sleeping trunks I'd come down the hall in, pumped my cock until it was hard, and rolled on the condom I'd brought with me. Getting my thighs under Phil's, I lifted his pelvis up to mine and only poised my dick head briefly at his hole before pushing in.

Phil grunted and twitched and his face contorted in pain as I slid into him, but he didn't awaken. When I was in all the way up to the hilt, aided no doubt by that medicine Phil had been given, I paused and rested, getting my own hard breathing under control. I couldn't believe it. I had my dong up beautiful, straight-jock Phil's ass. He was mine. He'd been had. He lay there stretched out below me, twitching and moaning quietly, but having taken all of me in. I began to pump him, and he moved with me. Could it be that he was receiving pleasure from this as well? I pulled his torso up to me and took his lips in mine. His responding kiss gave me hope that he was enjoying me as much as I was enjoying him. This thought was causing my cock to grow even bigger, and Phil's lips fell away from mine and he grunted in pain.

I let his torso drop back onto the bed and I took up his legs in my hands and wishboned him farther apart, opening his ass passage up enough to accommodate my enlarged size. And then I just slowly pumped him and pumped him and pumped him, until I'd come deep inside him. Then, almost regretfully, I pulled out of him, pulled my sleeping trunks back on, and retreated from his room to mine before anyone in the suite stirred.

The next morning, in the showers, a still-very-groggy Phil was complaining that his ass was still more sore from the exam than he had been led to believe it would be, but he showed no inkling of knowing his ass was no longer virginal—and certainly not that his ass was mine. I just hummed a tune and soaped myself off, trying not to relive my glorious fuck of Phil enough for my dick to respond for everyone in the shower to see.

I'd fulfilled my dream without doing any real harm to Phil that I could figure. I was just sorry to think that he probably wouldn't have to take another one of those colonoscopies for a good long while.

As we were leaving the showers, however, Phil pulled me aside and gave me a dreamy smile and a wink and said, just loud enough for only me to hear, "Of course, though, the exam was put off until next week, so I wasn't zonked with that medicine last night. But no one but you and me need to know that, eh?"

"Uh, I'm sor—" I started to sputter.

But Phil just smiled again and said, "I wouldn't mind being zonked again tonight either."

The Farmer Bill Cure

I couldn't be faulted for doing my best to fight off the depression from these urges that had clutched at me since high school. My parents, bless them, had done what they could to help me—my dad, especially, by guiding me through various sports programs, giving his all to the effort to give me the All-American sports hero life—using up all my time so I didn't have much of a chance to get into trouble.

I'd enjoyed the sports, and they certainly had toughened me up, but any effect they had on my "walking on eggs" depression was all superficial. I couldn't even begin to tell my parents what was really at the root of my problem. My dad would have curled up and died.

It was only when I was out of college—and beyond the consuming collegiate football and basketball programs—that I was able to seek help on my own terms, to give name to my urges and voice to how deeply they screwed with my life.

Dr. Shelton was the first one ever I told of my affliction—what I certainly did think of at the time as an affliction. I just sat on the sofa in his office and looked into his sympathetic and nonjudgmental eyes and poured it all out. It did feel a little better to have it out in the open to someone beyond myself. But that didn't get rid of the urges and of the guilty feelings they evoked.

I'd always thought that these shrinks didn't really suggest anything of use, that they were trained to make you face it yourself and come up with your own answers. But Dr. Shelton came right out with what I latched onto as a brilliant idea: retreat; leave the hectic urban life for a while, where I was constantly brought into contact with other people. Retreat for a while. He even said he could arrange it for me.

The town of Hamburg, Pennsylvania, was just north and west of Philadelphia, along the highway a bit past Allentown. But it was a world removed from urban, sophisticated, and enticing Philadelphia, the "city of brotherly love." The farm Dr. Shelton sent me to was north of Hamburg, right up against an eastern spur of the Appalachian Mountains. Amish country for the most part. Quiet and remote; neighbors who kept to themselves and their own ways and showed little curiosity about anyone coming to retreat for just a spell—coming to get their head on straight and put a spike in these depressions I suffered from because of the urges.

Farmer Bill was what Dr. Shelton called the man who owned the farm and worked it all by himself—and offered retreat and hard, honest work to some of Dr. Shelton's patients. He indeed was a farmer, Dr. Shelton said, but he also was trained in working with young men with my problem. If anyone could help me with this depression, Dr. Shelton said, it certainly was Farmer Bill. He was a man close to the soil, an expert in the basics and rhythms of life.

For some reason the day I drove up the Northwest Extension to Allentown and turned west was a light traffic day and the farm was a lot easier to find than I thought it would be. I was more than an hour earlier than I'd been told to show up. When I pulled into the farm yard, I maneuvered my Mustang between a pickup truck with the farm's name and logo on the driver's door and a Saab convertible with Maryland tags. I had assumed that I'd probably have to wait in my car until the appointed time, that Farmer Bill would probably still be out doing farm chores. But maybe not if there were two vehicles here at the house.

I got out of the Mustang and climbed the stairs to the porch of the white-painted, somewhat ramshackle wood-framed farmhouse with a fieldstone foundation. I went to the door, walking around a couple of smart-looking tan suitcases nudged against each other at the top of the porch stairs. The screen door was closed, but the front door was wide open. I couldn't see a bell, so I knocked on the door frame and called out whether anyone was home. Silence, although I heard what seemed to be a radio talk show mumbling from somewhere inside the house, not too close to the door.

This was the country, so I decided I wouldn't be shot or lambasted if I waited inside rather than out in the car.

I went in and wandered for a few minutes around a sparsely, but cleanly appointed room—undoubtedly the living room—which had several windows on two sides letting in the sunshine of a temperate-zone summer. But I kept hearing sounds from somewhere down a hallway that led off behind the foyer stairs. Maybe Farmer Bill was back in his study or something and hadn't heard me knock or call out at the door, I thought. I moved back through the dim hallway.

It wasn't a radio I had heard. The two figures, both naked, were stretched out on a double bed in a room nearly all the way at the end of the hall. Both were men, although I could only see the one on his side fully facing the door. He was young, not any older than me, blond and nicely muscled, these muscles now tightly strained at the effort he was making. His arms were stretched over his head, his fists wrapped tightly around rungs of the bed's brass headboard. His waist was lying on the arm of another man, who was stretched behind him and who had a ropy arm, bulging with veins, stretched around the young man, with a large hand wrapped around the young man's engorged cock. The other hand of the man behind was holding the young man's right leg up and away from his body. Focusing my shocked stare that the midsection of the young man, I could clearly see the churning base of the "behind" man's thick, condomed dick buried between the young man's butt cheeks.

The young man's head was thrown back and facing up at the ceiling, and he was burbling with exclamations of passion and highly pleasured taking. Groaning and moaning and grunting out for more, deeper.

I only caught a glimpse of the tableau before I withdrew back down the hall, but I couldn't get the image of the young man's beautiful body, undulating and glistening with a light sweat of being well exercised, out of my brain. And of that cock root churning in his channel.

The urges. This was exactly what I had been fleeing from for over half a decade. All of the enticements and spurned opportunities in the big city. The mental images of being in the place of that young man in the bedroom down that hall. And here, where I had retreated to escape all of that, here it was happening before my own eyes. I could only wonder, as I silently as possible stole back through the living room and out onto the porch, what Farmer Bill would do if he stumbled onto that scene.

I knew I didn't want to be here when that happened. I nearly stumbled over the two suitcases as I slipped down the porch stairs to my car.

I had arrived much earlier than expected. I'd just get in the Mustang and drive back to Hamburg and see if I could find someplace that sold smokes or could sell me a beer. I needed to calm down. I'd come back at the appointed time and just pretend I hadn't seen anything, and take my cue from whatever Farmer Bill had discovered—or not. But I *had* seen it—all that I had been running from. I needed a smoke. Or a drink. I needed both.

I had managed to find a tavern in Hamburg that dispensed both the smokes and a beer, and it was with calmer demeanor that I showed back up at the farm ten minutes after the originally designated time.

A middling tall, rangy man in, perhaps, his late forties was leaning languidly against a wooden column at the top of farmhouse porch when I pulled into the farmyard. He gave me a friendly smile, telling me I was expected. A handsome, square-jawed, if darkly tanned and weather-beaten, face on a spare, wiry frame. He wore a denim shirt and faded jeans over well-used, obviously serviceable work boots. Big feet for his frame and big, veiny, hard-worked hands too. A look of a no-nonsense, highly

330

efficient and competent, close-to-the-soil working man. Without at doubt Farmer Bill. And he looked much at ease, so I doubted that he had discovered what I'd seen in the farmhouse not much more than an hour earlier.

We were exchanging initial introductions and he was asking about the journey and the traffic on the highway as I walked up the porch steps to his level, my duffel bag hanging off my back. As I shifted the weight of that, I realized that the suitcases were gone from the porch. The Saab with the Maryland plates wasn't in the farmyard either, although the farm truck was there, parked in the same place it had been earlier.

"Come on it," he was saying. "I'll show you to your room."

I followed him back, through the foyer, beyond the staircase and into the hallway going into the back of the house. He turned near the end of the hall, into *the* room, and my heart leaped into my throat and I got all sweaty and trembly.

"I hope this will be OK," he said, ushering me around him and into the room. The bedspread was pulled tight now over the brass headboarded bed. No evidence of what had been going on there just a little more than an hour ago.

"This is where Dr. Shelton's referrals usually stay. Just had a guy from Maryland in here, but he was finished up earlier today and has gone home. Nice kid. Was glad to be able to help him."

I was listening to what Farmer Bill was saying—at least half way, enough to absorb what he was saying—but my eyes had latched on the strong, sinewy, vein-streaked hand he was gripping the knob of the bedroom door with as he leaned back against the door frame. Those hands, those ropy, tightly muscled, vein-bulging forearms. The man "behind."

* * * *

Dr. Shelton was certainly right. Farmer Bill was an expert in his field, in every sense. He treated me just like he would a skittish colt, and he took it slow and easy.

At dinner, in talking the theory of farming, he said, "It's all about sewing your seed in fertile soil, Ron. Knowing just where and when and how deep to plow. Respecting the soil, preparing it well, letting it run through your fingers. Winnowing and sowing and then being joyful in the harvest. Bringing it into season and plowing and seeding and harvesting. Making love to it, uniting with it, harmonizing with nature. Can you see it?"

Yes, I could. And he was being ever so charming and friendly and fathering.

And in the fields, doing honest, hard work close beside each other.

"It's going to be hot work, Ron, best we lay our shirts over there under that tree."

"A lot of this work is just repetitive motion, Ron, leveraging your muscles against the load, finding a rhythm and taking control. Thrusting against it and thrusting against it and thrusting against it. And knowing what muscles to use. The chest and thigh muscles on this here post digger."

And the graceful, repetitive undulation of his torso muscles against the fence post digger was poetry in motion. Sensuous, manly, overpowering. Each downward thrust of the thick post digger between his thrusting thighs into the hole and twist and retraction and repeated thrust both suggestive and enthralling.

"You've got to have passion in all you do out here, Ron. Whether you are digging a hole or filling a hole—digging, filling, digging—you've got to put muscle and passion behind it. You got to develop a rhythm. Understand?"

Yes, I did. And so did the urges.

Standing at the stockyard fence, big booted foot up on the first rail, side by side, both shirtless, Farmer Bill's arm loosely around my shoulder, him pointing with that big, veiny hand of his to the stud horse breeding a mare and the bull earning his keep.

"Whatever is in nature is natural, Ron. You know? Whatever is in nature is good and right. And everything comes into its season and, when it knows it's natural and right, then it's OK, it's good. You understand? Eventually, you've just got to let loose and let nature be nature. The great cycle of life. And you only live life once. You might as well get as much out of that life as you can, when you can. Preparing and plowing and seeding and enjoying the harvest."

And at the end of the day, the rule of not entering the house dirty. The outdoor shower by the barn. Stripping down together, rinsing and soaping up and rinsing off again under the showerhead, together. And drying off with towels as we raced for the house, buck naked, together. Laughing. Him slapping me on the butt cheek; me blushing and trying to stay ahead of him, not wanting him to see the effect the shower ritual was having on me.

There wasn't an ounce of fat on Farmer Bill—if you didn't count his thick cock and heavy balls, of course. The hard work farming required was evident in his trimness and his sinewy musculature. Beauty in motion when he moved, however. And a master craftsman and every inch in charge.

* * * *

When he first fucked me, I was ripe for the picking. We were out in the small vineyard he had on the first rise up toward the Appalachian ridge at the back of the farm property, well away from the rest of the world. He'd parked the truck in a depression below and let the tailgate down. After we'd picked several bushels of grapes and the shadows of the encroaching evening were quickly lengthening, Farmer Bill said he'd brought some wine from the last harvest out with us—and some cheese and bread.

We sat, side by side, leaning our butts against the truck's tailgate, stripped to the waist, dribbles of grape juice dabbling our torsos. Drinking wine and chewing on whole-grained peasant bread and sharp, locally produced cheese. Silently watching the sun set off to the west down the ridge and the lights of a few isolated vacation homes along the ledge twinkle on.

"I love it out here," I said. "So quiet. Silent. Lovely silence. Isolation."

"You're not alone, and it's not silent out here, Ron," Farmer Bill said in a low husky voice. "Listen again."

I did, and he was right. I could hear low sounds. A twittering and the sound of a frog in the nearby pond. And crickets.

"The sounds of nature, Ron. You hear them now, don't you? I don't think you were able to hear them at all before you came. But you hear them now, I can tell."

"Yes," I murmured.

"And you know what those sounds are now, don't you?"

I didn't answer. I knew where this was headed. I knew I was ready, but still the old reluctance, the twinge of guilt over the urges.

"Mating sounds. Nature coming into season. Doing what's natural," Farmer Bill murmured, his lips close to my ear, his arm around my shoulder.

"Yes," I said, my voice low and hoarse now too.

"I think you've come into season, Ron."

"Yes."

He pulled me over, leaning me back into his lap. His arms went around me, and his lips buried themselves in the hollow of my neck. He unbuckled my belt and unbuttoned my jeans and pushed them down my thighs. I pushed them the rest of the way myself, taking my briefs with them, and stepped out of them. His strong arms were squeezing me, and his broad-palmed, sinewy hands were roaming all over my chest and belly and down to my rising cock.

The first fucking was right there, like that, me being held into his lap, my butt cheeks nestled in his bush, as he leaned his buttocks against the tailgate of the truck. One of his hands on my chest, working my nipples and the other one on my belly, guiding the rise and fall of my hips on his buried, plowing cock until I'd taken the thickness of him inside me and had moved from pain to passion and gotten the rhythm of the fuck. Then that hand slowly descending to my tool, a maddening thumb latching onto the head of my knob and applying rhythmic pressure while the other fingers wrapped themselves and stroked me. Pent up as I was with years of unfulfilled urges and frustration, I spilled my seed on the ground twice before he shuddered and finished his studding of me for the first time.

Farmer Bill. Doing his job. Naturally. Studding me. Breeding me. And doing it masterfully; making me want it.

Then he turned me onto my back on the tailgate and hunched over me and licked the drabbles of grape juice off my torso and sucked me to a third spilling as he came into season for a second plowing and harvest. He wishboned my legs and nuzzled his pelvis between my hips and took me long and hard and deep, as I lay there, moaning and sighing, arching my back and writhing when he was riding me hard and lying back and languidly cooing as he took long, slow glides inside me, searching and exploring every crevice. Lying there, wondering why I had taken so long to give into the urges, and watching the stars flicker on over the Pennsylvania Dutch farm country.

And then again, later, as wisps of clouds scuttled across the early night sky, out between the rows of vine stands, studded like a horse, on my knees, buttocks lifted to him, my cheek on the soft moss, my fists grabbing at the soil, bunching up with each thrusting inside me of what he was breeding me with, a tool that would be the pride of any horse or bull—masterfully melting any mare or cow into burbling acquiescence. Smelling and tasting the rich soil of the farmland, doing what came naturally.

I stayed with Farmer Bill until I was fully comfortable fucking with a natural, joyful lust. But the day came when my Mustang was nuzzled out in the farmyard beside the farm truck, gassed up for the journey back to Philadelphia; my duffel bag was sitting at the top of the porch steps; and I was stretched out on my side on the bed in that bedroom for the last time, gripping the brass rungs of the headboard overhead for dear life, as Farmer Bill fucked me hard from behind in a farewell taking that put sealed to any reluctances or pangs of guilt I ever may have had. Exuberantly thrusting my hips back at his pistoning pelvis, while the knob of his master tool found my prostrate and rubbed me to new heights of ecstasy and lustful frenzy. The welling up and the release, followed briefly by murmurings and kissings and light tonguings across moist, hard flesh, and then the quiet, languid fuck of peace and mutual appreciation. Renewed passion and rhythmic fucking—and then farewell.

* * * *

One of the first things I did when I got back to Philadelphia was to try to make an appointment to see Dr. Shelton.

"I've talked with Farmer Bill, Ron," he responded to me down the telephone line. "In fact, I had a very long, interesting, conversation with Farmer Bill. You have no further need for my professional services. I can't meet you as your therapist . . . but I could meet you as your friend, if you want to see me and talk about it."

He scheduled me for after the last appointment of the day and waved his receptionist out the door as I entered his office.

"About Farmer Bill," I began, when he'd settled in a chair across from the sofa where I sat.

"You came to me depressed about your urges, Ron," he interrupted. "And you wanted relief. In our discussions of what was bothering you, I didn't really get the feeling that you, deep down, rejected the urges. You were just trying to suppress your natural instincts. And that was what was causing your depression. It was the guilt and resulting depression you needed to be liberated from, not the urges. That, at least was my assessment, and that is the last thing I have to say in any remotely professional therapist capacity. Was I wrong, Ron?"

I chomped on that for a few minutes. I had to be honest. That's one of the things Farmer Bill had taught me. To be honest with myself.

"No, you weren't wrong, Dr. Shelton."

"No, not Dr. Shelton. Hank. At this point, it needs to be your friend, Hank. And your depression? Did Farmer Bill help with that?"

"Gone," I admitted. "Farmer Bill gave me a whole new perspective."

"And in your perspective, am I, your friend, not your therapist . . . unattractive, Ron?"

ZING!

Well, I had to be honest. "No, Hank, you aren't in the least unattractive."

336

"If you'd like to just slip off those trousers, Ron, I think this would be a natural time to do a completely nonprofessional prostate exam."

Picking the First Fruit

I think I just might be the best peach picker in Virginia. Well, in Rockingham County at least. And that isn't just me boasting. That's what Brother Jeb said all the time I was picking peaches for him. And Mr. Howell said that to me too. More than once he said that. I've heard both men say that, in the peach business, it's getting the first fruit of the season to market before anyone else does that can mean the difference between a good season and a break-even or bad season.

I've been picking peaches—the last couple of years for the Mennonite, Brother Jebodiah, down near Singers Glen—for a good seven years now, since I was a boy. Brother Jeb's good people. Some Baptists here won't work for the Mennonites, thinking they are too peculiar and dress all old fashioned and stuff and just might not even be Christian, but I found them to be honest, fair, and themselves hard workers. Brother Jeb doesn't just send men out into his orchards in the heat of July to pick the first fruit to race to market with. He's right out there with them, working his butt off too. Of course in those dark clothes and that hat he has to wear, he has to take more breaks than most.

He goes over and leans on the fence next to the road, under the oak trees he's got his orchards bordered in. Standing there, he'll jaw with anyone who wants to stop and talk. This summer it's been mostly that Mr. Howell stopping in his big, new red Ford F-450 double cab. He's got his own orchards over near Timberville. I've heard tell about him being competitive and all, and some say he's a little underhanded. Not to his face, of course. He's one big, muscled-up sonofabitch. He'd take anyone apart who crossed him, I'm sure.

My uncle, Rick, worked in his orchards for a while, and he told me more than once, "It's good you want to work the orchards to save up for school, Johnny. But there's some orchards you'll want to give a pass on even if they offer good money. There's the Mennonites. They're strange folks and just don't mix well with good Baptists. It's never good to get in with the heathens. And then there's that Clarence Howell over in Timberville. He pays top dollar, but I'd stay out of the way of working under him, if I was you. He has more demands than a soul wants to talk about."

He'd give me a meaningful look, just itching to talk about it and daring me to ask why. But I never did. And I did want to earn up money for my electricians school as soon as I got out of high school, so after working for good Baptists for a couple of summers, and finding my paychecks shorted more times than I could count, I went against what Uncle Rick said and hired up with a Mennonite. And I hadn't had any complaints with Brother Jeb for two picking seasons.

The first week of the picking after finishing high school, I was out there, working just as fast as I could on Brother Jeb's peach trees. Brother Jeb had bragged on me at the end of the last season, saying I was his best and fastest picker. That meant something in Rockingham County, and I'd gotten some good offers from other growers here and about, but Brother Jeb had been fair with me, so I was fair with him and came back to him.

Speed meant something this year if we were going to be early to market. For some reason not that many Mexicans were coming up for the picking as usually did. I don't know if they were having trouble getting here or if conditions were better in Mexico than they were here this season. But, whatever, there were fewer of us picking. All told, the Mexicans were really the best pickers. They didn't have high expectations. It was hitting everyone, and for the first time, I felt the pressure to be working for someone else who could put more pickers into the field.

It was a Tuesday afternoon and hot as hell out in the orchard. I was down to my soggy and sagging gym shorts and working just as fast as I could, trying to help get enough bushels down off the trees for Brother Jeb to take a truck load down to the stores in Harrisonburg. Brother Jeb had already had to take two breaks, but I didn't resent that. The heat was really just too much for those black clothes he couldn't take off. The few others there, a couple of local boys, and a few Hispanics who either already managed to live here or who were so loyal to Brother Jeb that they managed to come back to him, were all as tongue hanging out as I was in the heat. Summer here in the Shenandoah valley was always a scorcher, and we were hitting heat records day after day this season. The white boys had been slogging along like zombies for some time, and now even the Hispanics and blacks, who could take heat better than most, were slowing down. Heeding the reputation I'd gotten and Brother Jeb's need to get a truckload of peaches to Harrisonburg before others did—and thus be able to pay me that time and a half he'd promised—I was working all the faster.

When I had to stop for a breath and a swig of water from my water bottle, the flashy red color of that big, new F-450 truck made me look over toward the fence under the shade of the oak tree. Brother Jeb was there, standing and leaning on the fence. And on the other side, one foot up on the fence's lower rail and looking pretty intently out at the orchard—at me specifically, so it seemed—was that Mr. Howell from over Timberville way. They talked for a while and then Brother Jeb came back to the orchard to take another crack at the picking. Mr. Howell went back over to his truck, but he turned and watched us for a couple of more minutes before he got in and drove off.

I was exhausted at the end of the day. All the rest, including Brother Jeb, had gone after we loaded up the truck. Brother Jeb was pleased because we'd managed to get a truck filled. He said he'd go ahead and drive those peaches down to Harrisonburg this evening to get a steal on anyone else racing for first fruit honors.

The few Hispanics that were working had gone off in the same ancient truck. It was load to the gills with pickers, all laughing and having a jolly time.

I'd overworked myself, keeping to my goal of being the best and fastest. I hadn't paced myself like they had. So, I just plopped down on my back under that oak tree Brother Jeb usually stood under, doused myself with water, and moaned and luxuriated in the shade. My bicycle was propped up against the tree beside me, waiting for me to get up the energy to ride the five miles east over toward Eddom, where I lived with my mother in a little country house. In the fall I'd be going down to Harrisonburg for technical school—if I had saved enough money—but I'd still be driving back to Eddom in Mom's old Cavalier every night. I'd have to work a couple of years as an electrician before I could afford a place or even a car of my own. And even then, I'm not sure my mom would want me to leave her all alone in Eddom.

I was dozing off when I heard the rumble of a truck. I expected it to pass on down the road, but it didn't. It stopped. I opened my eyes, and all I saw was a big blotch of cherry red on the other side of the fence.

"You look all spent out."

It was Mr. Howell, and he was standing by his truck and looking down at me over the fence. I groaned and sat up. I pulled up my T-shirt from under my back and folded it over my belly, suddenly feeling naked.

"It's been a rough day," I said. "But we managed to get a truckload picked."

"So soon?" Mr. Howell asked. "Taking it to market tomorrow, is he, is Jebodiah?"

"He's already driving to market with it," I answered.

I instinctively knew I had to speak polite and straight with Mr. Howell. He was one of the biggest growers around here. And a bull of a man in his own right. He was tall and thick necked and thick across the chest too. Maybe in his forties. He was one of those men who looked like he didn't dirty his hands but somehow had managed to work his body to high muscle tone. He was bald as a billiard cue, but he had a thick beard and mustache and a big patch of black hair pushing out the top of his buttoned shirt, which wasn't fastened down the top three buttons. It was like his chest was just aching to burst out of that shirt. He probably was fighting the heat as much as anyone, but he looked cool as a cumber now.

"Which market?"

"Harrisonburg," I answered. Not much that any of the other peach growers could do about that now, I knew, so there was no reason I could think of not just saying it. I was pretty proud of what we had accomplished for Brother Jeb today—not the least because Brother Jeb was right in there working with us as best he could and because he then knew which of his workers was giving him their best. It made me feel as much ownership of getting that first fruit to market as Brother Jeb did.

"Thanks for the tip. I'll send mine to New Market tomorrow then. A good tip is worth a ride home, if you're interested. You probably don't want to have to bike all the way to Eddom after a work day like you've had. I've had my eye on you. Everyone says you're the best and fastest picker in the county."

"Thanks. I like to give good work when I can. You know where I live?" I asked.

"Yep. Been checking up on you. Like what I see. So, do you want a ride home?"

"In that new truck?" I asked. "I'm not clean enough to be riding in that truck."

"If it doesn't bother me, I don't know why it should bother you. Here, hoist that bicycle over the fence and I'll put it in the back. If it makes you feel better, I've got towels I can lay down on the passenger seat."

It was not long after he started the truck up that he came out with the proposition. "I hear you're saving up to go to electrician's school down in Harrisonburg now that you graduated from high school."

"Yep, that's right," I answered.

"Pretty pricey school that is. Almost as much as going to a community college. Your grades not good enough for college?"

"I made good grades. The wages of an electrician are good and it's honest work that there's always a need for it," I

343

answered. "It's the fastest way of making money. College would be even more expensive and I don't have the time to put off making money."

"But a big part of going to college is to then have a college team to root for. You have a favorite college team?"

"Tech, of course. Doesn't everyone in the valley follow Virginia Tech?"

"I went to UVa myself, but I'll have to admit I follow the Tech teams too. They're a lot better. I even get tapes of their summer football team practices. I don't bother doing that for UVa."

"Yeah, Tech's good," I answered. I didn't know what else to say. I was intimidated sitting in the cab of that fancy truck of his. I'd slipped my T on, which wasn't too wet from sweat. But, even with the towels on the seat and back, I still did what I could not to touch any more surface of the truck seat than I had to.

Mr. Howell just looked over at me from time to time with an amused look on his face.

"You know you could be making a whole lot more money than you are at Jebodiah's. Maybe even enough for college and a car too. You wouldn't have to go around the county on that old bike. You've got a real good reputation now. In fact, I'd be willing to pay you twice what he is no matter what that is. It's a picker's market this summer. You could make enough to go to a junior college, not just to electrician's school. Or maybe both at once if you want to have a good skill to fall back on. That's a pretty smart idea, I've got to admit. And you hit me as a pretty smart young guy."

"Brother Jeb's good to me," I said. "I'm happy with him."

"Well, think about it. I'd be really happy to have you."

"I like working for Brother Jeb just fine," I said. I was trying to keep my voice polite, but it wasn't something I needed to think about or answer to more than once.

We were pulling up in front of my mother's house. She was out on the porch watering the hanging basket flowers with that old plastic watering can of hers. She did a double take at seeing the big red truck and dropped the can as well as her jaw.

344

"That your mama?"

"Yes, sir," I answered. "She's not used to seeing anything this new or big drive up and stop in front of her house. I'd best get out fast so she knows it's me."

"Looks like she broke that watering can when she dropped it."

I looked through the windshield and saw her holding the can up, with water cascading out of a rip in the plastic side. She had a forlorn look on her face. Mom didn't have the wherewithal to be buying a lot of new stuff like watering cans.

"Thanks for the ride," I said, as I climbed out of the cab. "Mom, it's just me. Mr. Howell gave me a ride home." I was already trying to work my way back into my mom's and my world. Mr. Howell's world was a lot more expensive than I could dream about.

"Give it a thought," he said as I stepped down on the ground. "I can give you a lot that Jebodiah can't."

"Sure, Mr. Howell. Thanks again for the ride."

"I'll be seeing you around, Johnny."

The next day when I biked home from the orchard, remembering with every huff and puff how easy the air-conditioned truck ride was in comparison with biking at the end of a picking day, Mom was out on the porch again, watering her hanging baskets. She was using a new, shiny-red watering can, and she had a smile on her face that went from ear to ear.

"Went to the market and bought yourself a new can?" I asked.

"Nope. That nice Mr. Howell who brought you home yesterday stopped and gave it to me. He said he was sorry that he had scared me and made me drop the other one. He wanted me to pass on his regards to you. And he told me he'd offered you a job with double the pay. He seems a right nice man, Johnny."

"I'm sure he is, Mom," I answered, "But Brother Jeb is a right nice man too."

* * * *

"Hope your mom liked the watering can."

My eyes popped open. Brother Jeb had called it a day early, because the swelter of summer in the valley was continuing and it was just too damn hot to be working outside. We were ahead on the peach picking, though. He was real pleased with that. Said it was mostly my doing. And it might have been; I couldn't remember much past noon today. It was so sweltering that I had just put myself on autopilot and tried to forget the temperature as I worked. Both Brother Jeb and those milling Hispanics and the other young white guys had piled in their rides and ridden off more than a half hour ago. I was laying under the tree working up the energy to bike back home.

I looked up and Mr. Howell was leaning there on the fence. He must have been really hot too, because he was shirtless. I almost swallowed my breath on how well-developed his torso was, especially for a man his age. He was really ripped. And he was hairy too—and deep tanned. Not hairy like a bear, really. I could see the skin through the dark, curly hair. But the hair pretty much covered his pecs and forearms and it trailed down his sternum and across his flat belly and then disappeared below his low-rise gym shorts. The hair on his body was quite a contrast with his bald head. The gym shorts were pretty baggy.

"Yeah, she liked it a lot. My mom doesn't get much new stuff, so that was a real treat. But you didn't have to do that."

"I caused her to drop and split the other one, so it was only fair I got her a new one."

"But you must have made a special trip to take it to her."

"Least I could do for that tip you gave me—that Jebodiah had taken his first fruit to Harrisonburg. I got to New Market first with mine the next day. Sold out in not much more than an hour. Getting the first fruit like that to the right market is real lucky. It sets off the rest of the season real good. Of course, if I had more help picking my peaches, I could really rake up the profit."

"It wasn't that great a tip. But I'm glad it worked out for you. It worked out for Brother Jeb too, so it's a win, win situation all around."

"Not that much of a win for you, Johnny. All you got was a watering can for your mother and a ride home. And you had to be back picking peaches the next morning."

346

"It was good enough. I got the time and a half Brother Jeb promised for making a first-fruit goal. He's real honest that way. I've had Baptist bosses that promised something but then didn't give it." I stopped, thinking I maybe went too far. Chances were good Mr. Howell was Baptist. I tried to smooth that over a bit. "But that ride home was real nice, thanks."

"You want another ride today? I'd be happy to give you a ride."

I thought about that—maybe for three seconds. "Yeah, sure, thanks." I looked up and saw that he was grinning down at me.

"I can't help thinking I should do more to show my gratitude," Mr. Howell said not long after we started off in his rumbling Ford F-450. "Of course, if you came and worked for me, I could make it up in wages."

"Thanks. I like working for Brother Jeb, though. Thanks all the same."

"Well, maybe some other way. Say, I'll bet you're hot as a fire cracker."

"Huh?" was the best I could answer with, considering what we usually used that phrase for around this county.

"The heat. The sun frying your body."

"Oh, that. Yeah, close to that, I think."

"Bet a dip in a pool and a couple of really cold brewskies would help with that."

"Yeah, that's certainly something to dream about," I agreed.

"Hell, no need to dream. I've got a pool at my house, and a refrigerator full of beer."

"You've got a swimming pool?"

"Yeah, sure. Not just a pond either. Concrete sides and bottom and everything."

"Neat. But . . ."

"And I know something else. We talked about films of the Tech squad's summer football practices the other day. I've got those on the machine. We could hit the pool and then watch the films while knocking a couple back. Waddya say to that? God it's a hot day. This air-conditioning is great, but once out of that, it's enough to roast a guy's nuts. Probably OK if you have air-conditioning at your mom's place, though."

We barely had walls at my mom's place.

"Well, I don't know . . ."

"And I could have Lynn put some steaks on for us. Make it an evening. I'd take you back after dinner."

"My mom will be expecting me home."

"I don't think she will. I was over at your house before coming here. She said she was going to a show with her neighbor . . . Mrs. . . . ."

"Steele. Mrs. Steele. She said that? That they were going to a show? That's strange. I've never known my mom to go to a movie."

"She said something about a rerun of *Steel Magnolias*. Said she was sorry she'd missed that when it first came around. So it looks like you need to fend for yourself for supper. As I said, I can get Lynn to broil us up a couple T-bones. I'm betting you could put that away after the hard day's work you've done. I made a killing off that first fruit to the New Market market. I'd really like to express my gratitude to you for the tip."

Well, if his wife was happy enough cooking up a meal for us . . .

Standing looking at the pool on the terrace behind his house made me want to jump right in. The pool was big. The house was big. Everything about his spread was big—and expensive looking.

"Too bad I don't have a suit with me," I said.

"No worry about that. It's just the two of us. Lynn's in the kitchen. Won't see a thing." With that, he stripped off his gym shorts, stood long enough for me to tout up his horse-hung cock and low-slung balls in the extra big category—a particular shock being as it was centered in that small V of whitish skin that wasn't deep tanned—dove neatly into the pool, and did a vigorous Australian crawl to the far side. Reaching that, he did a neat turn and stood up in the pool. "Your turn. Come on, strip and dive."

Embarrassed, I dropped my shorts and did an awkward dive into the pool as quick as I could.

We swam about. I couldn't swim very well. He was a regular sea otter, disappearing under the water in one place and surfacing someplace unexpected. A couple of times he came right up in front of me, his body bumping mine.

I was getting self-conscious, and worse, feeling myself getting aroused and going hard. So I swam over to the ladder and pulled myself up quickly. Turning away from him, I quickly toweled off and pulled my shorts back on. Only then did I turn back to him, seeing him dog paddling in the pool and looking at me with an amused look on his face.

"More hungry than in the mood to swim?" he asked.

"Yeah, pretty hungry," I answered. "As you said, I put in a long day. Quite a few hours since lunch now."

"OK, you go on into the house. I'll be in in a minute or two."

I happily did as he asked. I was having feelings I'd had before and mostly tried to repress. There was a guy a couple of times on the basketball team. Older than me. But that was just fooling around. We didn't do anything serious. But it had set me to thinking—and I'd been trying not to think too much along those lines. Going into the house would be good. Mrs. Howell would be in there. We'd watch the films, eat the steaks, and Mr. Howell would take me home. And that would be that.

I felt warm and trembly, though. Mr. Howell was so . . . built. I'd watched some films. But I didn't want to think about that. And especially by how his privates and tight, bulbous buns were accentuated by not being dark tanned like the rest of him.

I was in the house, waiting for Mr. Howell to come in, when a young guy came out of the kitchen and set some plates on a dining table.

"How do you like your steak?"

"Excuse me?"

"How do you like your steak? I won't put them on yet, because Clarence says you'll watch football films first. But I'll fix the steaks to order."

"Uh, medium rare, I guess." I hoped the confusion in my mind didn't sound that much like confusion. The guy wasn't much older than I was, and he was acting like he belonged here.

"And baked potato or fries? I'm Lynn, by the way. I cook for Clarence."

Lynn. Not a woman's name in this case. "Uh, baked potato, I guess."

We were sitting side by side on the sofa, Mr. Howell and me, with the DVD player running, showing Tech football practice. The lights were dim, and it was starting to get dark outside, although Mr. Howell had turned lights on in and around the pool, which we could see beyond a big, two-story window wall.

I was trying to keep my attention on the film, but I have to say that a college football practice is a bit boring. There's no scoring to keep track of and no school to cheer against. There was a brief flurry of excitement when I saw someone on the film I thought I knew, though.

"Hey, that looks like someone I went to school with. Wes what's his name."

"Wes Shelton? Yeah, that's who gave me the films. He's working for me this summer. Supervising the picking. I can't be there full time watching to see that everyone is working."

Yeah, I thought. You seem to be spending more time watching us work Brother Jeb's orchard than at your own. But I was feeling nervous. I knew Wes. I knew him real well. That's who I'd done a little fooling around with. Nothing heavy, I thought. Just measuring and seeing who was biggest and what might make us bigger—and then, admittedly, who could shoot the farthest, and whether you could get more by doing yourself or having another guy do you. There's nothing real heavy in jacking each other off, though. I do that just by myself maybe a couple of times a day. It's not that much more to do it with another guy your age who's just curious like you are. We both talked about girls and doing it to them while we did it. Of course, I'd never really done it with a girl. I was pretty sure Wes had; he really seemed to know what was what.

What was trying to get my attention more was the purple, bulbous cap on Mr. Howell's dick. He was wearing those baggy gym shorts and they were riding up his leg so that the tip of his prick was peeking out of a leg hole.

I was tenting up in my own shorts. I sure hoped that Mr. Howell didn't see that. It wasn't something I wanted to do—it was just happening without me being able to stop it.

He must have noticed my stiffening, because, without me being aware of it, he had snaked an arm around me on the top of the sofa, and the first thing I knew I was feeling fingers on my bicep on the opposite side of him, and he was soft stroking me there with his fingers.

"Umm, Mr. Howell."

"Don't be nervous, Johnny. I know you're interested. I can see you're hard." He had the remote in his other hand and, with a stroke of a button, he changed the DVD over to a sex film—a homo sex film. A hairy middle-aged guy—but in real good shape, just like Mr. Howell—sucking off a young blond guy.

"I don't think . . . I didn't come here for. I don't . . ."

"Wes told me that you did, Johnny. He told me that you were a real good fuck, that you begged it from him. And that he fucked you a lot."

"He told you that?" I could barely get it out. I was hyperventilating. In any event, Mr. Howell didn't seem to give a shit what I said about me and Wes. That Wes. He was always boasting. We didn't ever . . . "Ohhhh, god."

"Like that, do you? Hard for me, aren't you?"

I couldn't breathe, let alone object. All I could do was shudder and moan. He'd moved his free hand below my waistband and had a thumb on the bulb of my cock. He was moving the thumb around in the precum that had involuntarily oozed out there. I gave a little jerk as he tried to push into my piss hole with the tip of his finger.

"I'm going to be very good to you, Johnny. And you're going to be good to me too."

I wanted to object. To say this was all a mistake. And push him off me and stand up and go get my bicycle and start peddling home. I should never have . . . "mooooaan."

The hand on my shoulder had moved to the back of my head and turned my face to his. He took possession of my mouth with his, pressing his tongue deep inside my mouth cavity. I had to breathe through my nose, giving a rasping gagging sound. He pushed my shorts down to around my knees, and while his hand was off my cock, he grabbed one of my hands and pushed it under his waistband and onto his cock. Then his hand was gripping my cock again and pumping it slowly.

My hand had a mind of its own. It didn't come away from his cock. I didn't fist him, but my hand ran along the sides of his cock. I moaned again at the feel of how big and long it had gotten. And how hot it was. I could feel the pulsating, bulging vein running up the underside of it. That made me think of Wes. He was big like that too.

The kiss was over and he was kneeling in front of me as I sat on the sofa. My shorts were coming off and being cast aside.

"No, Mr. Howell. This is all a mistake. I've never . . . Oh, fuck. Oh shit."

His mouth had come down over my cock and he was deep throating me. I lay back, powerless. "Noooo."

I began to pant. Nothing like this ever before. It had to stop. I didn't want it to stop. Not ever. "Yesssss."

"You like this. You want this."

It wasn't a question, but I groaned my assent.

"You want me to fuck you. You've just been teasing me."

All I could manage was a moan.

He pushed me over on my side on the sofa, my head on the arm. Then he pulled me around on my back and was straddling me, his mouth working my cock. I grabbed his bald head in my hands, thinking I was meaning to try to push him away. That wasn't what I wanted at all. I was holding him there, instead, enjoying the rhythmic up and down movement on my cock between his lips and the bobbing of his head in the rhythm.

"God, Mr. Howell," I murmured, my voice feeling far away and weak even to me. "Wes lied. I've never . . . he lied."

He pulled his mouth off my cock and looked up at my face. "You've never been fucked before?"

"Ne . . . never," I moaned.

"Oh, fuck, this is delicious," he said in a guttural voice. "First fruit. My favorite. You want it. I know you want it. Your body doesn't lie."

I moaned.

"Tell me you want me to stop. We can just suck. You have to suck me too. But tell me you don't want it all—that you don't want me to fuck you."

"I . . . I . . ." it ended in a moan as his mouth came down over my cock again.

No fair, no fuckin' fair, I cried out. But that was all inside my head. I wasn't actually crying anything out. I was groaning and moaning too loud. And my hips were beginning to move with the rhythm of his mouth pumping.

I collapsed. I tensed up and then relaxed again. I tensed yet again as I felt a finger at my hole, entering me, slowly. Finding a spot that made me grip his ears and arch my back and moan a deeper moan than I'd given him before. I felt fireworks. Didn't hear them or see them. Felt them in a way I can't describe, as nothing like this had ever happened to me before. I shuddered and tensed. Then tensed even more. I couldn't breathe. I couldn't breathe.

"Oh, God, I'm coming!"

And I did.

After cleaning my cock with his tongue, he was lifting my legs, my ankles above my shoulders. His tongue going down across that ridge between the base of my balls and my hole. To my asshole.

I gasped. I groaned, I moaned. I was being tongue fucked. I was putty in his hands now—not that I'd put up anything like a fight before. He could do anything he wanted to me now. But that cock he had. The size of what I'd felt. I began to tremble. And to cry. Softly, trying not to let him hear. Trying not to be there at all. But the pleasure. The arousal. I was already getting hard again. My hand went to my cock, and I was slow pumping it.

I heard him laugh a low laugh. "You young guys. Love it. Fast reloaders."

He was hovering over me. His teeth were nipping at my nipples and I was giving little yipping sounds and my body was

353

jerking. I had no control. It wasn't even my body. I didn't want it to be my body. But, yes, of course I did. I wanted this pleasure, this ultimate arousal.

"Yessss, oh shit, yes," I hissed. I pushed my chest up, my nipples searching for his mouth. He laughed and raised his mouth to mine again and possessed me as before. I ran my hands down his chest, luxuriating in the matting of hair and in the hard curves of his muscles. Taking his cock in my hand, brushing my own cock against it, and then holding them together in my fist. His so much thicker and longer than mine. Both hot, hard, pulsating. His moving slowly in and out, rubbing across my fingers.

Shuddering again at the thought of what he said he was going to do to me. With that big dick.

He was pulling away from me. Rising up my body. His cock level with my mouth. "Suck it."

"Oh, God. I've never."

"Not that either?" He laughed. "Just open wide, keep your teeth off it, and don't gag anymore than you have to. I'll do the rest."

Holding the sides of my head with his meaty fists. Pushing inside me with that bulb of his. I couldn't take much, at first, and he didn't press hard . . . at first. Before he was finished, though, I felt that my tonsils had been battered and that he was a jackhammer machine.

"Can't yet," I heard him say, and then he was pulling out of me. "Not bad for the first time. Just about had me coming." Then he laughed his deep-throaty laugh again.

I wasn't sure my jaw would ever snap back in place. My nose was running, tears were streaming down my face, my tongue felt like it was twice its normal size, and the musky taste of him lingered on after he'd pulled out. My chest was heaving from the effort. But I was exhilarated at the experience. I'd done it. I always wondered what it would be like. The next time I'd take more control. I'd try to give more pleasure—like he did for me.

The next time? Oh, god, what was I thinking?

I lay there panting, not able to move. Thinking that this was when I should get up and flee. He was off the sofa, looking down at me. Smiling. He was fiddling with a small square packet. A condom! And he had a small can of something in his hand.

He really was going to do it. He was going to fuck me in the ass. In the ass! I'd never. I couldn't. No fucking way would I . . .

I moaned and tried to move. I was turning on my side on the sofa when I felt a hand gliding under my waist. A hairy forearm. He wasn't fighting me. He was helping me. To turn over on my stomach. But when I was about to put my leg out onto the floor and rise from the sofa, he was holding me firm, pulling me up on my knees on the sofa, my head on the armrest.

Crouched over me, he was moving fingers back to my asshole. Cold, wet fingers. Probing me. His torso over mine, holding me close. His teeth on an earlobe, breathing heavily.

"Steady, steady as she goes. It will only hurt at the beginning. Slowly, slowly I'm going to take you to heaven."

"I haven't. I can't. I . . ."

"You're honey. Meant to be taken. To be fucked. It's a man you want. A man with a big cock. More man than Wes was. I'm that man. I'm gonna fuck you. Here, now. You're gonna love it. Gonna beg for it. Love the pretending—that it's the first time. I don't think I've ever been this hard."

He hadn't been convinced. He still thought that Wes had fucked me, that he was competing with Wes, and that I was comparing him to a younger guy. He was right about one thing, though. I wanted it now. But I was scared, oh so scared. I started to squirm, feeling not thickish fingers inside me, but something thicker, slick, bigger than the hole but pressing in. At my asshole.

"Steady, steady." His voice was thick, growly. "God, you're tight. But we're going to do this. You're going to get fucked. And you're going be able to tell me I give it better than Wes does."

"Nooo," I moaned. "Oh, god. Oh, shit. Ohh. Ohhhhhh."

It was gigantic. A gourd, a watermelon. There was no . . . way. "Oh Fuckkkk."

Inside me. Expanding pushing. In, in, in. Stop and hold. Both of us panting.

"Tight, tight. This is going to be great."

He'd found the spot again. He was rubbing it with his dick head. I felt the jism rise. Hot . . . waves . . . of pleasure. "Ahhhhhhhhh, yess."

"Like that, do you?"

"Oh fuck, yessss."

I was building up the capability of saying something else, telling him the "however" part, when there was a searing pain, and I was fighting him hard, squirming within his grasp. Ineffectually. He was a big, strong man. And his dick was sinking deep inside me. Heavy breathing in harmony again. I began to sob, aloud. Defeated, taken, fucked.

And then he began to pump me. I came again and just went limp. He held me firmly, though, pulling me up to where my torso was erect. I was still on my knees. He had a grip under my chin with one hand, and his other, hairy forearm wrapped around my belly. His mouth was next to my ear, and his voice became thicker, more excited as he counted the strokes up his cock up inside me.

"Better now? I feel you relaxing. It's good for you now, isn't it? Better than Wes, right?"

I could do more than moan. But he was right. The pain was subsiding, the pleasure welling up.

I no longer cared. It didn't hurt that much anymore. And there was no going back from here. This was all his show now. As he breathed harder and his voice began to crack with lust and emotion, something else entered my mind. Power. Was it Mr. Howell who was controlling me, or me controlling his lust? I could tell he wanted me in a way he no longer controlled. I was the treasure. He lusted after me so much that he'd set this up and he couldn't get enough of me.

Maybe I could get him to come—to do so when I wanted him to. He'd milked me twice. Maybe I could control something here. I began to work my butt. Back and forth. Slowly. Contracting away from him and then slowly back on his cock, drawing him into me. Discovering that I could tighten and release my channel muscles on his cock and could tell that this made him moan—and made him harder inside me. He was breathing harder and moaning. Fucking faster, deeper. I moved my butt in circles, around his cock. Tightened my muscles and relaxed; tightened and relaxed. And with a deep grunt and release of his breath, he came, filling out the bulb of his condom.

Fifteen minutes later we were in better rhythm, more equal, as I lay on my back on the sofa and his knees spread my thighs, pushed under my butt, raising it to an angle that gave his cock deep penetration. He had greased up his staff and my hole more than the first time. There was more glide, less friction. And my channel was opening more to him now. I was more relaxed. My pleasure was heightened this time with the sensation that I had that gigantic cock inside me, that I could handle it. That he wanted to be inside me so much. Nothing to fight anymore. I had been fucked by a man—a real man, a horse-hung daddy of a man—and I loved it. I loved the connection, the wanting of me, the managing and controlling of such a powerful men—with such a big, vigorous cock.

My hands were running up and down his torso, my fingers nipping at his nipples as he gave low huffing sounds and grinned down at me. One of his hands was working my cock. I was moving my hips with the deep thrusts of his cock—and my channel muscles. Playing his cock as much as he was working me.

"Let's . . . try . . . to come together. It's a special feeling that . . . no matter, we'll try again later."

Later? I thought, having just come for the third time that evening. He thinks we'll do this again. That I'll let him do this to me again. What do I think of that? For the life of me I didn't know what I thought of that. All I knew at the moment was that I wanted to make him come. I wanted it to be something I did to his body that made him come.

Ten minutes later, after he'd come and we'd just laid there, cooling down, me feeling for the first time the sensation of a man's monster cock softening up inside me, he leaned over and whispered, "We can cool down in the pool. I want to fuck you in the pool."

"Get it like that from Wes, did you? He fuck you as hard or as deep, or as long? He make you beg for more of it, harder, longer, deeper than I did?"

"No, nothing like you?" I murmured in a moan, able to answer that completely honestly.

He was standing in four feet of water, with my butt plastered to his pelvis, feeling him soften inside me. His hands were gripping my waist and I was arched out toward the lip of the pool, my fists gripping the edge. The agitation of the water that his fucking motion had created was only slowly ebbing away. My ankles were locked together behind him, beneath his buttocks.

For the first time, we had come together.

"You are the greatest, Mr. Howell . . . Clarence. The absolute greatest."

"Call your mother and tell her you're sleeping out tonight."

* * * *

It had been a week. He'd come to the fence at Brother Jeb's orchard and watched and waited. But I'd put my bicycle on the other side of the orchard. And when he wasn't looking I'd been slipping off and taking different routes home.

He'd been to the house. But I'd managed to never be there. He'd bring little gifts for my mother, trying to get her to help me decide to come work for him—at least that's what he said he wanted. And my mother, knowing he was offering twice what Brother Jeb was and, being a good Baptist and never having been too pleased I was working for a Mennonite anyway, was doing what she could to get me to go with him.

She just didn't know what going with him entailed. She'd probably run off to the church and drown herself in the baptismal pool if she got even a whiff of what he was sniffing around for—what he'd already gotten.

After a week, though, I walked right up to him as he was standing, looking forlorn at the fence and said, "I sure could use a ride home."

He looked like a little boy in a candy store. He was all tongue tied and smiling.

"Just a ride home," I said, enjoying the teasing.

His face fell, but he just looked a little pouty and went around to the driver's side.

When we'd shoved off, I said, in a low voice. "You know somewhere private where we can pull this truck off?"

He almost swerved off the road as his head snapped around so he could get a good look at my face. I smiled at him, but I didn't use an "I'm just jerking you around" sort of smile.

He had no trouble finding an overgrown drive into an abandoned homestead and pulling in behind a collapsed structure of some sort.

I had him sit in the center of the backseat of the Ford F-450 double cab, naked, while I sat in his lap, facing him, and, leveraging off the heels of my feet on the carpeting floor, fucked myself good and deep on his hungry staff.

"Yes, I'll come work for you," I said. "You want me this much, I'll pick your peaches."

I'd thought long and hard. The morning after I'd slept in his bed with him—and with that Lynn guy too, with Mr. Howell going back and forth between us, having enough hard cock and stamina to service us both to exhaustion—he'd begged me to come work for him, saying he couldn't be without me, and that if I worked under him, there would be more opportunities for us to be together. He'd given me such a puppy dog look then—and when he'd come to the fence during the following week—that I finally gave in to him. I'd never had anyone want me that bad—or who gave me that much pleasure. I was in a whole new world.

* * * *

There were several young guys picking peaches in Mr. Howell's orchard. Young and good looking, white, black, and Hispanic. He had just as many working his orchards as Brother Jeb had—maybe more.

But they were a lethargic lot in most cases. Being as how I was Mr. Howell's boy now, I knew it was up to me to set a pace and an example. So I worked as hard as I'd done at Brother Jeb's. Wes Shelton was there, acting as field supervisor, just as Mr. Howell had said he would be. He smirked a little in my direction when I showed up for work on my bike. I hadn't decided, though, if I was going to call him out for lying about me to Mr. Howell. I couldn't very well work up a deep mad when

Mr. Howell had fucked me so well—and when most of my sleeping moments and some of my awake ones now were of Mr. Howell's cock working my channel deep. I didn't have much of a chance to speak alone with Wes for the first three hours of the day anyway.

I was working hard and fast, being a good example to the guys working the trees around me when I saw the big, red F-450 rumble up and through the orchard. When I looked up again, I didn't see it, though.

Twenty or so minutes later, Wes was walking near my tree and I called him over.

"I see that Mr. H. got you working here after all," Wes said. He was looking real good. All bulked up and tanned. My guess was that it was the football practice that was doing that for him, because he sure as hell wasn't lifting much other than a finger on this orchard picking.

"Yes. He pays double what I got before. I'm saving to go to school in Harrisonburg."

"I heard as much. There's a good technical school in Blacksburg, you know. Better than the one in Harrisonburg, I hear."

"I have to live at home. I don't have the money yet to live away as far as Blacksburg."

"Mr. H. is paying you double now. Maybe you could get him to pay you even more. You're the best of the lot around here, you know."

It didn't take much, I thought, for anyone to see that I was three times the worker that any of these other lazy pretty boys were.

"Speaking of Mr. Howell," I said. "Have you seen him? I thought I saw his truck come into the field a little while ago."

"Sure," Wes said, with a little smirk on his face. "Why don't you go look behind that storage shed over there."

I climbed down out of the tree. Wes was standing close to where I came down. Reaching out and putting a hand on my arm, he said, "You know you and I were getting to finding some real pleasure with each other. You go on and do it with anyone—go all the way?"

"No," I said.

"Not before Mr. H., you mean? You look well fucked by someone. My money's on Mr. H." He gave me a knowing laugh.

I gave him a dirty look, pulled away from him, and walked as steadily as I could over to the shed.

Rounding the corner, I saw the big, red F-450. That's not all I saw, though. The passenger door was open and one of the young Hispanic guys was laying, naked, half in and half out of the truck with the small of his back on the passenger seat. His legs were raised, and his toes were dug into the top sides of the door frame on either side. Mr. Howell, also naked, was standing on the running board between the Hispanic's legs, crouched over the passenger side, and was fucking the Hispanic's hole fast and furiously.

The muscles of the Hispanic's legs were undulating in rhythm to the fuck. The sounds he was making told me he was having a good time. And knowing what Mr. Howell packed between his legs and what he could do with it, my butt twitched in envy. I could see into the cab to where the Hispanic's arms were thrown over his head and his head was lolled to one side on the towel on the passenger side of the truck—the same towel I'd sat on that day of my first ride in the red truck. His tongue was lolling out of his mouth, and I could see even from here the dreamy look on his face. I knew from the thrusting of Mr. Howell's hips that he was fucking deep. The whiteness of his tightening and expanding alabaster butt cheeks in contrast to the deep tan of the rest of his body made me moan.

Red faced, I turned and walked quickly back around the side of the shed.

Wes was standing there in front of the shed. Not wanting to approach him, I turned my body back toward the truck. That was a mistake. The second view of what Mr. Howell was doing to that young Hispanic field worker, with the shock of the first sighting gone, was just too enticing now. I stood there and watched. Wes came up behind me and wrapped his arms around me. One of his hands went to my cock, having no trouble finding the hardness of it and holding it through the material of my gym shorts. His breathing was ragged, sounding like a low roar as close as his mouth was to my ear. I leaned back into him in defeat and just moaned as his hand went below my waistband.

"You knew what he was doing," I said, accusingly, but in a low voice that I hardly could get out.

"I sure did. And you should have known too. That's how he got you to come work here. That's his recruiting style. He's got the biggest dick in the county and all the guys who might be interested know that. They flock here—for the double wages, and for the fucks. What, did you think he wanted you so bad that you'd be his one and only?"

"You lied to him . . . about me."

"Best way I knew of to get you here and to be ready for me. He's good, but he's an old man, Johnny. I'm young and in great shape. I'll be better to you than he can be."

I couldn't say anything. All I could do is look at my feet. I felt such a fool. I had been stupid enough to think that it was I who was in control. That Mr. Howell. He just wanted his orchard picked fast and clean. And Wes. He was no better. He just wanted to control me too.

"Pretty shitty thing to do, I know," Wes said. "I know how you can get your own back, though."

We fucked right there inside the shed. I could hear the Hispanic's cries, so I supposed that Mr. Howell could hear mine as well. But I didn't give a shit.

The irony was that Wes was a better fucker than Mr. Howell was. He also was more susceptible to my charms and my growing sense of control. By the end of the summer he was begging me to go to Blacksburg rather than Harrisonburg and was willing to let me live with him—for free. And I had plenty of money to start junior college as well as study for my electrician's credentials.

Mr. Howell came sniffing around often, but denying him and letting him see Wes fuck me in the bushes made up for him plucking the first fruit off me. He reacted badly enough that I guess I did have some form of control over him. It wasn't as unequal as he thought. I was still best peach picker in the whole county. And, knowing that, he couldn't fire me.

About the Author

Habu is one of the pen names of a former supersonic spy jet pilot, intelligence agent, male model, movie actor, and diplomat. A wild youth in South East Asia was spent enjoying whatever sexual opportunities came his way, and much of his gay male writing is about recalling incidents from those days and inventing ones he'd perhaps have liked to experience. He now leads a very quiet and ordinary happily married family life.

An American, he is a published mainstream novelist and short story writer under another name and in another dimension of his life. He has written or cowritten (with Sabb) over 500 published short stories and nearly 100 published erotica e-books, primarily of gay fiction but also memoir, straight fiction and ménage fiction. His hand and creative writing can be seen in stories and books by habu, sr71plt, Dirk Hessian, Shabbu, and Stephen Kessel—among unrevealed others that might surprise readers. The fictionalized GM memoir *Flying High, Diving Deep* is loosely based on his life experiences. He can be found at the adults only gay male site **www.BarbarianSpy.com**, which he shares with Sabb and Dirk Hessian.

Our authors always like to receive feedback, and appreciate it when readers post reviews at Goodreads, Amazon, and other sites.

BarbarianSpy
FOR LITERARY HEAT

Not all books listed below may currently be on release.

BOOKS BY DIRK HESSIAN
Xtreme Erotica
The King's Men
Shores of Tripoli
Prophecy of Noto
General Erotica
Constantinople
The Beautiful Way
Blue and Gray
Colonel's Treasure
Beginning of Time
Labyrinth
Pretender's Fate
BOOKS BY HABU
Gay Erotica
Memoir Faction
Flying High, Diving Deep
Xtreme Erotica
Second Coming
Vortex: Sacrificed by Curiosity
Dark Angel Sounding
General Erotica
Death to Blonds
Gotta Keep Trying
Finding Amnad
Habu's Christmas Balls
My Neighbour's Spa
Finding Amnad
Beyond the Beaded Curtain
Hard Knocks U
Man's Man

Trip Money
Clint Folsom Mysteries Compendium Volume 1
Clint Folsom Mysteries Compendium Volume 2
Grab Bag 1
Grab Bag 2
Grab Bag 3
The Indian Doctor
Sailorboy
Home to Fire Island
The Sporting Life
Platres Conclave
Fetish Galore!
Choke Hold
Literary Gay Erotica
Cairo Surrender
The Handyman
Homeward Bound
Journey to Mirage
Menage Erotica
13 Ways for Halloween
Luther
The Indian Prince
BOOKS BY SHABBU
Finding Jason
Dirty Pool
Operation Black Jade
Cigars!
Angel in the Barn
Gayly Complicated
Despoiling David
The Tree of Idleness
I Met a Man
The Interview
Rough Road to Happiness
BOOKS BY SABB
The Legend of Holleystone Grange
Surprise Encounters
She is He

Wrong Man
Loyal to his King
Barbarian Tales - Book One - Traveler's Tales
Barbarian Tales - Book Two - Journeys Begin
Barbarian Tales - Book Three - The Inheritance
Barbarian Tales - Book Four - Road to Persepolis

~